THE BLOOD OF MY MOTHER

ROCCIE HILL

BLOODHOUND
— BOOKS —

For my grandmother, Nina, who always wanted to go home.

CHAPTER 1

1827 – LEAVING AMERICA

*W*e sailed out from the port of New Orleans with pale grey clouds overhead, but by the time we reached the godforsaken Mexican gulf a storm was churning across the marshy river mouth, so wracked and fierce the bellowing skies had turned to black. Along the horizon line, a seam of green light glowed through the dark like the devil incarnate, and the torrent pushed into our little cabin, covering us all with the smell of iron and brine and blood.

Captain forced us toward the nearest island, our ship rising up the waves into the lightning, high on a crest and then hurtling down the trough. And each time we dropped, every nail and copper sheath holding the hull together screamed through the rain. My father and uncle ran up deck to fight those demon winds with the crew, while the needles of hail cracked across the planks above our heads.

I crouched on a sour sodden mat, praying hard for forgiveness or mercy or whatever words might save our family on this fool's journey to our promised land. The Doc's jars of writhing river leeches tossed wildly across the floor where they had tumbled, and my older sister, Lou, pressed me close, shouting, "By tomorrow evening we'll be at our new home, Eliza!" She was only eight years old, her beautiful blonde hair drenched, her eyes gone cold with fear, and I knew she did not believe her own words.

We found safe harbor at the island bay to wait out the storm, and near to dusk the wind did begin to still. I could hear a lone piper over the softening rain, a mariner in the hold breathing out a weasel of a sad tune. Slowly then, the clouds parted to make way for the clean indigo night, and through the darkness we heard the captain call out fit and fair. At his shout, the tars jumped from their dice games. Pulling hard at the lines, they lifted the duck cloth tight and high, and finally set our little gaff schooner on down to the sea.

I sank into sleep below deck, dreaming of some Texias beach far from any stars we had ever known. We passed the night side by side, Lou and I, until hours later when we awoke to our boat lumbering over soft waves and the early sun seeping through the slats. We slipped on our skirts and climbed up top in time to see the dawn light skidding over the water like jewels thrown out. That open sea was as broad and blue a place as I had ever seen, with gulls and skimmers dipping low across smooth white beaches, while our *Lost Son* sailed on towards the bay at Matagorda.

The captain moored us near a land spit beside gold-blossomed Gulf acacias and palmettos, along thick canebrakes choking out the swamp willows. We all took the wherry boat to shore for the night while the deckhands repaired the storm damage to the ship. Lou and I crept off together through the brake, but within a hundred yards we found a slice of an old ship's hull cracked open on the rocks, the broken boards shifting gently in the waves.

Lou toed the wet sand around it and stepped forward to touch the wood. "It must be the Portagee ship," she said, and squatted to turn the plank over to look for a name.

"What ship is that?"

She cocked an eyebrow and looked straight at me. "I heard a story about an old wreck in this sea, carrying gold back to the queen of Portugal."

A pair of waterbirds nearby splashed up and down, cawing a ruckus and slapping the shallows with gleaming white wings.

"Let's keep hunting," Lou said. "We might find some of that gold hereabouts."

We walked on down the beach to another piece of the hull that was splayed out along the sand. Lou moved right onto the boards, pushing her way into the remains of the cabin. She was my older sister by nearly two years, braver than anyone in our family even when she spotted the brown beach mouse scurry across a swelled up purple foot in the doorway.

"Don't move!" she said suddenly, but I stepped closer to her, and we found ourselves balancing on a fallen jamb beside four naked bodies. "We better go tell Father."

I smelled a terrible rot from the dead flesh before us, but I pressed closer to look at those bodies. One was arrowed through, and another had bled out from his neck. I knew one of the women from back in New Orleans, and a boy from the schoolroom there. Last year he had been daring and prideful, making fun of my coarse black curls, but now he lay in the brack, his own red hair slithering round his head, smelling like a dead animal turning to shitewater.

I squatted in the sweet gummy mud and leaned over to stare at him. His face had begun to turn to mush in the shallows, but one arm lay exposed to the sky. I had never seen a dead person up close before, so I touched my finger to his skin and moved it up and down because my father, who had experience with dead people, had told me that when a body is exposed to the sun for a long time, the top skin pulls away from the second layer, and it slides back and forth.

"Stop," Lou whispered to me. "You know that could've been us."

"How?" I asked.

"Any old boat comin' through the storm. Could've been our *Lost Son*. Could've been our own family layin' there dead."

Turned out that ship wasn't Portuguese at all; it was the *Gaily*, the ship that Mister Stephen Austin had sent months before, filled with settlers like us. No word had ever come back, nor by sea nor by trail, and folks at the port houses in New Orleans had been wondering about its luck. Father and Uncle James found six other bodies lying up the beach and some more in the canebrake, clothes and guns and food all stolen from them.

We stopped two nights on that bay while Father did the burying. He made rough boxes from the shore trees and dug dry land graves, and when he was finished he stood straight, let his long rifle dangle limp under his arm, and took a small amber laudanum bottle from his trouser pocket. He uncorked it and gulped it all. His shoe prints were cut in the sand down the beach, and he stood quietly, staring at them.

"What's wrong?" I asked him, but Lou took my hand and walked me away, back to the wherry boat and to Grandma.

Later, Uncle James decided that only the dead Anglo bodies would get holy crosses because he said the others were not our kind. I laughed when he told us that, and my grandma slapped me, but truly, one body's just like any other once it rots to grave butter.

~

We traveled with our father and his mother, our uncle and kin, as refugee families did in those times, moving in packs like hounds for survival. Lou had lost her mother to fever in the Carolinas, and when the family got to Mississippi, Father took up with

Becky Bunch, a Melungeon girl from down the delta who saw to Lou and then gave birth to me.

Becky's skin was dark as wild walnuts, they said, and she had beautiful grey eyes. Father loved the strange ways of her people and decided to settle with them a while; when I was born he even named me Eliza Mississippi Green because he loved that swamp country so. But my mother died of yellow jack the year I was born, and after, we all moved on to Texias together.

Sometimes I see a falling star or imagine a hero, and I know it's my mother, dark curls and arms full of wild ginseng, come to me again like a slingstone from wherever she resides now, reaching to cover me from the anvil-hearts who hate me for her blood.

CHAPTER 2

e rowed back to our ship early the next morning, and the captain sailed us on to the village they called Matagorda, where Mister Austin had built a boarding house for the colonists, a smithy, two saloons, and huts for refugees like us passing through to headright land. This became our home for some months, while Uncle had our land surveyed and bought tools and provisions for our new life upriver.

Late in the day, Lou and I would hide together up in the wild waxy myrtle trees at the edge of the woods, waiting and watching for movement. One dusk I was perched on a big branch with the smell of the berries bitter around us, and the cuckoo and the corncrake crying through the twilight. I saw a huge black rat swaying on the briar below, clinging on the branch like a piece of infected fruit. Figuring it might come after me, I screamed as loud as I could to cause it to run.

"Get away!" I shouted, and Lou climbed up the branches to sit next to me.

"What's the matter?"

"Did you see that rat?"

She leaned over and touched my cheek, then took my hand.

"At least it's not a 'gator. A boy at the stores told me they have alligators here, sometimes crawling around the road in the dirt. One of 'em even ate a baby."

A moment later, I heard Father call out for us. "Girls! Girls! Answer me!" He began to sob from deep down his throat, and we jumped off the tree trunk to go to him. He was leaning against the raw cedar hut frame, his head thrown back, wailing like a lonesome old man at the end of a failed life.

Wild and deep, his voice brought others into the twilight, couples and their children crowding around our hut with their guns raised, staring at him through starlight.

"Father," I said, "we're right here," but he didn't speak, only stood there waiting like a spirit long ago perished.

The day we left Matagorda to travel up the Colorado River to our land, we woke at first light and started the loading in of our flatboat. Lou and I carried our own cases to our bunk mats, and then we leaned over the railing to wave at the Negro dock jimmies shifting cargo on the jetty. A couple of them straightened up from their work and stared at me. One wiped the sweat from his face and crossed his arms over his chest, shouting as loud as he could, "Hey girl, whatcha doin' on that boat? Come down 'ere!"

"Why are those wharfies looking at me?" I asked Lou. "What're they saying?"

"I guess maybe we shouldn't wave no more," she said and took my hand. "Nothing to worry about, Eliza. You just have the wild look like your ma. So pretty with your dark curls and grey eyes. They probably never saw a girl as pretty."

I had only just turned seven, but I could tell she was making that up. Lou was the prettier, with thick blonde hair and creamy perfect skin from her Carolina mother, and I knew that between the two of us, no one would stop their workaday for a swamp child like me.

The captain told us that the Colorado was not an easy sailing river because it hardly flowed at all. He did not favor the trip, but my Uncle James paid him to get us as far inland from the coast weather as he could. We had scrip for a *sitio* of land, more than four thousand acres, to divvy between us, stretching from the river swamps all the way out to the prairies where we could start our new life. The captain delivered us upriver through the logjams for ten miles, and when he couldn't get any farther, he shored us up near a huge canebrake along the bank and left us.

Uncle James had a thousand acres coming to him, and Grandma took two thousand acres south of his. My father claimed his thousand and called it Becky Creek, after my mother. Uncle James and his bad-tempered wife disapproved of this name, but Father would not back down. Lou and I knew they hated my mother from the moment she joined the family, but Father had the land surveyed and got his patent, so they could do nothing but leave us be.

Becky Creek lay south of my grandmother's property, and ours was the best black virgin soil where the riverflow turned back on itself and silted the marshes with cool crumbly earth. Uncle James started planting crops as soon as we arrived, but my father, no farmer to be sure, was befuddled at whether to put up shelter or put in seed first, so he befriended the traveling Caddo Indians, and asked their counsel. They dug a dirt lodge for us to live in and covered it with reeds while we got the crop in the ground.

What I remember of those days is furrowing into that soft marshy soil, using caney sticks like the Caddo showed us because Uncle James had taken all the proper planting tools. We walked the rows for a week, sinking deep holes and putting in maize.

Father welcomed these men to our table and paid them wages, and together, we cut the trees for fencing and smoothed the ground so wagons could move easily on our trails. When the crop sprouted up healthy, we cut logs from gumberry and pecan trees to build a house, separating the rooms with hemp sheets we brought from Matagorda.

Even though Uncle James was the oldest son, my grandma joined her land with ours, so she could cook and watch us girls because we were motherless. She handed over her money to our farm needs and taught me and Lou the things we ought to know for the future, like the alphabet and Spanish and our times tables. She also made sure that we started our hope chests, trunks of bedding we embroidered for when we married.

The day we pulled the corn off, we held a cookout among the rows in the hottest part of the day. The cobs were juicy raw, and our grandma roasted them over a wide fire pit and then smothered them in bricks of butter. Lou and I carried platters to the farmhands, and we all sat at plank tables, crunching into the corn with our Caddo friends, laughing at that hot sweet taste and their stories of the harvest.

My grandma brought a wide-brimmed hat to me that day, and whispered, "Eliza, you'll do well to stay outta this sun for it'll darken you up beyond recognition, girl, and then what man will marry you?" When Lou heard this, she asked for a hat herself, but Grandma just shrugged and replied, "No need for you, Louisiana."

A year later, the mosquitoes were thick as dust, and yellow fever came swooping up the Colorado River from the coast. We didn't even know she was sick, but my grandma passed during that season. On her last day, she sat in her chair at breakfast while the black morning still hovered at the windows. It was the Sunday of Palms, so she had put on her black dress to make special prayers.

She reached out to take my hand for grace, but then closed

her eyes without speaking. My father whispered out the prayer while Lou and I followed along, but Grandma was silent. Suddenly, she fell forward and didn't move again. My father put her atop the bed, told us to go to hear the preacher by ourselves, and then rode out in the rising red dawn to tell my uncle. When Lou and I came home from church, we looked for Father in the cornfields, but he wasn't out there. He was back under his bedcovers, whispering to himself.

"Father, you're scaring me," Lou said.

We sat him up in bed, but he was very drunk and needed help fastening his trouser buttons. Lou and I helped him stand and raised our arms to prop him under his armpits, and all I could feel was the soft webby skin of a weakened man.

"Didn't go well with your uncle, girls. Things are gonna change now," he said. "Be as kind as you can to each other from here out."

For Grandma's funeral, we had to stand on the road between two new buildings that we were not allowed to call churches. One was a little whitewashed hut that had been blessed by God via the circuit preacher. This was where the Baptists like Lou, Father, Grandma, and me heard the holy word. The other one was a logged cabin for the Cumberland Presbyterians, and Grandma always disapproved of their ways, so we stuck with the Baptists while our Uncle James sided with his wife's Presbyterian folks. I reckon it didn't make much difference which preacher told us his truth, since before they would even let us into Texias, Grandma, Father, and Uncle James all had to sign Mexican papers saying we were Catholics. I'm sure we were doomed to our God's holy hell the minute that ink dried.

The lady farming the acreage next to ours made peach cobbler and cut roses from her yard. She brought it all to the

Presbyterian cabin because some Negro folks had gathered at the Baptist one to say goodbye to my grandma, and that lady said the peach cobbler was not for them. My uncle and his family stood on the Presbyterian side of the road, and my father, Lou, and I stood behind them. Truth be told, Lou and I just stood near the peach cobbler and hoped for the best.

The Presbyterian pastor was a purple-faced blatherskite who ranted for an hour about God living among the cornrows, and our duty to bend our will to the Lord. The breeze smelled like peach blossoms as they lowered my grandma into her grave, and after the sermon, my father wandered off across the fields by himself until we saw him slump into the corn stalks as he found a place to kneel.

CHAPTER 3

Once Grandma's will was probated it turned out that Uncle James got everything, and from that day, he began building the biggest plantation along the Colorado. The Mexicans didn't allow any slaves in Texias, but before Uncle put the cotton in on the acreage he took from us, he went off to New Orleans and secretly bought ten Negro people to do his work. He became renowned for mistreating everyone: his slaves, his wife, and their children. My father said we would never set foot on the land that should have been part ours because his brother had become a thieving devil.

But our father was hard-pressed to keep our crops growing. He had never seen a drought back in the eastern deltas, and when the blooms of our victuals fell dry from the stalks, that unrelenting season broke him. We had traveled so far and fought so hard for our farm, only to find the stones in that dusty riverbed could transform ignorant foreigners like us into destitute refugees in a single month.

I remember Lou and me sitting on our rank clay floor, watching the cat lap at the last of the soured milk I had given it. Father stumbled through the door and squatted beside us, defeated finally from the sun and the dust-whipped wind. We came up short in that autumn of 1830, and by the winter we were cold and hungry, scratching the ground like starving chickens.

With no food and no cash money, he paid Uncle James with some of our acreage to take my sister to live with him, to educate her, clothe her, and keep her from starving. That was the first I understood about our differences. Father sent Lou away by herself because Uncle James would not have me. I came from people of the Yazoo River swamps, from a Melungeon mother down the dank delta from Vicksburg. I was younger than Lou, without her beautiful yellow hair and porcelain skin; I was a girl without value.

A wintry hoar fell the week Lou parted, and the small lanterns across our stoop threw greasy shine over the dirt. I had packed her a basket of our scrawny carrots for the wagon ride, and her small hands were warm when she took it. She was steadfast, and she never once lamented being sent away.

My father was to take her early, while the cold fog still lay upon the river. Lou stood in her heavy old shoes by our wagon posts, looking to the ground where mushrooms grew up through the dark-clumped grass.

She put one hand out to touch mine and I grabbed hers quickly, loathing this day.

"Don't forget me, Eliza," she said and reached her arms out to fold around my shoulders.

I ran to the bench of the wagon and shouted at my father. "Don't make her go! We're a family, aren't we?"

He stepped down and stared at me. "We had some bad luck, Eliza. Nothing else to do." He put his hand on the top of my head awkwardly. "I'll be back before nightfall. You stay inside now, and lock up the door and windows."

I watched them drive away, and went to sit on an old box laying in the weeds. I bent over my knees and put my hands together, praying hard for my feckless father and his lost dreams, tears sliding down my cheeks.

In the spring, a few neighbors rode up to our homestead late in the day as the horizon was cooling and turning pink and purple. Father was still in the fields, and the riders went right out to see him. These men knew my father's reputation as a sharpshooter, and offered to pay him money, cattle and pigs too, if he would ride with them to Galveston Bay to the little fort at Velasco. They needed him to pick off some of the advancing Mexican army, and since we were hungry, he said yes. He asked our neighbors to watch over me, and off he rode that very evening into the dying dusk. When they arrived at the garrison, they fought the Mexicans for two days and finally won. Later that week, he came home covered with dried mud caked onto his buckskin, drunk and happy as a lemming under a spell.

After that, our life on the river bottomlands was one battle after another, sometimes with the Mexicans and sometimes with the Indians. We had plenty of food and money because my father had found his calling, and at the first news of a threat, some sanctimonious Texian republican always rode up to enlist Father to help with the killing.

Deep in that dark cropland, the two of us might go weeks without seeing a single soul. When strangers did ride through our gates, our hackles rose immediately. The Caddo were reliable, but sometimes the Karankawa would pretend to be Caddo, and once they got inside, they could skin a woman in less than ten minutes. That's why Father taught me how to use a rifle, for those times when he was out in our cornfields still hopelessly struggling to bring food from the damn plants.

The day in March when Three-Legged Willie McCann came with his young friend, Micah, I waited out their approach with my rifle lodged on my chest, staring at the two riders through the afternoon mist. When I saw Willie's third leg sticking out akimbo from the left side of his horse's saddle, I knew him to be my father's friend, and I lowered my gun.

That old leg caused him certain pain because it had grown deformed from bone disease when he was small. For years he used crutches to walk because it stuck straight out sideways from the knee and try as he might he never could get his left foot to touch the ground. But my father had taken a liking to him and carved him a wood leg, an oak stump he could hook onto his thigh so he could move like other people. He was deep grateful, and because of that, we trusted him.

About fifty yards from where I stood, Willie stopped his horse and called out to me. "Hey there, Miss! Put that damn rifle down before my ranger here shoots ya!"

He was laughing, but Micah had drawn his gun, as if not knowing what to expect. They both slid off their saddles and led the horses to the porch posts.

"Ranger McCann," I chuckled. "Bring yourselves inside."

Micah was staring at me, and so I stared back hard at him hoping he would look away.

"What's the matter with you?" asked Three-Legged Willie glancing at the boy. "Never seen a woman before?"

I turned to watch them follow me inside. I was not yet fourteen, but I had lowered my hems to the floor and started pinning my hair up, so I guess he was right to call me a woman.

Willie and Micah took places at our table, and I put two tin cups filled with hot coffee and grog in front of them.

"I'll go get Father. Have some of this for now."

"God's hooks, girl!" Micah shoved the cup back to me. "You don't understand. We have no time. You haven't a minute!"

I looked at Three-Legged Willie, and he nodded. "We're here to move you on, Eliza."

I heard my father coming through the rain that had begun to fall on the path. The coal bucket just outside our open door was covered with black shimmer in the wet daylight, and as he passed I saw him drop a tiny amber vial into it.

"Hello, Willie," he said.

Willie nodded. "We need to move you on, Ben. They're coming now from San Antonio. The fort fell."

My father sat at the table. "We'll be fine here at home. Becky Creek is far from that Alamo mission." He leaned forward and coughed deep, from the bottom of his lungs until his throat was clear to breathe again. He pulled his jacket up around his neck and scrunched his shoulders and arms together to hurple the cold away.

"Dickinson's wife made her way out of the cottonwoods to Gonzalez," Willie said, looking only at me. "She says there are six thousand Mexicans headed straight for the Colorado River and your Becky Creek. They are aiming to annihilate the lot of us, Ben. Keeping on past the Brazos, torching every one of our homes on the way. What do you intend to do?"

Without responding, my father began to empty his pockets. He pulled out another little bottle and a fistful of wild garlic, laying them gently on the table. The over-sogged roots fell on the oak, and a faint smell lifted.

Micah stepped forward toward us, his childlike face turned scarlet. "Mister Green, even the men who signed our constitution are running. They're charging to Louisiana today to escape with their lives!" He was a tall boy with bright blue eyes that sparked with gold dust, and looked unafraid to take on the men who stood about him.

"This is no runty calf, this Micah," my father said. "Where'd you find him?"

Willie slapped a hand flat on the table. "We don't have time for conversation, Ben. Even a crack gunman like you can't stand up to this alone. Houston's moving out from Gonzalez, and he needs marksmen now. And your girl needs to get to safety."

"What is your intention?" Micah asked.

"Boy, I'm just a farmer with a slingshot, but I will be of service. Willie knows that."

"We are all Texans now!" Micah barked.

Father did not even look his way; he just frowned and glanced out the door at the rain coming down through the alders. "Better get your clothes, Eliza. Anything warm. Blankets and all the provisions you can find. You and Micah load the mule cart."

"When it's over she will be residing across the Sabine and you can call for her there," Willie said.

"But how will you find me?" I asked my father, "and how will we ever find Lou again if everyone's running? Uncle James hasn't let us see my sister in years, and we might lose her forever!"

Father had already walked to his yauger rifle and laid it on the table alongside the tiny purple garlic blooms. Without answering me, my father pulled a hatchet from the gunbox and a pepperbox pistol, standing tall and proud, useful again like a perilous violent boy.

Micah and I went out in the mist to the muddy yard; we loaded the cart and he hitched up the animals.

"I'll see you in America," Father said, and suddenly I put my arms around his waist, holding him as long as I could. "Go on, Eliza," he said, sadly and without affection.

CHAPTER 4

*M*icah and I set out over the mud in pelting rain that was slowly shifting to hail. We had no cover on the cart, but once we turned on the farm road east, I realized we were the lucky ones. Hordes of refugees, mostly women and young children, joined us along the trails. They came on foot, carrying or dragging their dearest items, sacks filled with blankets and food, clothes and dishes, anything they could grab from houses about to be torched. Many wore shoes for the first days, but the mud seeped and settled inside the leather infecting their skin, so the women removed their shoes and walked barefoot in the storms.

When the night fell the temperature dropped and though we covered ourselves with bedclothes, the wool soaked through till the only thing to keep us warm was our own shivering. The first night we scouted cover from the rain, but never found any. Micah and I slept under the flatbed of the cart among the sodden blankets and food. In the middle of the night, he woke up and moved closer until I felt his body warmth and awoke too.

"What are you doing, you dung-molly! I was sleeping."

"The reason I stare at you is because you are.... *effulgent*." His voice was sweet and earnest, like he had made a scientific discovery.

"What does that mean?"

"You are prettier than anyone I ever saw."

I took a quick breath of the cold night. "Oh?"

"Of course. Your mama and father never tell you?"

"My mother is dead, and Father is not that kind."

"You could see it for yourself anyway." He reached his hand toward me, so slowly, but I pulled back. "I'd like to touch your hair. I never saw hair so curly like yours. Glossy and curly and black. And your eyes, big and smooth like the color of old silver."

"I don't even know you," I whispered. "And my father trusted you."

"I didn't mean nothing. Don't want nothing. Just making a statement." Micah rolled away from me and faced the rain. "I'm here to see you safe."

During one day of weak sun, we rode nearly thirty miles and by dusk, scores of people emerged from among the stands of sycamore and hazel pine that scattered wild over the prairie. At nightfall, hundreds were walking with packs and long sticks made from stripped branches. All of us were refugees, seeking sweet asylum back across the Sabine River in the United States.

One night when Micah went out to hunt for food, I sat on our pack with my rifle cocked and waiting. The black sky was dry, as though the birds were building their nests out of thorns. And then an old fellow rushed upon me from down the bank, smelling like river fish and moving silently through the darkness, grabbing for my arms and head, for anything he could take for himself. I jerked my rifle high and pulled the lever clean and swift. That was the first time I ever killed a man. You want to know what killing him felt like? Didn't feel like anything.

We had to cross two hundred fifty miles to the Sabine, and then over into American safety, and often we took in trail orphans, starving children whose families had been lost or killed. All of them had soiled themselves with their own urine and shite, for nothing mattered as they stumbled along that evil ground, children as likely to pass with the night as to sleep. We fed them when we could and held them when we had nothing else to give.

One night we camped in a circle for safety, but Comanches emerged from the woods on horseback and stole our mules and horses. With no animals to pull the cart, Micah and I took what we could carry and walked with the others. We trudged across the counties to the Brazos and found the west bank of the river jammed with vehicles, worn out carriages, ox and mule wagons, and we waited our turn to cross, the smell of sewage rising around us.

We reached the eastern bank and walked through the mud all the way to the San Jacinto River, where thousands of people waited to make their way across. We camped in the rain for days before we could get to the other side, and then pushed east to the Trinity River, which had broken its banks and was covered with driftwood. All manner of disease lay upon us. Measles, sore eyes, whooping cough, and every other sickness had broken its boils among us.

At Liberty, I saw a baby die in his mother's arms. I was worried about how close Santa Anna was, but the baby didn't care. He just put his little head on his mother's forearm and stopped breathing.

We were still at Liberty when we heard a sound like distant thunder. The cannons were firing at San Jacinto. The cannonading was so brief that we were certain the Texans had been defeated, and we started east again at best pace, only to be overtaken by a man on horseback. He rode up and down our miserable shank of people shouting, "Stop! Go home! The Texans have whipped the Mexican army!"

That night I laughed for the first time since Becky Creek. We all shouted thanks to God, dancing and clapping our hands. The old men and young girls and all the others, hungry and smelling of trail sewage, flung ourselves around in circle jigs. We stood on the damp prairie in between the rains and praised the Lord for our safety and our good fortune.

The next day we reversed direction and went back home to start our lives over again.

Micah delivered me to Becky Creek, but he left me on the doorstep saying, "You got walls and a roof, Eliza. More than most. You have the fruit of God's grace here, so see to it."

"Where you headed?" I asked him.

He came boldly up two steps. "Our new Texas needs an army, and I'm calculating to be part of it. We're a republic now, and we need all the soldiers we can get." His baby face had such fury, and he stood there like a fierce little lamb of Jesus.

"Good enough," I said. "May I offer you some drink before you go?"

He followed me into my ravaged home. Although the walls and roof were standing, all else had been pillaged and torn, destroyed by Mexican and Indian anger at our Anglo occupation.

"Terrible," said Micah. He harrumphed a bit as he saw the crumbling walls and torn sheaths connecting one room to the next.

I nodded. "But who's to say we wouldn't have done the same if our land was in the cross-hairs?"

"I have to go," he said. "They need me. And you need a watchman."

I shrugged. "I am the watchman."

CHAPTER 5

I had no money and no family, nothing but Becky Creek. I was cut off from the few settlers on our frontier, but I made up my mind to build our farm back up. Some days I would sink my fingers into our crumbly soil and with my eyes closed, I could imagine the reflection of the sky on the surface of our well. I found that my particular skill had all along been growing food. Redding our planting land early each morning, I knelt like an unschooled magician in the dirt; neither understanding nor protecting my instincts, I merely dug.

A few wild peach and fig trees were dying near the creek, and so I set to work to save them by mixing the earth with fresh horse shite from an old animal that the butcher in Matagorda kindly offered me. The squashes and the pumpkins eventually did well, and I was able to keep myself from starving by adding in the eggs of a couple chickens I had caught running loose in the dead cornstalk rows.

My father returned home several months later, on the summer solstice when the sun shimmered on the horizon like a golden bowl. Bedraggled and breathless, he stood in the doorway with the glow covering his shoulders. He looked around the room and smelled the vegetables roasting over the fire.

"I'm hungry, Eliza. Got anything?" He sat on the stool.

I set his plate on the table, leaning close to kiss his cramp-jawed face with quick affection. But he didn't look at me, just lifted his spoon and pushed food into his mouth.

"Last time I ate was days ago. In the Cherokee Territory, I think."

I filled his plate again. "What were you doing up there?"

"This home is beautiful," he said and tried to straighten his neck. "You still a virgin?" he asked suddenly, his arms and face filthy with shadows that were really dirt.

I nodded.

He flicked his fingers across the plate, as though a demon had approached. "I need to sleep, Eliza. Is there a place?"

His bed had been stolen, but I lay blankets out for him, soft tufts of cotton that I had sewn into quilt pads one peaceful day so long ago.

"Here, Father. Sleep as long as you need to."

He had lost blood from a sword to his arm in those eighteen minutes of battle at San Jacinto. He also lost a finger on his left hand that he said he would no longer need anyway since he was right-handed. As he sat at the table, he held up his shaking grimy hand to show me. He started to count his fingers aloud, but after 'one' he hesitated.

"Which comes next?" he asked.

"Pardon?"

"After 'one'?" He shook his head in disgust. "I can't count anymore, Eliza. I don't know why. One day I woke up hungry and did not have the knack."

"Well, now your belly is not hurting, maybe your numbers will come back." I stood behind him with my hand on his shoulder blade, stroking him. He smiled, but he couldn't stop shaking.

My father died in the winter after our next harvest. I decided not to send to my uncle for help, and by myself, I laid Benjamin Green out in clothes he had kept all the way from the Carolinas, dug him a hole, and put his body on my quilt, rolling it out the door and across the mud. I sank a thick post into the soil at the back of my house to mark where I would put him, and then I lifted the side of the blanket and shoved him into his grave. He had stiffened like a crossbeam and fell into the gap with a sharp thud, and it took me two days to shovel enough soil into his hole to fill it. After that I said his favorite prayer and took my quilt down to the river to wash it and cover it in fresh mint leaves.

By February, the folks of Matagorda became aware that I was alone and sent the new sheriff out to poke in my affairs. Sheriff Zoller and his fudgewit wife showed up one Sunday afternoon, circling round my property.

"Not seen you at church," Missus Zoller said. She was wearing a pink ruffled dress that made her look like a stacked cake, and she screwed up her dishpan face like a dung beetle on the hunt.

"What's this?" asked Zoller, pointing to my father's pole.

I turned to look at the sheriff. I moved from one foot to the other, not knowing whether to tell the truth until all at once I blurted out, "That's Benjamin Green. Show some respect, will you?"

Zoller came toward me and I took a few steps back. He kept moving forward and finally caught hold of me.

"Eliza, you out here all by yourself?"

I closed my eyes and for some damn reason tears squeezed out. I took a deep breath, but the tears kept rolling down.

"You can't live on your own," his wife said, her voice twanging like catgut. "There's Karankawa faring forth. And Comanches. No one is here to defend you."

Zoller held me at arm's length. "Your papa was propertied and you aren't of age to administer it." He squinted down at me. "How old are you anyway?"

"Fourteen years, but I know how to run this farm."

"Who's your guardian now?"

"No one."

"You must have a guardian, girl. What did the judge say?"

"Not been a judge. No one's been to Becky Creek in weeks and weeks."

"You can't be chasing plows on your own. Has your uncle seen to you?" Zoller sounded slow and crabby like the corn cracker from Kentucky that he was. I could have said that to him, but I was afraid of him.

"My uncle? I haven't laid eyes on his fat belly in years."

Missus Zoller straightened her shawl around her shoulders and chest. "You'll come with us until this is settled."

"No, ma'am, I don't want to leave Becky Creek. It's my home."

I half expected her husband to lunge at me. But I didn't care; my sister had been sent away, my grandma was dead, and my father's body lay in the ground at my feet. We had traveled together to this land at the world's end and it was all I had left.

"Yes, girl," said Mister Zoller, "and it always will be. But now you must come to safety until the judge appoints a guardian for you. Your community will protect you. I'm the new sheriff, so you are obliged to obey me."

Come March, I stood before them all in a broken-down shack they called the courthouse on the bay at Matagorda. A pot-belly stove was behind the circuit judge, but I shivered on the damp floor planks on the other side of his desk. He had a great hulking body and he smelled as foul as a hangman.

"Mister Zoller will take you in and report to this court each year about your welfare. His compensation and your lodging will derive from the sale of or rent from a measure of the land previously belonging to Benjamin Green, your father." I listened to the judge's pronouncements, while the seeps of winter darkened into my caving stomach.

"What about my sister?" I shouted. "Where is she? What about her? Becky Creek belongs to us!"

"Miss, you are mighty malapert for a young woman in such a pickle. You would do far better to think before you open your gob again." He leaned back in his chair so far that I prayed for him to fall and crack that evil skull. "Your sister is being cared for. Yours are two different cases. Your uncle, James Green, has prepared a document describing the origins of your mother, entirely different of course from Miss Louisiana's mother. In this Republic of Texas, pickaninnies do not inherit property. Pickaninnies are themselves property."

"Pickaninny? You lost your wits? My mother's people were Melungeon, not Negro."

He slammed his flat hand down on the desk so hard the noise caused me to step back. "Keep quiet. Your uncle has made us aware of your true nigger blood."

I could see he was clearly and egregiously so bad and so powerful that he could and would steal a girl's only possessions.

"Yours is a more complicated situation, of course," he announced, "because your father was a hero of our Republic of Texas. You have his blood too, and we do not dispute that. Consequently, it is my decision that this community will care for you until you reach the age of eighteen years. You will live with Mister Zoller and he will educate you as necessary. You will then be a free citizen of this country."

The judge stared, waiting for my appreciation of this freedom, expecting me to dip and bow for what he deemed a gift. I merely stared back at him for the buzzard ogre he was.

"However, the remainder of Benjamin Green's property is

from this day ceded to his brother, James Green, for inheritance by Louisiana when she reaches the age of sixteen."

My breathing quickened with my heartbeat, while Mister Zoller grabbed my arm so hard that I had those bruises for weeks. He pulled me down the steps toward his wife who waited at the hitch, and all that was left to me was a glance at the far blue bay and the waves folding to shore.

That afternoon the Zollers took me in the back of a buckboard to their home at Live Oak Creek. They sat on the seats in the front, drintling like turkeys as we rolled over the hard road to their acreage. Missus Zoller's voice droned on, and every time she turned to look, her frogeyes glared at me. Between deep catches of breath, I jostled about on the flat cart-bed, knowing I had been finessed by the lot of them.

When we reached the plantation, I entered through the front doors of the home for the first and last time. The Zollers preceded me down the short narrow corridor, into a house that stank like it had once been flooded with riverwater.

Then I fell upon the hallway look-back glass.

I had been told by my sister that I looked wild, and Micah had said I was pretty. On this queer afternoon, I stopped abruptly in front of the polished glass. Those were the pieces of me put together now. I couldn't move. That was Eliza, hair dark and curly, and wild like a hurricane. Skin the color of swamp wood. Eyes pale like grey forest jasper. I could be Melungeon or Mulatto; I was what they wanted me to be.

I turned round and saw my captors. I looked back at the mirror and saw my life.

CHAPTER 6

*a*t the Zollers' home, I was put in an attic room, small and dark, and I hated how quickly I came to know my place. My first morning at Live Oak, a tin whistle sounded out back and shortly after, a watch master dragged me from my sleeping cot, stumbling down the rough stairs and out across a clean tiled floor to a mudhole behind the ovens. He pushed me to my knees in the stinking sop of scraps and tore my sleeping shift from my shoulders until I was naked to my waist. The cook brought a blade from the shed and pulled my head back, shaving my hair from widow's peak to neckline, again and again, until all around me lay my hair, the only thing that had been left to me, settling into the mud.

"You won't need all that hair, girl," Missus Zoller said as she stared, contented at what her people did to me. "You be working from here on. Better off without it."

The watch master nodded while bootless runners carrying tools passed us. "Go on," he said to the cook, who turned and went inside.

"Now girl," Missus Zoller said, "this is your first day at Live Oak, and it's time to give you the mark of our home so you will never be lost from us." I lurched to stand, but the watcher pushed me back to the mud, face down and splayed out like a dead girl, and he put his foot on my back.

He squatted at my head and took a rag, dipping it into a pot of oil and rubbed it across my shoulder. "Now it won't stick to your skin," he said.

When the cook returned, she carried an iron that glowed red in the weak morning light. The watch master took it, and the two of them held me with my face in the mud, while he put that iron to my left shoulder, holding it there while I screamed.

Finally, Missus Zoller said, "All right. That's plenty long," and he lifted the iron off me although the pain did not stop. The cook pulled me into the house to a stool near the hearth, where she instructed me to sit. And I did, my body shaking, my head shaved, and my shoulder scorched with pain.

Every time I thought they had taken everything, these devils managed to find another piece of me to steal. Truth is, whatever little we have left, it does become our joyful heart, and so I sat on that stool for a very long time, picturing Becky Creek, the home they stole, the eye of my heaven.

I worked for the Zollers for one miserable year, sweeping and fetching and mopping. When they caught me growing plants out back, they beat me and chained me to my bed at night. I soon learned how to knife through the tiny iron works of their shackle locks, and late some nights I would free myself and sneak into their book room.

I had not forgotten the lessons my grandmother had taught me. She said that people could take away everything you owned or loved, but they could never steal your mind. Some nights I would take a book to work through. I knew the alphabet and I could put some of the letters together, so I promised myself I would figure out new words, sound them out and discover their truths.

When I was fifteen the judge decided I should be allowed to stay with the Zollers another year. Weeks later, Zoller came to me at night wanting sexual pleasure, and I kicked him in the knackers and watched him howl. He whipped me for it and one of the stripes he left on my back never did disappear. But a short time thereafter Mister Edwards from Wharton was named my new guardian, and there I was transported, farther still from Becky Creek and farther from Lou.

I was allowed in the front door of the Edwards' Cairo House Plantation and when I finished my chores, they let me set on the bank of the Colorado, summoned by my dreams to drink the river water in the summer's richest hours. The bees flew through sunlight beside me, while I imagined the edges of a home I might have one day, always with a broad porch where I could rest and rock.

Despite the kindness of the Edwards family, I slept every night in my room with my back to the wall while covering a small kitchen knife in my hand. But in that room I had my own glass, and in it I saw my mouth and plump lips, my skin the mix of Carolina farmers and swamp Melungeons; I saw my eyes, clearer than all else, sharper and truer than a singing thrush.

Edwards had twin sons, gawky young teenagers who could barely read. Their father had the greatest pride and hope for them, but they made a mux of whatever they touched. They were slow but sweet, and so I began to teach them their letters and their numbers all over again. As they learned their alphabet and read lines, Mister Edwards called me by my name.

Then one miraculous day, a friend arrived at Cairo House Plantation. He rode up in a uniform on a glossy black stallion of seventeen hands. He slipped from his saddle and saw me standing in the vegetable garden.

"Mary Mother of God!" he exclaimed, and looking up at him, with the wind and light working off each other, I came close to believing that even Lou might round the house and put her hand in my own.

"Three-Legged Willie, my old friend," I whispered. I threw my arms around him and pulled him so close.

"You are choking me, Miss Eliza!"

"I'm sorry." I stood back swaying with laughter like a navvy half seas over. "I'm so happy to see you."

"You have become a handsome woman, Eliza." He looked at my costume, spun from the cotton grown in these fields, dyed a deep Dresden blue by the sad prisoners bound to this estate.

"A new dress," I said. "A gift from Missus Edwards."

"I'm not referring to your outfit. You are so pretty you'd cause a man to plow through a stump."

Three-Legged Willie could make Old Scratch smile.

"You are a flannel-mouthed liar," I chuckled. "But I love you for it."

He hobbled toward me and put his arms around me again. "What are you doing at Cairo anyway? Are you here for the wedding?"

"No. Who's getting wedded?"

"Why, me. To the Edwards girl. You didn't know?"

I looked behind me to see if we were alone among the pumpkin vines. The back of the main house was snow white against the wisteria, and the broad green meadow lay beyond. I had been blessed here; though not of pure blood like the Edwards, I was given washed clothes, sufficient food, and I could not remember the last time I had been locked up.

"No," I whispered. "Mister Edwards has my title deed."

"What? Where is your father?"

"He passed over in the winter of '37."

Willie pushed me out to the length of his arms and stared at me. "I'm sorry, Eliza. What the hell happened to Becky Creek?"

"Damned Texans stole it. All of it. My uncle and the Zollers and their judges. I expect even Edwards got some of our acreage."

Willie shook his head and stood helpless in front of my tragedy. "It was some of the best land around."

"They stole it, Willie. You can see that. Father died and they saw an opportunity, so they took everything that was mine and Lou's."

He reached out for my hands.

"I am owned now," I whispered. "By the family you are marrying."

"I would stand up for you if I could."

At my feet lay rocks I couldn't lift from the rows, and the sad snout of a dead vole, all wound in the vines. "Yes, Willie."

"You know I can't give up this marriage. After all these years looking, the Edwards girl is the only one who would have a man with three legs." He stood tall in trim starched trousers, yet his forehead was lined and his eyes tilted sadly. "Forgive me."

"I do," I said. "I understand."

"Your father gave me back my leg," he said. "I would do anything to help you if I could."

"Nothing to be done. Marry and have such a life you won't be looking back." As I said it a magpie dived hard at the dung-covered carrion beside us.

CHAPTER 7

*E*dwards was a kindly owner, and the slaving families said he would be saved because of this. They gave sacred testimony for him on Sundays in their lord's house, desiring to keep our master safe and prosperous. But let me tell you this: there is no place in Zion for people to own people. I know a fact or two and that's one of them. Melungeon or Negro or Indian, none of that matters to those of us who are bought and traded for seed and horses. The end times will show my truth, and there will be no salvation for these slaver devils. Edwards thought of me as an animal, and any pretense to kindness died in that.

Willie rested at Cairo near a month, learning the ways of a slaving plantation, finding me when he could to bring sweetmeats given him by the Cairo cook. On the rise of the new month, families began arriving for the wedding from the farming counties and the near coastal counties like Brazoria and Matagorda, and I prayed that Lou might be among them.

It was years since our father had sent her away to live with Uncle James, but I searched for my sister with every wagon that let off young girls. She would be nineteen years nearly, married perhaps, or she might arrive in a gown with her hair pinned up.

In my mind, I could hear her voice while I lay in the rustling grasses beside the river, and I wailed like a beast hoping she might hear me from wherever she was. But none of them came, not even Uncle James. And then one day near the wedding, Edwards told me he had not invited them.

"They are not our sort of folks," he said.

"I'm not fretting. He is not my sort either. I was just hoping to see my sister."

Edwards nodded and looked at the ground. I knew he was embarrassed. After all, I was only a creature to him; as kind as he might be, I was not expected to think or feel.

On the day the Edwards girl was wed to Three-Legged Willie, I climbed the slopes of the cutting to watch. I was eye level with the white flutes of the lilies set upon their poles; they curved and sagged like swallows into the deep blue sky. Alone on the riverbank that afternoon, I was so small and unimportant that I could have passed through the eye of my grandma's needle.

In the distance, I saw the bride standing awkwardly in the center of her neighbors, her head bent forward and her shoulders rounded, yet wearing the loveliest white lace I had ever seen. She wrapped her arms around herself, nervous and holding her own body tight, with her big tadpole face gazing at Willie as though he could light a lamp in the deepest winter. Then they all sang to the Lord and declared His glory. And I, outsider to them, clung to the grasses of the cuts still praying my sister would come to me.

I fell asleep on the bank and when I opened my eyes the rough shoots clung to my face. I brushed them away and sat up. Night was about, and the wedding had turned to a shivaree. Lanterns down the meadow filled Cairo with a beautiful yellow glow, while those guests danced and clapped and ate the rich pastries I had watched the cook bake in the kitchen that day. I had missed supper and my stomach was sharply empty, so I pulled my legs up to my chest to shush the hunger growls.

Beside me, something moved. I was far enough from the

house that it might have been a polecat or a coyote. I turned quickly to cause it to run, but instead I saw that boy, Micah, stepping into the moonlight to peer at me.

"Hey, girl. What you doin' out here? Why aren't you at the shindig?"

"Not invited," I said and shrugged. "How did you uncover my hiding?"

He put his hand out to help me stand, and I took it.

"There's always people who know where people are. Three-Legged Willie, for one."

"He's not drunk yet?"

Micah shook his head with a grin as broad as the crescent moon. He had grown tall from the red-faced boy I knew before, into a handsome belvedere of a man standing beside me in his best bib and tucker.

"I marvel at you, Eliza." He took my spread from the ground, nothing but a bolt of frayed old lutestring ready to line some potato scrappings bucket; he took this and held it for me like a robe of ermine.

"Thank you, Micah," I whispered. I thought of the teenager sleeping alongside me underneath the cart in the rain, and I understood that the cord connecting us was buried deep now. "What brings you to Cairo?" I asked.

"Willie got word to me that he was calling quits to his mollynogging ways and taking a bride. So out I come. I been working the mines in Mexico, looking for silver."

"Find any?"

Micah chuckled. "Ain't no easy silver for folks like you 'n' me, Eliza. Whatever we get, we always have to work hard for."

I laughed and Micah did too. We were a songbird's full flight from the party, so Edwards could not hear us.

"Micah," I whispered, "you offer some smiles."

"You got anything here, Ellie?"

"What d'you mean?"

"Anything here you are feared to lose? Property, clothes...anything?"

I chortled out loud. "Property? They took it all. Every stitch I wear belongs to Edwards or the judges. I got nothing now."

Micah nodded and touched my hand as it lay upon the grass.

"They didn't do right by your pa. I know you got no dowry, but it doesn't matter to me."

"Dowry, boy? What are you talking about?"

He stood and gazed into my face. He wore a broad straw hat tilted to the back of his head, and I swear I saw a shooting star or a single drop of light beside him. "This is wedding season. We could run off tonight and never come back."

"Get away! Why're you coming here telling me these silly things after all these years?"

"I guess you might say I missed you."

"Such fulsome horse shite."

"I'm telling you true. My uncle is over in Ticklefoot at Grimes County, resting with my sister. I'm heading there in a day or two, but we could leave tonight and neither Willie nor Edwards would ever know what happened. My uncle's a preacher back in Alabama. He can marry us, and then you will no longer belong to these thieves."

Micah was rare and I knew it. I looked straight ahead at the sycamore trees in the full moon. Some slave had left a pitchfork leaning against one of them, some young man abandoning his work for a beauty in the cotton rows. Suddenly it was a spear, aiming through my open heart.

"We all know you shouldn't be slaving except for satisfying the crimes of these men," Micah whispered.

"They're claiming I'm Mulatto. You heard that?"

"I did. Willie told me your uncle swore to that. You don't deserve any of this."

I shrugged. "Whether it's true or not, I been slaving for a few years and I'll tell you, Micah, nobody deserves that life. But I got the brand on my shoulder to prove their story."

"Maybe it doesn't matter, Eliza. Maybe I just don't care."

"Well, whoever my people were, I won't always be a slave. In six months, I'm eighteen, and then I will be free. It's written by the court."

"Tonight," he repeated. "Right now."

"Come back in six months," I said.

"You can't trust any of 'em to keep their oaths."

"But can I trust you?"

He stepped up to me and put his fingers on my cheeks, a rough touch from a workingman's tools. He grazed his tongue over my lips but stopped at once and grinned.

"I knew your taste would be sweet." He turned me around and I felt his fingers fumbling at the opening of my frock. He breathed deeply as he tried to slip the wood buttons through the eyelets, and having undressed me beneath the arch of my back, he slipped my sleeves down and touched the old branding wound on my shoulder.

"Don't matter, Ellie. None of it." He laid his head against that jagged mark on my skin, and though I couldn't see him I knew his body was making a prayer.

As my breath ruptured to tears, a hare limped onto the riverbank before us, its fur silky from the moonlight, and Micah did up my buttons.

"Come with me," he said and took my hand. High over the moonlit fog, I heard the cock crowing on the red ridge tiles. This man was so eager to please me. What could be the downfall of love?

We mounted his horse and he teed it to a gallop. He was beating his hat against the flanks of the animal, and I was holding on for my own life, pressed against the warmth of Micah's body as we pushed across the open wind of the plain. He well knew the road to his sister's ranch up north, and he set us flying. When we approached the Brazos, a wild curled river glowing in the moonlight, we stopped to water the animal.

"You are a mighty driver," I said, gulping at breath. The muscles in my legs were taut and sore, and I stumbled a step in the black night. Micah reached for me, helping me to find balance, and though he probably did not see it, I turned and smiled at him.

"I been working on the Rio del Norte for a couple years. Out there we got the best animals in Texas." He put his hand on the dark silk of the horse's neck. "This is Cash. Pretty much all I got in the world."

"You planning on going back there after we get married?"

Micah was tall and lean with light hair that fell across his forehead so that even in the moonlight I could not determine his expression. "I'm not a miner anymore, not a ranger either. Those are jobs for rough men and bandits. My sister's husband is a farmer so I guess I'll be learning that trade from him now." And with that, the burden of my heart was rolled away like the stone from Jesus' tomb.

Facing the trail again, we held hard and fast, reaching the piney grove at Ticklefoot by first light.

His horse was drained and drunk on sweat, and we fell silent, beaten by exhaustion. We crept through the gates as the light lifted a yellow line across the flat horizon.

"Wait." I slipped down from the saddle to stretch. "I'll walk from here."

The path was lined with enormous sunflowers, and in between them were scrawny red poppies tangling at my feet. I loved those yellow and red colors crossing together, and all I asked for in life was a home like this with some flowers. I looked out at the dawn over the dusty plain and felt I was in heaven's fields. God save me, I never wanted more.

"I can still feel the wind swirling," Micah said, and he jumped down beside me.

"That's dreamin', boy."

"Sometimes dreamin' is truth." He grabbed my hand and we walked up the road to the front door of the farmhouse with the smell of chimney smoke rising to the sky.

Inside, the husband of Micah's sister was stoking the stove with chunks of pine and he waved us close to the fire's roar without opening his gob. We stood side by side, warming our hands till we could feel them move again, while the sweet smell of charring wood filled the room.

"Morning," said Micah, pulling tall to his full height.

"Micah." Neither showed surprise or affection.

"This is Eliza Green. We are betrothed and I aim to get my uncle to do it for us."

"I expect he will. Still sleeping yet. Where's the girl's pa and ma?"

"Dead," Micah said. "Where's my sister?"

"Fetching eggs." The man nodded, staring at me. "I reckon the two of you are unfed as yet. Looks like you been riding hard. Girl, go out to the hutch and tell my wife we have two more for the meal."

I started for the back door, but Micah stopped me. "I'll go." He disappeared out back while the smell of dung crept in from the yard.

"Where ya from?" asked this ginger-haired fellow.

"Yazoo River's where I was born. Been in Texas since I was little though."

"How'd you come to know my wife's kin?" His voice was deep and suspicious, but I figured he was all the family I had right then so I smiled back at him pretending he meant no harm.

"He ferried me to safety in the Runaway Scrape."

He nodded. "You best go clean up for breakfast. You'll find a well out there."

I scurried out and was glad to be free. At the well, I dipped the ladle in the bucket to clean my face and hands. I pulled my dust-bound hair back into a bun and smoothed the wrinkles and dirt from my dress, pitifully trying to become a lady for these people who were now my protectors.

Micah and his sister came upon me, arm in arm, like children.

"Ellie!" he called out. "This is my sister, America."

Blonde as her brother with a smile as bright, she took my hands and held them, gazing at me.

"He will be your husband, girl. Thank goodness." She put her arm around my waist and we walked up the steps to the kitchen.

We sat to table with the others, two grown sons and three daughters, all of them dressed in frayed work clothes. Micah's uncle sat next to me, watching for my first wrong gesture. But I had been a stranger for more years than not, and I had learned well the ways of pretending to be part of someone else's family.

"I will be happy to join together the two of you," Uncle Moore said. "But I need to have your parents' permission, as you are not of majority."

"They're in their graves now. I'm an orphan."

"Then who is your guardian?"

I looked at Micah.

"She had a godly mother, Uncle. She passed when Eliza was born. Her father fought at San Jacinto and has moved to his Maker." Micah's rawboned face was strained, and he struggled for the right words.

"Who is in charge of her?"

"I am," said Micah.

Uncle Moore stared. He lifted his eyebrows but said nothing.

"Truth, Uncle."

"You are not touching the face of God, son. What are you two running from?"

Micah's brother-in-law rose. He shoved his chair across the wood floor loud enough to make the animals scatter. "I'm going to fetch the cows. If it's true she's an orphan, and I believe it, then marry them. What's to lose?" He walked to the door, calling his sons behind him. "Get on with it," he said to Uncle Moore. "We got chores and I could use their help."

The children followed their father into the daylight. Micah and I stood by the fire with his sister, his uncle holding a huge preacher-size Bible, and this is how I became Eliza Moore and left Green behind, while the others were out with the cows, some believing my story, some not, and some not even caring.

After, Uncle Moore lay the Bible on the dining table, and looked about the room for a jar of ink. Empty handed, he glared at Micah's sister. "I'll do the recording," he said, pulling a clean goose quill from the center fold of the Bible. "But I'll need a jar of ink, America."

"Uncle, I'm afraid we don't have much use for ink on this farm. But I promise we will write their names and this marriage in our Bible as soon as we can afford to purchase some."

Our wedding feast was a pottage from scraps, and legumes we had plucked out of the dirt. After dinner, Micah and I helped with chores until we were so tired we fell asleep in our place in the haybarn. Long into the darkness he came to me, lay his body across my own and began slipping in and out of me. He whispered strange commands, but I was covered with fear and softened by wonder, allowing him in and nestling him close.

CHAPTER 8

Two days later on the Sabbath we aimed to go with the family to the Baptist tabernacle tent. The others went in the mule cart together, while the two of us stayed behind to finish the cows before we set out. I stood on the edge of the weedy plain, waiting for the sun to rise and for Micah to finish his chores. I pulled his sister's hat around my head, squashing the dark curls to my cheeks against the wind whooping off the horizon. And in the distance, I perceived an animal, or perhaps a rider, some object approaching nearer and nearer. Its outline grew more and more distinct, until it seemed to be leveling straight at me, fast and heavy.

As the animal approached, I saw it held a man, and that I knew this one.

He skidded to a stop near me.

"Miss Eliza," he said. "What're you doin' here?"

I shook my head, wishing to God that Micah was near.

"Get away! Leave me be!" I shouted.

The man leaned forward over the pommel of his saddle, his third leg swinging back uncontrollably. "Eliza, girl. You can't run away. They will find you and harm you bad."

"Who?" I asked. "The lawgivers of Matagorda? Or your Edwards family who took me as their slave? Those are thieves, Willie."

He was sweating from the ride, breathing hard and near to crying. "I'm here to bring you back," he said, void of course and just as lost.

And then I heard Micah's voice behind me. "You ain't taking her anywhere, Willie. Stop there."

I turned and saw him, holding a rifle to his chin, trained on Willie, his friend and fellow ranger.

"Leave it, Micah," Willie growled. "They gave me authority to arrest you both."

"This is her place. With me, Willie. We are married now."

"Boy," Willie sighed. "If you keep running, you won't ever be able to return to this county. Nor put your foot on the soil anywhere on this coast." Willie looked at both of us, quickly and scatter-eyed with pain. "If you come with me now, I will tell them you never ran. I can lie that you were upriver and lost. Listen to me, son; if not, you and Eliza are walking into a life of sorrow."

"Get back to your new family, Willie," said Micah, obstinate as a quarryman. "Get back to your wife and I will stay with mine."

Slowly, Willie removed his hat and rested it on the pommel. He pulled a small Bible from his saddle bag, unclasping it gently like a book of the arcane intents. He let it fall open, sobbing while he read, *Do not be deceived: God is not mocked, for whatever one sows, that will he also reap.* He stopped, choking back hard on the next words. "I can't," he whispered, and dumb with despair, he threw that damned book to the dirt.

I walked closer to him. "Willie, we're not going with you."

He wiped the sweat and tears from his face with a road-dirty hand. "By grace, I am an unworthy servant. I dishonor everyone."

Micah stepped beside me and said quietly, "A friend you are and always will be," but his rifle was still aimed at our intruder's heart.

"Run, girl," Willie said. "Know that I never came here today, and I won't tell tales to your master, Eliza. You and Micah, run till your legs won't carry you no more. And one day when you think on it, say a blessing for those of us who got left behind."

He set his hat firmly on his head, turning his horse to an easy Canterbury gallop down the road to the gate, and out into the open prairie.

Micah and I sat alone near the hearth, with the old iron stove surrounded by hot bricks and the cook plate still steaming coffee. I brought the pot to him and filled his cup.

"The life we have will be different from what I hoped," he said. "You afraid?"

Unsure of myself but unbending, I put my fingers on his arm without answering.

"You understand what I'm saying? We have to leave. Before the others come home. And Willie was right. We can't come back here, anywhere down here."

"But these are your kin. I don't want to cause you to run like this. What will our lives be like?"

He slammed his heel into the floor and my heart thudded.

My breaths labored shorter and shorter, until disembodied and faithless, I leaned away from him. "Do you want to send me back?"

He did not touch me but said, "Eliza, I been loving you for a few years now. I tended to you in my dreams out in the desert." He sat quietly then, while a hundred thoughts raced through me.

"I reckon the best place for us is to ride north to Nacogdoches," he said at last. "There's Caddo there, good people, and a friend of mine from my New Mexico ranging days has a home nearby. Although there's also some Comanches. But we'd be close enough to the border that we could escape quick into the

United States if we needed to. Otherwise, we'll hide there till you come up eighteen. As long as we don't cross into these southern counties till then, we'll be safe."

I took a step back and he stared at me. "I'm acquainted with Caddos. When my father was alive they were trustworthy to us. What about the Mexicans? Your brother-in-law said they were storming our borderlands, making war against Texas."

"That's only the southern border, Ellie. Anyway, my friend is Mexican. Tejano. If he takes us in, we'll be safe."

"As long as Edwards doesn't get the truth out of Willie. If he does, they'll be packing after us."

Micah took a knife and a small chunk of whittling pine from the table. As he put the blade to the wood he said, "Do you think you are worth all that to these people, Ellie?"

"It isn't a matter of what I'm worth. It's what folks think they lost. They took my home and everything I had. Now it's their pride they'll be coming after."

"Then pack up a coupla days' food from my sister's storage, and I'll get the bedrolls onto Cash." Micah leaned over and took my hand. "We'll be safe, girl. I'll make sure of it."

"Do you regret taking me on?"

He put his arms around me and put his mouth on mine. I could smell the wood chips on him, and the soapstone ashes too. "Never. Not now or ever."

CHAPTER 9

We set onto the El Camino road north to Nacogdoches territory. Holding to the ranger practice of camping for the early eve long enough to cook supper, we let the smoke swirl about the landscape. As soon as darkness hit, we would take off on a gallop as far as Cash could carry us and throw down camp for the night. In this way, any pursuers would be chasing only our cook smoke.

A few days later, Micah, me, and Cash emerged from the thick chaparral of central Texas, road-weary and filthy. We were far from any town or Caddo camp, but I saw a dark line in the distance, and as we grew near, it became a cleft fence stretching till I couldn't see it anymore. The glowing red dust of the sunset hung over the horizon, and we trotted up to a high carved gate, no name painted across, just a wood plank suspended over the road by tall pine poles.

"We'll walk from here," Micah said. "You lag behind a ways but stay close enough to me. Rafael Bereminda is my dear friend, but his guards don't know that."

We passed a row of *jacal* huts that had one room and a porch, with workmen lounging about and staring at us. Micah asked in Spanish for the *hacendado* owner, and they answered him without hesitation. I could smell onions frying somewhere, and beef smoking. I was so hungry I thought my knees would give way to those smells. Already, we had come far but we kept on, walking Cash slowly as though we weren't starving. Somehow the horse knew to be silent, and we moved carefully to the final gates where men stood with firearms. Painted across this grand entry was the word 'Bereminda'.

The home was surrounded by a high and thick clay wall with a small porch behind the tethering rails. I stood beside my new husband in the sharp sunlight, thinking that a cool sip of water would bring such a revival in me, when suddenly the huge oak doors opened and a man stepped from the darkness within. Short and stubby, bald with a sweet wide grin and elaborate moustache, he strode to Micah as a lost brother.

Micah threw his arms around him. "Oh, my Lord, Rafe! Seeing you again is sweet! And this," he held his hand out to take mine, "this is my wife, Eliza."

I had never seen a man dressed in such a costume as Rafael. He wore brown velvet pantaloons with tiny gold studs down the sides, an ivory cotton shirt embroidered with white silk, and a bolero thrown across his shoulders that was as brilliantly colored as Joseph's own coat. He was not haughty, but his face was tilted up to the horizon as though he was waiting on instructions from an angel of God.

"Welcome, Señora." He smiled broadly. "Please come," and he pointed to the open door.

We entered a vestibule and kept on through smaller doors into a square open area where children were running wild in the soft powdery dirt.

"What brings you to Bereminda?" he asked Micah. "Have you traveled far?"

Micah nodded and subconsciously put one hand on his Paterson pistol. Rafael's eyes flashed to that. "We drove hard for days and nights. Needing protection now, my friend."

Bereminda held his arm out to us without question, and we followed him through another door. The minute we moved beyond the dust and sunlight, I felt cooler. I nearly collapsed into a huge oak chair, and a woman came to us, carrying tall drinks of sugared water and citrus. We grabbed them.

"My God," Rafael exclaimed, "when is the last time you drank?"

"Oh, not long ago."

"Yesterday?"

Micah laughed. "Maybe."

The woman offered us more and we kept drinking, the faint taste of limes sliding down my gullet.

"Is that pleasing?" Bereminda asked.

Micah put his hand out to touch mine. "You could not even dream it, dear friend. *The fountain of the river of life.*"

Rafael nodded slowly. "We saved each other's lives a few times, Micah. Lost as we were on the escarpment where the air smelled like a coffin." He turned to me. "Your husband was so fearless, even the Comanches said he was possessed of a double backbone." Rafael smiled kindly at Micah. "As long as I have a morsel, Sergeant Moore, half of it belongs to you."

Bereminda led us through his home, each of the rooms connected to the others around a garden of bougainvillea and gardenia and lilacs. In the very center was a pond with huge sparkling white fish, swimming like pets, chubby and determined. We followed our host until he stopped at rooms that he intended for us.

∽

Late into the dark of that night, I heard the *guitarristas* playing in the hacienda square, and I felt beside me for Micah only to find him gone. I threw my old clothes and shawl around me and went to the porch where I saw him leaning over the polished pine railing. Two women sat on a wooden veranda across from us, and they were dressed in lace, beautiful colors combined in swirls of yellow and crimson.

In the open plaza between us were more musicians and couples dancing. Before us a small boy was pulling a wooden quockerwodger toy across the plaza, tugging it along by a purple ribbon. The moon was gone that evening, but lanterns were fixed along the eaves and a pit of wood fire flamed in the center.

"Why are they all up so late?" I asked, standing next to Micah.

He turned and smiled at me. "This is not late, girl. You just rode so hard your hours are ajee." He put his arm around my shoulder and I shuddered. "Don't be afraid of me, Ellie. You're safe here, and here with me."

I nodded. The smell of roasted pork was around us, but I hadn't rested enough to give urge to my hunger. Instead I looked hard at the happiness before me. "We are at the New Jerusalem surely?"

In the distance, a perfect blue roan stallion stood tethered near the vestibule, high-necked with a broad strong rump. A man dressed in white muslin over worn wool pants sat astride securing a bow and a long rifle to his pack. He pulled an old Spanish-style silver helmet onto his skull and waited while servants pushed wide the heavy gates for him alone.

"Come and see," Micah said. He grabbed my hand and led my bedraggled self down the steps and across the wondrous party before us, heading for the warrior in white. "That is Teddy Blue Corlies from my time out ranging. Come, let's greet him before he sets out. I fought with him out in the far territories."

He hurried me across the plaza toward the rider, and I pulled my old wool around me tight. I was mortified walking through this hidden compound of men and women in bright cotton and silk, such a distance from the chaparral frontier outside the cleft rails. The ladies wore delicate lace *mantilla* headscarves, draped from ivory hair combs down to their shoulders, and to me, a swamp girl slave, I thought they must all be Mexican princesses.

"Eliza, come! This is an old friend. What's making you lollygag?"

"Look at me! Dressed like the lowest rank of churl."

"Oh, girl," he whispered sadly, "your pride makes me lonely."

"My pride?"

The silence between us was raw, and I knew I had offended him. But I had only said my truth. We both looked to be Texan tramps among these refined Tejanos.

"One day," he said, "I will give you all you believe should be yours, and on that day, you will see the poverty of your pride. Be proud of your courage at the plantations, or of your bravery in the Scrape. Don't make your testimony about your frock."

He put my hand inside his own pocket, holding it warm and close. He nodded, and we walked quickly forward together to Teddy Blue Corlies.

"You damn fool! I know you!" called out this Teddy Blue.

He dismounted suddenly and threw his arms, covered with unembellished white muslin, around Micah. "When did you arrive? Your face is a kindly sight!" He was tall and muscled, and wore his curly light brown hair to his shoulders. His eyes were the deep blue of lake waters, and he looked to me, winking. "Why, you are not alone, Micah."

Giddy and smiling, my husband replied awkwardly, "This is my wife. This is Eliza."

Teddy Blue Corlies held his hand out. "I am very pleased, ma'am. This man has needed a wife for years." He bowed his head to me, and turned to the horse, lifting himself with deft ease into the saddle. They paused a moment, both of them glowing silvery blue in the lantern light. He nodded to us and as sudden as a spirit, clucked up the horse with a sharp, *C'mon Sam!* and rode through the gate into the darkness.

"Why is he dressed in an undergarment?"

Micah paused for quite some time, but I kept looking to him for the answer to my question. "Out in the territories, we called it Satan's frontier. The days there are full of heat and harm." He shook his head slowly. "Before us, each farmer with a rifle called himself the law. But when we came, homesteaders were grateful because we killed so easily. Satan's frontier. They called us Texas devils and that was not a lie. And Teddy Blue there, he even belongs to the Temple of Dead Boys."

Micah nodded toward another man lounging close to the women and the music players. "He's one too. Men who swear they will never forget a dead child's face. Rafael brought a few around him here, fierce men, but men who have gotten their souls ready to be laid flat on the prairie. They got burial clothes on when they ride out."

Smoke from the roasting marled around us, the sweetest smelling pork I had ever known. Plenty of foods were piled on tables before us, on huge platters painted with big brush blooms of many colors. Micah was so hungry he brought it all, roasted pumpkins filled with meat, squashes smelling of fresh comino spice, thick strips of sizzling beef, and soft-crusted sweet bread of which I had never tasted the like. And he gorged himself, tasting every food and gulping at some to swallow them whole.

During our meal, people danced before us, and Rafael Bereminda was one of them. He moved to the *seguidilla*, a proud courting dance, fast and driven by *vihuela* guitars and the deep pounding of the *bombos*. He danced with a black-haired woman of the greatest beauty, whose skin glistened the color of milked coffee. But when he saw us nearby, he stopped abruptly and approached us, holding her so gently and leading her toward us.

"My friends," he said, "this is Lariza, my dear love." Her eyes were black and wide, and as she held her hands out, she brought the scent of honeyed cloves. "Lariza is from the highlands of Michoacan. Her father was Purépecha, which is why she is so graceful and beautiful."

Lariza looked immediately away. "Please," she said to Rafael, her cheeks flushing. She held back slightly, stepping behind him.

"You have arrived on the night of my father's birthday," he said to us. "Did you know that? His grave is alongside the fishery. My father always cherished his fish." Then Rafael laughed loud and long, grabbing a piece of persimmon pie from the table. "*Los caquis* grow wild by the bayou. We have tried with other fruits and orchards but have not been successful. Still, *la torta caqui* is excellent."

"Is this your natural land?" I asked.

"Oh, no. I am from the Spanish state of Coahuila long before Mexico took over and engaged our impossible dictator and his mutton-headed army."

"Santa Anna?"

"Yes, Señora. When I refused to join him, he printed my name for all to see, as a devil traitor." Rafael put one arm around Micah's shoulders and shrugged. "Such is my fate out here at the end of the world," and he laughed out loud again.

"Don Rafael, I thought I saw pomegranates on the walk to your home. Is that right?" I asked.

"I don't know why God lets pomegranates grow here, with our swamp and mush. But yes, we do have wild pomegranates. But you must not venture beyond the plaza without accompaniment. Tomorrow, we will show you these trees. Tomorrow, during the daylight."

Bereminda put his hands on Lariza's shoulders, gathering the attention of many, and she, in turn, dipped her forehead to the heat and dust of the night.

"I must speak to our cooks," she said, "for just a moment and then I will return," and she slipped away into the shadows of the eaves.

Micah handed me our plate. "And I need to feed Cash and water him for the night."

Once alone, Rafael said, "Did Micah tell you that I lost my first wife? She died in San Saba when I was starting for the Alamo. I sent her to Mexico to escape the cholera, but it traveled straight to her anyway, and brought her down."

"I am so sorry, Don Rafael," I said. "So tragic to lose someone you loved so dearly. Do you have young ones?"

"We did. We had a small daughter. She traveled with her mother and died in the same way."

Boldly, I touched his arm and bowed my head. "You are a sweet man, Señor. You did not deserve these losses."

"Some nights I hear them pounding at my doors. If I am late, I know they are following me home. But most times they leave me be, as long as I am obedient." And with a sudden smile as broad as the lantern lights hanging about us, he added, "Lariza saved me from my agony."

Just then a priest, glossy as a young crow, approached us from his rooms.

"Father Esteban, this is my guest, Señora Moore. She and her husband have come to reside with us. Señora, please meet Father Esteban Molinaro."

His face was smooth and pale, but his hair jet black. His eyes were also the blackest of carbon, and he looked more a mascot than a man of God.

"My girl," he said and offered his cotton-soft hand to me.

"Are you here taking a last look before your prayers?" Rafael asked him.

The young man shook his head. "No, but I thought this

evening I might deserve one more piece of that fine persimmon pie." He spoke through his nose in short squeaking words.

Rafael paused, and narrowed his eyes at the man, hesitated, then suddenly, he swept his hand out to the table laden with pie. The priest nodded and walked to it, turning his back on us, and suddenly I saw him to be a shape-shifter, replete with multiple darkened souls.

My husband returned, wearing his Paterson in its holster at his waist. "All is well, Rafael. But my wife and I need to sleep."

"Of course, friend. I understand. I will see you next with the sunlight."

Someone had set the fire in the clay *chiminea* near our bed, so our room was warm. I slipped from the wool shawl and dress, and stood in my filthy cotton shift. I put one knee on the thick mattress padding over the bed, but Micah came to me and lifted me to stand again.

"Wait," he said. "We are both too rotten to get into these clean sheets."

He went to the washstand and took a soft cloth, dipped it into the warm soapy water and brought it to me.

"Pull your shift away," he said.

I hesitated a moment then lifted the cotton over my head, stretching tall and then letting it drop beside me. I was not embarrassed. He had seen me naked several times since we married, although never staring as tonight. He rocked back on his heels to keep his balance, and went to the table to pour himself a cup of *pulque* drink.

"That's not your first tonight, is it?" I asked.

Without answering, he swallowed it, and came toward me. He put the washing cloth to my neck in clean gentle strokes, and then swirled it around my breasts. At last he threw the cloth on the floor, and put one hand between my legs, slipping his fingers so slowly up into me. He bent slightly and put his lips on my nipples, sucking and teething so gently until I could no longer stand it and stepped away.

"Come back here, girl." He pointed near to him, and I stepped inside that place, where I could feel his chest rising and falling with my own anticipation.

CHAPTER 10

$\mathcal{W}$e set off the next morning with seven fierce men as our protectors. Neither Micah nor Rafael was intrigued by exploring for pomegranates, so the woman, Lariza, was my company. Our guards were Mexican, and they rode stocky Callahan ponies that could withstand arrows yet could run like Spanish horses. We traveled at a slow trot for an hour alongside hundreds of sinewy cattle, ruddy like Hades with long curved horns, more cattle than I had ever chanced to see, loose in broad pastures on either side of our trail.

When we reached the banks of the Angelina River, I found it to be an ugly muddy concoction of branches and silt, its sandbars stretching across the dark mud. We dismounted into the deep soil and stood beside a pomegranate tree that had grown strong from the marsh, and even King Solomon would never have expected to find such fecundity in this sickly dung hole of a stream. The ripe fruit was beginning to burst with deep red seeds that were filled with sweet juice clinging together in a fragile creamy membrane.

"Oh, pick them, please," I urged Lariza. "These are wild and perfect, and we may never see the like again." I took the small knife from my sack and made cuttings of the silken branches in the gulley. I wrapped them in cotton soaked in the Angelina and placed them in a bag on my saddle. We stopped for our midday meal in a humid patch of tall grasses, and being the only women in our party, Lariza and I sat on our own. As we tried to chew our venison, we were soon covered with tiny biting red bugs devouring us in the same manner.

"Have you lived at Bereminda long?" I asked.

She nodded and smiled at me, beautiful and guileless. "Several years. I met Rafael when I was a child. The first time he saw me I was covered in mud." Her black hair, thick and glossy, had begun to slip its combs and she let it fall across her shoulders and collarbone, shaking it out and then repinning it high on her head. "I am much younger than you think, Señora. My life has brought me some misery, mixed race and all. Maybe you understand?"

I said nothing, but she continued to watch me, stare even, kindly and simply seeking a friend. For a moment she reminded me of my sister.

"You are so pretty," I blurted.

Lariza blushed deep and hot, and lowered her head.

"I'm sorry," I said.

"Please don't be. I have been lucky." She looked up again. "Rafael's father paid for me and died shortly after. He wanted only me, not the others in my family, so I was alone until Rafael came home from the wars." Her voice was quiet but not sad, and I wanted the courage to tell her I had been sold as well, but quickly she asked, "Where is your family?"

I shook my head. "Micah is my family. The others died, except my sister but I haven't seen her in many years."

We sat on the shaded bank watching each other. Lariza waited a long time before speaking again, the outline of a forgotten smile on her lips. She lifted her hand from the grasses about us and put it across my own.

"Well then, we are both lucky with our men, aren't we? Such kindly partners for two women like us."

∾

Working through those wilds was painstaking. With grassy tufts embedded deep in the gullies that were also overgrown with dwarfish trees, we trudged heavily through the brambles to make our way from one pomegranate to another. By the time we emerged, the sun had moved halfway down the sky, and our guards called out end of day to hurry us home. We quickly secured our booty to the saddles, driving the reluctant animals from the mushy river bank up onto the trail. We followed the muddy winding Angelina along the bluff, our line of horses and tired riders darkening against the horizon. At one bend, the lead man paused in the shadows beneath the wild sycamores. Lifting his broad *vaquero* hat and baring his damp forehead, he slowly scanned the wide plain and slopes about us.

Suddenly and for no apparent reason, he waved that hat violently. Leaning forward, he heeled sharply into his horse's flanks. "*Rapido! Rapido! Vamos!*"

The other men followed and four-beat to a gallop alongside us, slapping the rumps of my mount and of Lariza's. The earth around us began to shake, the bullrushes trembling at the waterside, and thunder rumbled across the plain. And finally, my heart falling to the pit of my gut, I saw it too.

Out of swirling dust clouds on the plain, a group of Comanches charged toward us, coming straight and riding hard on the fastest horses I had ever seen.

I loosened the reins and my horse surged forward through the tall grasses, its neck jutting toward the horizon. Screaming, I rode hard into the distance, unaware even of the fate of my companions until one of our guards advanced close beside me, grabbed my reins, and took my pounding horse to a faster gallop across the dry landscape. Feverish with fear to save only myself, I allowed him to drag me on, the bags of pomegranates bouncing uselessly from my saddle.

The Comanches shot at us with rifles and bows as we fled, and one of our soldiers tumbled from his mount to the ground. Another rode to save the body, but we lost him as well, and the rest of us pushed ahead furiously, covered with hot fear, toward the safety of Bereminda.

One other of ours fell to Comanche bullets before we entered the gates, but it was not until I stood inside the compound, gasping and stricken with horror, that I saw Lariza was no longer with us.

When the guards told their story to Rafael, they estimated seventeen Comanches in war paint, carrying evidence of prior battles, putrid flesh dangling from their saddles. The warriors had carried lassos over their saddles, whirling them high and flinging them toward Lariza until she was roped by three Comanches and held motionless in the dirt.

Within minutes of hearing this tale, Micah was in our rooms, loading weapons and changing to thick leather chaps and leather jacket that might withstand arrowheads. He collected two Colts, a musket and a rifled gun, and then untied a hidepack roll of knives.

"Will they kill her?" I asked.

He walked to me holding a small double-edged knife, curved and pointed, much like the old circumcision blades I had seen at Cairo Plantation. Without putting this down, he spread his arms around my shoulders.

"We may be back tomorrow. Or we may be...a few days." He smelled like animal hide, and I realized that what he truly meant was that he might not be back at all. I reached for his wrist and held his knife-hand in front of us.

"What is this one for?" I asked.

"This is a hard country, and we are no different from the Comanches."

"Micah, promise you will not commit savagery."

"I have never taken an oath I couldn't keep, Eliza. The Lord is testing me now, because I want to make that promise to you, but I can't."

A small group was left behind to protect us, and each of the adult women was armed with a rifle as well. Since the hacienda occupied the inner rise of one *sitio* of land, these four thousand acres and well-stationed permanent guards gave most of us in the compound a sense of safe haven. Bereminda had never been attacked in its entire lifespan, and several of the elderly men referred to it as the 'holy hill'. That evening the cooks made us all a simple supper, and after this early meal, the other women and children were abed.

I had known how to shoot from the time I was a child, so I joined the guards at dusk in their hideaway lookouts. The first who saw me climb the ladder shook his head hard and waved me away without speaking. I ignored him, reshouldered my rifle, and moved up to the parapet ledge. The men were hidden within secret spaces in the thick *adobe* clay walls, focused keen on peepholes that would fit the barrel of the Sharps rifles they held. I took a place alongside them, in a slender space, dark and moist, and smelling of filth and urine. Beside each guard space was a willow-tied ladder, leading down to the ground.

Near to the high night, while the rising moon was casting a glow against the clear black sky, I heard rifles click around me and saw the men lift their barrels to slot them into the holes. I followed, but still could not see the threat.

"Where?" I whispered to the man next to me.

He nodded at a dog near our feet who had perked its ears to a far-off smell. "Now you must return to your rooms, Señora."

I did not follow his instruction, though. I had seen folks fall in battle and was not afraid. I shook my head gently in response.

"You must!" he whispered furiously.

My mouth had gone dry to coughing, so I picked a small stone from the ground and cleaned it on my skirts. I put it between my lips and sucked, to make my mouth water, all the while staring at the moonlit low brush on the dusty fields before us. The sure explosion of a rifle thundered near me. Through my own peephole, I saw a man scurrying toward our wall, a Comanche with face painted black for war, holding his own rifle as he moved low through the thorny weeds.

Suddenly, a guard near me leapt into the black night, howling like the Comanches themselves. He ran to the man and threw his body across the other to stop him moving. Too close for rifle attack, they both pulled knives.

I kept my body low and saw the guards beside me hold back from shooting, for if our courageous man lost, each of our soldiers would have the time to train a rifle on the Comanche. If our own won, the message to any in the woods would be sent that we were armed and ready.

But the guard alongside me shouted, "Are you wild? Go down and back to your rooms at once or you will have us all killed!"

I edged down the ladder, and at the bottom slipped from the dank opening in the wall and sat on the porch breathless, with my rifle laying across my knees, and all of me knock-knocking together.

By dawn I had not moved. The poor lone Comanche, dead and scalped by our soldiers, had been a single scout to Bereminda's palace, hunting us and haunting us and ultimately dying upon us. They had dragged his lame body into the plaza and it lay not far from my feet. The other women slept with the safe silence of the night, leaving only me to stare at the crazed black eyes of this man. Lucky those eyes remained; often we would scalp and gouge each other's faces, we Anglos and Comanches, until the eyes rolled into the dirt. Micah was right, and I knew that. No man in this land was different. God had long ago slipped from our Texas.

CHAPTER 11

*R*ising at light, I watched for our men. I did not return to that foul hiding place but moved to an oak bench near the gates, and I stretched out upon it as the light opened the sky. I put my head back on the planks, because the guards told me that in this way I would hear the men and their horses pounding before I could see them. I took the hot early coffee that Rafael's cook offered, and gazed out the crack in the cuts, hoping for some sight of Micah, Lariza, and the others.

Hours later, the morning was a clear blue sky, spread across the horizon, and fields away I saw a swirl of shadow, and I heard the guards shouting with relief and excitement.

"They're coming! All out! They're coming!"

I helped the men swing the gate wide, and the women emerged from their rooms, dressed in sleeping gowns and slumber eyes, lazy and trusting as they had been the whole night through.

First rode Rafael, Lariza astride his mare with him, his arms tightly round her. Several men came behind, including Micah and Teddy Blue, all spattered with blood and carrying scalps tied to their saddles; unclean and damned, every one of them.

But Micah slipped from Cash and came to me. Behind him followed a boy tethered to him by hemp rope. A child not more than ten years, blond hair and tanned skin, his pale blue eyes staring fiercely at us all.

"We took them down," Micah said to me, and put his arms around my shoulders. His clothes were damp and bloody, and he was sour with the stink of death. "Found them by the river where their scout hid in a hollow trunk." His shadow bobbed against the sunlit clay wall behind him, as he waivered with exhaustion. "He came on us in the dark. The others too. I took three with clean shots. I thought we had lost Teddy Blue when they knocked him down with a bullet to his left thigh, but he's a fierce one. He pushed himself up against that same hollow tree and brought most of them to earth." Micah rested his head on my shoulder while the specklebellies circled above us against the stark sun.

"Where are the bodies, Micah? Did you bury them on the plain?"

He lifted his head and stared at me. "You don't understand yet?" Trembling, he said, "We won all their guns, four of 'em, and some silver. But their flesh will rot. By God, nobody buries an enemy out here."

Micah turned to the child and said sternly, "Come here, boy. This is your mistress, Señora Moore. You will do everything she instructs."

The boy did not understand and looked angrily from Micah and back to me. I'm sure on that day, had he been given an opportune pause, he would have merrily cut our throats.

"Eliza," Micah said, "he's yours for now. The Comanches called him Arakka, but we don't know his real name. He was their captive, probably for years because he's lost all his English. We will keep him until we can find his family."

"What will I do with him?" I asked, and the minute I said it, Arakka scowled and turned away.

"He can be your servant, and truly I fear for what the

Bereminda cowhands might do to a wild Anglo boy like him."
Micah nodded at the boy. "Arakka! Come here."

Arakka stood a few yards away, the rope trailed on the ground. He was afraid and unrepentant, a child cradling the memory of his birth cord cut too soon, a look-back glass to my soul.

Rafael's father had built a *temazcal* bathing hut at Bereminda, and I came to know it as a place of deep quiet where I could wonder in peace on this world. Built of baked *adobe* bricks in the round domed shape of a bread-baking oven, the bathhouse was a man's height across the ground and barely a woman's height tall, so we needed to crouch to our knees to enter. Inside, rocks lay heating until the *curandero* poured water for steam. We used the steam to release bad smells from our skin, and cool water and laurel branches to clean ourselves. The men also partook of this hut to relieve battle terrors, and women used it after our bleeding and after giving birth.

On that first day belonging to Arakka's new life, Micah took him naked into the *temazcal*. Many of the hacienda women surrounded the hut to watch, because our young white boy howled and fought hard to stay away from the doorway. He was overcome with anger and fright, squirming and punching out at Micah, until Teddy Blue tied the boy's hands and feet. Micah knelt and pushed him through the opening. Inside sat the curandero and his attendant, waiting and laughing at this poor Arakka, come for cleansing.

The young priest Father Esteban joined me and sat in the rocker on my porch, preaching about the suspicious ways of those who frequented the bath hut.

"Our Lord frowns on this place," he said in the loud voice of a blateroon.

"But, if you do not use the *temazcal,* how do you bathe, Father Esteban?"

"Don't be impertinent, Señora. You may not ask this question of God's men."

I had been called impertinent before, and I well remembered the man who did it, an untrustworthy Texas judge and thief.

"Forgive me, Father. But if the bath hut is not godly, how do we clean ourselves?"

This greasy blackbird put his hands to either side of his head, slicking his hair back while he sweated like Herod on judgment day.

"You love many things more than Jesus," he said suddenly. "Child, your life will not end well. I fear for your heathen ways." He closed his eyes then and bowed his head, and a halo of darkness rose around him.

We waited on the porch till the sun hit the top of the sky, when at last the men reappeared to us. The boy had been scrubbed with laurel, his hair cut and pomaded, his tongue and teeth washed. The attendant removed ticks from his skin and scraped the crust from his feet. The curandero applied basil and rue to the naked bodies of all three, these herbs to pull the hell and darkness from them.

Micah brought him to me, still tethered to his thick hemp rope, and handed me the coil.

"Now he is clean and he's yours, Ellie."

Teddy Blue Corlies stood beside him chuckling. I scowled at him and he pulled his face straight. "I'm sorry, Eliza. But this child is fiercely strong!"

"Please take the rope from him now!" I said. "I cannot have a child who is a slave."

"Ellie, he would kill you as soon as look at you. We can't unleash him just yet."

I waved the two of them away and took the boy to my rooms. I pointed at the cushions on the floor for the child to sit. So tentatively, as though I were the soul of treachery, he lowered himself cross-legged to sit beside me, and I untied him.

"Your name is Arakka," I whispered. "And my name is Eliza. You and I are similar, boy. We began like two of the same breed, not belonging anywhere." I tried to talk in the rhythm of a lamentation, soft and droning so I would not frighten him. "I will not let them hurt you. I understand you don't know what that means and wouldn't believe me if you did. But if you could only trust me somehow."

He lifted his hand sharply to strike me but I had well learned the ways of those who wanted to hit me. I put my left hand out to stop him and took his wrist.

"I am your only friend, Arakka. I am not the enemy," I whispered.

I swear I saw him nod, but it could have been a dream sent to me. Then I sighed and he heard it. The gold flash in his eyes dimmed. He seemed desolate and faint. And as the fire rose in my bones I saw the shadow of a yoke lay across his shoulders; surely it was only in my mind, but I saw the deep brown wood, lathed and smooth, and heavy on his back as it had once lain on mine.

Arakka refused to sleep in a bed. At night he would often take a single blanket and spread it on the floor of the porch outside our rooms, and there he would lie, alone but for the universe. I called him son of the morning, for he rose before dawn and brought Micah and me coffee and fruit in bed. He hunted alone for meat, and when he succeeded in bringing a carcass home, he would fling it in the dirt before the Bereminda kitchens.

Slowly, he learned English words, and once while I was teaching him about families, I saw him smile as I described the word 'brother'. I wanted to believe that his childhood language, or life, was returning to him.

When he understood our words a little, Rafael and Micah interviewed him to discover the whereabouts of his Anglo family. He told them he had been with the Comanches for seven years, and he described being taken from a family farm while he was waiting for his father to return home. He said his mother had been killed that day but didn't know what happened to his sister or older brother.

When Micah questioned his age again, Arakka became agitated. He stood and went to where the horses were tethered. There he sat, stone silent between the legs of these huge stallions, sullen and unafraid of being trampled.

Rafael sent word to the militia at Nacogdoches that Bereminda held a young white boy who had been a Comanche captive. They also sent out descriptions of him to farms across Texas, and we waited for his kin to step forward, but broadsheets were rare then, and the ability to read was even rarer.

Months passed with no return on our efforts, and in the autumn bower that was Bereminda, Arakka became our follower; by spring, this strange imperfect child had become our son.

CHAPTER 12

*S*hortly before my eighteenth birthday, Rafael gathered together his surplus cattle. The news had come in the *New Orleans Daily Picayune* that they were fetching a hefty sum in that city, and so our host decided to drove his excess eastward. This was not an easy ride, crossing gator swamps and the devil's land of outlaws on the Sabine, still thriving alongside our dog poor new Texas nation.

The cattle drive set off early one day; I think it might have been a Monday because it was near after our weekly worship with Father Esteban. Their plan was to follow the Angelina River south toward the Opelousas Trail bound for Louisiana, crossing to the east of the deep harsh Neches, down to Beaumont, and on to the New Orleans stockyards.

Ranchers brought their beeves from across Texas because of the price that year. A steer sold in Texas fetched five dollars, but in New Orleans the price was thirty-five. An enterprising *hacendado* such as Rafael could drove a thousand cattle, pay his cowpunchers well, and still come home with money enough to last for the rest of the year.

Thousands of animals were taken across the Sabine River in a single day. Along the way, drovers found stray Spanish cattle running wild and unmarked since the Spanish priests abandoned the mission ranches. They branded them as their own, managing to grow their herds, knowing that every wild steer would be worth another thirty-five American silver dollars.

Swimming the drove was a dangerous job, and only the best cowpokes were handed the task. So many steer drowned in that river near the new town of Beaumont that Teddy Blue, who had been named Rafael's trail boss, was obliged to post bond before crossing. On the far side, he paid six dollars for each dead cow the city elders found floating in the river. Into Louisiana, the cowpunchers took the herds across swamps slithering with poisonous snakes, and bayous where a man or a horse would sink to his chest. The steers were familiar with grazing thick prairie grass, or the tall grasses between the white pines in Angelina, but in Louisiana those cows only found bad bog holes filled with cypress roots.

Micah made this hard journey in order to earn cash money. He knew that when I turned eighteen, I would be a free woman and no longer needing to hide behind the Bereminda walls. By their return, I would be a free citizen of Texas, not an escaped servant or slave, nor bound to any human being but him.

Lariza and I spent easy days in their absence, often taking our meals together in Rafael's private rooms, trading the unsalted stories of our youth. We designed a garden of vegetables, and Arakka helped us seed it. We three spent hours at this, and our chat brought us rolling with laughter, gamboling about in the soil like mischievous children. Father Esteban did not stop to inquire of our troubled souls during his rounds about the hacienda compound, but I often saw him watching us from afar, rocking on a chair or merely standing in the deep shadows of the eaves.

On one of our days, this snoutfair priest with his tallow-combed hair picked his way into the planted rows to face me.

"Señora, señorita, you have been struggling long hours these past weeks," he called out in his high-pitched twang.

I looked up from my seedbed and squinted at him. He was an unwelcome sight, and I hesitated to speak.

"What are you planting?" he asked, flapping his delicate hands across his cassock to brush the dust away. He clasped his fingers together across his lower stomach, pushing his hands hard against the flesh to disguise his growing paunch. "Is this boy working hard enough?" he asked. "Perhaps I could coax a few more hours from him." He frowned toward Arakka, who was bent close to the ground with his work, staring at us. "Would you like me to give him some lessons about respect for hard work?"

Arakka, docile with me and Lariza, glared and moved his small chin from one side to the other. Scarcely visible to those who did not know him, this small flutter indicated dark intention.

"Father Esteban," I said, "we are all working hard to finish our planting before the men return, and that will be any day. Arakka is doing his fair share, to be sure."

Esteban shuffled closer to me down the row of clods. In the polrumptious tone of someone too vain for the priesthood, he said, "Your boy needs to learn our ways." He gazed at Lariza. Calling her 'miss', he added, "Wouldn't you say so, señorita?"

At that point I stood. "We are all busy, Father. Lessons are for later. Please excuse us from this interesting dialogue."

Arakka stretched tall for his boy's frame. He sensed that I was irritated, and I could see him slip one hand into his trouser pocket for the small knife he kept. He edged toward us without speaking.

Listening to our conversation from her place among the cornrows, Lariza was striding toward us.

"Father," she said loudly as she approached, "Father, we all have work to do."

"Of course, girl," Father Esteban replied sharply. He put a

hand on the tendons of her shoulder and dug his fingers into her back. "Of course, my dear."

Lariza said bravely, "I will consult with Don Rafael when he returns about the availability of the boy for your teaching. For now, Arakka has other chores." She turned the boy round and took my hand, pulling us out of the priest's sight.

Once away, I whispered, "Thank you."

Lariza nodded, smiling, but I saw that her hands were trembling.

~

Two days later, on the afternoon we finished our beautiful garden's toil, Lariza's maid brought tangy *tejuino* drinks for us, and we three sat admiring our work. The *mayordomo* had constructed a shaded area for us, covered by the fibrous henequen cloth of the agave plants, and we lounged there protected from the hot sun until the sky turned to purple dusk.

"I am dear tired," I said, "and my soft mattress is calling me. Arakka, you go with Señora to supper. I am going straight to sleep." I stroked his head the way I imagined a real mother would.

I reached my room and changed into my sleep shift, pulling the cool bedclothes around me. I do not remember a single thought from the time my head touched the goose feather pillows until far into the night when Arakka began shaking me awake.

"Please, please, oh please," he repeated over and over until at last I opened my eyes.

"What, boy?"

"Please," he said again. Then he stopped. His eyes were red and droopy, and his hands hanging on me.

I sat straight up in bed. "What happened?"

Behind him stood Lariza, shaking her head, her arms crossed over her breasts. "He must leave at once, Eliza."

"Please," he whispered.

I looked again at Arakka, and saw that his fingers were tipped in blood. "Arakka, what did you do?" I asked, terrified.

He shook his head hard.

"He saved me. We were heading to our rooms after supper, but we took the short way behind the fishery. We should not have trod in the dark like that. Esteban must have been following. He came for me. For me! The don's woman. Took me from behind by my shoulders and shoved me to the ground. He lifted his robes and was hard and tall, heaving on me. Arakka jumped upon him."

Her voice had risen and her breath was harsh and uneven.

"He kicked the boy away, but Eliza, Arakka cut his throat so wide that the priest bled out within the moment." She growled the rest from her throat. "And so he should have. Bled to the death. If Rafael were here, he would have done the same. But Eliza, our good boy must go quickly."

"No," I said. "If he saved you then Arakka is a hero. Rafael and the rest will respect him."

"Oh, my dear," she whispered. "There are no half-breed heroes." She said these words while watching me intently, a secret vein of shame pulsing between us.

"He is not a half-breed, Lariza."

"You don't understand the people here. He is a savage boy to them and he killed a priest. A priest!" Her voice dropped to a whisper. "And all he has on his side is the word of a *mestiza* whore. He must go. Now." She shook her head, gently and with such sadness. She clutched my sleeve, and I felt the tug of a child. "Come," she said, pulling at me so many times.

"He is by himself, Lariza. We cannot let him go alone. He won't survive outside the gates." And with that, I put my arms around the boy and held him. "I will go with him," I said, and rose from bed. "Will you give us horses and food? And a weapon?"

Lariza nodded. "Of course."

"And tell Micah why I have gone. Tell him the truth. He will know what to do."

"Where will you go?"

"The only person I have in this world besides Micah is my sister. I heard she married a man over near Newtown Crockett, so that is where we will head."

And within the hour, we were gone from Hacienda Bereminda, onto the long morning road.

CHAPTER 13

*W*e headed for the piney woods on the west side of the muddy Angelina River. Two days' journey out from Bereminda, we came upon the three ancient hills that had been built and then abandoned by the Caddo when they moved farther west to the Brazos River. Those men had lived among the mounds for almost a thousand years until we drove them out. How well I understood their desperate days. There between those three hills we sheltered, hidden and packing in food for the rest of our journey.

Arakka kept us off the roads between Nacogdoches and Crockett until we reached the dank sweet forest that smothers this land. That was the fine silt river bottom between the Neches and the Trinidad, where the pines reached a hundred feet even on the prairie, and a man could hide behind their broad trunks. Often, Arakka insisted that we dismount and walk our horses through the creek water that penetrated the soft pineland, and I followed his instruction because I believed he could hear and see things I could not.

On the forest trail we moved slowly, hiding from the occasional human sound, whether it be Indian, Anglo, or

Mexican. If Arakka sensed a presence in the deep pines, rather than sally out to confront it with our rifles, he made us hide our horses far away and wait for hours in the darkness, patiently lying upon the damp needled earth until the vibrations had passed us by.

One time, when a group of men were riding too near, we covered ourselves with those needles and lay with the worms, watching the distant hooves come toward us. Arakka taught me to shallow my breath rather than hold it, and to keep still that way for hours.

Out of the forest, our journey changed. We edged up to a sawmill where a dozen men toiled at the cut pines and oaks. We were only twelve miles from my sister, and I pondered whether or not to stop and make inquiries. Arakka was strongly opinionated about this. He shook his hands and head wildly as we stood on the edge of the forest, telling me that we were not safe. I saw the shaft of sunlight split the shadows open around us; and I watched this boy so confident in himself in this raw landscape.

As we approached the outskirts of Newtown Crockett, we found the farms closer together, and at one there assembled a large number of citizens. Though Arakka and I had cleaned and costumed ourselves to be like the townspeople, a murmur rose among them as we arrived. We were offered food, as was the custom for strangers in these Texas lands, and we sat uncomfortably on wood stools, poised to run if the need arose.

Our hostess, an older woman, introduced herself. "Have you traveled far, you and the boy?"

"Fairly," I said. "We are seeking my sister, Louisiana Baylis. Do you know her?"

The woman took a step back. Her grey hair lay in tight tufts about her face. In measured words, she said, "Levi Baylis lives outside of town, to the west side."

"Will they be at your event here today?"

She shook her head, smiling. "Not seen them for many months. Mister Baylis recently pulled his efforts out of farming and stock raising. Got hisself involved in some other business. Some around here might call it swindling."

Arakka gulped the beef on his plate suddenly. Swallowing it whole without chewing the moist tender pieces, he looked at me proudly.

"Can you point us in their direction?" I asked.

"Of course. But won't you stay for our dance?" she asked. "We will be celebrating the corn! A large impossible haul."

I shook my head. "I think we should press on to my sister's home. But thank you for your hospitality."

She gazed hard at Arakka. "What's the boy's name? Your brother? Your son, mebbee?"

I hesitated too long. If I told her his Indian name, she would understand we were not a normal family and might notify the sheriff; I did not know his Anglo name. I was cobbed for an idea, and my delay caused her to scrutinize me.

Suddenly, Arakka spoke. "I am Moses," he said, and I blessed his heart in my relief, for he smiled easily as well. And although this blond boy did not resemble me in the least, the woman nodded.

"Follow this trail to the Baptist Church on the other side of the village, and then head north to the river. Keep on the south riverbank for a mile and you will ride straight into the Baylis place. Go quickly," she added. "Dusk falls early and hard now. You won't want to be traveling out toward the Baylis land in the dark."

We thanked her and mounted. As we rode on, I glanced back to see her still watching us, her arms crossed over her chest.

I did not speak to Arakka until we reached the river, clear of Crockett's Anglo settlers.

"Who is Moses?" I asked.

"I am," he said, and we both slowed our animals to a walk. We rode in silence a few moments until he spoke again, choking on his thoughts until words slipped out. "The Cherokee killed my mother and father. They shot my baby sister. They took me and sold me to Comanche. I never saw my brother again. Now my father is a healing chief in Comancheria. He gave me clothes and food and I became his son. Your husband stole me."

We rode on as the falling light cast a dull gleam on the water beside us.

Finally, I asked, "Arakka, what do you desire for your life?"

"I will see you safe, and after go home."

I spent my eighteenth birthday eve riding along that river toward Lou's ranch, and we crossed the gateway in a drizzling rain and total darkness. The road led to a small house without windows. I insisted that we wait in the wet mud until daylight so as not to surprise the inhabitants, and Arakka's unerring Texas rifle was pointed all those long hours toward the porch, while he scanned and surveyed the dark outlines.

As the dawn rose, we perceived another three buildings surrounding the main one. All were rough and crumbling, and empty of human movement. None had windows, but all had vertical gun slits across the boarded walls. I had traveled far and lay low now on the ground near bushes of sharp willow branches, before this forsaken farm, seeking the very last memory of my childhood that I believed might still make me whole again.

And then I saw the sight I had been hungry for all these long years. Lou stepped through the pitched doorway in a dark blue dress and black boots, descending the broken steps and watching the horizon. She carried a bucket, and walked through leafy tangled vetch toward the near well. I wanted to call out and run to her, but instead I knelt in the mud and raised my head. At last, Arakka put his hand on my back and stood tall.

The arc of light across the corrals made me smile and it made Louisiana smile too. Cottonwoods leaned upon the sides of the house, their leaves overgrown and raw green in the sunlight. I stood alongside my boy, planting myself in the road before the Baylis house. This was my sister, no matter what had become of our lives.

"Lou!" I called, and she turned, then suddenly ran at me.

"Eliza!" she exclaimed.

Our arms were about each other, and I felt her palms and fingers on my back, the press of her small chest, the pumping of her heart so hard against my own.

"Lou," I whispered, tears tumbling down my face.

"Sister," she said, "I thought I had lost you forever."

That evening the waning gibbous moon rose slowly. Arakka sat on the rough pine steps, watching the plains and waiting to taste a rich-smelling venison that Lou roasted in a heavy pot over the fire. He pointed his rifle toward the dousing light of the skyline, careful of the tall grasses in the distance and the herd of wild deer. The mist blurred the far end of the cart track, but he was constant and patient as our only protector because Lou's husband, Levi, had taken his men up to St Charles for work.

Lou stepped toward the doorway behind me, resting her small hand on my shoulder. "Supper is almost cooked." At twenty years she had no children yet, and was on her own with nothing but a rifle for safety.

She squatted next to me, and doing so, the frayed edges of her frock spread across the old plank.

"Why didn't your husband take you with him?" I asked. "I imagine the city would be exciting."

"Someone had to stay here," she said, "and see to our place."

Like an old jobber disapproving of new ways, our boy grunted.

"I have so much to ask you, Ellie," she said. "So many things to hear and share. But first, please tell me about Father. Where is he now?"

I dropped my head to hide the sudden tears. "Father died," I whispered. "Uncle James didn't tell you?"

Lou padded gently past us down the steps, then turned and stood in front of me. "No." Her voice fluttered and rose, and from deep in her throat she added, "He told me nothing. When he left me in peace, our uncle, I could manage. But when I lost my temper, he sought me a husband and promised Levi part of Becky Creek."

"You and Levi own Becky Creek now?"

"No, Eliza. Our uncle and Levi sold it all." She climbed up the termite-riddled porch planks and settled beside me.

"We come out of the belly of hell, ain't we, Ellie?" she said at last. "How did Father die?"

"Went to battle at San Jacinto. Came home and passed after a few months. Till the end he believed he was bound for the kingdom of God, Lou. Till his very last day." I just stared at my sister, this girl who was all that I had left of my childhood.

"How was it with our uncle, Lou?"

She sighed and shook her head. "I learned my lessons. I can read and write. Count up too. Then they sold me to old man Baylis."

"You're pretty, Lou. So pretty. I expect you had several suitors."

"Texas is a hard land, and being pretty doesn't really matter after a while. Dries you out in this cold. And Levi is a harsh man."

I reached over and put my hand on her cheek. "You have us now. Micah and me, we are your family."

"No," she whispered. "I belong to Levi Baylis. He stole

everything I had. And if I leave, he will find me and kill me. He told me that." She shrugged suddenly. "Do you think Father went to the Lord, Ellie?"

I waited a few moments before I replied. We heard the ponies snorting in the corral outside, and the cold wind spitting off the evening plains. Finally, I said, "Heaven ain't my business, Lou."

A scatter of straw lay across the porch planks and I brushed my hand nervously through it.

"That's all that's left of our dog's bed." She clenched a handful and threw it to the dirt. "Old Billy died of poisoning in the winter." Dark hosts broke over her, sinking in her life's losses. "Like I said, Levi told me he would kill me if I tried to leave."

"When Micah comes for Arakka and me, we all will escape and be free. I'll take an oath for that. He will want you with us." The mist had dissolved over us, and her skin was luminous in the moonlight. "People who have nothing suffer hard in this life," I said. "Our uncle sold me to a farmer when our father died. To slave. But there's better things and we can find them. I'm dearly hoping you will come with us, sister."

She smiled, with tears creeping down the apples of her cheeks. "Why are we talking of all this?" she exclaimed. "Time for supper." She took my hand, and Arakka's, our fingers curling across each other's, and like the poor often do, we praised the Lord for our blessings.

CHAPTER 14

*T*he next morning, Arakka had gone to hunt meat for us, while Lou was in the barn putting straw to the animal stalls and hay to their baskets. I stood in the dawn among the ponies left behind when two men rode up to the paddock and slid to a rough halt. They paused staring at me. A hundred years hence, when the worms have eaten our poor flesh away, our skulls will look the same, man or woman, Tejano or Anglo, but on that morning to these two men I appeared just another servant, disheveled and sweating in the paddock.

"Girl, direct me to Mister Baylis!" The loud churl did not introduce himself for I suppose I appeared to be of a class unworthy of learning his name. He held a rifle across his saddle and did not deign to tap his hat to me.

"Good morning, sir," I said. "Levi Baylis is not here. How might I help?"

The man who had spoken leaned forward across the horn, seeming to ponder my skin, not quite tawny in the early light, yet staring square at my light grey eyes. A mixed breed, he knew, but mixed of blood he could easily hate? Or something more difficult. A Mexican or Spaniard, or even perhaps an Italian? It wasn't the first time I saw a settler rouse his own confusion just by looking at me, and imperiously, I remained quiet and unafraid.

"I want to get a look at that white boy you got staying here. My wife said his Christian name is Moses. I saw the picture the Sheriff sent out last year, and I believe him to be gettin' on for the age of the poor white babe kidnapped years past by those Indians at San Felipe. His name was Moses too."

"What cause do you have to believe that?"

He narrowed his eyes fiercely. "Don't question me. Go and fetch Missus Baylis."

"I am Missus Moore, guest of my sister, Louisiana Baylis. Kindly calm yourself, sir."

"That may be," he said, and pulled a broadsheet from his saddle bag. "The drawing on this document is said to be the same as the boy brought recent to our settlement." He shook the yellow page in front of me. "This boy killed a holy man over by the eastern border." He leaned back on his saddle sharply. "I will speak with Missus Baylis now."

The second man walked his horse closer to me. "I'm Sheriff in this county, girl." He pointed to a star, which was bent and hammered from tin that was fixed to his hat. "Go and get her."

When I returned with Lou, she smiled at the men.

"Hello, Sheriff," she said, suddenly and a little too sweet. "I understand you are looking to see Levi. He's at business up north and won't be back for weeks. What can I do for you?"

The lawman dismounted and walked toward her, coughing while he brought the tobacco wad forward in his mouth and began secreting the bitter brown juices.

"I want to talk to that boy calls himself Moses."

"He's clear gone," she said. "He ran away a few days past."

"How could that have happened, Missus Baylis?" His jaws puffed round and solid, while his heavy brow bulled out in a frown.

"Got no men here to hold him, sir. He's a boy but he was plain strong."

"Silver reward on his back now, ma'am. Good purse for whoever returns him." The sheriff paused and asked, "Why was your sister riding with the boy?"

Lou drew herself tall as her spine would allow. She grabbed my hand and took a stride toward the man. "My dear sister was seeking help, sir. A woman captured by a skilled boy with arms. What would you expect?"

The sheriff waited, watching me and Lou, one to the other and back. "I will talk to your husband about this. Don't forget it."

Lou nodded at him. "You are always welcome at the Baylis homestead, Sheriff."

We watched them ride to the horizon before Lou spoke. "We must find him, Eliza. If the sheriff knows about Arakka, then everyone in the county will soon know." She put her arm to my shoulders. "Silver reward, Sister." Gently, she said, "Arakka can't stay here anymore. They will all be seeking him. When Levi comes home, he will be after him too. And God help us, Eliza, if they find you helped him escape, they will jail you. You must leave with the boy."

Arakka returned in the dark before the moon crescent had lifted to the top of the sky. His packs were full of butchered meat, and I caught him as he began to shoulder them into the crib.

"Leave those, boy," I said, and brought our satchels to the paddock. "You are hunted and we must go."

We stood between the turf-face and the worn wooden rails, between fermented earth and starlit sky, my sister and I touching our hands together one more time. Resolved beyond grief, she did not tear up again, but handed me sacks to keep us fed on the trail.

Then she stepped forward, kissed my cheek, and said this, "Coming to me was the sweetest gift, Eliza." She handed me a black sash with old stitchwork across it in the palest blue silk threads. "I was making you a present. It's not finished but take it."

I tied the old cotton around my waist. "I'm deep sorry to leave you here, Lou."

"We'll find each other again one day, sister. But what shall I say to your husband if he arrives? What is your destination?"

No thoughts came, nor any words. The places I had been we could not go back to. South no longer existed on my compass, nor east. I looked to Arakka, who knelt in the soil fastening the last pack, and shook my head wearily at this scurfy hell.

Finally, I said, "The only way is west. We'll head to the Trinidad River and shelter there."

Arakka and I mounted and heeled our horses to walk on. When I turned to wave, Louisiana had her back to us, and was passing through the slip of light into her broke down house.

We rode till we reached a broad sandy beach of the river, open to the stars and a cloudless indigo sky. Arakka led us into the stand of water oaks down the bend, where we threw our bedpacks alongside the most impenetrable swamp he could find. Beneath the shrill alerts of the roosting kites high above us, he and I lay waiting for sleep to fall.

Toward dawn, I heard the squeal of a wild pig in the morning sunlight, then heard it stop suddenly, and I saw Arakka's dark shadow move toward me. Coming up on twelve years of age, he had grown tall the past year, and now like a man feeding a family, he carried the legs and intestines of the headless animal.

He tossed the guts in the dark mud beside me, and began gathering tinder.

The sound of a tin whistle rose above us, and slowly I realized it was the kites again, shrieking at the first light and the blood of the pig.

"I will cook the pig," he said. "We will travel far today. You need good food."

An hour later we sat side by side tearing ravenously at the roasted flesh of the pig. He told a story of his father, a kindly healer, and children with belly rashes, of applying balm and giving caresses to them, and he said it all plainly, without emotion.

Suddenly the grasses around us moved, and the cane at the water's edge rustled. A hissing came through the water then, a deep slapping of tongue and teeth, and just above the muddy waterline I saw a black-scaled alligator advancing, its upper teeth displayed.

"Arakka!" I shouted, and he snapped his head to the sound. He grabbed his old Virginia flintlock from his belt, raised it, and aimed.

The water exploded with the shot, and the gator thrashed brutally while the rank smell of fish surged around us. Arakka's attack had missed its fatal mark, and the reptile slithered back into the water, slinking along the bank, huge and heavy, away from us.

"It's young," he said. "Curious, only. But others will smell pig blood and we are in their country. We must leave now, quickly."

My chest still heaved with fear, but I stood and grabbed our bedrolls and remaining roasted meat, tying these onto our animals. Once astride our mounts, we trampled the grasses to reach the bluff top, but at the crest, I stopped my horse.

"We need to find a crossing, Arakka. Those men'll find us easy if we stay on the east bank."

Sunstruck and with his neck bared, he said, "We'll go north to bayou fork. We can cross or hide there." A bird with a dropped wing dipped low across our heads, its glimmer of light across the muddy green river bearing downstream until its cawing plea faded. He swaggered then, this young boy, filled with his knowledge of the land and the birds. "I tell you, Eliza, we will find safe haven in one hour."

When we reached the summer hedges of the fork, the mesquite and ivy wound together choking each other, and we lay on the bank, waiting in the damp afternoon light until, in our exhaustion, we fell to sleep.

CHAPTER 15

*W*hen I awoke the light had slipped away, and I felt strong arms close by, a grown man's arms touching me. I flashed my eyes open, and jumped to sit in the darkness.

"Oh girl," whispered the voice, and I put my hand out to touch the man's face, for this was Micah, beside me so close, his familiar breath palpable against my skin.

"How did you find us?" I asked.

He lifted his arms, strong and tanned, and I pulled myself closer to his body, and warm it was from the ride. I couldn't remember not having known him; from that moment I believed he had always been a part of my life, and that whatever might befall us could never change that.

"Did you think I wouldn't? Arakka has the talent of a Comanche to cover his trail, but I've been a tracker longer than he's been an Indian." Micah sat up and put his left hand across my bodice. His fingers were muddy and he left that mud smeared over the cotton covering my breasts. "You lyin' here quiet in the mud and cane like this. You injured?"

I breathed in the night mist, waiting a moment and watching

him. "I'm fine, boy. Just so tired of this midnight road. I'm so damned tired of running. You saw Louisiana? You know we can't go back. Nor to Bereminda, nor to Crockett. A priest killer and an escaped slave. We got nowhere to go." I put my hand in the grasses, brushing them through with my fingers. I felt a hard, smooth stick, and when I raised it I saw it was a piece of bone, flute-like, porous and yellowing. I dropped it quickly, then touched it again.

"I got plans. This is a big country. We'll get to the other side of this river and our scent will wash out." Flaming cardinal flowers grew beside us, and water willows. "Time to get tramping on, Eliza. We'll cross the river in the dark. No one will expect that. If they come this far, they'll probably ride north from here."

"And once on the other side, then where? There's nowhere for us to go," I mumbled. "Can't go back anywhere. No home anywhere."

He stood and stomped the thick mud from his boots. "You got little faith in me, Eliza." The bogbank shone in the moonlight like mother of pearl. "You think I drove those beeves just as a favor to Rafael? Damn well brought money back from New Orleans." Micah held his hand down to mine. "You never did believe in me, girl. Since the day we met, you been afraid that I couldn't provide for you. Since the day we met." He withdrew his hand and turned his back. "Come on, Arakka," Micah said gruffly. "We're crossing the Trinidad tonight."

I bowed my head and said under my breath, "I been alone my whole life. Never anyone on my side. You think I can conjure faith in you like magic?"

Any point in that wood would have swallowed my words, except where he stood, back to me, listening for me. "Let's go, Eliza," he whispered. And he whirled round and faced me square. "I'll tell you, I brought cash enough for us to buy a place. Cattle're worth a good price in New Orleans. Rafael and I sold 'em all off."

Micah held his hand out again, far from me, but I stood and

walked through the mud to him. "We'll buy some acres," he said. "Raise little ones and farm. We'll be safe up by the Brazos and away from the devils of your childhood and the devils who hunt Arakka. Old Clack Robertson has land for new colonists."

I put my arm around his waist, slipping my fingers under his shirt like a road gypsy.

"Fine farmland," he said. "You'll see. We could grow corn or pumpkins or cotton. We could even have cattle and horses. I saw this land once."

"I do believe you, husband," I said.

He nodded stiffly. "New Nashville out on the Brazos River. Some families are farming there already. And there's a militia unit there, so I could be sure to feed us even if the crops don't come in. They won't find us there. I been thinkin' hard about this," he said loudly. "I been planning it. You're eighteen and free, and Arakka'll be hidden with us out on the prairie, far from Nacogdoches, until the next killing happens and they forget about our boy."

"He won't come. He wants to go home."

"Home? Ain't his home with us?"

"No. He wants to return to his Comanche people."

Micah didn't move. I saw his muscles stiffen where he stood, and I moved to take his hand.

"Damn, Eliza. We can't send him back to the Comanches. We might as will kill him ourselves. You don't know. You never saw what they do."

"I have seen some things. Maybe not everything you know, but out here we all live scared."

"Shite. Don't you know what happened down at Bexar? The Republic, our people, invited the Comanche chiefs to meet for peace, and then killed them while they were sitting in the council room. The Comanches are coming for us all. I don't know if they'll leave any white boy alive now."

He turned to Arakka, who stood alongside the muddy,

moonlit river, balancing deftly on a limestone outcrop. The water glowed faintly from the Mexican perch seeking smaller prey, and Arakka stared at the darting lights, ignoring Micah.

"Boy, you understand what I'm saying?" Micah's face was twisted, his voice beaten. "You can't go back to your tribe. You're not one of them and they will kill you."

"I do," he replied, and stepping from the rocks, approached us. "But you do not. These are my people. They will not hurt me."

"They got deals now with the Kiowa and the Apaches. Our land is ignited from all sides. Safest place we can be is among our own kind," Micah said.

"What kind are those?" Arakka asked.

Micah fell silent, withdrawing his thoughts like across a chasm to yonder. He leaned forward to the boy without touching him. "I don't want to leave you, son."

Arakka shook his head deliberately. "I am not your son. You and your people stole me. Now I'm going home." He kicked mud into the fire, and grabbed his flintlock. "It's time we cross the river," he said to my husband, haughtily.

Micah nodded. "We'll get you as close to Comancheria as we can, and then we'll go on to our new home.

Once out of the bayou, we swam the river on our mounts, arriving on a hard-packed sandy beach, where we slept a couple of hours till dawn. When I awoke, the two men had packed their bedrolls and our food for the journey, first to the Comanche canyons and then onto Milam County. We traveled to the cliffs of the Brazos River, near the mesquite and the tangled scrub oaks, the early chill misting still about us.

We dismounted by the turnout trail up to the caves and hoodoos of the painted Palo Duro Canyon. My emotions were so high when we parted that I cannot remember my words, but I believe I said this to Arakka, "Come to me whenever you need. We will always be loving you."

He stood beneath a barren mesquite tree near the colony line.

His hair was washed clean blond and cut short, and he still wore the vestments of a Texas son, rough wool pants, and buckskin flaps over them, with a white cotton shirt. His lips were plump and set together, and he folded his hands carefully at his waist, obstinate till the end.

I whispered to him, "Come back to us, boy."

He turned away without speaking and walked a few steps to his horse, suddenly swiveling to look straight at me, nodding silently in return.

He stripped the white man's clothes away, and when at last he stood naked, his body was lean and of perfect proportions, his back muscled and bronzed in the early sun. He tied the leather strings of an old breechcloth about his waist and vaulted easily onto his horse. He did not look again but clicked his ride to a trot out into the vast land before us.

CHAPTER 16

*W*e were among the Anglo founders of the County of Milam, hundreds of miles first parceled to empresario Leftwich before the Revolution, then taken by Mister Austin, and finally given to Robertson, a new man with a new promise for our colony. Robertson controlled the area between the Brazos and the Colorado Rivers north to the old Camino trail; curvy, flat land that was pie-easy to farm. The country shot out to the far purple horizon, dark rich dirt just waiting to be planted. The prairie grasses blew gentle across a broad landscape sheltered by wooded hills, and there we claimed our acreage on this vast and uneffaced place.

Micah and I journeyed to the new town called Nashville, named after old Mister Robertson's homestead in Tennessee. The congregation of small log and board cabins had been built on a bluff overlooking the Brazos. Near the old Tenock crossing north of town, the river dug deep into the fresh silt of its own floodplain, and the bottomland was dense with thick timber and underwood. Micah and I greedily claimed all that was offered to us, four thousand acres, which were far too many for two poor croppers to work on our own.

We rode into town seeking the home of Captain Erath who had rangered with Micah in the western counties. He lived in a logger built out of cedar, nine feet high and twice that long. The floor was covered with oak planks, and small huts sat on either side, the smokehouse and the corn crib. Erath welcomed us and fed us, and I did remark that he lived in a palace for the size and polish of it. His wife had not accompanied him to the frontier, but his two serving women provided us with sleeping pads and food all the days we spent in the Erath home while Micah was signing the deeds, surveying our headrights, and paying for them.

Some of our neighbors helped us to erect a log fort, and we paid them well for this.

"They might do it for free," I had told my husband. "These are country people who depend on each other."

"We are perfectly capable of paying wages, Eliza, for anything we need," he said to me.

When at last we were finished with our farm, we possessed a dozen pigs, two goats, and a few strong horses. I refused to allow slaves on our land, so we employed an Irish woman named Mahoney to be our cookie, as well as a farmhand and a cowpuncher.

My husband bought a hundred head of cattle from Bereminda, and paid Rafael highly for droving them to us. On the day the men from Bereminda arrived to deliver our stock, Rafael, Teddy Blue, and my dear friend Lariza were in the party. The don rode as the point out in front of the rest, dressed in gentlemanly *charro* finery.

We stood on the porch of our new home, watching the procession launch through our cattle gates, and when Micah saw his friend, Rafael, looking about from under a broad-brimmed hat, proudly wearing his best silver-studded jacket in matching color, he said to me, "Look, Rafe's admirin' his own shadow."

Our two gyp dogs ran out to meet them, ending up instead at the feet of Teddy Blue who leapt from his mount, dropped to his knees, and rolled in the dirt to hug them both. The *vaqueros* parted around the explosion of their dust ball, laughing at the sight, and soon the drag rider brought up the straggling rust-colored steers with their huge crown spreads of six feet. Micah leapt off the porch like a young boy and climbed onto his waiting Cash to meet them.

Cookie Mahoney had piled chuck bags at the far end of the porch planks. Together, she and I had scrounged the landscape, filling sackcloths with anything we could find on the wild land, plums, dandelion greens, and purslane; acorns for mushing and grilling, and prickly pear. She came now and lifted a sack in her arms, groaning in the shadows of the overhang.

"Cookie?" I asked.

"I'm good, ma'am. Not old, just unused to this toting." She straightened and leaned against the wall boards. She was a tall one, and round as a cow with calf. "It'll come with hard work."

"Let me take that, Cookie."

"Oh no, certainly no." She wore a pea green cotton frock with deep pockets, and in the left one she carried a carving knife. Her face was chubby and pink, and she wore her hair, light wavy auburn, pinned back into an old-fashioned white cap.

"At least I can help," I said.

She nodded. "This is my job though," she mumbled. She had come out of Selma to Nacogdoches and before that we never knew her story. She had no husband or land of her own, but was a fine worker who could feed a cavalry out of a single wild turkey. "Thank you," she said simply and looked away, embarrassed. "But I want to earn my wages."

By the time the crowd came through our gates, Cookie had pulled the last of her pies from the outdoor oven, apples and rich cream smelling of autumn. I stood beside her, passing the plates from her hands to the bench, and when we were done, she said, "You're a kindly one, ma'am."

In truth, our Cookie Mahoney was by far the better of us, an unafraid and loving soul who wanted only to be worthy of a home.

The punchers herded the new animals, all of them the color of burnt-out sienna, into the meadow. The flanks of our new steers were steaming, and they stood shoulder-deep in the big field of high prairie grass, with wild scarlet paintbrush and bluebonnets as far as we could see. All hundred of them chomped through that prairie like they were moribund from the droving.

Teddy Blue leaped up the steps and threw his arms around me, sing-songing, "Ellie Ellie Ellie," over and over like an old barn swallow in flight. I pushed him off, singing 'Teddy' back at him and laughing. When we stopped to catch our breath, we looked out to see the cattle populating their new home, and it was a sight to conquer the clammy heart of any swallow-catcher.

"What's to eat, Eliza?" He turned from me to saunter inside the open door to our cabin.

"You stay away from those pies," I said. "That's for the *barbacoa*. Sit down and I'll get you some bread out of the oven."

"Smellin' it already, Eliza, and I'm thinkin' what a fine woman you are."

I pulled one of the warm loaves off the stove and put it on a cedar plank atop the table. I sliced through, running slabs of butter across the top with a wooden spoon, letting it melt into the crevices.

"Thank you," he said. He grabbed a hunk and shoveled it into his mouth as quick as a starving brush mouse. "Want to ask ya something," he said quietly. "Micah asked me to stay here with y'all. Work with him and live here. Okay with you?"

"None of my affair, Teddy Blue, unless it's my personal opinion you are looking for."

"Of course, Eliza, that's why I'm asking. You're the boss of this place."

I smiled at this. "We both have dearly missed you. The more

strong men on the ranch, safer I'll feel." I leaned back against the table. Micah came in just then and asked our topic.

"Our family is growing, husband, and Teddy Blue is welcome here."

~

In the morning, our guests lay soundly upon their sleeping pads through first light. Cookie had already lit the stove and gone searching for brush wood, leaving only Lariza in the kitchen.

"Is it just us?" she asked.

"Yes. You know the men will be sleeping off their bourbon. I doubt if we'll see them till the high sun."

She nodded and sat at the table. "The last I heard you were off to find your sister in Crockett. How is she faring?"

I hesitated too long to answer, remembering and thinking until tears tumbled down my face.

"Oh, my friend, I'm so sorry. I didn't know she caused you pain."

"She didn't. My sadness comes from knowing her life. And about her husband."

"She's not happy then?"

"I'm happy, Lariza. You are happy. But the rest of Texas womanhood, who knows? Find a decent sort and all is well. If not, those homes ain't homes for anyone." I looked across the room at the baking trays and pot of flour. "Come," I said and took her hand as we walked to the paddock, where we saddled up our mares and rode out into the cool morning mist.

We could see the far hills, covered with the mist and dark bluebonnets, a horizon brushed in Frenchy blue paint covering the hill. We rode at full-out gallop across the meadow and up to the top of the ridge, where at last we dismounted and lay on our backs, breathless on the carpet of bluebonnets.

When she caught her breath, Lariza rolled over to look at me. "What happened to the boy Arakka?"

I shook my head. "He went back to his people."

"You and Micah were his people, no?"

"No," I whispered.

She paused a moment. "This is beautiful land, Ellie." She reached her hand out to touch my arm. "What do you think you'll call this place?"

"No idea. I expect naming it will be Micah's privilege."

"You know he loves you so dearly he would let you call it 'Dunghill' if you wanted!" We both laughed long at that. "If it were my task, I would call it Bluebonnet Ridge, after this spot right here. Right here this minute, because exactly now you are happier than I have ever seen you."

CHAPTER 17

*T*he cattle drive to New Orleans brought more money than Micah had dreamt, and he was determined to spend it quickly. Instead of a mere cabin for us, he wanted a compound, house and barns and crib and paddocks, all built to his imprudent vision. When word of this reached our neighbors, farmers for miles buckboarded out to see our holdings and were astounded at the broad buildings of cedar and the new crops in clean lines out to the horizon. We were not as much visited as we were watched by the Milam families and their slaves.

I waited beside the pecan trees that Micah had planted on either side of our house, seeing this parade of colonists, waving to them, and hoping they would dismount and greet me. Failing that, I decided to approach them. In high sun and through tawny mud, Teddy Blue and I brought a cart filled with lunch buckets to the families, inviting them to take hands with us and to drink from our well. Half-confounded, the gawkers refused my offer, wheeled round, and left on the road they had come.

Teddy Blue stared after them, and gathered the buckets back into the hand cart.

"What did I do wrong?" I asked.

"Nothing. You can't be a friend to them unwilling." He hitched a rope to his backside and leaned low to the road, pulling the cart through the mud toward our beautiful empty house. Sootflakes blew off the chimney across us, spotting my face, and as I wiped them away, tears smudged black down my cheeks.

"I wanted more. I thought it might be different here."

"Everywhere's an underworld, Eliza. You're a tip apart from the rest, bronze-buffed skin, color of whiskey. Don't mean nothing but sweet beauty. Yet most folks see their nightmares in strangers, not their kindly dreams. Here ya got the run of river shallows, ya got Micah and a pearl of a farm. We don't need the others."

That autumn, Micah and Teddy Blue built a liftable crossing over our stream, much like a castle drawbridge, inspiring more resentment among our neighbors, and in fact, that bridge collapsed without explanation within the year.

Indian raids were common, and though they burned the fields of nearby farms and stole from their herds, nor the Comanche nor the Kiowa ever touched ours. Some farmers said witches slept among us at Bluebonnet Ridge, and some believed we bribed the tribes with beeves and harvest.

By the end of our first year we had lost two of the pigs and both goats, their torn flesh left on our land as though a mountain lion had had its fill. Teddy Blue hunted it for a day and a night but never found an animal predator.

At the turn of our second spring at Bluebonnet Ridge, I found a stranger standing boldly in our yard, gulping water from our well-cup. A wiry canny fellow, stiff and straight in his bearing, he drank his fill and then drenched himself with more. I came toward him from the near corn rows I tended, and he stood unflinching with his crisp cotton clothing glistening in the broad sunlight. I had a feeling that he had come to us from a dark story, but I strode up to him all the same.

"Well," he said, smiling with taut thin lips, "you're quite a beauty." The smell of woodsmoke surrounded him, and he asked, "Ya seen a horse anywhere behind the hedges, girl? I lost mine late yesterday." His voice was loud, and ominous as a hangman's.

I owned the land this man stood upon, but that did not erase my fear. Trembling with the memory of plantation voices of my childhood, I tucked my straggling hair under the brim of my work bonnet. Melungeon though I was, free mulatto as I was counted, we lived in a land of slavery, and I looked the part of anyone's dream or hate.

"Welcome, stranger," I said. "Sorry to tell you that we've not seen your horse." He was handsome, dark hair and moustache, though no taller than I. "Your name, sir?"

"Frederick Braun. I've come a ways on foot just now and I'm in need of food. I'll take a plate on that sweet porch. Go and fetch it and then fetch the title holder." He began to move forward past me toward the steps of my home, but Cookie came to the porch and blocked him, pointing a rifle toward him as an open spout.

"Who have we here?" she asked.

"This is Mister Braun," I said quickly, but did not move. "He has lost his horse, and would be grateful for some food. I'll clang the bell for Micah, who he requests to see."

I invited Braun to the kitchen where Cookie poured us up large cups of cool cider she had been storing in the dark shed. We sat on the porch in the thin spring sun, eating dewberry cakes while he told me a tale of Missouri where his parents left him an orphan.

When he finished the cider, Braun struck the cup on the porch rail to call Cookie. "Honestly, girl," he said to her, "I'd sooner have whiskey now."

"Oh would you?" she asked. "You're quite a shillaber, ain't ya, Mister Braun, there."

He jolted to stand and whirled on her abruptly, but my husband and Teddy Blue came over the ridge carrying their rifles, their strides tight with the disturbance.

"Well now," said Cookie, "here the men come."

Micah nodded at Braun and touched his index finger to the brim of his hat. "Hello, sir."

Insolently, Braun did not speak. The sun before Micah scrubbed his face with broad bright light revealing his impatience.

"I see you have eaten," he said. "Moving on?"

Braun wiped his fingers across his dark moustache and sat down again. "I hear this Bluebonnet Ridge is the biggest producer of victuals in the county."

Micah nodded silently.

"Well, I am establishing a post for trading with the farmers and soldiers in this vicinity and my intention be to purchase from you when possible."

He paused, waiting for Micah to react.

"What're your needs?" Teddy Blue asked. "Like is, we won't always have your wants met. We feed our own first."

Young Braun drew his lips tight. "Maybe that be changin'." He pulled a sack of coins from his breast pocket and took to clacking them together. "Niggers don't need that much to eat. They work just as hard from scare as from sustenance."

Micah jolted forward into the mud patch between them. If it hadn't been for Teddy Blue grabbing hold of his sleeve to stay him, my husband might have felled the man right there.

Teddy said, "Mister Braun, we are interested in trading our surplus with your operation, of course, but Bluebonnet Ridge ranch is sufficient unto itself, and not a single slave is part of this society. Wages for work, and that's the long and short of it."

Braun nodded, but his lips pulled together in a scowl; shortly thereafter he walked on to the road into a far stand of oaks, and so briefly, I heard the sound of horse hooves.

Weeks anon a tale of the new store reached us, and Micah and I visited that first month, strolling through his sacks of flour and beans, commenting on his establishment. Braun had built a table before the little one-room building, and stood behind it, taking Mexican coins and promissories, and trading products like soap and cotton bolts from Nacogdoches. The Bluebonnet Ridge needed little, so we sufficed with purchases of ribbons and sweetmeats. Upon our leave, we stood at the payment table handing our coins to him.

He wore a tan broadbrim and a long leather duster coat. In the weeks since his Bluebonnet Ridge visitation, his moustache had grown down the corners of his smile to the affectation of smirking anger or madness, or both.

"I thank you for your patronage," he said.

Micah touched the front of his hat with one finger but did not speak. His aversion to this Braun could not be disputed.

Braun spoke again. "We are having a small meeting here after worship on Sunday afternoon, Mister Moore. I expect you will want to join us."

Micah sighed hard. "Who is the 'we' you refer to, Mister Braun, and what is the topic of your meeting?"

Braun leaned back against the log walls of his store. The building was unfinished, thrown up quickly, and smelling sharp and sweet of hewn lumber not yet seasoned. He pushed his hat back on his skull. "Neighbors gathering to discuss topics of interest to all. Stories ruminating over this country and what might be our action."

"What stories?" I asked.

Braun looked away from my husband, dogging me with his

gaze. He nodded to himself and grabbed the stems of red-spotted buffalo clover from his table. He offered me these flowers, saying, "These are for you, Missus Moore. This discussion is for Mister Moore."

I took them from his hand and said my appreciation, lifting them to smell their wilting petals. The very moment they passed from his hand to mine, he added, "Go on, girl. Your man and me have business now."

Micah's eyes widened. I dropped the flowers and put my hand on his arm, begging for calm, but the breeze around us was foul and possessed of some larvae rotting nearby.

"Sir, you will be respectful when you address my wife," Micah said, "and you will now apologize for your rudeness."

Braun leaned forward to fetch the blooms, lingering silently, weighing his response.

Micah shifted quickly toward him, grabbing that duster collar tight and pulling him high. He swung a clenched fist at Braun's face, knocking him to the dirt. Quickly he lifted his fists over Braun's head and hammered down, while dry dust puffed around as my husband beat the man into the ground, splitting the day with his own grunts until at last, Braun lay dazed and silent.

"An apology then," Micah repeated, standing over him.

With the broken voice of a crow, Braun wheezed, "I am most sorry, Missus Moore, of course. I meant no insult."

Micah took my arm and we turned to our wagon cart, stillness swallowing me all the trail back to the Bluebonnet Ridge.

Micah never again traded so much as a corncob with Braun, bringing to swift end that man's frail economy. Our victuals gained a reputation for ripeness and taste none other could claim, so folks came direct to us for provisions. Teddy Blue took on the job of drying beef and smoking hogs for selling, and the fur trade went back upriver to Torrey's post.

We hired in a stock raiser from County Armagh to help him,

an eager man previously starving in the north of Ireland, who could accommodate the requests for our cattle meat. As quick as Braun had established his supply store, he lost it all again to the Bluebonnet Ridge and the old settler businesses up and down the Brazos. He disappeared from the county by September, and it was years before we heard of him again.

CHAPTER 18

For three harvests, we worked the open land, loading its banks and grasses with the bounty of that sweet black earth. We grew our farm and waited for a family to come, but that dream of children eluded us until one late winter, a babe formed deep in my gut causing me stabbing hurt every day. By April, my belly had rounded and Micah lit our bedroom tapers each morning with the smug grin of a man who has caused a new life.

I was out in the blueberry rows, determined to work until I gave birth, when my legs suddenly trembled, and I fell hard like through a gallows against the rough planks of the hauling cart. All my strength had slipped away, and for a time I could not move. I bent at my waist and vomited across the dirt. A great weight pressed upon me, and I clenched my back so tight that I could no longer stand.

I doubled over, lying finally alongside the cart, the horses snorting and scuffing beside me. I called out for help, for my husband or anyone who would lift me to some soft feather bed in a cool room. My groin cramped tight, and the impossible heft of the small gummy life came spewing out of me. I closed my eyes, and my breathing seemed to stop, and when at last the pain stopped too, I was able to open my eyes again, but I saw only black with glints of red and yellow and blue embedded. I lay behind this dark veil, waiting for a savior to lift me to safety.

"Miss Eliza!" a woman's voice called. "Miss Eliza, what is it? What happened here?" It was our Cookie Mahoney, the deep strength of her voice giving me hope. "You are bleeding, ma'am. Help! Help! Come quick!"

She lifted my head and held it to her soft chest, but I couldn't see her because the blackened veil still lay across my eyes.

"Help!" she continued to call out until the farmhands ran to us. "Look here! Missus Moore is injured, and we need a doctor. She must be moved to the house. Where is Mister Moore? Quick! Get to work!"

My stomach pumped with pain again as they sat me upright. "Please, Cookie, please get Micah."

"He's comin', ma'am. Don't you worry. He'll be here in swift seconds." I waited with my eyes open but seeing nothing, and I was still in the dirt when I felt his hands take me by the shoulders and hips. I slipped my arms around him, trusting as never before. I said his name once, and then I don't remember speaking or moving, and when I awoke, they told me I had slept for days.

On the first morning I opened my eyes, I cracked my lids with the sweetness of consciousness, but still saw black. No shadows, no people, no pictures, or men looking over the bed at me; nothing in the room but Micah's voice.

"Oh girl, you scared me. I thought you were done for." He put his hands to either side of my face, holding my cheeks in those big warm fingers. "Thank God you came back to me. Don't matter about the babe. I got you back now. You're the light of my life." He put his cheek on my chest and rested there.

"I can't see you."

"I'm here. Right here." But I had started to cry, and he felt my tears on his skin. He pulled back and touched my forehead. "What do you mean?"

"Can't see you. Can't see anything. Micah, why is that?"

For weeks I lay abed. Micah ordered the surgeon to come from Austin and examine me, but he determined my harm was so deep in my skull that he dared not cut it out. He had no answers or cure. My eyes had simply dimmed over for no reason.

A month later, I finally ventured to the bottom floor of our home, feeling my way with my hands and toeing the steps carefully, and I sat to table at breakfast. I wore lace and light blue cotton that brought my grey eyes to cornflower, so Micah said. I pulled my hair back to a bun and waited for him to sup with me. I knew I had not survived this illness well. I was no longer lovely, not graceful, nor even pretty.

He sat across from me at the oak table. Our Cookie Mahoney served us johnnycakes made of corn meal and butter, with hunks of roasted pork. Micah was ravenous, and I listened to him eat, recognizing those familiar sounds like old friends.

"You aren't hungry?" he asked, still chomping.

I shook my head, hoping he saw me.

"Come here," he said.

"I don't know how," I whispered. "Where are you?"

I felt his fingers touch mine from across the table.

"I will always be here. Just put your hand out."

"You can't want a damaged beggar of blindness," I said.

"You aren't damaged and you aren't a beggar. Stop saying those things."

"I'm a blind woman. A blind woman who probably can't even give you children now."

I heard him push his chair back, and his footfalls came closer. "Eliza, you're my heart."

"I'm so sorry."

"No," he whispered, standing then beside me.

"Every day I dream of jumping from the porch like a wild girl, running out to see the lilacs or the river. But I can't. Instead, I sit here in the dark, helpless." I shook my head. "You woke up so early yesterday and butchered a deer in the yard, didn't you?"

"Yes."

"You were so quiet, husband. I'm sorry I've become this, Micah. I'm your damaged wife."

I sat in a cedar rockerman on the porch for weeks, learning to identify smells and sounds of folks, while I waited for Micah to come and go with the day's work. Teddy Blue Corlies ate to table with us, although I surmised by his halting conversation that he had grown frightened of my blindness. I could sort out Teddy Blue's footsteps, because they were the heavy ones, clomping like a steer up to where I sat.

When he and the farmhands were near to me, I smelled paddies of rich dung; when Cookie Mahoney came from the kitchen I knew her by the scent of molasses and butter soaked into her garments. I was fair proud of myself for knowing who was before me, until one day as the light fell to dusk, I suddenly realized I was not alone on the porch.

I sat quite still to figure who might be the presence, and whether it be human, carnivore, or ghostly. Slowly, I recognized the honey smell of sugarberry bark closing on me, but I knew no one who came so surrounded.

"Who is here?" I asked.

I swear I could hear the creature smiling; it held this smile, and the unfamiliar bark smell, and when it leaned forward to touch me, its body was closer than I thought possible.

"You are sick," the man said heavily, and I reached both my arms out to Arakka. "I heard this from others up our canyon. They call you the blind woman on the Brazos."

"What others?" I asked but I had already clutched him close.

"How did you lose your seeing?"

I shook my head. "It happened when I lost the baby. No one knows how."

"What baby?"

"Micah and me had a child coming."

Arakka was silent and still, until at last I released him and he sat beside me. "I have come to help you."

"I am so happy to see you," I said, immediately knowing I had used a word that meant nothing to me anymore. "But you must hide, Arakka. This whole prairie is alight with fires your people set on us. Our Milam neighbors are out for Indian blood and scalps." I touched his naked arm with the palm of my hand. "The Comanche and Kiowa have come for all of us. Soon Texas will become a corner of the United States and the biggest army will hunt you all down."

"Who came for you? Did people fight this ranch?"

"Not Bluebonnet Ridge, no...." I stopped and pressed my lips together while my thoughts exploded. "It was you, wasn't it? Why no Indians harmed us?"

Arakka had become a man in those passing years, grown and opinionated, with deep stubbornness. He did not answer my questions, but simply changed our topic and said, "I will speak with *cocinera* about your food. That is cause of your illness."

He forced Cookie to prepare a corn dish they called hominy, a soppy bloated mess of liquid kernels floating in paste. He insisted I eat this every day, along with fresh liver from antelope that he would hunt down himself and spice with an herb he called *trompeta*. He instructed Cookie Mahoney to keep my gardens healthy, and to pick vegetables of bright colors and feed them to me without roasting or boiling. Although I thought this the vilest tasting meal he could have concocted, I was blind and had no choice: the rest of the population of Bluebonnet Ridge had placed its faith in our white boy's Comanche medicine.

Six or seven weeks passed, and I began to see shadows. Whether this was due to Arakka, the presence of such love around me, or the plain healing of time, I do not know. A month hence, deep into a warm October moon, I lay abed on the quilts, wearing only my sleeping shift. Micah had gone to see to stirring horses near the house, and I waited for his return before I could fall back to the midnight quiet.

The door to our bedroom opened, and my husband stepped over the threshold. He flung his hat on a chair, and unclasped his buckle, pulling the heavy leather belt from his pantloops. He dropped it to the floor, and unbuttoned his fly, and even in the darkness, I saw all of this. When he wore nothing but his cotton shirt, he came to bed and lay his muscled body over mine. He grazed his lips across my neck and face, sighing and uttering such things of love as he never had before.

And as he moved on me, I opened my eyes as wide as I dared and whispered this: "I can see you, husband. I can see you again."

"Oh, my love," he said, and pushed into me with all his strength.

The next morning, I stood on our clumped rows in front of the house. I could hear a plow cutting through the air in a far-off meadow. The foresters and handies came one by one across the black earth, carefully spilling seeds from their sacks. We were planting our new crops, and I was supervising, the like of which I never imagined I would do again.

Cookie Mahoney, with her timid disher girls, stood in the

Bluebonnet Ridge house to watch us, peering out the door cracks as if we could not see them. And I, on that bleak grey horizon, was no less filled with the future's brilliant light.

After our work, I sat on the porch rocking the afternoon away, and watching our Bluebonnet Ridge fields in wonder. I closed and opened my eyes quickly, again and again, silent and smiling.

Micah and Arakka soon came from the corral with their horses and tethered them to the near post. They sat on either side of me, both with hands touching mine. The sun had thinned against the cold dry light.

"Arakka is leaving us tomorrow," Micah said.

I looked at our boy. "I don't want to hear that."

"I need to be home," Arakka said. "They wait for me."

"I still don't want to hear it." He put his arm across my shoulders. "When will you come back?" I asked.

"In spring. When we come from Palo Duro again."

We ate supper in silence, for none of us wanted to speak of the following day.

At dawn as I lay abed, I heard noise in the corral and ventured out to see the cause. In the dying of this soft night, dreamy stars were still pulsing over us, while out on the prairie our farmhands were already at work, mulching up the seed mounds. The cows had gathered round to watch from their field, and Teddy Blue was sitting on a split rail beside them, chuckling at the audience. And all of it was washed in yellow light glowing from the bottom of the horizon, while the blue birds and martins and mockingbirds held the oratorio.

Micah came gently behind me and hung his arms around my shoulders, whispering in my ear, "Arakka is gone, Ellie. I'm sorry."

I shook my head and stared at the ground without speaking, my memories licking across the soft dirt.

CHAPTER 19

The next Monday suppertime I stood at the edge of our kitchen garden, my arms full of fresh-plucked winter honeysuckle. The skirly scream of the fat frying in Cookie's pans rose and fell around us while she turned the pork chunks top to bottom and side to side in the deep rich grease. I lay the flowers on her work table and when I straightened, a shadow caught my eye across the garden, a hunched frail fellow, a stranger, who watched us from the near path. He marched toward me, shuffling along with an old limp and one hand stretched toward me.

"I watched y'all," he said with a rough tobacco-scratched voice.

"What you doin' here at Bluebonnet Ridge, stranger?" Cookie asked. "Do we know you?"

Just then Micah pulled Cash up to the post and slid off, wrapping the reins round the cedar log. "Who we got here?" he asked, and crossed in front, separating me from the old hawbuck man.

"I watched 'em sprig up them victuals," the stranger said. "They did good jobs, ma'am." He was addressing me plain, not looking at Micah or any others about. The man nodded and pulled his hat from his baldy skull. "And you did good, Miss Eliza."

"Who are you?" Micah insisted. "How do you know my wife's name?"

This man was near to the color of a blue-washed sheet, glowing like a ghost against the dusk. "You don't remember me, do ye, girl?"

"This is my wife, and you will please speak with respect," Micah said.

The old man nodded. "She is your wife, and she is my niece. My sister's kin. I come clear over from the Yazoo Valley to see her and bring articles belongin' to her mother."

"My uncle?" I whispered. "I didn't know any of my mother's kin was yet living."

"I'm the last, Miss Eliza. I be Frank Bunch, or Moon Eye Bunch, as I am called, though most of our clan was moon eye folks."

I walked closer to him, not believing that he might be true blood of my mother, Becky Bunch. My confusion welled up in me till I trembled. Micah took my hand and led me inside, while Cookie saw our stranger through to table.

We sat silently, the dying sun dapping through our open windows. Light lay on me, on our plates, and across the walls, leaving Moon Eye squinting his eyes almost closed.

"How long you been traveling?" Teddy Blue inquired.

"Coupla weeks, I think." Moon Eye kept rubbing his eyes, and when they opened a crack, their color was pinky blue.

Finally, in the middle of eating our stew, he blurted this to me. "I see better in deep night, my dear. Most Bunches did, exceptin' your Ma. She was a merry mixer who didn't care. I need to find some shade now, as my eyes be a' hurtin'."

I climbed the stairs before him, leading to a room where he

might sleep. Over his shoulder he carried a sack made of old carpet pieces sewn together, and when we opened the door, he put this sack down. Kneeling beside it, Moon Eye pulled from it a ragged square of cloth and laid it on the floorboards.

"Eliza, come sit with me a-piece."

I knelt, and he put his hands on my shoulders, his fingers wrapped tight to me like ivy.

When I looked closely, I saw that he held tears in his eyes.

"Your Ma was dear to me, Eliza. A kind woman, and a fair beauty too. There was none could catch her spirit but yer Pa." Moon Eye shook his head, bobbing in and out of the shadows. "A 'Lungeon maid, her soul clung to all she touched. She be gone a long time now, but I held these items safe for you. Ya know it took me some years to find you, darlin'. Yer Pa traveled you far." He smiled quickly and wiped his eyes dry. "I come now to put her to rest with you. Here then. Let's a' looky at what I brung."

He put the items on his soiled cotton square and stared at them for a time. He was an odd sort, like I had not seen before. Blondy-grey straight hair hung from a protruding ridge at the back of his skull, and his eyebrows too were this light color. His front teeth were shaped like tiny shovels. He was an unhealthy-seeming soul, his face and arms the color of an old cow's milk. He moved slowly, like his joints were crying with each step, and though he was the age my mother might be, all those fifty years lay heavy on him in a way I did not believe they would have touched my spirited mother.

"Weren't much there by the time I traveled over from Newman's Ridge. Your Bunch family had long gone. Those left in the village gave me what I asked, but pickins was small. I'm sorry, Eliza. I brought you what I could."

"It doesn't matter, Moon Eye. I don't even remember her. I'm happy you are here with us now."

"You don't remember me either, do ya?"

I shook my head.

"Here y'are," he said, handing me a small ring. "Folks tell me it's a emerald, a big old polished emerald, but I don't know. Could be glass. Pretty anyway, and it was your Ma's ring, and our mother's when she was a girl. Back beyond our kin in Tennessee, I don't know."

I ran my pointy finger around the inside of the gold, amazed that my mother's flesh had touched where I now touched. It was tiny and didn't fit me, but the gleaming green glass, huge and clear, filled my soul. I could not see my mother's face in my mind, but somehow I felt her looking at me again for just a second.

Moon Eye took a tiny silver dish from the floor and handed it to me. Bent and darkened, the piece had one scrolled word engraved in the center: *Mama*. The edges were scalloped with sharp thin swirls, tarnished as well. He handed it to me, and it was so small it fit in the palm of my hand.

"Came from New Orleans," he said. "One of our brothers brought it back to your Granny Bunch after he run away from Newman's Ridge to fight with General Hickory. 'Course, none of the family forgave him, but Granny Bunch kept this silver piece all the same. She loved that boy so deep, more'n the rest of us. She always remarked to us leftover children how handsome he was. When he died in the pirate raids of '22, she gave this to your ma."

I put the ring on the tray and set them beside us. The cool clean smell of waterweed rose from the old cloth he carried with the items.

"This is a hard road, Moon Eye," I whispered. "Finding my mother like this."

"Here's another," he said as though he had not heard me. He unfolded a big old straw hat with the widest brim I ever saw and he put it on my head. "You look like her, Eliza." I pulled the brimsides down around my cheeks and stared at Uncle.

My breath was shallow and my voice harsh. With great fear I asked him, "Why did you bring me her trinkets, Moon Eye?"

"I have one more," he said. "This ten bill from the Mississippi Territory Bank. Ain't worth nothin', of course, but your Ma thought it was. She sold some eggs to a traveler and he gave her this. She hid it in her knickerbockers so no one would find it. My Lord, she thought it was worth a fortune, and not any of us could tell her otherwise. Here," he said and shoved it into my hand. "Old damn crinkly thing. Bank's gone bust now." He leaned back, looking at me and these few items. "And that's all's left of Rebecca Bunch, your ma. Exceptin' 'a course, you."

I looked down at my hands, for I could no longer look him straight. I had left my Ma's grave to the overgrowing weeds, and never looked back. I knew it didn't matter that I had been tiny when my father took us from the Yazoo; I had never paid respect.

Suddenly, the harsh rattle of a crow's voice scraped outside the window and Moon Eye said, "Mine is the tail end of a bad life, dearie. I was hangin' on till I got these to ya. I'll stay the night and be on my way, if that's acceptable."

I nodded, but his silence breathed back to me, and I asked, "You cannot stay with us a while?"

"Not long."

"A month even? Just a month with your niece who is joy'd to have you near?"

"Maybe, child. We'll see."

Throughout the winter and spring, and then into summer, Moon Eye rested with us, favoring me with stories of my grey-eyed mother and their rascally games down the Yazoo swamps, of her very own light walk through a gathering of beaux until at last she met my father at the dock market in Vicksburg. Benjamin Green, a sad widower with hungry cropper kin, who was simply looking for a place to light and a mother for his small babe from Carolina.

By day, we worked the plantings together, me and Moon Eye wearing his broad brimmed hat to cover his eyes, cutting the brown and dying leaves from the pumpkin sprigs, and laying straw to save the pattypans from molding against the earth. By evening, he began his tales, and he walked sentry in the dawn as grains of light fell trembling in the mists.

And one evening early up the August moons, Micah came into supper with special care in his voice.

"The silks're on the corn, Ellie. We got another two weeks or so and every one of us will be picking them milky cobs." I was at the cookpot by the kitchen fire, and he came up behind me and put his hands around my waist, standing up close as he could. He kissed my neck and put his face beside mine. "I had hoped you'd be carryin' a new babe by now." I sensed a soul was waiting for Micah and me to crack the earth's door open, but as hard as we tried, we could not jar it.

"I'm sorry, Micah."

"Ain't your doin', girl. Maybe it's mine. Who knows?"

"Maybe the reason I haven't got our baby yet is related to my own mother."

"Your mother?" He stood back and leaned against the warm chimney stones, smiling. "Now you're cornering that cart on two wheels, girl. What's your Ma got to do with it?"

"Well, I have questions, husband. Moon Eye arrived suddenly and from then I couldn't make a baby. Been months my uncle stayed with us without intending. I do believe now that he came with my mother's soul. How did he find us anyway? There wasn't a trail to follow."

"Ellie, he said he searched for years. Once he found your father's grave, and my sister, he would know where we are."

"But how did he know to go to your sister? And why did she not write us he had come?"

"Aw, Ellie, I don't know. He's here. He's a good man, helping us on the farm such as he can. Why can't you just accept? We got work to do. We got babies to make." He came forward again and put his arms around me, pulling me close until I relaxed into his lean body.

CHAPTER 20

Three weeks hence, the corn kernels bulged heavy with milk, and Micah called every farmhand from the county into the rows to pick. We sold them for weight not by count, so the quicker we could get the ripening cobs to town, the better off we would be. We harvested corn early morns, and I worked alongside the rest, standing in my boots on the dry earth clods and smelling the delicious sweet fragrance of fresh bursting corn.

Moon Eye and me worked together, both wearing our husking mittens to protect our skin. He started at one end of a row, twisting the cobs and hooking them off the stalks, and I worked the other end, until we met in the middle, quietly acknowledging each other. And then one day as we turned and moved to the next row, I heard him speak to me.

"You have a chance ta' know grace."

"What did you say, Uncle?"

"I think you know your mother is waiting on you, Eliza."

I removed my gloves and stashed them in my pockets. "Do you talk with her sometimes?" I asked timidly.

"No. But she is calling to you. She be waitin' to say goodbye."

His words hung around my shoulders, touching me for days. Long after we had finished the corn and sold it on, I ruminated the days away about my mother calling out.

That was a cicada year, and the first morning I heard those five-eyed bugs singing to me, I knew the autumn rains would not be far off. I had come to a plan, and whether Micah approved or not, I had to act before the weather turned against me.

I saddled up my mare and pulled her out to the trail heading to the far steer pasture. Micah and Teddy Blue had been working the steers for a couple of days on that prairie, and I rode into the gentle sun bringing them dinner because I thought my corn bread and honey-pork roast would soften Micah's reaction.

I came upon the men in the scrub oaks on the Brushy Creek, parsing the big branches into stakes. Micah stood shirtless in the sun and watched me riding up, staring quietly in his calm, knowing way.

"Bad news is not welcome, Ellie," he said. "What you come out for?"

I pulled up on the mare and sat astride, staring back at him. Teddy Blue came to me offering his hand to help me dismount.

"No bad news, husband. But I brought you boys lunch."

"Don't lie to me, girl."

He smiled when he said this, but he had never been one to enjoy mystery. I took his hand and gave him the basket of food. We spread old hemp cloth over the prickle weeds, and I passed them each a napkin holding their dinner. I had begun to perspire in the noon sun, and so let my hair fall free in order to repin it higher off my neck. Micah lay back on the cloth, staring at me.

"You are a beauty, Eliza. How did I come to have such luck?"

"The Lord made a mistake that day," Teddy Blue said laughing. "Must've got you mixed up with some other soldier."

Micah grinned and moved closer to me, putting his arm around my waist.

"This is damn good pork. Now tell me why you're here.

There's a reason you're covering." He had always been a frank fellow, straight and fearless.

I leaned over and brushed his sandy-colored hair from his forehead.

"There is something I must do before we can bring our first baby. I know you will not agree, but I am called to do this."

He nodded at me, without condescension, and waited.

"I must travel to my mother's grave in the Yazoo Valley and pay my respects. And I have to go soon. Before we get the rains. I'm not walking across Texas through those rains again, like we did before, you and I."

He braced himself and stood, a handsome man grown nearly six feet tall. I knew I was the lucky one, but he did not say another word on my subject.

"Let's finish up, Teddy. We'll be back in time for early supper, Eliza." Although he spoke to me, his silence on what was in both our minds was raw. He turned to grab his axe from the meadow and walked away.

After supper when our bellies were full and we lay abed together, I scrambled up my conversation again. "Are you angry, Micah?"

"No. I just been wondering how to organize things. We got the pumpkins and squashes and sweet potatoes, the tomatoes, and the cotton of course. Even the damn pecans. All of it coming in the autumn. I expect you mean to go soon. Maybe in October? Well, you can't go alone and I can't go with you in October."

"Or I could take Cookie Mahoney to Bereminda, leave her there and go on by stage to Natchitoches. We don't have as much Indian trouble now that Texas is part of America."

Micah lay quietly. The pecan tree outside our window, lush with leaves, blocked the starlit sky from us. We heard the squawk of a snipe flying across the moon, and after, the night fell to silence.

"We can't spare Cookie during harvest. Ya know that."

"Does that mean I may not travel?"

He put his hand under my shift, and spread his fingers over my stomach, sighing. "You really believe traveling out there will unwrap a child for us?"

"I do." I put my fingers on the bone of his brow.

"I want a babe so bad I would venture anything. If you think this journey will work, then I do too. I'll send Teddy Blue with you and Moon Eye. Teddy will see you both safely through the journey, and you'll have no worries from him on the way. Only one thing though; I want you back by Christmas. I'm not spending those dark days without you."

CHAPTER 21

ookie packed up a wagon of harvest for the three of us, Teddy Blue, Moon Eye, and me, and we set off well before dawn heading down to the Old San Antonio Road. Moon Eye, frail as he was in daylight, drove a few hours each morning, turning the oxen over to me as soon as the sun began to climb the sky. Teddy Blue took his horse beside us for safeguard during the days.

Like most rangers on the road, he was possessed of a fleet horse and a steady arm, buckskin breeches and moccasins, and he wore a red shirt and cap to identify himself. He carried a knife or two in his belt in addition to the Anglo firearms, and he knew every ranger and every Indian in the area who might be a party to our journey.

Teddy Blue and I worked hard on that trail during the hours of light as we waited for Moon Eye to wake into the darkening horizon and help us. We were vulnerable crossing the open creek beds, and each time, I could feel Teddy Blue hovering ready over his weapons.

The second day delivered us safe to the western hills outside of Crockett, and we reached my sister's ranch at mid-day. We drove the oxen up through the cottonwoods, and found the land spongy with heavy moisture, because over the intervening years that river had meandered close to the corrals and pioneer cabins. A few scrawny longhorns moved slow across the paddocks, but there weren't any good grasses growing for them.

"I see someone out on the porch of the cabin," called Teddy Blue, and he held his left hand up for me to stop the wagon. "Old guy, just settin' there. Don't see much activity on this ranch, and two of them side roofs need some patching. Let's stay a while back here, Eliza. Give the cowpunchers time to come out and find us. Ain't never good to surprise men hard at work." He lifted a rifle from his pack and lay it across his saddle.

"That'll probably be Levi Baylis at the main house. My sister's husband. We'll be sleeping here tonight in warm quarters, boys."

Teddy Blue nodded but kept staring at the cottonwood cluster and the buildings ahead. "We'll hang back, all the same. Something's not right here."

The man I thought to be Baylis saw us and climbed on his horse. A bedraggled ranch hand came out the front door and did the same. When they reached us, Teddy Blue greeted him.

"Hello, sir. You Levi Baylis?"

"That be me. You lost?" he said, and brushed a filament of smut hanging from his hat brim. "If you folks're lookin' for food, we got little to offer ya." He jammed one hand in his pocket and pulled a fistful of seeds. "This land's a mistake. Nothin' but floods and drought for us. This is all that's left now."

"Looks good clean seed to me," said Teddy Blue.

Baylis looked at each of us but rested his gaze on Moon Eye. "What's got his color? Sickly sight, ya got." He turned his face to watch the sky, thick with a dark swell of coming rain.

"Mister Baylis," I said, "then I am your relation. Louisiana is my sister. We come from over Milam, headed out to the Yazoo, and thought to stop the night with you. I am Eliza."

He watched me for a moment. "My wife's sister? She's visiting to my brother's family this week. But if you're kin, we can spare a dinner for ya."

"Dinner will be welcome," said Teddy Blue. "For all three of us."

Baylis dipped his head. "Come then." He clucked his horse toward the compound, while Teddy Blue and I stared at each other.

As we reached the buildings, we saw a thick front hedge behind the wallflowers, filled with thorns and tight choking flower buds that hung dead on stems. The hatchet birds chucked at us, scratching and sucking the air without a song.

"Come," said old Levi Baylis, "we'll dine on the porch. He sat us in strange chairs made from willow branches that had once been chopped and fashioned but still sprigged leaves at our arms. A ranch hand brought broth for us. "This is good soup," Baylis said.

"I had hoped to see my sister." I smiled as broad as I could, but I had begun to follow Teddy Blue's scent, and knew that all was not quite right. "When will she return?"

"Ah, days from now. Who knows? She up and decided to travel to a friend in Sarahville. Who knows?"

"I thought she was visiting your brother."

"No," he muttered, and did not elaborate.

I nodded to him and continued chewing. Gradually, I identified a noise that at last showed itself to be distant gurgling. Old man Baylis jumped from his chair and ran to the sound, swearing all the while.

"What the hell is this?" he asked, but no one answered. Milky water had begun flushing from the undergrowth beneath the porch, draining from a pipehole out of the basement. Baylis's ranch boys were scurrying to find a solution, and eventually he too disappeared into the night, leaving me, Teddy Blue, and Moon Eye to wonder.

"What the hell do ya make of that?" asked Moon Eye.

"Man's cooking up whiskey below, I'd guess," said Teddy Blue.

"Never seen nothing like it," Moon Eye replied. "Leaving guests here to fend of a sudden to see to pipes."

Teddy Blue laughed. "Not much fending to be done, Moon Eye. We're going to sit and wait, I think."

That moment a knocking started: hollow and regular, beating out a rhythm on metal. It thumped for a few minutes and then stopped abruptly.

"What was it?" I asked Teddy.

"I have no inkling, Miss Eliza. I expect it has to do with the leak. For now, we are just setting and waiting. Like the days before San Jacinto."

"You must've fought long and hard, Mister Corlies." Baylis had slipped through the door and stood at the doorjamb.

Teddy Blue nodded without surprise. "Be a custom for all western rangers."

"You on muster now?" Baylis asked.

Teddy shook his head. "I'm delivering Miss Eliza on behalf of her husband."

"Why're you dressed as a fighter then, if you're not on muster?"

I knew Teddy Blue had never liked being questioned too deep. He leaned back in his chair and hooked his fingers through the pistol latches on either hip.

Baylis saw this, and added, "I mean no harm. A matter of idle curiosity only."

"Well, Mister Baylis, as ranging men travel afar we like people to know our allegiances." He added, "And our talents." He said this quietly, seeming to look down at his feet, although I knew from past experiences that he could see every movement on the porch.

Baylis ran his hand over his bald skull and sucked hard at his gums. "I hope your dinner was to your liking. I got cowpokes waitin' for me and I must be back to the pastures. I will say my fare-thee-wells now, folks. I'll tell Louisiana you stopped for a meal with us, of course."

After he had left, Moon Eye exclaimed, "We been dismissed! What the hell?"

"Yes, we have. No warm beds for us tonight, Miss Eliza."

"Teddy Blue, I fear for my sister. We must find her! I don't believe she has traveled for visits. I'm sure she's here somewhere."

He shook his head again slowly. "Nothing we can do. I pledged to your husband to deliver you to your Ma's grave and bring you home." He pondered this for a moment. "If you desire to change our destination, I will be obliged to communicate with Micah first."

The thought of Lou being harmed gnawed at my heart, yet I knew that Teddy Blue, me, and Moon Eye would be a paltry battle force against Baylis and his cowpokes.

"I, for one," said Moon Eye, "am still feeling piggish in my belly. I suggest we ride on and throw camp for the night under some big oak near the forest."

"Eliza, we'll be journeying back here in some weeks," Teddy Blue said. "We can bring a helpful army of fellows from Bereminda and look about for your sister then."

I let them reason me away that day. We saddled on as Moon Eye suggested, lighting at last just before dark at the western edge of the broad forest separating us from the Hacienda Bereminda. Teddy Blue killed a couple scrambling quail birds, and set about roasting them alongside the sweet potatoes that Cookie had packed in for us.

Deep down the evening, the wolves and panthers screamed in the night at the scent of blood from the carcasses. Nearer they came, until our horses snuffled and brought Teddy Blue to his feet.

I do believe the scream of the panther, so like the plaintive shriek of a human being, is the most fearful sound I have ever heard.

CHAPTER 22

The next afternoon we arrived at Bereminda and I sat astride my mare, staring longingly at the clean wood of the hacienda gates. I leaned back on the horse and drank from the horn of water left hanging for travelers. The cooling shade of the pecans spread across me, and we rode through, on toward the house. Lariza ran to meet us as soon as she heard about our arrival, and though she swelled full with their first baby, she came quick and threw her slender arms around my shoulders.

"Oh my Lord." She laughed. "I knew you were coming from your letter, but still I love this moment so."

She took my hand and we passed through the heavy oak doors into the square. I had not returned to this place for years, not since Arakka and I had escaped. The pink papery blooms of the bougainvillea hung across the interior walls, and I stopped in the dust to stare at them. Bloodline or not, in this world only two things make us kin, and those be joy and sorrow. In between, I see folks separated by their own desires, but that day when I happened on my memories of Bereminda, I had both pulsing in me, the great happiness of those past days, and the terror of the way I left them.

"Eliza, what is it?" Lariza slipped her arms around me again.

I smiled, feeling a fool and wanting to push her attention away from my muddly heart.

"You are so beautiful with that babe in you," I said quickly. "Would you show me what I have these years much coveted? I have never been that round before."

"Of course."

She led me across the plaza to her rooms and locked the door. We sat on satiny bedding covered with tiny damasked roses, and she lifted her white cotton blouse. She untied her stays and displayed her naked breasts and belly, all swollen and the color of polished jasper. I put my palm over my open mouth in surprise. Her skin was stretched tight holding the baby, so huge with life.

She took my hands and put them on either side of her stomach. When I felt it move, I lurched back.

"I never seen this before," I whispered. "Was that your babe I felt, getting comfortable in there?"

Lariza smiled. "That's him. Here, put your cheek on't and tell it something."

I lay my head upon that taut skin of hers and closed my eyes.

That night we sat to table with the Bereminda workers, a hundred of them by then, old ones and children and young 'tweeners in love. Slender tree branches ripe with blossoms framed most windows and arches, and the balmy eve allowed us to supper in the plaza, with lanterns of different and bright colors bouncing around us. Rafael's cooks butchered a young steer, and seared its slices over a blazing fire. We ate until we could not take more, and then in the firelight, lovers danced.

Rafael turned gently around the plaza with Lariza, his arm tentatively across her back to support her, his silver-tipped boots clicking the tiles. Our old codger, Moon Eye, was in his finest moment, watching the young women and hoping for an invitation to a dance. 'Even out of pity,' he whispered to me, 'I don't care!'

The next morn we departed on the road for San Augustine, a small village just our side of the Sabine woods and the Free State. In this foreign terrain, there lay only the brittlest crust of gentility. We rode into town looking for succor, finding instead the dark side of their ways. Black men and women were exiled to shanties along back streets, while the poor whites huddled in the bayou water, prideful of the paler color of their skin. These swamp boys were eloquent on how much they loved their Augustine town, but they never brought a damn plant from the soil themselves, and never even learned to speak properly. We rested the night in boarding rooms, eating sour broth and sleeping on bugged mattresses. The next morning Teddy Blue Corlies woke us early to leave that river town and head into the wooded Sabine flatlands.

"Glad we're gone from that place, Teddy," I said. "Dross of hate smoldering around it."

"You and I ain't like 'em, Eliza. People like us fought hard to be left alone, and we're just a little more pleased with what we get. One thing's sure, they're lookin' to kill or make coin on strangers who ain't the same as them."

I puzzled a look at him and took the horn of my saddle.

"Boarding house widow told me privately last night that I could get a good price for you. Damn bitch! I woulda taken her down if y'all hadn't been here and at risk."

I nodded silently, still perplexed. Flushed, he lifted his reins and rode on quickly down the trail.

～

The Old San Antonio Road shot straight across the last miles of Texas and into the old French territory of Louisiana. Though the land was now America on both sides of the Sabine River, folks still called it the Free State, the wild place between what had been New Spain and the French territories, even now occupied by freeloaders of the western lands: assassins, preachers, and brigands. We reckoned to make Louisiana by early dusk, and all three of us held rifles and knives ready, knowing the bandit folks were still hiding in the tall pineys.

Deep into that cool trail while Moon Eye slept in our wagon, I blurted out to Teddy Blue a thought that had been burning at me since daybreak. "May I ask you something?"

"Anything. You know that."

"Back in Augustine, you said that you and I are not like those of that town. I know why you say that about me, Teddy Blue, my mixed blood and all, but why did you add yourself in?"

He nodded and clicked his horse on without speaking. At last he asked, "You don't know my story then?"

"No."

Finally, he raised a weathered thumb toward me, and lifted his voice quickly. "You know I would jump a bleedin' bear to save your husband, right? This is because he saved me." Roadside muck speckled his hair already, and his hands were clenched tight around the reins from the cold air.

"Micah told me of your fights in the western deserts."

Teddy Blue turned to me, this man who had become my only brother, his eyes brimming with bewilderment. "Sure, we both did that." His voice started out hoarse, with fear dragging at his speech. "But I'm talking about something else." He stopped and lowered his voice. "He killed a man on my behalf, Miss Eliza. A man who heartily desired to kill me."

We were riding behind the oxen cart that Moon Eye drove. Teddy Blue stopped his horse, and put his hand out to take my reins. "Man didn't like what I was made of."

"What do you mean?"

Teddy Blue looked me straight. His face had turned bright red and sprouted with tiny pricks of sweat. "Hard sayin' this to you. I ain't a man like others. I ain't one for you ladies."

"Teddy?"

"My father called me Nelly, Miss Eliza. Kept me locked in the henhouse so neighbors wouldn't know. I lived at the foot of the yard for years. They fed me, sure, but wouldn't have naught to do with me, till one day I broke out and ran." He dropped my mare's reins so gently I hardly noticed. "Traveled all the way from Culpeper to Nacogdoches. Never stopped till there."

I sat staring into the forest. I had heard of men like him; so many out in the far prairies or up the peaks left behind their women, found themselves rough sawn love, and never returned to our touch. Some were born that way, and some fell on it. Some ponied from one side to the other depending on the calamitous times around.

"I been thrashed for it too many times to admit my truth aloud to them who won't treaty me."

We rode on until he asked, "Eliza, you disgusted with me?"

I shook my head. "You and me been on a tide all our lives, Teddy Blue, fighting off the folks who hate for hating's sake. I never met one like you before, except I always loved you as my brother."

"You met more'n you think." He nodded. "I knew you were a kind woman the first day I saw you. You deserve more than you got in life, but then you got Micah, so maybe you and the Lord are even now."

We crossed the Free State to Natchitoches and pulled alongside the Caney River where my family had made its home before we traveled down to New Orleans. Once we were on Front Street in town, we stayed our horses and oxen, and Teddy went to fetch us water. Me and Moon Eye watched a dozen wharfies by the river loading timber off the docks and onto broad flatboats. They piled these trunks high as a building, working smooth and quick.

The shift from cotton to logs had caused the river economy to grow and the town ways to change. Women in hooped skirts sauntered from uptown to down, along the boardwalks and in and out of the sundries store and teagardens. I even saw a store with big printer boxes in the window, selling books and papers from New Orleans, for so many citizens had learned how to read.

We spent that night in a grand house, owned by beef customers of Rafael Bereminda. We came with his letters of acquaintance, and each of us was given fine rooms on the second floor. I do believe that was the first time I slept on the same level as the owners of such a stately home. One of the daughters of the local Creole planter had married a planter from Cane Lake, and now lived in town in this immense dwelling.

We were greeted at the doors by their slaves, who took us to a sunroom where the gentle mixed-race owners joined us and discussed our journey in quiet voices, just the way I imagined town people might talk. I was led off by a soft-hearted older woman they called Nunnie, a decent lovely person, milky tan in color, who had fallen on her luck and become indentured to the owners late in life.

Nunnie took me to the bathhouse and filled a huge tin tub with steaming water. She offered to bathe me, but I balked at this, and so she left me with soap bars and perfumes and softening oils.

Our hostess arranged for our dinner clothes, giving Teddy Blue a red silk frock coat that reached to his knees and brown velvet trousers. Moon Eye passed his bath hour arguing against the house fashions, and eventually opted to dine alone in his room wearing but his trail clothes.

Nunnie pinned my hair high off my shoulders and dressed me

in a pale blue velvet dress from her mistress's wardrobe, a hooped skirt, cinched-up waist, and plunging neckline that took me right into their royal Creole clan. The finest pieces though were the satin slippers that the owner loaned me, such smooth comfort for those dry cracked soles of mine.

Our meal was from paradise, such as I had never tasted. The young chef, a Frenchman from Tarbes, boiled a pot of crawdads and shrimps, and mixed it with garden tomatoes, onions and peppers. They told us he worked it all day, boiling it up and watering it down over and over again, adding layers of their rich butter from the Bereminda cows, and finally mixing in a powder made from sassafras leaves. The chef himself served us, scooping the thick soup over dirty-colored rice on golden plates from France. They gave us great chops from the hog, and bananas from the Turk Islands in the Gulf.

Late the next afternoon we prepared our journey again, and the Frenchman filled our oxcart with dried and preserved foodstuffs. Nunnie stood on the porch of the planter's home, holding something I could not see, but holding it so close to her I thought the truth of autumn must be in it. I walked to her, and she to me, coming sure-footed down the steps. This was an afternoon of raw cold, silent even with wind that tightened around us. She bowed her head, dawdling a moment, and then lifted her fist from a front pocket.

"A favor, ma'am?"

I nodded.

"I had a daughter once," she said. "A beautiful girl. I called her Nicole. These people sent her away because they said I was not a good enough mother. But last year a traveler came through and said my girl might be a bride in Natchez. If you journey that way and find her, please give her this. Please tell her that her mama is still loving her and waiting to see her."

She handed me the envelope. I was about to explain that we weren't going through Natchez, nor was it likely that I would happen across her daughter based on such small detail. That was the truth. But her eyes were wide open and she gazed at me, hoping.

I rocked back on my heels, took a deep breath, and grabbed the wrinkled envelope. I put it in my pocket, understanding at last about the gleaming comfort of our hope in this black world. Nunnie might spend the rest of her life waiting for the delivery of this letter and the return of her child. That girl might lie long dead, or concubined to a pirate, or might even be disinterested in this mother who longed so for her. But whatever the girl's truth be, it was the silver edge of hope that I could offer.

"I'm sure I will come across her, Nunnie," I whispered. "And I will tell her you are well and long to see her."

Nunnie's face flushed red and her eyes brimmed with tears. She had been living on the lip of sorrow for so long that it came to her very quickly now.

"Why, Miss Eliza, I think you must be one of the kindest folks."

"I am nothing, Nunnie. A look-back glass to persons I meet, is all." I smiled and put my arms around her. "I will see you again, my friend. When we return on our homeward travel."

She nodded and turned her back to me, starting for the house.

We were two days easterly bound on the old Chickasaw and Choctaw walking trails. These were slow-going surfaces rutted deep in the mud by Indian wagon wheels that had carved their way across the wet plains. We rarely saw a soul, neither settler nor Choctaw, riding down their fates.

We rode on toward the village of Vicksburg at the joining of the Mississippi and Yazoo rivers, and on that evening when we reached the fork, we stood on the cold shady banks before the broad mud-covered slobber, watching for it to burst into sacred life.

Each of us was chilled through our marrow, soaked and shaking in the night. I heard the last scraping of the wings of geese homing across the sky; I lay under the cart on a damp blanket and slept until dawn.

CHAPTER 23

$\mathcal{M}$y father always said he buried my mother unmarked, in a field below the Yazoo River. By the time we chucked down that road twenty-five years later, bouncing and bobbing over the ruts, all the Bunches were dead or moved on. My kin didn't have holdings like our neighbors, but Moon Eye told me we had some cabins on both sides of the Yazoo. He said our men stuck together for poaching purposes, and us children never went hungry. Moon Eye told about our family days, Sundays after Mass, where every single child had a sharp knife, and played mumbley-peg down the creek for swigs of liquor that he had stolen from the corn shed.

He told us that my mother was the best cook of the family, making his favorite chocolate gravy. She had a knack for making leek cornbread and frying up pies, using whatever old fruits or vegetables were leftover, and he said every last Bunch, even the West River ones, complimented her on these. When she was young, Becky Bunch grew the purest ginseng in the whole Yazoo Valley, and made money by selling it until the white folks called her lawless for it.

The farther we rode down, the more I learned about my

mother, some from his stories, but lots from the look of things. The Yazoo Valley was deeper than the Cane Lake lands of Natchitoches. Folks hadn't farmed here for twenty years or more, so the old trails were just sunken paths, overgrown with wild azaleas sprouting pink out of the dark. He pointed out the big magnolia, one hundred and sixty years old, he said, where my mother's father hanged a white man for stealing a table-full of hamantashin pies at Easter.

Once we reached the bottom of the valley, we three squatted on the wet grasses and watched the black-billed wood storks in the river shallows poke through the sour water for snails and flying bugs. Old water oaks lined the banks, their cracking branches hanging heavy with scrambling spiders and the moss they lived in.

"A 'Lungeon is all alone in the world, Eliza. That be our lamentation, because we look odd to them whites and we have our own ways. We never been part of a town's life, never got a vote. Our children and women never even had shoes." Moon Eye leaned back on a cedar trunk that had fallen across the water, sitting and squelching on the swampy mud. "Ain't no telling what folks like us will do. We cook our own shine and dance till the sun comes up. We use knives to keep our women safe. That's why towners never let us in. And us Bunches just kept on dyin' from their damned sicknesses, one by one, till we was all gone except you and me."

He was calling out so loud for his past days to return, for my mother and their mother to be with him. I reached over and took his pale hand, held it like a crystal, staring at it.

"Where was the house, Moon Eye?"

He put his arms around me, cradling my body.

"Here, baby girl. Right here." I looked down and saw a dead mole beside us, half covered in the Yazoo mud, small and cold with little points where its eyes had been. I touched its back, a pelt of fur and grass woven to one by time. "Yer Ma were born right here in this room on old Christmas, just as we passed to the next day. Around about the midnight time."

"My father always called her birthday by that name, old Christmas."

"Those born that night have souls that will live forever. Maybe in sorrow, maybe in glory. The sixth day of the new year is more holy than all the other days set together." A smell of cat piss rose around us through the oak branches. "There be night panthers here, girl."

Teddy Blue had been quiet for a time, but I could see he was shivering.

Suddenly, he blurted, "Well, Moon Eye, are we on our way to Becky Bunch's grave, or are we freezin' here for pure pleasure?"

We were so deep in the overgrowth that Moon Eye could open his eyes wider than I had ever seen.

"Becky Bunch ain't buried down here," he snapped. "Becky Bunch is buried in town." He turned to me. "See, after the yellow jack took her, your Pa made a pine box and put your Ma inside it, like she was safe in her own bed. Hammered it shut and carried it on his wagon into town. The towners supposed she was white like your Pa."

"He always said he buried her in fields down the Yazoo bottoms."

"He was protectin' her by sayin' that. Never gave up keepin' her safe. I'll show ya tomorrow. Now I need some food and sleep. My bones're tired."

We spent the night at a boarding house in Vicksburg, a big home that smelled like lavender. After dinner, I sat on the bay seat of my room looking onto the bare cherry trees below. I was watching lantern lights dip back and forth through the branches, flashes hovering beside the bushes or pluming up to the indigo night. I swore I heard iron clanking against itself, a gate swinging on a busted hinge. A beam shot straight to my window, and then

I heard his voice wailing for me, old Moon Eye limping on the darkened path through the camellias.

"Eliza!" he called. "Eliza, I'm cold!"

"Of course you are, Uncle. It's November on the river loops, and the fog is eating to your bones."

"Yes! That's it!"

"Well, come inside and get yourself warmed again." I laughed.

We met in the hall, and I wrapped him in the matelassé coverlet from my bed. He sat beside me, shaking with the cold.

"I been up Cedar Hill graveyard. Makin' sure your Ma's stone is there." His voice was tired and slow. "I be a little clammy tonight, Eliza, but I will take you on tomorrow no matter what." His face held the look of porous marble.

"We'll see how you are in the morn, Moon Eye. You need rest and warmth now."

He sighed, and smiled at me. "I be broken in mercy tonight. I forgave 'em all for what they did to us Bunches, and now my life load is cut in half. Remember that. You must forgive, even those that do not know to ask. Don't spend yer days piercin' yer own side."

Moon Eye let his head fall upon my shoulder. He lay against me, his chest lifting faintly with each breath.

"Just sleep now," I whispered, shaking my head.

"How can I keep from singing?" he asked, but not of me, and in a deep voice that seemed to timber from the moon, he said, "Come now to the table."

His breathing shallowed so softly then, and my breasts heaved against that frail little man as I sobbed hard painful gasps.

"Your Ma prayed me to be your witness. We'll go see her tomorrow."

"Let's get you to bed, Uncle."

"Seal it with an amen for us, girl. Go on."

I put my hands on his, and as I held them, the cold knobs of his wrists changed to stone. I put my lips on his damp forehead, whispered *Amen* as I kissed him, and went to fetch Teddy Blue.

The town people would not let us bury Moon Eye in Cedar Hill Cemetery. Although his skin was frost-white, in their scrawny thinking they knew him to be our Melungeon blood. Me and Teddy Blue rode his body down the Yazoo bottomlands, and put him in a hole we dug. Deep down that swamp, we looked about for hard wood. We found a couple wormhole planks and set them as a Melungeon burial shack over his grave. At last, we found a broke-neck dulcimer from the old days, buried in the swamp but made of better tree than the boards and fallen branches. Teddy hammered it up sideways to look like a cross, and we set this atop Moon Eye's last visitation.

Late that same afternoon, we hitched the oxen again and headed back to the hills of the graveyard in Vicksburg, where it was easy to find my mother. She was lone on the plateau in a broad field, a hunk of sandstone atop her. I guess my father had carved out her name, Becky Bunch, and gave up after that. But there she was, lying under my feet, deep in the earth in the box he had made her.

I tipped like a soggy harlot from side to side as I walked to her. I knelt and put my head on her mound and spread my arms wide out. I didn't cry; I never knew her. What I came for was release from her shawl of mother-tide. What I came for was myself.

At last, I sat back on my heels and crossed my arms over my chest. In the thin light of dusk, I read my mother's name again, the rough letters gouged by my father into her grave marker. There lay his love, deep in the stone, past the gleam of this day, or any day. He had dragged me from her resting place away to lands so far, but sometimes I saw her spirit sitting at the foot of my bed, still watching me and thinking.

I took a gulp of milk from the can that Teddy Blue handed me, and across the Glass Bayou I saw a swan swimming to the far bank. Beside me, sprouts of barley were growing up out of my mother's grave. There are no instructions for escaping, nor for letting go. *Lift that shawl*, I prayed. *Let me breathe and love me still.*

CHAPTER 24

*W*e crossed back to Texas before Christmas, journeying through the piney woods south of Weches town. This land was a sweet sight for me and Teddy Blue, for we had not found prairies of peace in Mississippi or Louisiana, only dying peoples, striking inward and downward as we watched. We were two days at Bereminda with Lariza and Rafael and their new baby boy, and while there I laughed heartily with her as we watched the child's tiny tongue and sparkling black eyes. Rafael had named him Jose Maria Joaquin Bereminda, after his father and without Lariza's family name because being a Purépecha Indian, she had none.

"If I die young," she said when we were alone, "he will not have my name and may not remember me." She blushed and fretted at this, lost in the saddest dream a woman could dream.

"You forgetting about my recent journey? I've been seeking a mother I hardly knew, but remembered all the same. One way or another we carry their spirits, like stitching between our days, Lariza. Your boy will know you forever."

On our homeward trip we were joined by hacienda cowpokes, heading to Bluebonnet Ridge to trade for our cattle. As we pulled out from the woods, the rain began to spit and didn't let up till we joined the bayou just north of Crockett.

Teddy Blue and I brought the oxen round the bend where the creek became a coulee we could cross. We pushed them hard up the rise toward old Levi Baylis's land, until we saw those Bereminda boys scattering fast ahead.

"Stay back," Teddy Blue said to me, and he leaped onto the mare beside the wagon.

Suddenly one cowpoke came back, riding hard and shouting, and waving his broad sombrero at us. Teddy kicked up his horse shouting to me again, "Stay back!"

But I could already see a billow cloud of smoke sliding up the sky in the direction of my sister's house.

"Fire!" screamed the lone cowpoke, wheeling his horse around and riding, hammering the earth toward it. "Fire!" he shouted again, and he rode on for the gate and the burning house beyond.

I followed them, kicking the oxen hard, arriving to see the Baylis workers scrambling out the doors and jumping to their horses to ride fast away.

The flames burst and the ground around us swelled out hot and hard like a griddle plate. The ranchero boys made a line out to the well and tried to quench that blaze by pouring pans of water on it, but the wood slat walls had tindered up before we even got close. Waves of heat rolled at us, and my eyes were burning from the smoking haze. Ash fell from open windows on the second floor, and I called out my sister's name as loud as I could.

I grabbed a bucket of water and a couple linsey-woolsey blankets from our cart and ran fast toward a far door not yet filled with fire. Again, I called out hard for my sister, but I couldn't see or hear anything except the exploding fire everywhere. I ran through the smoke along the flaming crib barn next to the house, and heaved open the far door.

Levi Baylis lay squirming on the sod floor, moaning and moving.

"What?" he shouted. "What is going on here, goddammit!" His words tumbled out in the voice of a drunk, and with the heat pressing down on him, all he could do was roll his wiry body over the dirt.

"Get up, you fool!" I shouted. "Where is my sister?" My voice was strong and full, but he just hobbled over, sat in the dirt, and closed his eyes. I grabbed his hands and pulled him toward the door.

"What are you doing?" he asked.

I kept dragging and pushing his old body nearer to the closed door, and suddenly I recognized the sound of boiling across the room. I looked up to see two copper vats, steaming and hissing above a firepit dug into the floor. A third vat lay bent and reddened from the heat, its corn mash draining out at our feet.

"You cooking moonshine? You damn sap-head! Put that fire out!" I shouted, pointing to the flames underneath the vats. I ran into the heat and emptied my bucket onto the pit.

He stood and teetered toward shelving filled with clay pots. He grabbed as many as he could carry and started for the door, clutching them to his chest like jars of gold.

"Where is my sister?" I shouted, but the crackling had turned to roaring above us.

I raced out and back to the house, searching and shouting for Lou. A roof timber had fallen into the main room, and the flames from the fireplace shot straight up past the ceiling and out to the sky. I hunkered over, and with the blankets wrapped around me, forced myself into the center of the room, covering all but my stinging eyes from the fire. When I could not push farther, I dropped to my knees and crawled through the searing heat, feeling the floor for any solid hump that might be a body.

Lou lay by the front door. I felt her skinny arms and hips, and then moved my hands up to touch her face. She did not move, but I called her name so close I hoped she would feel my breath if she could still feel anything. I threw the blankets over her and stretched my arms to the edge of the door to shove it open, but that damned sucking fire held the door sealed tight.

I shimmied myself upright and threw my shoulders against the door again. The hinges cracked open only about a hand's width, so I slipped back down to the floor and put my body over hers, and as I did I felt her chest pulsing.

A Bereminda poke and Teddy Blue yanked at the other side of the door, pulling at me and my sister, prying that crack wider and wider till they could slip us through and carry us to a grassy damp knoll far out from the house. They gave us water and wrapped us in blankets. Late in the night, the boys went back to the house to carry out anything else worth saving. Lou and I sat propped against a cottonwood, watching the fire in the dark. We watched the hedge holly leaves twitching hard in the fire until they were a row of cinders near a couple planks, guarding nothing now.

Come up midnight, my sister leaned her head on my shoulder. "Where is Levi?" she asked.

"Don't know," I replied. "Do you even care?" Embers were all that was left behind, her sad life turning worse in this night leaving nothing worth saving.

She didn't answer me, but only slipped an arm around my waist and said, "He's my husband, Eliza. What else can I do but care?"

Next morning, Teddy Blue came upon us and squatted on his haunches with his kindly bedraggled face, wanting to talk.

"Teddy?" I asked.

"Yes, ma'am. Levi Baylis is gone."

My heart skittered with secret joy. "You bury his remains yet?" I asked.

"No, Miss Eliza. That isn't what I'm saying. Levi Baylis is just gone. No trace of him. Must've run off last night."

My sister shook her head and tried not to cry, but deep solid sobs overcame her like she was Lazarus himself.

I put my arms around her, holding tight to her undernourished frame, feeling her heart and her sobs and anything of her that I might touch

"Eliza, do you have a home for me tonight?"

"Oh, sister. Of course, my love." I had spent years waiting in fright for the gun-butts to come cracking at our doors with news that her head be split in two by Levi Baylis or her body left by the road. "We're a family again."

The boys packed us up and we left that hour, intending to get a day's ride away from Crockett. I drove the ox cart along the camino, while Teddy Blue and the Bereminda boys rode the rear with the pack horses. By the time we reached the river road to Bluebonnet Ridge, the sky was bright, cold blue and cleared of clouds; the earth was quaking beneath the heavy hooves of our horses and oxen.

"You ever wonder about your mother, Lou?" I asked. "You been through so much, you ever wonder what she makes of it all?"

"Honey, my mother's been dead longer than yours. I understand that you're coming home from poor Becky Bunch's grave now, but my mother passed and never has had a word to whisper since then." Suddenly, Lou pulled herself beside me on the seat and slipped off her bonnet. "You'n me, we're all that's left, Eliza."

She took the reins from my grip and chucked up the oxen until we could hear our bench springs creaking. We were tearing so fast that the tongue of the cart shaft had slipped the iron bolts loose. I laughed, gulping deep and shouting into the crested wind. I grabbed her waist with one arm, and cinched up to the bench rail with my other. Holding her that close reminded me of our younger times, for her face had changed from a frown to a wild miracle.

We slept hard those first days back at Bluebonnet Ridge. Micah left early to collect our cattle for the *vaqueros* from Bereminda, and I slipped into Louisiana's bedroom, lay myself alongside her, and put my arms around her. Lou sat upright in bed, come to life of a sudden.

"Christmas is coming," she said, almost giggling. "We should be fashioning some presents for your farmhands."

We went down to the kitchen where the lamp lay still unlit. Cookie Mahoney was stirring up some dough with Bluebonnet Ridge flour and fresh butter.

"Aye, you two young ladies. What can I do for you?"

Outside her kitchen door sat a rookery, brooding and breeding crows cawing with the dawn.

"What's that noise?" asked Lou.

"Honey, that is our birds getting ready to cover their young ones." I went back to the outside gate to shoo them away. "You rest now, my dear. Your last days have been a nightmare of harm. Have some milk and go back to your bed."

Lou's skirts brushed softly against the woodsmoke of the rising fire. She shut her eyes and said, "I know, I know, but I have to make sense of what is to come." And then she said something that made me shudder. "It was never my intention to leave him. You understand that?"

Cookie Mahoney shook her head. "He burned your house to cinders, child!"

I opened my arms wide and wrapped them around Lou. "I am here," I said and dropped my head. "Micah and I, we love you."

She smiled shyly. "I remember when you and I were the 'we'. Weren't no other 'we' but Eliza and Lou. Makes me kinda sad that we both got others now."

One last winter pear lay on a wood plate on the table. I rolled it over and saw that the backside was rotting to brown mush. Like a child, I put my fingertip on the soft part and then pushed hard into the juice.

"I have nothing to go back to," she said. "Levi disappeared, our house and his business destroyed." I dragged along behind her as she walked over to Cookie and put her arm around her big waist. Lou and I wore my warm dresses of tweel that I had dyed deep purple from blackberry juices. "What will we do today?" she asked in a shrill wiry voice.

"Well, my dearies, I need you here making pies with me for them boys from Bereminda. They are heavenly hearty eaters," Cookie said.

By dinnertime we had put up a dozen fruit pies, some for the meal and some they could take on their homeward ride. We dressed the midday table for the men, and then carried warm tea in jugs to the porch for ourselves.

"I am beat," Lou said.

"Of course you are," Cookie replied. "We been doin' good hard work. This is the good kind of tired."

"No, Cookie, it's something different. I feel like the bottom of a dried-out lake, just aching in every bone and empty."

I blurted, "I know you're tired, sister, but do you at least feel a little free of your former sorrows?"

She closed her eyes and put her lips tight together. A couple of tears dribbled down her cheeks.

"You gals can talk all day long about how ya feel," Cookie said. "Just wastin' your time, ladies. What's real is what's real. The

Lord don't think on your feelings as bein' all that important." She leaned back in her chair shaking her head and took a gulp of tea.

A couple of the boys straggled up the steps chuntering about work and tipped their hats to us. Cookie rocked her bulky body forward and stood. "I better go get some hot food into those hungry men."

I reached out and put my hand over Lou's. "I hope you will be happy here."

Cookie shook her head as she stumped into the house. "Don't hope this side a' heaven," she called over her shoulder.

"I was also happy in Crockett, Ellie," Lou said.

"How can you make that claim when old Levi Baylis was such a cruel one. You told me his doings years ago, Lou. And his sisters and father. They stole everything our father gave you and left you with a bundle of old rags."

"I served him for ten years on my own. I never wanted for bread, and Levi never let anything befall me."

"He's a drunk who set fire to your home!"

"Jesus called me to be Levi's wife."

"Did he call you to be beaten and locked away by your husband? Louisiana, you are safe with us. No one can harm you, long as you stay with us." A floodtide rose in my heart, but what was left to say? We could not change our path from the Carolinas; we could not redeem the stolen headright on the Colorado. But I would protect my sister until death.

I noticed Micah standing at the bottom of the steps, oddly passive and carrying a ball of tight white string. "What do you have there, husband?" I asked.

"A measuring for your sister's rooms."

I laughed. "He always did prefer marking a foundation to marking time."

"Ellie," she said, "lives just aren't as saber-straight as you think."

CHAPTER 25

On one of the slow bright river evenings, we rode down to the Brazos. Micah had been talking a hallelujah about his river bass since our first night back, and he took us to earshot of a beaver dam where the bass, he said, were as big as pigs. We dismounted by an elder, and he ran like a barefoot boy down to the water. He unsheathed his pole and hung his prized lure onto the hook.

"Come on!" he called. "We'll catch the old one first! You're going to testify to what I'm saying then." Teddy Blue followed him into the shallows, slapping his own pole across the moonlit water.

Micah believed his aging wood rod was as near to perfection as an old craft could get. When my dear warrior cast it, the spring of its dark satin grain bounced like a flame across the river, and Micah smiled with unabashed glee.

Lou and I squatted in the grass, sparking up a pile of dried weeds and wood to a cooking fire.

"You pull 'em, and we'll fry 'em, boys!" I called out.

I heard the tide slap across the bank and smelled the sour leaves from the elder floating in the brackwater. I built the fire to a hot blaze, and took Lou's hand to pull her gently beside me on our hempcloth spread. We heard a splash and then a wild joyous crow from Micah. I jumped to my feet and ran to see this bass of men's legends.

"Look, girl! Big as a pig!" he shouted, guffawing his heart out as he carried a teeny fish dangling from the hook. We laughed hard until they returned to the river to hunt through the water again, and I to the fire.

Lou's bare silhouette lay before the light, as still as an anvil, her arms furled about her waist. Her hands were covered with soil, and her face as well, for she had rubbed her cheeks with the gummy river mud. I ran and knelt beside her. She wasn't crying, just looking ghost-eyed at the flames blazing.

"Lou, what happened?" I took hold of her hands, heavy as stones, but she didn't move. "Lou?"

Her face was dazzled dumb in the firelight until her pupils grew bigger, blacker, smothering her pale blue irises with the dark and flash of feral madness.

"I will find comfort with you," she whispered slowly. "But will you find comfort with me so near?"

"Of course. Now breathe and relax for you are with your family now." But around her I saw a rosy of red light like a lariat, glinting off her face and neck until I had to look away.

Once home, I fell to sleep in bed with her, our bellies full and warm, our arms around each other until late in the afternoon when I awoke to the sound of a tap-tapping against the door.

"Who is it?" I called, half-whispering so as not to wake my sister.

"It's me," said Micah.

"Come in, husband. You never hesitated before!"

"I have a visitor for Louisiana. Here with me."

"She's sleeping, Micah." He opened the door and craned his face through the crack.

"It's her husband, girl. Levi Baylis is here to see her."

Micah slipped in the room smelling of buttermilk and cowhides, tall and handsome and belonging to me. He knelt beside the bed and put his hands on the quilt. "Her man wants to see her. We can't deny that." He put his hands around my face. "You know what's right. She belongs to him under the law."

I shook my head. "Does he mean to take her back? We can't let him."

I saw he wore his holster and gun, and I lifted my eyebrows, because he seldom entered our home without removing them.

"Let it unfold."

I slipped from Lou's bed and joined him near the top of the stairs.

"I'll just wait here on the landing," said Micah. I saw Levi Baylis standing in the shadows. The old man's eyes followed me like I was stripped to the skin.

Micah let Lou's husband enter her room, but he waited on the other side, listening. After some minutes, he joined me and Cookie by the hearth, shaking his head.

"Damn me, what do you think? She's going home with him."

"No, Micah! We can't let him force her."

"He won't be forcing her. He cried to be pardoned and she did. He cried for her to forgive his sins, for starting the fire, and she agreed." Micah unstrapped his holster and left it atop the table. "And that is the end of it."

An hour or so later, Levi Baylis appeared to us, his hat pulled far down his forehead, dark as a devil. Behind him trudged my sister, her head bowed.

I stepped in front of him and blocked his path to the door. "You're not taking her!"

He glared at me. "My wife and I have made a new covenant, girl. She is coming with me back to Crockett, under the law of God and of this land. And this is not your business! You stay away from her."

Lou's face was stark white, her cheeks rouged up with fear, and her poor eyes were sunk into sick grey skin. "Please, Ellie," she said. "This is my doing. We promised each other again upstairs. You remember the Book of Jeremiah? The Lord requires us to forgive." She moved close beside me and took my hand, whispering, "Just believe, Ellie. And love me anyway."

"I failed you, sister."

"No." She pulled a black bonnet over her head and covered her gold hair.

Baylis strode proudly to the open door, and Louisiana followed him.

"They will know I am a Christian by my love," she said.

Quickly, I followed them out the door, but Micah grabbed my arm before I could leap down the steps.

"Let them go," he said softly. "It's the law, Eliza."

"Whose evil sends a woman back to that life? Don't let him do this!"

"Your sister agreed," he said with a firmness that left me completely graveled. "And if she hadn't, he could take her anyway."

I slipped down to sit upon the steps and watched them ride off. The sounds of that horse's hooves were heavy on our land, their very pounding teaching me a thing or two about hate.

CHAPTER 26

*O*ur dear Evelyn Polk Moore, our first and prettiest babe, was born that year, and Sister Edana, a distant relation of our Cookie, came all the way from Tampico to bide with us during the last days of my time. Sister Edana was a midwife nun from that little Mexican town, come to soothe the birth. Having never had a mother to teach me the ways of carrying a child, my knowledge of this condition was scant, but Sister was filled with stories of how to shoo away the animalcule particles she swore lived around us in the air, too small to see. And each morning she would burst into our bedroom, commanding Micah to leave even as he lay before her in his tow shirt. My husband was annoyed, but as midwives go, Sister Edana was said to be the best.

The day arrived when my pains began, searing, hot and deep in my bowels until I screamed. Micah came charging into the bedroom that morning, believing the kind sister to be harming me.

"Oh, you!" she called out. "We are now getting to the pinch of the game. Your babe will be with us in a few hours. Go downstairs and think of a name, boy."

I gave Evelyn her first breaths that day, while the thin late sun circled through the panes. Sister held me upright and leaning against the back of a chair for hours, until my legs gave way and all I could do was squat while the babe's face pushed out my underside. As long as the balance held, I could hold, and I felt Sister gently tugging, shimmying the child so slightly from side to side as it appeared to this world.

The nun's voice was soft and deep, as I imagined my mother's might have been, doing the job my mother should have. Living without my Becky Bunch had felt a powerless forever for an orphan girl on the frontier, but here was Sister Edana now, stepping close to my pain and countering it with a gift so strong she could have been my kin.

Our Evelyn was always graceful, a dancer even from those gurgling days. By the spring, we would set out to Hog Island for a meadow meal, and she'd sway those tiny feet through the beach gravel like a fine actress. I held her, balancing her little body, just to watch her try to dance on those silky chubby legs. She was willful and lovely; she stood without wings but sounded like the sweetest thrush whenever she laughed.

The next year our little James Henry set down, a boy of soft voice and pale skin who carried cogitations of sadness in his eyes from the day he was born. Micah loved that child too, and from the first days, carried his son off to the corner lands near the county line where the soil was mostly clay and where we could never plant. He held him close to his chest and talked him through farming and riding and protecting his own. By the time James was one year old, he had listened to Micah's calm biblia and had learned to grin when his father's gentle voice was about.

Our third child, Louisiana, came two years later, and as always, Sister Edana returned to us for those final months. Lucy, as we called the child, came out with a flattened face, a broad nose like a Negro but pale white skin and hair the color of old sheep. She was plain although spirited and serious, and she watched us without cries.

When it came to touching her own skin or my breast for suckling, she was hesitant and a little frightened. Sister Edana recognized this, and helped me to put my hands on her, holding her against my chest and whispering to her.

Towards the end of Lucy's first month, Sister noticed a faint sway in the babe to its left side, and often, as I pulled my poor girl close to me, I would feel her chest pounding. Doc Leahy told us she had a tilted heart, a condition not fatal but one that would keep her close to home for life. When she began to crawl, she did so slowly, always inspecting items laying before her with her tiny blue-shadowed fingers. She would sit back and lift some fragile leafless twig in her hands, stare at it, then ruefully claim it.

Micah and I had hoped for a dozen children, but with the birth of Lucy I grew tired; drawn and drained. I could scarcely walk across our little stone bridge over the stream, and it was all I had in me those first weeks to carry that babe in my arms. Sister Edana rested with us through my nursing months, and on the day Lucy finally pushed from my teat, Sister carried my babe for me to a fallen sycamore log along the sweet-smelling bank, where we sat side by side in the sun, sucking the perfumed flesh from wild figs she had picked.

I was shin-deep in damp bluebonnets, watching the tall pecan trees as though they were spires of some lost castle. "I'll hold Lucy," I said and put my arms out to take her, but the babe would not come to me.

"This child is strong-willed, Eliza, but weak in body as Doctor has told you. You will have some heavy tasks because of her." She lifted Lucy high against the bright sky and added, "Put your arms out again. You must not allow her to call the game." With that, she put the sobbing girl in my arms.

Lucy slithered against my body, and I loosened my hold

slightly. "She is my third child, Sister, named for my own beloved sister whose husband refuses my visits. So all I have is this girl here to love as I always wanted to love my Louisiana Baylis."

Sister Edana did not reply straight away, but settled on the log to face me square. "She must be your last babe, Eliza. You and mister should stop here."

"Oh, no," I said, and forced a laugh, smiling sharp. "We need many more children to work this farm."

"I will speak with Micah too before I leave. Your body is tired. If he cannot be true to this, you get you a cotton rag and soak it in vinegar. Keep it inside you at night, in case." She lifted the baby back to her own chest. "Look at you, girl. You're tired already now. Your soul is owned by God, and I'm telling you this on His behalf."

As with many life instructions, we heeded her words for a few weeks, but once she returned to the convent in Tampico I began again to call Micah's name in the dark silent house.

CHAPTER 27

I believe we were again to April sowing, when I saw the young marksman standing in the road before our land. He trained on a hawk across the sun, and in an instant one more man had come through the shadows. The younger was in a uniform, looking to me like an old-worldy soldier, so I ran to the far field to fetch Micah. I held the children and walked behind him up to the spot where the first visitor squatted.

"Sir!" called my husband. A couple of our ranch hands were hidden in the woods, as was the custom when strangers were about, but Micah walked forward, strong and unafraid.

"Sir!" he called again. "You come to the Bluebonnet Ridge for crops? I'll say you are out of luck. You caught us at planting time."

The young soldier turned to my husband. "I felled your hawk, gent. Let me recompense you." He reached into his pouch and pulled out two paper dollars.

"Who are you? And why are you here?" Micah asked, brushing the worthless bills aside.

"I am Private Absalom Johnson from the new Third Judicial Court of the State of Texas. We are looking for dinner, and for Mister Moore of Milam County."

Without a flinch of recognition, Micah replied, "Let's hear you out, man."

The two young men waited in the sun before us, both wearing near to rags and starving skinny enough to bring shame to their mothers.

"Judge Three-Legged Willie McCann be traveling this circuit, sir," said the boy. "He arrives in a day or so."

At the sound of that name, the sinews tightened along Micah's neck, and he turned slowly to the speaker. "You wear the coat of a territory ranger, boy."

Absalom nodded.

"You earn it or steal it?"

"I was with Scott's men when he captured Veracruz. And the hill they called Gordo." The boy paused, eyeing my husband and cradling his rifle.

"Were you on with Scott to breach the Mexican capital?"

"I was. And thereby met Three-Legged Willie in the ferocity."

Micah stood in the hogweeds and stones, still wearing his broad old work hat to block the sun. He carried but a long hoe from the field, with not even his Paterson at his waist, and suddenly I froze, thinking this day might contain his reckoning. Over his shoulder, he said to me harshly, "Go on back to your chores!"

Branches on the cottonwoods and pecan plantings stirred in the still afternoon, as the boys stepped forward at Micah's unusual gruff tone. Teddy Blue appeared, his polished Colt rifle extended in his arms, trawling with it like a spoonbait.

Still holding our babies, I walked a few yards back toward the house.

The boy looked at Micah. "You remember Willie, sir?"

"I do. We rangered by shoulders together out in the Staked Plains and the far territories."

"He instructed us ahead to find you. He be hoping to take a meal while he's here judging."

The sweet trembling whistles of the curlews spun above us, as they swooped over the pasture. The strangers looked up and smiled into the sun, dark shadows falling across the angles of their faces.

"Ain't no call better," said the boy. "I been afar too long. Good to put feet on this land, sir. You got a fine farm here. We are Texans, not been paid for our soldiering for months, and so damned hungry."

For one long minute we all waited while my husband sought the pulse of these intruders. Micah and I stood on the far side of ten years since we ran away, but in this slow land, ten years hardly scrubbed away the dirt of a past.

And then I saw my husband's shoulders soften as he sighed. "I am Micah Moore. Last I heard of Willie McCann he was farming cotton at Cairo Plantation. Married to that Edwards girl. Not judging out here on the prairie circuit."

The boy put his rifle butt in the dirt. "He's been lawyering for some years now. Wife died in the cholera of '45, most of 'em at Cairo didn't come through it."

Micah nodded once. "Come to table, men. You are welcome at our family dinner."

Three-Legged Willie set his first judging session down under a spreading live oak tree at the two forks of the San Gabriel River near to the new Milam trading town of Cameron. Absalom secured two empty whiskey kegs and dug them upright into the soil, laying a rough-sawn plank across for a judging table. Three-Legged Willie sat on a nail keg and leaned his rifle and walking stick against the oak tree. He laid out his own law book and gavel on the plank and pronounced court in session.

Folks from east and west of Milam County gathered around the oak tree to watch, having ridden for miles on hot horses to see the sight. Willie called for order, but the crowd was too excited to pay attention. The more he emphasized, the rowdier they got, until he reached for his long rifle and laid it on the table, cocking the hammer and putting his finger along the trigger.

"The court is coming to order," Willie pronounced. "And if it doesn't come to order right now by God I am going to kill somebody, and I'm not particular who I kill."

Micah invited our old friend to rest with us, and he bided at Bluebonnet Ridge for months. Gentle, kind, and simple, he was a fine ruffian. Not a grandly schooled man, he was still curious about all of nature, sitting on the porch boards with Evelyn, Lucy, and James, laughing at their little fingers and funny smiles. One time I even saw him stand for an hour in the shadows watching a bird bring grubs and flies to its young nesters, just watching it fly out and back, out and back.

He traveled a broad circuit, from Rutersville to Nashville, and was often mistaken for a preacher. Towns sometimes would ask him to pray for rain since a drought had all but folded our crops the prior year. Three-Legged Willie set aside certain days for rain prayers, and said at these times, "Lord, thou knowest how much we need rain for man and beast. We ask thee not to send measly sunshowers that will only make our corn nub out. Lord, we need rootsoakers and gullywashers. Amen."

He judged and he prayed, and he often pretended to heal the bones of our aching farmers. He charged one bit for prayers, a pistareen for healing, and a silver dollar for judging. If a man came with a pelt, Willie offered all three. Once a neighbor flashed him a wad of notes from the busted Galveston bank, but Three-Legged Willie ran him off the river that day.

Often, he did his judging beside the oak fork, where the river ran hard one way and glistened the other; where the mud rose to the surface and ladled there in great globs. Years on they named that part of Milam a new county, and that place beneath the oak became the permanent courthouse, where Willie had first set up his whiskey kegs.

~

When Nashville's church moved far out to the new platted town of Cameron, on Sundays at Bluebonnet Ridge we let Willie speak the sermon preceding supper for our families and workers. All came to us every week for these devotions against hunger, and Mister Three-Legged Willie McCann slipped into his rightful chair at our table, helping and praying and loving our Bluebonnet Ridge like me and Micah, Teddy Blue, Cookie, and all the others.

Only once did we open our hearts with questions of our old Cairo days. Cookie and her girl had just laid the food, warm acorn bread and golden Johnny cake, roast pork covered with honey, and plenty of pumpkin squashes with butter and molasses. Willie leaned back, drawing in the fine odors and smiling. He put his big hands over Micah's and mine.

"I'll warrant you are the best hosts in all of Texas," he said, nodding at his own words.

"Thank you, Willie," I said.

Cookie put before us a platter of baked wild apples stuffed with small, dried fruits. Willie put one on his plate and knifed it in half, the steam spooling out into the cool Texas afternoon.

"I was sorry to hear about the passing of your wife," I said quietly. "She was a good and kind girl, as I remember."

He stared at me while his eyes brimmed up. I was dearly regretting mentioning the Edwards girl and stirring his sad days, when he said, "I held some deep sorrow when she died, Eliza, but not as dark as the day when I chased you and Micah Moore." Lines around his mouth cut deep, and his voice was dry and low. "Nothing can fix what I did to you, making you run on for your life. I knew your father. I loved him. I had a duty and I gobbed it."

"We landed well, Willie. Let's forgive, you and me."

"I'll burn in Hell, Eliza. There is no forgiveness. I'm a judge, and this be judging."

And that was the first and last time we ever discussed it, and from that day Willie kept his truths deep and asked few favors.

CHAPTER 28

*A*t the rise of the early spring of 1852, Micah and Willie's old comrade, Peter Bell, came to rest with us. Although long known to our Green and Moore families because my father was with him at San Jacinto and my husband had rangered with him in the New Mexico territories, Petey was then in his second term as the Governor of Texas. Politicians were not of the habit to pay social calls to simple farmers, however far out on the frontier we might live.

The first night he joined us, I took the children to bed after supper, although I heard the men deep into the dawn staggering about the porch below our bedroom, laughing and chuntering on the subject of battling. Petey's men had never rangered, so he sent them off to scout our property, but all of our own were qualified to join him. Micah, Teddy Blue, Three-Legged Willie, and even young Absalom were part of that drunken discussion.

I leaned against the window in the moonlight listening for men's secrets, but upon hearing their sloppy jubilating laced with whiskey, I was pleased not to be in their company. Petey had brought with him a wood box of Larrañaga cigars smelling foul in my sweet Texas night, and eventually I latched the glass against them all.

Next morning, the truth of his visitation was out. We saw a dozen men camped beside the trail to our land. They had brought with them a small drove of handsome sleek mustangs from down the Colorado River, and the cavalry buster was breaking and training them one-by-one for the soldiers, because Petey's gang of men was just that: a company of soldiers. Micah would not question the Governor's plans, so I took it upon myself to get to the reason for his visit to our little farm.

After much cajoling by me, Cookie consented to feeding them all. The farmwomen, including the wife of Bobby Drumgool, our new Irish stock raiser, attended to our Cookie, butchering pigs and beeves and setting the fires to blazing deep in the ground for the roastings. We put out pies of pecans and sweet cane syrup, corn fritters by dozens, and we baked the huge squashes leftover from the fall harvest in our deep brick ovens. To think of the plenty we had those years, girded with roots and seeds, nurtured by stream and sun in every artery of our land; what magic it was to feed an army.

I set myself beside the Captain Randolph Marcy, a balding old coot from back east who had been schooled at West Point. He was a harsh fellow, and the stories we had heard from riders traveling through were all about his skill fighting Indians, particularly the ones residing in the western lands. Since our Milam County was as far west as people ventured, I was sure old Marcy planned to lead his column of men into secret mischief.

"Welcome to you and yours, Captain," I began. "We are seldom visited by so many accomplished and handsome soldiers."

Leaning back in his chair, Marcy waved a pork rib dripping with honey across his plate. "This is the finest roast I have tasted, Missus Moore." He was guarded by a Delaware Indian who stood behind him against the wall, shifting his gaze back and forth across the room for hours while the rest of us ate our fill.

"Thank you," I said. "We're a simple frontier planting, but with the Lord's wisdom we have grown respectable food."

Marcy looked around our dining room and out to the porch where others were seated to the meal. "And so with no niggers. How is it that your economy grows?"

My face turned immediately afire, my eyes growing to full moons. I began to speak but closed my mouth quickly. A second later I realized I had rested my hand on the stray strands of my hair. Dear Cookie Mahoney, stood at my shoulder and understanding my surprise, she said loudly, "With a vegetation magician like our Missus Moore, we don't need an army to work our land."

"Thank you, Cookie."

She gathered herself, rearing up to her full height beside him. "I'll see to the girls in the kitchen."

"We are family," I said quietly to Marcy.

"Where I come from in Virginia, our slaves are also our family. And after all, the valiant state of Texas did entreat to join our United States of America as a supporter of the slavery economy. You are supporters here at Bluebonnet Ridge, are you not?"

Another word from me would have laid my story at his feet. On the far frontier it had never mattered what color of picker worked the land, because every one of us was needed, and even the Queen of England herself would have been obliged to sit on the milking stool or hunch over the bitter smell of the squash rows.

I had placed Petey Bell on my left side, and now he barged into our conversation.

"Captain Marcy, are you aware that Missus Moore's dear father fought with me at San Jacinto? He was a hero and a great Mexican killer, just as you are one of the greatest killers of Comanches this state has ever seen."

The prideful talk of these battlefields and the downing of

folks collided with the truth of my forlorn father, returned home after the fight at San Jacinto, slumping to his grave from the loss of his spirit and his faith. That was the real promise of their glory.

"And Missus Moore," continued our governor, "Captain Marcy and his troops are about to conduct one of the biggest surveys ever devised by our nation. They'll be tracing the river, your Red River, to its very source. We have dreamful tales from scouts, of a hundred thousand prairie dogs up the lower fork, living in a prairie dog city, and caves and hoodoos in a canyon so immense that ten thousand men could harbor there."

And with that I realized their true intention, for the land he spoke of was the Comancheria and the canyon that Arakka had called Palo Duro and that he now called home.

Marcy's men still bided with us through the summer season when the wild fruits were heavy and ready to harvest from the deep swampy heat. In those last weeks, the cavalry readied their provision wagons for the long journey, and our fortune turned to silver that year when the expedition cooks bought every single item we could dry or preserve for them.

The soldiers lived at the near bend of the Little River below the Sugarloaf Hill, working their horses and drinking corn whiskey to sing themselves to sleep. But when they ventured up to our Bluebonnet Ridge they came as boys, and I often found them playing with the children in the yard, as soft as men could be. At times, Cookie baked up some sweet biscuits, hard like tack from the hot back of the outdoor oven, and those soldiers were happy just to sit on the steps and gnaw at the sweets.

One of them identified himself as a fine shot, and I, having grown up with a father who was the finest shot in Texas during his good years, I asked to see this boy's feats. This became a

Bluebonnet Ridge challenge, with a couple of his army rivals, and our own Micah, Teddy Blue, Bobby Drumgool, and Three-Legged Willie all vying to be champion shooter.

They ate early of grilled beeves and cornbread, then off to rake and level the shooting range, the rancher and soldier alike cooperating like friends. As was the wont of the cavalry, they sipped their whiskey beginning early morning with the foolhardiness of boys. Some wore their new buckskin breeches, stiff and yellow and newly issued, and others wore their wools to give them free movement with their rifles. Our own lads were sober as was the custom with rangers, never imbibing fermented drink while holding weaponry.

Having become partial to the soldiers over these summer months, our two kitchen girls sewed up little flags to wave for their preferred shooter, simple colors of cotton that matched the kerchiefs given to them. The rest of us worked hard in the fields to tie up our chores before the afternoon. We set benches behind the shooters, who lined up like circus bears along the gun line, tasting the breeze and flattening their shoulders against the split rails.

When all was prepared, I gave Evie and her older friend, Adeline, tiny apothecary bottles to place on the paddock posts that had become the targets. Adeline was the child of our stock raiser, Bobby Drumgool. She was a thin girl with straight Irish-red hair, wild eyes the bright green color of horse apples, and a laugh loud enough to stop the corral.

The two held hands and teetered through the field, chuckling from nerves as they went. They set the glasses along planks balanced on the posts, until each shooter had his own target. The rules were laid out. Each had one shot of their chosen rifle to burst the glass, and all would fire at the same time. A shoot-out would then be held for the winners, and another, until one man was left as the champion.

The men were itching to pull their triggers, Micah included.

THE BLOOD OF MY MOTHER

But none was allowed to bear down until Cookie Mahoney slapped her bunting flag down to the dirt. The men formed a line, nodding and dodging and nodding again at their marks, some sliding their fingers along the slender hooks of the polished brass while the others grinned and nozzled the iron plates. I walked among them, thanking them and admiring their weapons, while Cookie counted off the start with *One! Two! And three!*

At once the sharp knells rang, hammers bursting, the start, the flight, their howling bullets pummeling the target line with the shattering of the bottles. The noise echoed over our heads, exploding till I turned and suddenly the litany was dead.

Three rounds were shot, with Three-Legged Willie falling in the first round along with Absalom and a couple of our hands. In the second round, the girls moved the targets farther back, placing the planks over barrels with the help of Teddy Blue. This round brought down Bobby Drumgool and most of the younger soldiers, leaving only two cavalry officers, Micah, and Teddy Blue. For the last round, Cookie insisted on moving the target line five more feet back, and chuckling as she went, she helped the girls set whiskey barrels parallel to the shooters, and they put a longer plank across those.

Again she raised the bunting and cried out her one-two-three, and our men, less itchy fingered at this point, took good time to aim.

"Come on!" Cookie shouted. "Feared for the results?"

The four let their bullets sail beyond her heckling, and we were so far from the range that the girls ran to it and brought back the bottles. Cookie exclaimed the winner in her best and loudest voice, *Mister Teddy Blue Corlies!*

We ran to him, and I hugged him close.

"God sakes, Eliza!" he shouted, but the crowd from our ranch gathered round him quickly too. He moved sideways from us escaping toward the small donkey cart holding the shattered glass that had been swept up by Cookie's kitchen girls.

I pulled Evie to me, and without much thought, I said, "Evie, go fetch Adeline for pie."

But Evie just stared at me, shaking her head and frowning.

"What?" I asked, and then in a louder voice, "Evie, what's wrong?"

Micah heard me, and strolled over to us, his rifle balanced across his shoulders. "Girl," he said calmly, "why are you shouting out?"

I pointed to Evie. "Something about Adeline."

He squatted in the dust and whispered, "Where is she, darling?"

Evie put her little fingers on her father's arm, shaking her head. "She plumb run away."

The shooters had ceased their celebrations and clustered around us. Adeline's big brutish father, Bobby Drumgool, moved among them and hoisted Evie on his shoulders, smiling.

"Adeline!" he called out, looking around the tight clamor of men. "Where'd she get to?"

"She took off after the contest," Micah said. "She'll be back for Cookie's pie though."

But she wasn't, and by sundown, our lads and the soldiers set out to search our land for her. They returned long after dark while I sat with Adeline's mother on our porch, watching the column of lanterns along the dark trail back to the Bluebonnet Ridge. Micah slipped down from Cash, trudging up the steps to us. Weariness clung to them all, and he looked me straight in the eyes, shaking his head.

"Nothing, Ellie. We couldn't find her."

Bobby Drumgool took his wife's hand and said, "Come, we'll get some sleep now, and start out again early in the morning."

CHAPTER 29

Our ranch boys and the soldiers hunted together for three days until one evening Micah came home and made his decision. "Can't keep doing this, Ellie. We covered every foot of our land, and the acres around. Coyote probably got her."

"You wouldn't stop if it was Evie." He didn't give me a discussion, so I climbed into our bed and closed my eyes hoping for sleep.

The next day our pokes were back at their chores, the horse soldiers were back training their animals, and not a man took to the hunt, not even Adeline's father. That day I drew my babes around me, irritating them by holding them so close. Harsh as giving up the search might sound to folks from Montgomery or New Orleans, out on the edge of the world where we lived, those who were caught outside our boundaries often vanished, and our lives were too lean to spend energy on lengthy searches. Panthers trod in the night, and our life's lessons were patched together from our losses, not from our successes.

One more day passed before Adeline showed herself. She came teetering up the road, shoeless, her clothes hanging in shreds about her bleeding body. She dragged herself into the front paddock and sank exhausted to the soft soil. Evie saw her first and came running to find me, shouting her story at the top of her little lungs.

Micah and his men were in the far fields, so Cookie and I lifted Adeline from the dirt and brought her in the house. I held her while Cookie cleaned her sore and bloody parts, both of us feeling for bone breakages. Her strength overtaxed, she could not speak or even sob, but sat on a bedmat while I, Cookie, and Evie hovered and held her, rocking her till sleep let her escape our damned world.

We sent one of the girls to fetch Bobby Drumgool and Micah, and they arrived breathless and sweating, charging up the stairs to where Adeline lay.

"Where she been?" asked her father, kneeling beside the slumbering girl.

"Can't talk," Cookie said. "But them ain't animal wounds."

Her father began to lift the blanket from her, but I stopped him. "She needs that sleep, Bobby. By God, let her find her voice by herself. Cookie and I will get broth in her as soon as she opens her eyes."

Micah put his hand on the big man's shoulder. "Fetch your wife," he said quietly. "Adeline'll be needing her mother soon."

Adeline slept through our dinner and supper, while we stood around her, waiting for those speckled green eyes to open again. She all but jumped herself awake like out of a nightmare, and stared at each one of us as though she were seeking someone in particular.

"Oh, my little love," her mother whispered, sitting beside her on the mat and holding her as close as a woman could. "Thank you, Jesus."

"I'm goin' to get her some supper," said Cookie. "And I don't want anyone askin' her anything until she has eaten it all. And you, boy," she snapped, pointing to Absalom, "you go get on yer horse and fetch Doc Leahy."

Such was Cookie Mahoney's power over us that we fell silent and allowed Adeline's mother and father to hold her in peace.

The girl supped her broth until poor Evie could wait no more. "Addie, where'd ya go?"

Adeline nobbled a thick corner of bread between her fingers without answering. She held out a scratched and bloody arm to my child and tugged at her to climb beside her atop the bed. She stared at us as a blind girl looking out at darkness, though surrounded she was by candlelight.

"We'll take her home," her father said.

"The doc will be here soon," Micah replied, and went to poke the embers in the fireplace to bring them to light again.

And before Doc Leahy bolted up the stairs to us, the girl turned to Evie and said, "Men was ridin' round me. Everywhere."

"What do you mean, girl?" asked her mother softly.

"One pulled me up on his horse and rode round and round till I fell off the saddle. I ran, but they got to me." She didn't cry at us, but lay quietly telling this story.

Doc opened the door with Absalom behind, shooing us all out but for Adeline's parents.

We gathered in the kitchen, a few soldiers with Marcy, me and Micah, and our boys.

"Did we come to the wilderness for this?" I shouted at those who stood beside me. "Blood everywhere! Blood on the chaff, on our breasts, our floors. What is our apology to these children?" I started to cry in a way the girl never did, gushing sobs on Micah's chest, and through the uneven windowpanes of Cookie Mahoney's immaculate working place, I saw glints of the new moon haunting us.

"We'll be off tonight," Marcy said. "We'll find the Comanches and take their scalps. And because we are ready for the mapping, we might as well be moving up the Red River into the canyon."

Marcy was unyielding and ambitious. He breathed anger as he

spoke to us, and I understood that his army job of exploring had all along meant killing Arakka and his adopted kin.

"They are long gone, whoever they are," Micah replied. "Girl's only seven, Captain. We have not got to the truth yet about what happened or who did it. Could've been my men. Or yours."

"Mister Moore, the Comanches have been the evil doers in this county for many years." His voice was tight. I had heard stories from Teddy Blue that this man had tongued the raw brains out of Indian skulls, and I did believe it now.

"We got a few local bands," Micah said. "Could be Lipan, Kiowa or Comanche, if not our own kind."

"We will find them," said Marcy, "and we will send their scalps to this girl's family."

Judge Three-Legged Willie replied, "Well, Captain Marcy, serving the wrong truth could start a war with the Indians that would bring the settlers of this place to annihilation."

Marcy, moderated in the face of our local law, nodded. "You have a point, Judge McCann. But I want to interview her. And my troops will be off before the Sabbath."

Micah learned from Doc Leahy that the girl had been harmed in many ways; stabbed multiple times, dragged through the prairie, and finally raped. Doc bandaged her knife wounds and the deep scratches, and stroked her little bruised parts with balm. He confessed he could do nothing to crush her memories though, and worried into midnight how long she might survive.

She spoke little about the days she spent away, least of all about those who did the torturing. Her mother and I took turns sitting vigil over her, but she never even rose from the bed. I took up needle-yarning to calm myself, me with my fumble-fisted talents setting in that dim room and passing the time as this child grew weaker.

Marcy pressed the doctor for a question session alone with Adeline. True to his word, he forced Doc's hand on the Friday and by Saturday morn, the army had collected their belongings and new mounts. Our cowpokes and kitchen girls delivered them one more oxcart filled with provisions, and while Marcy's men finished their packs and goodbyes to our little Bluebonnet Ridge community, he unfolded his plans within earshot of all. Micah and me stood with him near the fresh springs as he related a story of Adeline's attack. "She was taken by men from the Comancheria."

The chaparral cocks were clacking and whining that dawn. Chilled as it was on the hover of autumn, a few lone wild geese came scouting overhead for their winter homes.

"But how can that be information the child possessed?" Micah asked.

Responding with grace to questioning was not Marcy's habit. He blurted in a rage, "I have deduced it from my conversation with her!" Damp ring-wormed chestnuts lay at our feet, and their musky morbid smell surrounded us. "We will give them their own back, sir, and clear this prairie of their kind for the safety of you and your little ones."

They rode off in an even column, down the Bluebonnet Ridge trail, proud and tall on their animals, with justice, such as they saw it, on their side.

Adeline's little life expired that night, and her holy service was held at the graveyard on the east of town. The oaks had begun to turn and spot by then, the leaves shaking in the cold winds as though the dryads themselves were singing with us. By the afternoon, every soul in the county had heard this tale, and every heart had filled with rage.

We sat round our old plank table at suppertime, taking each other's hands while the fearsome future unfolded.

CHAPTER 30

$\mathscr{B}$y the spring, more horse soldiers had arrived to build a new and bigger fort up the Brazos River. When the timber was up and the walls carved with gun slits, a line of cavalry crossed the counties of Milam and Robertson from the east, circling round the Bluebonnet Ridge road on sturdy horses, with their dogs and their women workers, with carts of food and weapons, and a hundred walking soldiers.

Someone, a naughty child or some outlaw, had strung a line of brittle yellow wolf teeth from tree to tree across our trail, knocking several hats off the cavalry, and our protectors were none too happy for it. Some of these new men rode stiff and tall on their mounts, proudly carrying scalps strung from their saddles like prized sacks of jackstraws.

They swore to us that they would keep us safe from the devils of the frontier, not understanding that for us farmers, the devil could be the footstep of a neighbor or a soldier, either one. On their way to the site of the new fort, they purchased from Cameron Town casks of wine and whiskey for the officers, and soft sheets for their wives.

Our wild birds had long flown north, and that meant the

Kiowa and Comanches would soon be scouting the Staked Plains together for buffaloes migrating south. The Lipan would be fighting all of us for food and acreage, and sometimes just for the ferocity of the fighting.

The ring of safety that Arakka had afforded us blew apart that year, because every single one of us was blooded with blame for Marcy's gluttony. Each day we crept to the fields carrying weapons as well as hoes, trying to bring in corn or cotton or peaches from our land before the Indians knew. One early morning Micah allowed our James to ride over the little bridge and onto the stream banks, searching for berries with his oldest sister, Evie. He had dressed them in leather undershirts for protection against arrowheads, and had chosen the fastest mare for them, covering them with his own rifle the while they were away.

Once at the hedges, they slipped from the horse, and filled three bags before a band of Kiowa Comanche came into sight. Micah leapt upon his horse, Cash, firing his rifle in merciless fury. But our small boy, James, jumped on his mare and pulled Evie up with him, riding like the devil hounds to our compound where the Bluebonnet Ridge boys were ready for anything.

We lived that day with no dead to bury, but most days brought the killing of at least one of our people. Some days deep inside I all but heard my mother's voice calling me to hide, so I grasped my babes and went to the canebrake swamp, holding them silent when the tribes came for us. Micah fetched us when the battles had finished, sometimes minutes but more often hours later. Soldiers who saved us told of the broad prairieland upriver that was covered with skinned rotting buffaloes, butchered by Marcy's men to starve the Comanches.

Eventually, Micah forced us to move to Cameron. We pitched up with Three-Legged Willie in his cabin at the back of the new courthouse. He had been hired to judge through the summer in town, and there lived enough men to protect us against the raids.

On Friday eves, our women would cook up pots of stew from the Bluebonnet Ridge victuals and pigs, and the men set out tables in the center of town where we might eat in peace or face the marauders together. Soldiers came to shield us and for the good cooking we provided, and we all sat round, guns leaned to table, my heart shredded with fright.

～

Toward the end of our meal on one late summer night, we heard shouting alongside Willie's new courthouse, a commotion drawing Micah to the far street crossing to observe. Other families scurried to their homes, but our lodging was with Three-Legged Willie on the other side of town, so all I could do was to pull my children close and hold my rifle to my shoulder. I heard a gunshot, and then another, and Willie's voice roared above the folks gathered.

"This man is not a criminal till I do the judging. You got claims against him, bring them to me tomorrow at judging time!"

The soldiers walked us to the courthouse for sleep, and our neighbors turned to their homes like docile beeves.

"Indian, it was," Micah said as the babes and I mounted the steps to our quarters. "They were about to hang him, but Three-Legged Willie pulled his gun on them."

"What crime?" I asked.

"Don't know. Man just showed himself. He's in the cage now, and I need you to come there with me."

He and Willie took me to the jail where the Indian crouched behind iron bars that had been forged in San Antonio and shipped up the river to us for our criminals. The man's face was painted chalk-white on one side, and red on the other. Brass loops hung from his earlobes. He was slender and wore a breast-plate of white tubes covering his unclothed chest from neck to waist. He wore deerskin leggings and a breechcloth tucked into his belt. His hair was greased with rancid buffalo fat and covered with white clay, and he had parted it down the center into braids, and mixed with the reek, the paint of the plains dirt lay across his scalp. Before me squatted a wild angry man smelling of the deep earth.

"Willie," I whispered, "this is not a Comanche. He's my son."

"What're you saying, Eliza?"

But Micah nodded the moment I spoke. "He's a white boy, Willie. One of them that was captured in the early days. We've known him since he was young. Rescued him twice myself."

The flame wick at the back of the cell was jumping as we moved in the dank air. Nothing else shifted around us, inside or out, but all the same I knew a siege was being laid for us, driven by folks of our town and the rise of the new dawn.

"You can't judge him, Willie. Not tomorrow, not ever. He belongs to me and Micah."

"Name is Arakka," Micah said. "Or Moses. Raised with families on both sides."

Normally prideful of his judging talent and logic-tongued in the face of neighborly murder, Three-Legged Willie's lips dropped open. "Goddammit, how can he be yours?"

I said, "We are needing to save him from the morning. I'll give him a wash, while you and Micah sort our answer."

Willie was speechless and did not move.

"Go and get me some rags and water!"

Both men turned their backs to the dim jail light. Micah carried a lantern throwing the halls in flame-shadows, and I faced the young man, my heart in cinders.

I sat on a stool, low as a milking prop, beside Arakka. He had not spoken a word, but I shoved a comb in his hand and began unbraiding his hair. I wiped the red clay off one cheek, then the white side, and I lifted the breastplate from his body. Micah had brought some jelly soap, and I dipped a rag in the tallow and held it out to him.

"Me or you?" I asked.

Arakka stared at me. I was not even sure that the boy was able to understand my language anymore, so I began washing his shoulders and chest. I noticed a deep wound on his left arm, a letter that had been carved by a human hand and scarred over. I put my finger in the jagged rut to clean it, and realized it was the letter 'W' branded on him with hot iron. I cried to see this, remembering my own mark, but he only stared at me, unchanged after all these years.

We passed into the deep night, my boy silent as I wiped the dirt and grease and paint from him. Finished with the chore, I took his Indian clothes and threw them out the door of his cell. I called to my husband to bring trousers and a shirt from our room.

"I need pivot scissors," I said to Micah. "And burn these, please." I kicked the Comanche clothes across the dirt floor. "Now," I said to Arakka, "boy, you will talk to me. What has come to pass?" I looked at his face, his golden skin and hair shining in the flickering light. Only a few hours of darkness remained to us and I said urgently, "What, boy!"

Suddenly, he talked while I cut his soft blond hair to his jawline.

"I lived with my father until Lipan killed him. I took our people farther up canyon to find new fields. Last year your soldiers found us. We knew this by the little dogs near the river barking. But we were caught."

He reached for me and grabbed my Holy Ghost finger where I wore Micah's ring. Bowing his head, he pressed his damp face against my hand, swaying his cheek back and forth over the line of blood I held there that would always go straight to my heart. He gentled against me that long moment, and then lifted his face to watch me cry.

"Your soldiers came. Pushing people up cliffs away from the river. They killed my wife and son. They killed hundreds. If we were able, we slipped between them." Nervous birds fluttered outside our walls, marking the dawn across our prairie. "Men came in my cave and found me. They put a rope on my neck and sold me to a man called Waggoner but I ran. I have run a long way to come to you."

A sound gorged the room, bellying down like a trap door sealing. Several of our Bluebonnet Ridge men stood across the sod floor, one of them wearing a butcher's apron, another drumming his fingers on the log wall.

"Well," said Micah, standing among them. "I think it's time we left."

For the second time, Arakka and I ran together across the dark stony trails of the prairie. Micah gave Arakka a good horse, and the three of us set quick for home. Cookie supervised the packing of the Bluebonnet Ridge's other belongings into our old Conestoga and the oxcart and they rode out after us the next day. I never heard what tale Three-Legged Willie explained to the townsmen about the Indian warrior, but he and Absalom must have been convincing because they survived the morning and lived to keep on judging.

The Bluebonnet Ridge was a day's ride for our folks, but a fleet unpacked horse could make it in a few hours. We set out riding our animals low and fast, raking hard down the old Camino and putting those miles between us and Cameron Town before the light lifted. When our mounts could push no farther, we parted the trail into the trees by the river for rest and water. I took a sack cloth of butternut biscuits off my saddle and handed them to Arakka and Micah.

"Thank you, Eliza," my son said. Tall as Micah, he swallowed the fist-sized food in one gulp.

I shook my head at him. "If we are going to tell folks at home that you are our adopted son, then you better call me Mama."

He smiled awkwardly and mouthed the word, new and sharp to him since he had never known a mother.

We reached the Bluebonnet Ridge by afternoon. Micah found an armload of dry tinder in the kitchen and built the night's fire in our bedroom. He sat beside me on the dusty abandoned bed pads, and took my hand.

"I'm sorry I ever brought that boy to you. This won't be easy now. Comanches one side and folks from town on the other."

"We got four children, Micah. Three babes and Arakka. You brought them to me in different ways, but they are each belonging here. And I will kill a person who tries to harm any one of them."

Micah leaned back against the wooden wall and smiled. "You are dangerous, Ellie. And earnest. I always knew that. A bad combination, you ask me." He put his head down and kissed my face.

"I thank you for your complimentary thinking, husband."

He laughed loudly and stood. "I gotta go help Arakka get the ranch open and ready for work tomorrow."

"You mean Moses," I said, but none of us would ever blot out my boy's Indian name.

I worked that day's hard chores, polishing the prairie dust off the floors and blowing the webs out of the cupboards. In the late afternoon, I stood by our well, bucketing up the clear splashing water, that sweet Bluebonnet Ridge water, drinking it down and washing off my hands and arms. A couple of coyotes stared at me from the other side of our front corral, but our dogs smelled them and chased them off. I drank three goblets of that water, one right after the other, and turned to carry the bucket back to kitchen.

"I will," said Arakka, as he came silently beside me.

"You scared me! You became a quiet one."

He took the bucket, and all washed clean in Texan clothes, he looked a sad man.

"You have lost a lifetime of love," I whispered. I put my arm through his and grabbed his wrist in my fingers. "We can't give you that back. I'm harmed so deep to think of what they took from you."

"Your people killed my wife and son. My father. Losing them is cutting my arms off."

"What the Ridge can give you tonight will satisfy your hunger but not your heartbreak. I know that. But I can still love you, can't I?"

Arakka nodded and turned away from me.

"I would heal you if I could, boy."

"Then tell me why these soldiers slaughtered us."

We sat to the long Bluebonnet Ridge table, all of us together again, our waiting girls, pokes, family, and friends. Having imbibed too much whiskey at the meal, Teddy Blue brought out the guitar he had won at a New Orleans game of brag long ago, made by the luthier Christian Martin himself. Teddy chose songs we all knew and sang them to us in his strong beautiful voice, smiling wider when his family sang with him.

I could not stop staring at them all, Teddy, Bobby Drumgool and the rest, sitting with this boy of ours and asking no questions but on the subject of his skills. Yet Arakka's face furrowed like a wet rope, and I wondered if the soul of that child was ever going to mend. Long ago down at Cairo Plantation, a Baptist preacher explained to me that a soul weighs about as much as a mature jacksnipe, yet the soul in Arakka set him an awful anchor of hurt, pulling him down that long, long trail of grief.

Almost as though he could hear me thinking, and I do believe he might have, Micah rose from his chair and came to stand behind me. He put his warm hands on my shoulders and spoke to all.

"I am introducing you to our boy tonight. Some of you know him as Arakka from a long ways past, but his true name is Moses, Moses Moore. He is a boy adopted by me and Missus Moore before we come to the Bluebonnet Ridge. He's home now, and tomorrow he'll be ranging with us."

Teddy Blue picked up his spoon and clacked the bowl of it on the table. Others followed, beating theirs against the long plank of our community table. An evening dragonfly the deep color of periwinkles rose above me, swooping across the table to a new perch.

When the hammering ended, Micah returned to his seat.

I nodded to him in thanks and turned to Arakka. "You are already loved then. Remember that when you fall to sleep."

CHAPTER 31

The town of Cameron kept growing, and up the river, old man Menifee built a supply station that was named Bucksnort by the U.S. soldiers after he added a saloon. The military established more posts across our state, and as the army calmed the far borders by killing more Comanche and Lipans, Anglo settlers claimed land farther out into the prairie, leaving our little Nashville town to wither.

At the Bluebonnet Ridge, we kept on with beeves and hogs, and victuals of all sorts, but the new planters in Milam County put down only cotton because of the money it brought them. With cotton they needed more slaves, and they brought them out from Georgia and Mississippi, African men and their families forced into shanty huts.

Some Negro men were four times a father, some ten, all of them fighting without battle-tackle to keep their sons and daughters alive, their only weapons being their false smiles for their white owners. When they ran off or were beaten to death, our neighbor planters journeyed all the way to New Orleans to fetch replacements, buying new people with silver and copper, just like they bought flour or cloth.

Evie was about seven years and James about six, little Lucy hardly four, when I began to grow again, my belly warm and rounding under cinches that I could no longer pull tight.

"Whatcha got for me this time, girl?" Micah would ask whenever he saw me in the light of dawn standing beside our bed and wearing no clothes. I knew my years were piling up behind me, making me tired before the child was even heavy. Some days I could not even climb from our soft sleep covers.

Finally, getting on for July, I felt the heat pounding hard over me, while Micah called in Doc Leahy. I was commanded by both to bed for the next four months, a feat I told them was neither admirable nor possible. Then late one freezing November morning, I gave life to my strongest child, little Stella Rosa. The Doc said she would be my last, and that she was.

Stella sucked out my milk all year, drinking till she was woozy with warmth. When she started toddling along after us into the fields, Micah built her large square fencing in front of the porch where she and my other ones could amuse themselves in safety, watched over by Cookie Mahoney and her two kitchen girls.

My biggest surprise was how each child was so unlike the others. Evie, still graceful and musical even at her awkward times of starting her bleeding; James, trying so hard to be a man while surrounded by his fog of sadness; Lucy, a plain but cunning little chitter-chatter of a girl; and now Stella, strong and smart, letting the others lord over her while she waited to grow taller.

Three-Legged Willie came frequently to do judging, staying with us and still preaching those Sabbath sermons to our people, bringing up hope that was sweet as dreams. One morn he called out to our congregated Bluebonnet Ridge families, "Because your suffering lives have come to truth, you are now and forever covered with immortal light."

I thought he was talking straight at me, but it turns out so did Micah, and Teddy Blue, and Arakka. Each one of us in the audience that day believed that Three-Legged Willie had singled us out as the object of his pastoring; well, that be the trade of a preacher or poet, or even a charlatan.

On into the year, we sat to sermon in the summer meadow, with a visiting minister preaching. He wore a black suit showing only a stripe of his white shirt beneath, and for all the world he reminded me of a skunk-man come to stink us out. Micah introduced him as Pastor Sam Baldwin, a fellow who had studied the holy scripture with Micah's Uncle Spencer Moore back in Georgia.

Pastor Baldwin opened by softly quoting the Book of Daniel, but so few of our people could decipher any letters at all, he could have been reading out his own words. In fact, his story was just that. Rather than quoting a holy book, he told his own account of the end times, when planters across east Texas, Louisiana, and Mississippi, would fight against armies of other states. He gulped communion wine from a goblet beside the pulpit stand, and chanted about the oncoming Negro war, when the darkies would rise to defile white women and slaughter old white widows.

"Sleep with your guns abed!" he shouted at our men.

I tensed hard with each of his thoughts come to life, for I was one of them who had been owned, my childhood sold by my uncle for the small value of my labor. Careful as I was to hide my Melungeon looks by keeping my hair tight-bunned and wearing broad brimmed hats so my skin wouldn't darken more, I had heard my neighbors worked to frenzy and to hanging or burning, and I knew a man such as Sam Baldwin could single me out.

Micah took my hand, laid it on his thighs, and stroked it across. But I was perched like a lost blackbird under the gospel tent of Baldwin's god, where love and protection had been abandoned.

Baldwin blustered about Armageddon in the valley of the Mississippi, when southern men would unfurl their combined might to crush the soldiers from the North and to chain up

Africans again. At his swirling, screaming finish, the men round us clapped and stamped their shoes hard, because the savior Jesus Christ was on Baldwin's side, even though Micah paid their day's wages.

After the preaching, our workers drifted off to roasted hogs and blueberry pies that came from our kitchens, their children running round the yards with my own. Arakka and Teddy Blue circled in front of me, and Micah held both my hands.

"I didn't understand him to be this kind, girl. I'm mortified in front of you," he said.

Teddy was in a fury. "I will be rid of him."

"He will be traveling on tomorrow anyhow," I said. "No reason to cause trouble tonight."

We all looked to Micah. "Couldn't have been a worse Sunday preaching. But folks here don't know your past. To them, we are all the same blood."

"We aren't safe now," I said. My eyes were burning so I shut them to the sun and leaned against my husband.

"We're sending him on," Micah whispered. "Before the night."

From everywhere came the courses of change. Men from a store at Marshall made their way across the state, stringing wires to treetops as they went, to Waco, Marlin, and on to Cameron. From shivering branch to shivering branch, those wires carried tapping from New Orleans and Natchez that our Texas folks turned into words, and these words in turn brought us tidings faster than the pony mail.

Within days of them happening, we heard about robberies and shootings, elections, visitations and drunkenness. Stories of people we never knew came in a rush, and before we understood, we had opinions on the subject of who was hanged in Kentucky, the value of gold in Sacramento or of slaves in Louisiana.

Nothing could turn back those tidings, and we never lived quietly again. I sometimes wakened in the dark dawns to shouts of our Bluebonnet Ridge boys stating their thoughts about the faraway news, fighting among themselves over telegraph information.

In the summer, Teddy Blue rode up to Marlin to deliver goods to Zenas Bartlett's store. He brought us back promissories and furs and dark stories of the English ships off the Galveston coast ready to set down slave deliveries. Most folks in our counties traded cotton for food, and the more cotton they planted, the more Negroes they needed, same as Carolina, Georgia, and Tennessee.

Teddy told me of watching a speaker on the Rat Row in Marlin. He said this rouser, loud as a prairie bull and shaking the air with his rebel anthem, appealed to his audience for joiners to the newest association of angry men, called Knights of the Golden Circle, and that this recruiter was none other than Frederick Braun, the young trader whose business we had broken.

In January of '61 we got the news that just before Christmas, one hundred and fifty-nine men had sat together in the Baptist Church at Columbia, making up their minds that South Carolina would no more be part of America. Baptist men all over Texas joined the Circle, and we lost more horses and cattle to midnight.

By the end of the rains that year, the Golden Circle men gathered with the lawmakers in Austin to carve Texas for what we already saw in other cotton lands. Come March, the people's vote was in, Governor Houston put out of his employment, and we joined yet another new nation, with another flag, called the Confederate States of America.

~

One late morn I stood in the kitchen, ladling the flesh of wild damsons into a steaming pot, watching the jam cook up, thick and smelling of heaven. I stared at the bubbling slop and stuck my finger in it, scooping the biggest lump of jam I could find and shoveling it between my lips.

That was when the smell of the damsons, sweetened by our own honey, mixed with the faint odor of cinders. Cookie sashayed in to stand beside me, her nose scrunched and her eyes narrowed.

"You burnin' that jam, Miss Eliza?"

"Don't think so."

She took the ladle and poked around the pot, and as she did, her big flanks shook under her cotton layers.

"It's the smell of a mow fire! Outside! Where're the littles?"

I scrambled to the porch to see all four beside the porch steps. Once in the air of the prairie, I saw the haze of smoke covering the far barn.

"The hay!" I shouted. "Cookie, Evie, take the children to the cellar in case we got Comanches on us."

I lifted my skirts and raced down the path. The men were already there, forming their lines to the well, and I stepped between to help. Micah and others had been out ranging the beeves, a couple pokes had been with the horses; not a soul was tasked near the hay that morning. The big cart sat blazing, jutting into the open barn doors.

Just like a box of crackle-wood catching, a hay spark devours quick and continues on till not even the barn posts are left. We bucketed out more than a hundred times over those red devil flames, until Micah called us together. We gave up on the hay and ran the water over the grasses and paths shoring up to that barn to keep the rest of the farm safe.

The next day it had burned itself out, with nothing left but heat and char. Micah, Arakka, Teddy Blue, and me went out early that morning, poking hopelessly in the ashes for a reason.

"What will we do, Micah?" I asked. "We lost the winter holding for the animals."

"And our best quality was curing in there," Teddy grunted.

"There's no good reason for combustion," whispered Micah. "Dedicated the barn to hay. Checked for heat pockets each day." Lightly, he shouldered against me. "Just burned up all at once."

I stared at him. His voice was hollow, those kindly blue eyes glazed over with dark innocence.

Arakka broke from us, circling the ruins of the building, walking round and round without so much as a pause.

"Must be something left behind in the char," I said. "Some clue."

Arakka looked up at me from across the burned-out foundations, his eyes wide. He held a long stick in his hand, and his cowpoke hat lay at his feet. He stirred the ashy mounds with that stick, and then poked it hard into the ground, stabbing again and again until the drops of his anger bled out in the earth.

Micah called us away from the devastation. He led us over to the old pecan tree, the first one he had planted when we came to the Bluebonnet Ridge. The bark was ruddy brown, turning to its autumn wood. Micah pulled his shoulders wide and stood straight.

"This is a hard place. We knew that from the start. Now we'll be cinching up our belts," he said. "That's all there is to it. Sell more victuals, drove more beeves out to New Orleans. We'll trade for hay this year. Maybe we cut the herd some. We had more bounty than we ever needed anyhow."

Arakka squatted on his haunches next to the broad trunk. He folded his arms across his chest and bowed his head.

"The Lord's sign, maybe," Micah said. "Take hands." He reached to me and Teddy, and we formed a circle. "Arakka, come. Take hands to do some praying now."

Our boy put his tanned fingers to the crown of his blond hair, but did not move. "It is not."

"What?" asked Micah.

"The sign is not from your lord." He spread a hand on the base of the pecan tree, at first I thought for balance. I leaned over to take his weight, and then I saw the mark. The symbol of a rising sun within a circle had been carved into the bark, and underneath the letters KGC for Knights of the Golden Circle.

"Damn it!" blurted Teddy Blue. "Damn them to the long burnin' of hell."

"It is your mystery here." Arakka tapped the tree gently and stared up at Micah. "No god. Just angry men who hate us."

A couple of our pokes, Noah Clay and his son, were free Negroes who came to Texas from Alabama years before. On the day our barn burned, they came to me and Micah declaring their parting.

"Where to?" Micah asked them.

"We can stay no longer here. We're aiming for California."

Micah smiled. "Looking for gold then?"

They shook their heads. Like so many cowpokes, they wore the only clothes they owned and were dead proud of their guns and ropes.

"There won't be a war, be sure of that," Micah said. "And if you stay, I'll see to your case once this is all over. California may well secede before you even get there. Then what?"

"I guess we'll head on to the Sandwich Islands then," Noah said.

Micah chuckled softly, but I do believe Noah had confidence in his intention.

"We'll fill a prairie schooner for you," I said. "You'll be needing food and good horses. Till you get to the desert you will be in dangerous hands."

"When're you leaving?" Micah asked.

"This day," said Noah's son. "Just heard the Knights strung up some poor niggers at Marlin. We gotta be gone, Mister Moore."

Standing on our porch out of the frosty eve, I watched those two good men ride out. I lifted my arm to wave farewell, my heart calling out silence to their silence in the night.

Micah came up the steps and stood beside me. We had been Americans no more than fifteen years. We had rights of way, fields, and cattle in our keeping, but the bringers of bad news were among us and I had no one to run and tell.

I could not find a lord to pray to that day, and I never again have.

CHAPTER 32

hree-Legged Willie came home to us in the spring that same year. With Absalom at his side, they moved with their belongings to the Bluebonnet Ridge. The boy rode a calico that looked like buzzard bait, yet he sat up proud on its back for the world around to see. Willie drove his old buckboard piled with books and whiskey. I ran from my chores to greet them, finding only men in need, but hunger is one thing we never abided at Bluebonnet Ridge.

Willie uncorked his whiskey and poured all round.

"You'd be better off with a cup of hearty milk," Cookie snorted, but old Willie just grinned at her. "Y'all 're hungry. Liquor bound to push you over the edge."

"I have been loving you for many years, Miss Mahoney," he replied. "If you weren't so ornery I would have married you a long time ago. Come on, give us a big hug!"

We fed those men until they could eat no more. They removed their belts across their puffed bellies and leaned into the whiskey again.

"I gave up judging," Willie said. "Nothing but swarms of ugly rough people now, different only in their degrees of ugliness.

Hundreds of snakes and redbugs everywhere. Mystery fires abounding at Cameron." He stood slowly to light his pipe in the fire. "I am aching like never before, crusted from the center of my heart out." He took a step or two and wobbled, and his poor third leg knocked a jug off the hearth. I jumped up to set him straight, and he put his old arms around me.

"Thank you, Eliza. We come through a lifetime together, haven't we?"

"Railroad's building out this summer," Teddy Blue said. "More work, more trading. You'll see."

"Maybe." He shook his head like he was staggering a pilgrim's hill. "I guess I'm needing some sleep. My teeth are hurting and my brain is holding too many grudges."

I took a lamp and accompanied Willie to the guest room that faced the horizon, thinking the morning sight of gold showering our ridge of bluebonnets would ease him surely into the next day. I filled his pitcher with cool water from the well bucket and set it on the old oak commode that Micah had long ago hammered up. Willie lowered his painful body onto the bed, and slipped the leather strap from his wood leg.

"You still walking the limb my father carved for you?"

He smiled gently. "Ah no, Eliza. Absalom made me a few over the years, painted them and all for different occasions. This is the traveling one."

I sat beside him on the quilts, but he didn't meet my eyes. His face was flushed and damp as though a fever started from deep inside him.

"Darkness everywhere, Eliza," he whispered. "The earth is staked with the squealing noises of the pigs lining up for stabs." From his pocket he pulled a handkerchief of colored sweets. "I brought these for you, as you've always been a kindly child." The sugar lumps were old and dusty, and his voice had dropped so low I could barely hear him.

"Lie back, Willie. I'll get that boot off for you. You need a good long rest."

He slumped to the side against the rough pillow rolls, and in that same ghosty voice, asked, "Did you ever hear tell of the skulls they keep in San Antonio? Some with full teeth, even. Keep them buried underneath the plaza. Soon as General Twiggs turned the garrisons over to McCullough, the Knights of the Golden Circle started digging them up, Mexicans and Indians, all those skulls brought into the profane sunlight, score-taking if you ask me."

The lantern beam buckled over his face, and I heard the door latch lift behind me.

Micah said, "I come to say goodnight. See if our old Uncle Willie is ready for peaceful resting."

"We have no blood between us, boy, but I am grateful you consider me uncle." He closed his eyes and asked, "What is your destiny, Micah Moore? Men in Texas have but one side left to them. You go with the confederacy or eventually they will hoist you from an oak tree." Trailside muck clung to his greyed hair. The skin on the tops of his hands was shiny and bruised blue, and he dropped his head to his chest. "I'm so tired, children."

Three-Legged Willie passed in the night, well fed and cosseted among friends. We buried him in our little graveyard, alongside Adeline Drumgool and all the other departed infants and farmhands. With no preacher among us, Micah took that floodtide from his heart and brought us a few honorable words. My husband had long believed in healing wells and miracles, winning square and looking to the kinder shore.

In silence he laid a shovel in Willie's box for his use if he awakened, and we dropped fistfuls of red soil across. The men trowled him over till he was but a dark mound in the meadow. All but me joined hands as Micah did one last prayer to their lord for the safekeeping of our friend's soul.

We were pulling off the pumpkins and corn that summer when a couple of our boys joined up to the Milam Greys. They took off one night for the volunteers at Cameron and didn't return to the Bluebonnet Ridge. I never saw them again nor even learned where their bodies got buried after they fell. We heard news by August of the South winning Manassas, and more of our pokes scrambled to take the Confederate side. By the time we started on the apples, Micah rallied the men to make their own choices, but pleaded with them to work the farm till after the harvest. Finally, Jefferson Davis invited our Texas governor to visit him up at the Confederacy capital in Richmond, and deep into that season, Texas men from every prairie and hill were leaving the fields to get into their greys.

The morning Micah set out for selling our victuals in Houston, he gathered the men remaining to the Bluebonnet Ridge, shared them among the wagons, and looked to me for a last word. His band of ranch hands were waiting on me to bid goodbye to my husband before they could depart, a womanly wave or gentle call was all they expected, as was the custom. But something bold came to life in me that moment.

I headed for Micah, striding slow and steady through the bare cornstalks. My skirts brushed and tugged against the teasel sticks in the ground, but I kept on to him. I made the men wait, staring at my husband's face and hands, unashamed in that gleaming dawn light for the irritation I caused them. For I had learned to read by the reek of kitchen garbage, and had smelled the skin rot of whipped friends in my youth. If times were hard, I could be hard too.

"I got no one to leave with you but Arakka and Absalom, girl. Keep yourselves safe."

"We've been on our own before. Do your trading down at Vinegar Hill and bring us back some coins this year. That's all."

A basket of ripe berries lay on the step beside us, sweet purple ones I had picked the day before to give to Cookie for a pie. I handed the basket to Micah, but he shook his head.

"No room for that."

"These are the sweetest our Bluebonnet Ridge has to offer. I plucked them right at their hour."

He gave me a gentle smile. "It's hard to bear this life after the pleasant times we had. We lived with flood and ebb, but never saw this hard lot. If you are in need, go to Bereminda, Eliza. That's where I'll look for you if you're gone from here."

Sunlight and wind fell together now through the thick leaves of our pecans.

"Boy, you forgot I slept alongside you under a wagon in the pouring rain with no cloak or shoes. I got more mettle than you think."

He took my hand tight, and I stared at his dark mouth and bright eyes, nor scared nor sad were they. "We'll be home the next new moon," he said. "Only a month." He leaned over to touch my face and kiss me, as he seldom did before our people, and soon after, the clacking and rolling of their wagons moved down the uneven trail toward the Houston markets.

Come our summer's end, towards the first of the gold-glazed month of September, we had little to do at Bluebonnet Ridge but watch the children play shuttlecock on the banks of the creek. Cookie was putting up jams, Arakka tending the cattle left behind, while I just sat in the smoke-mirled days, waiting for my husband's return.

It was usual for the Bluebonnet Ridge to be quiet as our neighbors had already come to buy their fill of our victuals before Micah left for the Houston trading season. Absalom and Arakka stayed close to home, setting fire bright as Betelgeuse to our shorn fields, and carrying Colt guns wherever they rode across our land.

We waited for Micah and the boys, biding the noise while folks' anger swung around us and against us. We stayed closer and closer to the compound each day, until only Absalom ventured out to the far prairie on patrol. One day he found a Negro hoisted from an oak and burning against the dawn skyline. He lifted him down and rolled the gentleman's poor self in the dirt, hoping his spirit was still vigilant. We put the body in our burial yard, alongside Three-Legged Willie, with a marker saying only the date of that morning, September 10th 1861.

A commotion for our goods had occurred in Houston, cotton and victuals claiming such prizes the boys never saw before. Yet before Micah returned, Texas volunteers for the Eighth Cavalry were mustered in that town by Benjamin Terry. Men who had rangered with Micah stepped up to enlist, and young boys who longed for a fight and a butternut yellow shirt did the same. Colonel Terry took them all onto a train for New Orleans, and Micah and Teddy Blue brought the abandoned mounts of our boys across the flats to home.

I heard them coming in the afternoon before I even saw them. Those ragged wheels and the hooves of seven tall horses pounded the trail through our river thicket. They could have been Comanches or Apaches, could have been neighbors coming for us or Union soldiers running. Such were our times that all manner of fear and marauders scraped through our land, but I ran out anyway, without even rifle or blade. I scampered down the musty thicket through swamp plums and wild twisted grape vines, creek snakes and brakes, until at last I could see them coming toward the Bluebonnet Ridge house. Each drove a wagon with hitched horses, crashing through the field of red thimble flowers, speeding more the closer they lurched.

I ran toward Micah, and he pulled his wagon to a steep stop and jumped down to me.

"Eliza," he whispered in my ear, his arms round my shoulders. "You are a kindly sight."

We stood for minutes in the dog daisies, pressing against each other like hot stones of longing. Teddy Blue drove around us, keeping on to the houses and the children, and the sparse community left to us.

We found him before dark, bending to a tea chest packed with salt and foraging for hocks and vivid-fleshed bacon while Cookie Mahoney scolded him from the kitchen. We stood in the open doorway laughing, and our children rushed around their father, pulling him to the floorboards.

October dusk at the Bluebonnet Ridge came in piles of purple and gold over the ploughland, and we joined this sky as it emptied out across our porch. Evie and Lucy went to do Cookie's bidding for supper, while Micah held Stella close as he always did. We each had stories to tell, but Micah could not contain his and so we listened, and James sat at his feet intent on learning some new truth from his father.

Once the horizon went dark over the ridge and the fresh air of the fall settled, Arakka lit the lamps for us to see one another. I closed my eyes and looked again to the spirits of Micah and Teddy Blue living inside me. At supper our hearty table was filled with a hasty slaughtered beef, roasted with yams and corn, pounded and rolled with wheat bread and apple stuffing. We drank milk out of crocks, and buttered the food until we were bloated pioneers.

We told our stories to each other, prying our fears off one by one. Micah and Teddy Blue displayed the Mexican silver, barter for our products. But when Absalom discussed his patrols, and the poor Negro gentleman he tried to save, our dreams of wealth were silenced.

"I saw him in the fire, screaming like a baby at birth," he said. "By the time I rolled him to the dirt, he was dead. I never seen it before, sir. White mist covering the ground around him, steaming off his own smoking chest. I can't abide seeing it again."

"Well then, boy, I release you to the west or the north, because these are our times."

Absalom shook his head. "Not leaving, sir."

We had more acres than we few could work on the farm that winter, more horses, cows, and hogs. Arakka and Teddy set to burning and tilling over, and watching our land go fallow. Cookie and I pulled what was left of the pumpkin and potato harvest, and by Christmas we had a trove of coins and Confederate paper money. The winter asters were my darlings, and I tended them close, watching their scarlet juice clotting in the frost behind.

Each week we sent Teddy and Absalom to Cameron to trade off the victuals that wouldn't keep. I remember standing in a stiff winter wind, and Micah reminding, *Don't tarry in town, boys. Neighborly friendship is a temporary thing; now they need the food, but deep down they remember we hold no slaves at Bluebonnet Ridge.*

And so they returned to us over starlit prairie every single time, never biding with townfolk or drinking in the taverns. By the late winter we had no more to sell, and with the growing sightings of Stars and Bars on farms down the Old Trace, we kept ourselves to our home chores and our own community.

CHAPTER 33

The sun rose late those days on the last edge of winter, the children running wild with their battle games between our kitchen garden rows. James ran the slowest, but sweated first, and stripped to his shotgun chaps, his poor pale skin nearly grey. He was thirteen that year, and prideful to take his chores with the men, burning off new fields with Arakka. But what I knew about James was something I could never fix.

I toiled with it and often said aloud to my boy that he was brave, knowing instead that he was covered with inexplicable sadness. Times I would meet him on the trails through the woods, and the dark hush around him caused me to shake. I told myself he needed comfort, but Texas was at war, the Bluebonnet Ridge was hiding in clear sight of our neighbors, and I scarcely afforded James the tenderness he craved.

Before the Union took our wires at Vicksburg, we still got our weekly news with maps and tidings. I heard some northern Negroes got freedom, and I read in the broadsheets about New Orleans, our largest southern trading port, falling to Farragut's Union ships. Every week was a new battle, and the blues and greys were downed on both sides by Frenchy minie balls.

So many men had been taken to the ground, that Jeff Davis called again in the spring of 1862 for anyone left at home to belly up to the war. All males between eighteen years and thirty-five were commanded, but this being a rich man's confederacy, planters were allowed to hire boys to die in their places. Miners, river workers, railroaders, and politicians: none of these were forced. But for farmers or stockers, this was the order to war, even out on our prairie. We kept to ourselves and protected our eligible soldiers, Arakka and Absalom, hopelessly hoping that the Union would put swift end to the fighting before the year was out.

Come October, we heard of a town to the north along the cattle path where the Butterfield stages had brought a hundred settlers from the east, new folks with tidings traveling even quicker than the telegraphs. They called their town Gainesville after a wealthy man, a general, who long ago stood with his troops on the Sabine River border to Texas during the battling at San Jacinto, keeping American volunteers from helping us.

Absalom informed us of this dark Gainesville, describing rough new shacks and hard-tossed farmers wielding but their bare hands to plough their plots. Plantations of the old empresarios grew there unperturbed, their holdings valued from the heads of their Negroes, while the immigrants scraped a bitter life, haunted by the abundance of their neighbors. In that place, the bad luck of a slow harvest struck down marriage beds, and what infants were born often died as soon as they breathed.

It was no surprise then, when talk came to us by a renegade rider escaping the secessionist massacre of Union supporters at that town. He rode to our gates, scattering the mares and hogs and children to the trees. The man wore a shirt torn from shoulder to wrist, and had lost his hat along the trail.

"I come for water," he said, and slipped from his horse, crumpling to our porch steps.

Cookie handed him the bucket, but he did not wait for the

ladle, just scooped deep with his hands, gulping the water until I saw that he had begun to cry.

"I'm no spy," he gasped. "Know that. Not me. Water and a fresh horse and I'll be moving on."

Times as these, every town had a vigilante court; the farther north in Texas, the harsher were the judgments. When the tidings of a jayhawker uprising fell on Gainesville, the court set out at dawn to round up near to two hundred men for judging. A simple majority was all it took to convict the confused men. A few were freed up, a handful escaped, two were shot, but through the next days the rest were strung up from an old elm tree east of town. Every single man stood pale and trembling, waiting for his turn at the noose and the hanging tree. A few each day were left to strangle in agony until their necks snapped, while the rest were made to watch that damned tree and the shuddering movements of each of the dying.

Our renegade was one of the lucky. He told us they had tied his hands behind his back each day and shoved him into a wagon for transport to the place of execution. Crowds collected from every direction to watch, and such was the deep and dangerous condition of the excitement that any man talking of mercy was brought across to join the wagon of those waiting to die. Shooters guarded either side of the cart as it traversed the broad street to the old tree, and the judges set their chairs on a hasty platform to watch.

On his day, the hanging proceeded through darkfall, two by two until the crowd heard a cracking of bones. Fifteen men in all were hanged, our boy being the sixteenth who somehow slipped away at dusk through the canebrakes of the Red River, aided by a Disciples preacher.

"You can stay on here," Micah said.

"You are far from Gainesville now," I added. "Just stop that sobbing, please."

"I need a new horse. I'll be gone in peace, the way I come."

Teddy Blue brought him food, a repeating rifle, and a hook-blade knife. "Here, man. Take these. I'll saddle a rested horse for you." He brought a fast eighteen hander to tether and helped the renegade to his mount.

"They know you," the boy called to me. "That preacher told me to come to the Bluebonnet Ridge ranch for help. Now they will hang you too." After sharing his bald wisdom, he rode off in the dark to Mexico or California, across prairie and desert, to starve or to flourish, I never knew.

When the high wires brought us tidings of this slaughter, the stories were righteous on behalf of the fine work done by those awful juries. We were few on the Bluebonnet Ridge, and we kept our hearts down our gullets.

And so it came that one night during the month of May, Micah sent Teddy Blue Corlies on a secret errand out east, to test for the welcome of our clan at Bereminda, figuring that behind those gates with Rafael and Lariza, our family might be safe from these wartimes. No sooner had Teddy ridden out from the Bluebonnet Ridge, our sleep was disturbed by a sudden and violent thunderstorm. The rain descended in torrents for more than two hours, and at dawn Absalom rode out to find our poor soggy messenger. By dinnertime, he returned alone.

Two days later, Micah whispered to me, "He's always been the strongest rider, the best shooter. Our Teddy Blue can skirt the houses and pound those roads like God himself."

I watched the horizon every morn, across the windblown blackberry hedge, listening for the horse bringing our friend home. But a week hence, we had yet no word from Teddy Blue, nor any gossip about a murder on the Old San Antonio Road.

Micah called us to table after supper, those few who were left at Bluebonnet. Cookie sat beside me waiting for him to speak while she softly hummed a tune about mothers welcoming home their raggedy soldier sons. Though she never birthed her own children, we had shared mine all those years. We both knew

James was old enough to bugle if they got their hands on him, and Cookie Mahoney had plans to put him in hiding before she ever would allow my boy to wear the grey.

"We'll be closing down the Bluebonnet Ridge until the war is ended," Micah said. "You women may stay but know that tribes will be returning here now the men have gone to battle, Indians and Anglo marauders looking for harm and food." Evie stood beside her father, and he took her hand. She was a tall woman, coming up fourteen years and near in age to my first meeting with Micah, although so much softer and prettier than I could ever claim. "We Moores are packing tomorrow and leaving at dawn on the next."

A bloated moment passed, and I shall never forget Cookie Mahoney's look of astonishment. Her lips trembling and her eyes full of tears, she exclaimed, "Has it come so soon to this?"

Neither larger heart nor nobler spirit ever grew in any woman as it did in Cookie.

Micah reached across the table to touch her arm. "I expect you will accompany us," he said to her, "as you have long been a Moore."

She lifted herself slowly without consent. For me, no prudence or sanctity will ever heal the sight of her wounded stare at the loss of her home. She sashayed pridefully out to the porch, where the beautiful useless wild roses had begun to dry from the late spring sun. I trailed her out and sat beside her, Micah joining a few moments later.

"You ain't coming back, are you?" she asked. "I can see that. You and Micah'd never leave this home if you planned on coming again. Damned neighbors will have it all."

"You know we can't stay, Cookie," I said. "Those left in this county are clear: they hate us, hate me. And I expect our neighbors'll take this land one way or other."

"Well, Eliza, I won't be going with you. I be staying here, caring for the Bluebonnet Ridge. Keeping it safe." She nodded after her own words, breathing heavily through the quiet. "I ain't going," she said again to no one in particular.

"We will need you with us," Micah said. "To help with the children. If you stay here, the locals will come for you."

"No," she repeated, looking out at the pecan trees and the corral.

Into the dark, she helped me put the children to bed, and then warmed some milk and honey for us to sip against the lantern light. We were ruminating, each of us without chatter but staring out on this land we had loved so many years, when the grasses in the field shifted without a breeze.

"Looky there," Cookie said. "Poor old ragamuffin." She pointed to the horizon, the air brilliant with fireflies. "Coming through the blackberry hedges. Man out there got hisself a bow saw."

Quietly, Arakka put his cup on the porch and stood.

Micah nodded. "He's a hungry forager, and we are leaving soon. Leave him to it."

"That man is stealing," Cookie said.

"No reason not to, now that most men are off to war."

Cookie walked to the doorway and grabbed the rifle leaning against the jamb. She looked me straight and lifted it to rest on her chest. "I see you, man!" she shouted. "And I know you!"

"Damn all you know!" he yelled back, standing square and daring this woman with his fearless hunger.

Suddenly, I heard the lever clack as she pulled the hinge out and back. Cookie lurched slightly when the ball flew, slapping back to the doorway to keep from falling. She made a good clean shot in the dim light, and the man went down with just the one.

Absalom shouted, "What the hell?"

Cookie handed him the rifle. "Just another thief in the yard."

CHAPTER 34

*W*e took the mules and horses, and moved out of the shelter of Bluebonnet Ridge, our wagon loaded in with food, tools, weapons and a few satchels of spare clothing. I sat on the backboards with the children while our brave men drove us on. It was not yet daylight and my two youngest yawned and nodded over as we parted from our home. But Evie, James and I held our arms high overhead and waved hard to Cookie. She and her girls stood in no more than their muslin housedresses, cold in the May morning, but waving back at us fiercely for the last time.

We stayed wide of the Opelousas and the San Antonio roads until we cleared the ranches of our neighbors, crossing our far unfarmed prairie thicket that was clumped with dwarfed dogwoods and spice trees. Into the county of Robertson, we entered the upland prairie fields, seeking an old cattle trail Micah remembered from his ranger days. Our first night we threw camp in a deep meadow overgrown with moonflowers and morning glories.

Next morn we rolled our team forward over old deep ruts that my husband identified as the Trace he had sought, covered with the tumbling stalks of butterfly weed. Micah chose a near wood for our midday camp, and I filled our stew pot with brown beans and wild onions, boiling it up until they were ready for eating. The girls played their games while they waited for the meal, but James sat with me, sometimes stirring the pot and sometimes staring at the fire. When the voices fell, I could hear a sound of cogs whistling somewhere beyond the thicket of blackjack oaks where we sat.

"James, get your rifle and go to the farthest tree. Go see what that sound is."

Such an obedient child he was, he left his post at the cookpot and stepped quickly toward the clump-edge.

"It's a shack, Ma," he called back. "Old house with a teeny yard and a milk cow."

I nodded and waved him back to me for safety. "But you hear the sound? What is that?"

Arakka squatted beside us and put his arm around young James's shoulders. "This is a wheel spinning. No danger. Only a woman making cloth."

Micah crouched and took hands to say thanks for our food, leaving me to stir and fill the bowls without their prayer. "We reach the loblolly forests this evening and will pass near to the Huntsville penitentiary. Folks around here spin up the cotton and take their bolts over for prisoners making new uniforms. It's the only trade they have left now." He spooned his lunch till he emptied the bowl, then lay back smiling against the oak and held my hand. "Girl, you are a grand cookie."

"Thank you, husband."

"Isn't your mother a good cook?" he asked the children.

"That's what our Teddy Blue always said," James whispered, staring again at the trembling corona in the fire.

"We don't know what became of him," Micah said gently to our son, "but we know this. Wherever he is, he'll be safe because he is Teddy Blue Corlies, a man of skill and bravery."

James nodded. "I seen his face in the fire. Under a clay roof. Rising up toward the Bluebonnet Ridge."

I put my arms around my son, pulling him close to me as though that would heal his little soul, but he shook me off and stood closer to the fire.

"You don't believe me, but he's there!" he cried. "I seen him."

"Oh, child," I whispered, my lips grazing his soft hair. "My love."

Micah called out for us to move on, and one by one, we packed the wagon, leaving James to extinguish the flames.

We pushed along the Trace toward the piney forest, into the bright blooms of the wild coneflowers. As we ventured farther east to the county of Leon the soil became soft and dry, for following our last rains, the greatest drought I ever knew had begun. Traveling the outer cuts we saw few, neither people nor work animals, until one evening we approached the postal shack at the tiny crossroad hamlet that was called Leona. A small rough log lean-to propped against the postmaster's old home, this building had served as a provision store for soldiers, mail call, and former counting house for the farmers when the men were still at home.

Mobs were common on the war frontier, but I had never seen a gaggle of women and children clamoring with such murderous shouts as stood before us at that town. They waved rifles and knives, uncontrollably raging for the simplest cause of all, for food from the military storage to feed themselves. A dozen of them stood round the open-ended shack, seething at the vision of flour and salt beef, and screeching for the blood of poor Mister Postmaster. The ragged man, too old to soldier in the war, held them back with a single loaded rifle.

Micah halted our little caravan, staring at the old man. "He's got a damned Henry."

"Probably stole it from some Yankee deserter. Load it once and fire all week," said Absalom. "He could kill off this whole town before the women even raise their guns."

"Eliza, get this wagon back to the creek." Micah climbed off the seat and unhitched his mare. "We'll go on in and help as we can."

I took the reins and knock-knocked them to bring the mules around, while my men walked in the opposite direction. But high in the dark there came another man's voice, clear and strong, a barometer of calm. As soon as my children heard this, the four of them lurched to the back of our wagon to watch.

"Ma!" shouted James. "Ma, it's Teddy Blue! He's over there in the shack and he's bleeding out!"

"Why folks," our Teddy said above the crowd, "my brain is dried up and my stomach's shrank to a cinder, but I still know the right side of this life from the bad."

I pulled the mules to break and turned round to see him. "What do you mean he's bleeding, boy?"

"There's blood all down his face, Ma," James whispered. "I should go help, don't ya think?"

"You stay here. You and me are protecting the girls and our wagon."

Before he could protest, a rifle shot cracked over the heads of the women. We held our breath, staring into the darkness for the shapes of any who fell. Micah and Absalom stood, rifles raised, beside Teddy Blue and the old man.

"My dear ladies of Texas," said the postmaster, "If you steal these stores you'll be stealing food from your soldiering southern men out fighting on your behalf."

I walked quickly through the cobwebbed grass to the muzzles of our horses and took their halters to quiet their snorting. "Lie down, girls! Get down and stay there."

Arakka appeared beside me, glowing out of the dark in his white cotton shirt. He climbed silently into the box of our wagon and lay his arms across Evie, Lucy, and Stella, keeping their heads beneath the rails.

At that moment, we heard iron move sharply against iron, as Absalom dragged the bars of a rusted gate, closing it across the opening of the shack. The old man stepped back into the darkness with his Henry rifle, scraping it over the dirt floor.

The hungry women crept forward toward those guarded sacks of flour and boxes of salted meat behind the gate.

"Ain't right to be stealing," said Teddy Blue, "but we are all Texans, and ain't nothing wrong with your postmaster lending you food for your children. Line up then!" He lifted the first flour sack high up over his head to prove his intention. "Line up! 'Course, each who takes food tonight must swear an oath to replace what you take before the army ships it to your men."

They emptied the lean-to while the witless old postmaster sat on a three-legged stool against the backboards, his scrappy grey beard grown long over his chest, his bones poking out under a flannel shirt. He waited in the dark half of the half-shack, watching his numbered boxes of beef charky disappear, until this poor Belshazzar could watch no more. He rose up from his sad throne and muttered, 'I have fought the fight and been whipped,' as he slipped through the back doorway.

Hours later we parted Leona town and threw our camp beneath a clump of cottonwood trees. The men lit a simple lamp to steel our little community from Confederate rovers, and I instructed Evie to begin the supper preparations. I tended to Teddy Blue's wounds, my Bluebonnet Ridge men together at last, leaning back in the bitter hogweed while the shooting stars burned above us.

A shallow line of parted skin began at Teddy Blue's skull and furrowed to the sharp cut of his jawbone. Blood had seeped and dried over his eye and cheek and nose, leaving this dear handsome brother of mine a Cyclops mask. Yet, as I cleaned away the crust and sewed the curled flesh together, he blessed all in earshot with his sweet tumbling talk of his journey to Bereminda.

"I rode through the storm till it stormed no more. I journeyed as a ranger wearin' red, for I was in sight of villages and farms on that old hunting Camino, and I wanted no fight from folks regarding my allegiance."

"Teddy, man, we want to know of your journey, but tell us first, will they have us at Bereminda?" asked my husband.

Teddy could not look at Micah because I held his face in my needlework, but I believe that without the sewing, he still would not have shifted to look at my husband.

Without so much as a muscle tick, Teddy Blue said, "I got two newsy items to give you, and here they are. I stopped at the Baylis homestead near to Crockett, and was well fed. My horse watered and rested. But there are no Baylis people now, and no sister of yours, Eliza. At Crockett is a new family, Methodist people who had heard of old Levi Baylis but said the farm lay repossessed and empty for four years before they purchased it from the bank. The Baylis' whereabouts are an uninvestigated mystery. In truth, I think the Crockett neighbors are pleased to be rid of the Baylis family."

In turn, I could not flinch from my handiwork threading his skin, for even a sudden start of my shaking heart would have caused him more pain or a lifelong scar.

"All along that road you see non-combatants scavenging, you see children traveling by themselves. Hence a week, I reached the Angelina at the point of narrows, where those big trees locked their arms across the water. The dark was the deepest I ever saw, from the mustang vine and the creeping ivy. Saw an old rowboat in the river night with a damn gumsucking fool living in it, laughing his brains out as I scrambled up the gobshite mud on old Sam's back."

At this moment I tied off my silk thread, knotting it close to the edge of his jaw.

"You must not shave yourself on this line. Not till I say to you."

Teddy's eyes widened, for I don't believe a woman had ever before directed him in his personal habits. Seeing this, Micah shrugged and patted Teddy Blue's shoulder.

"And then," Teddy continued, "My Sam and me came upon the welcome gates, and the road to the compound. But now I tell you my number two item. There is nothing for us there. No walls, no protection. No persons. No furnishings. No food. Those houses are skeletons and carcasses. That beautiful fortress is gone."

"Burned?" Absalom asked.

"Some of it. Some thieved. I traveled on to Nacogdoches and met some baldy skull stockman who told me this. Rafael took Lariza and the children home to Mexico. Back to Saltillo. That white-bellied Nacogdoches bounder stole the Bereminda beeves after our friends went south, and held them from the foodless families for the army's prices. And then he galled to say to me, 'We are rid of them Mexicans at last.'

"So my friends, whether we go west or south or north, I'm not bothered. But traveling east can't be our plan. And wherever we go, we bear the scorn of these Texias people along the way."

He called it by the name we knew when we first arrived, when we believed it our land to own. And here is the mystery of this damned place, nor labor nor silver, nor loving nor spite, none has ever gained title deed to its crops or prairies or persons.

CHAPTER 35

*T*hat night, after we lay the children in their wagon beds, four in a row under their quilts, I spread a bedmat underneath on the dry earth with my head close to a wheel for shelter. Waiting for Micah to join me, I thought of our Bluebonnet Ridge, of returning there and fighting for the war's duration, and fast off I fell into sweet dark sleep.

Before the morning chuckawill songs and before any light from the far horizon, my husband crawled under the wagon beside me. He pulled a quilt around us and took the ties from my hair plaits. "What was it I said, girl?"

"When?" I whispered. "You are always saying some damn thing."

He grinned at me. "Long time ago, under the wagon in the rain. I said you were beautiful."

"You said effulgent. Took me a few years to find a book that wrote the meaning. Didn't mean beautiful."

"Did to me. And still you are tonight." He raised my muslin so he could feel my breasts and belly, moving his favored hand between my legs.

"You telling me some news?"

Micah's fingers were calloused and cool, and he was gentle with them until I heard his breathing shift and deepen.

"What is it then? We aren't going home to Bluebonnet, are we?"

"No, we can't."

"Are you and I parting tomorrow?"

"You know me. You know me every minute."

He put that tough, lean body over mine, warm now and warming me as he lifted and fell inside me like to be my own skin. I spoke no more, but lifted beneath him, and listened to his clicking tongue in my ear, Micah's own soft sound of love. I opened for him, higher and harder to reach, and the quilts held our sweat slick as dew. And when he burst, I knew there was no babe in his cry, but I did not care. It was love all the same from this man, and we had enough children for this awful time already.

Moon-drinkers, every last one of us was awake early to see it still stamped in the sky above us. I directed the children to parcel out our provisions, dividing them equally between our two parties.

"Teddy Blue and Absalom and I will be traveling north," my husband said. "Crossing the Indian lands and seeking Union commissions in Kansas. Teddy Blue says the governor is pleading for volunteers, for more cavalrymen, and there are none better than us rangers from the territories."

The two moved forward to where Micah stood, standing shoulders with him while I nodded quietly. I knew the man, the steam of his mouth and the hardness of his tar when his own fight was called.

"We'll ride on till we can muster with the jayhawkers," Teddy said, "then sell what remains to buy us some blues. We'll get word to you and the little ones if we can."

Micah said nothing more, and I knew that once separated, I would not likely see him again in this life.

"Arakka will take you up Palo Duro," said Teddy, "where the Comanche canyons are calmer now that all the men are fighting the other side of the Sabine."

Micah held his girls and then released them. He took James's shoulder firmly, saying, "You and Arakka are in charge of the women. Keep them safe. I am giving this responsibility to you, James, because now that you come up thirteen, you are of age for it."

Before Micah climbed his mount, he took my hand, cradling it until he could no longer. And quick as that, they chucked the animals hence, onto the ancient hunters' trail, Micah sitting a handsome sight on his mare as his outline faded into the horizon.

"Your father's a fine soldier," I said to my children, turning away so they could not see my face.

"Yes, he was a ranging man and he will be fine," Evie replied with the great and ignorant pride of a child who has been kept from life's truths.

We set off that morn with the sun rising on our backs. Arakka at our lead meant that we followed the ways of his Comanche family, never near the known roads or working homesteads, always troubling the horizon for a running watercourse. We kept the Old San Antonio Road to our south, and headed for the Brazos River and Waco village, a two-day journey at our fastest pace.

That first day Arakka kept us close to a timber ridge, and we set our camp a few hundred yards west of an abandoned log house, cut from pines in the old times. James and Arakka went to hunt our supper in the late afternoon woods, while the girls and I watered our tired horses and mules, and lay the items for dinner.

Once Evie had finished her tasks, she said to me, "I'll be

scouting up at that cabin, Mama. Might find some things we can use for our travels."

"No, you will not. We will stay together until James and Arakka...until the men return."

She laughed when I called her brother a man, and opened her mouth to remark, but saw my face and silenced herself instead.

A few moments hence and the two returned with our supper and the first tale of our journey. James had been digging in the brush by the piney woods and found a pile of Indian blankets. Thinking they would be useful for the cooler autumn nights, he began pulling them from the sticks and needles, and stacking them.

Yet inside the blankets lay a bundle of bright-dyed scarves, bloodroot red and goldenrod. He separated this bundle from the blankets and found tucked inside a newly dead Comanche babe. He gave that poor soul a grave, shoveling and crying, and after, he sang 'Nearer My God to Thee', his favorite tune from the Baptists.

We steered wide of our Milam countryside so as not to meet those who might know our opinions, rising early to travel in the dark as best we could across the bare prairies until we reached the falls of the Brazos, where the young river becomes crisp and clear as it winds upsource to the canyons. The only spot with a rocky bottom for crossing a wagon, it was a place of whirling frantic water voices. We found a cool grove of elm and willows to shelter us from the top rise of the sun, and took that first meal alone, charky and squashes with the squirrels the men had brought down.

My boy was feeling his given job that day, and said seriously to Evie, "I expect you girls to create a better meal come the night."

Evie rushed at him in a wild gallop and slapped him hard across the face. Arakka grabbed hold of James before he could reply in kind, and I took Evie to hand as well. We waited with them as they shrieked and lunged at one another, but the water coming down the cliff was louder than either.

"You children are making me sour," I said. "Pack yourselves up quick, because we are moving on now." They heard my anger and quieted. Arakka took James off to load in the wagon, and Evie went to help her sisters. For me, I stayed dreaming to my roots in the stink of the bracken riverbanks, wondering at the loss of love between those two. My chore was to keep the truth from them, that any day might end in our death, and to suckle love between all four, although I had not the furthest idea of how to do it.

Much against Arakka's Comanche judgment, I insisted that we enter Waco village to trade for such victuals as were left. We passed but a few hours in that dried out town, finding little of consequence but a table of old nails and a few cuts of fly-covered pork long-past saving. We departed north along the Brazos, with Arakka smiling to himself while declaring to me that he would nurture our bellies once back in the wild lands.

Out on the marshy banks the river shallowed, and each night we found protected grounds for our camps under pecan trees and with fresh water for drinking and washing. I had known this Brazos since I was a child myself, muddy as it was when it chucked into the broad gulf sea, but up here it sparkled clear in the hot sun.

Arakka fed us with squirrels and wild turkeys, roasted acorns and some dried corn we meted out sparingly by pounding it into flat Comanche cakes. Along the way, he taught my girls to ride astride the bare backs of our horses, and Evie excelled at vaulting the mare to a gallop whenever he would let her.

The land opened wide to the sky, and changed from marsh to scrub, from dark farmers' soil to red rocks and loam, and all along the Brazos we left footprints on the sandy banks. The main river split, and despite the heat on the unfettered horizon, the cold streams kept even my wild children from drenching themselves.

As we moved across the prairie, we joined the forsaken trail to Palo Pinto, a land long disputed by Anglo settlers and Comanche. Drawing into town we pulled to a halt before the deserted courthouse, where not a soul tarried at the crossroads. Since the men had mustered into the Confederate army, the women and children had scattered, leaving their homes out on this frontier for any brigand with a good eye.

"Hold your rifle up, James," Arakka said. "You are a warrior. I will go inside." But when he returned, he told us the building was cleared through, leaving neither jailer nor ruffian.

"We will take supplies here," he said.

"Supplies?" asked James. "Ain't nothing left of this old town."

Arakka took Evie to the hotel to scavenge and returned with wool blankets.

"You see," he told James. "When people leave, some things do not fit their wagons. Those things we take for ourselves."

"That's stealing," said my little righteous Lucy with the squint eyes of a preacher, even as we stood in this empty wilderness, in this empty town, in the middle of this desolate war.

"Ain't stealing if they leave it behind," said James.

"Be very quick," said Arakka, sending the three oldest for goods. "People may be watching."

I waited with Stella while my little family scurried off, bringing me back their treasures to judge for use. Yes, to the dried-out corncobs, to the salt and the cups; no to the pencils or the ledger books from the saloon. A single red-stone chimney drew a dark tower against the far-off fields, all the hamlet abandoned for a week or more by the look of the tools and dead victuals laying to rot.

As the girls returned, we packed a tight wagon for the uneven trail. Evie mounted a horse to ride alongside Arakka, and I took the reins of the mules with the little girls beside me. And my James, fledging still into manhood, insisted that he needed to check the jail for bullets that might remain or other useful weaponry.

Arakka slipped from his horse to join him, but I spoke against it.

"Son, give him the Henry and let him go alone."

I saw James smile proudly at that, and he took the modern rifle from Arakka, moving quickly through the heavy oak doors.

Only moments passed before we heard voices, James calling out firmly and another tiny eddy of sounds, high and whining. Before I knew, Arakka leaped up the jail steps with his strong grace. But after a silent void of firing or shouts, I handed the reins to Lucy, took my own loaded Tyler, and followed him.

I passed the gates and the jambs into the cool dim room. The office counter was covered with dust and slender light shafts, and on I went into the far room of darkness where criminals had been chained to protect the finer folks in town. I heard my boys jawing softly before me, and a new smell, bitter and foul of filth, smothered us all. Within a tiny minute, the dark room loosened to shadows and I saw both of them kneeling on the floor beside the thick bars of the iron cage.

"What're you boys doing?" I asked. "We got a journey to ride."

"Mama, look at this. Some Indian child all chained up. Now what?"

I walked across the sod floor to touch the bar, and I saw the child lying on the other side with wrists and ankles locked in chains, a boy not more than six, long hair the color of ink, his little body thin as the shaft of a pen. All the while he trembled, trying to roll away from us, and as he did, he covered his limbs again with his own shite and spew.

Arakka cajoled him gently in the language of the Comancheria, but the boy did not respond. His lips were cracked and paled with flaking skin, and his little belly was swollen with the last days of hunger.

"Get him out of there," I said. "Get him out now."

"There is a lock," Arakka replied.

"James, fetch water quickly. He's about to die." I leaned forward and put my hand firmly on the child's shoulder. He shuddered at my touch, and though he did not speak words, the vowels from his rummy heart called out to all of us. Soon my children stood behind me, and little Stella crept closest, her grey eyes wide. She put her fingers through the bars and held his arm as though she had discovered a new friend. She pressed her lips together calmly and watched him.

"What'd he do, Ma?" asked Lucy.

"Ssh!" I said. "All of you, look for the keys!"

And what answer could I have given her? What could be the crime of such a small child enough to merit being caged and left, forgotten or worse, starving to his death in the dark. Poor godless soul that I had become, I pined for bread of life that I could see plain, and for a kind truth to tell my children.

We tore the jail apart for keys, but none we found would release the child's chains, nor open the cage-lock.

"We can't free him," James said. "Maybe we should pray for him."

I stared at my helpless son. "We will not leave him here to die. I would not leave any of you, and we will not leave him."

Arakka spoke to the boy again, deep and gentle with Indian words and sounds to comfort him, yet no word of any tongue was spoken by the child.

"Maybe he's not one of yours," I said.

Arakka grunted and stood. "I tried three languages. He needs strength and safety to speak. But he is Comanche. I know that." Arakka crossed his arms over his chest and shook his head sadly.

"Give me your dag, boy," I said quickly to this eldest of my children. Arakka slipped a slender knife from his left boot and handed it to me. "If we can free him from the cage, we will take him and worry the chains later."

I leaned over the heavy padlock and tinkered the springs and tiny shafts inside the keyhole. As a child I had taught myself this lesson, a silent pitch for liberty those sad nights with the devil Zoller. Terrified to have this child's death on my heart, I sweated deeply while turning and lifting the point of the blade, listening closely for the last latch to spring. Such knowledge rides with us forever, I think, and so I picked that iron clean until the swing shaft sprang free.

"Lift the boy gently," I told my children. "All of you, do it together. Make sure he isn't hurt, and then lift him to the wagon. We are moving on now and will clean him and feed him as we go."

CHAPTER 36

or two days the child lay covered in the wagon as we traveled, his eyes open wide with fear, his little bones rattled to their marrow by the rough trail. Evie and I took turns ministering to him with broth and water, careful not to kill the boy with sudden abundance.

My daughter, coming on fifteen years and soft as a catkin, helped me wizard open the iron cuffs on his wrists and ankles. I gave her ointment to stroke into his angry painful skin, which she did with the greatest devotion, all the while singing to him that song of wartime love, 'Lorena.'

Stella sat beside him as we drove on, and he had little choice but to let her hold his hand for those long hours. And me, well I slept with my arms round the child in the dark, not knowing if the dawn would find me holding a corpse whose sad soul had at last escaped.

His body improved as we made the trail west toward the Indian territories. When we closed on old Fort Belknap, the farthest settlement now emptied of soldiers and families, Arakka took the boy to see the abandoned huts of Captain Marcy and his soldiers, the men who had killed his family.

Days into the rolling plains, the child partnered James and Arakka on the hunt, and sat with the girls at campfire, yet he was still not smiling or talking.

"When you have no more to say, you might as well be quiet," James told us, but this small child did not even have a name; we could not attest his story or treat his far secrets and I longed for Micah's wisdom to bring peace to the boy's ailing world.

Across those western lands the sun grew hotter and the mesquite tangled toward the sandy river bottom. We followed a north feeder fork of the Brazos, a shallow diminishing water source that Arakka determined would lead us to the canyons he knew along the Prairie Dog River in the Palo Duro. As we saw the rusty spine of the Caprock along the horizon, soft red soil clung to our clothes and tools. The canyons below the Llano Estacado were our destination, cut deep into the high plains where we intended to live until the war was over.

We had reached a land unfamiliar to my own children, places of golden sky and blue dung they had never seen, of horned lizards that lay in wait for white folks like us Moores who strayed from home without skill. But these must have been the birthing grounds of our new young boy, because he took fine pleasure in its secret gullies. As we traveled deeper, he and Stella spent their nights playing Five Marys with her precious set of tiny bones and wooden ball, but nothing she did would bring words from him. We journeyed closer to the Caprock, along the red cliffs, and with each mile this child grew stronger.

Top of the sun was when this small boy first heard the sandhill cranes honking in the cloudless sky. He looked up with the slowest grin, nudging my girl to show her the diamond trail of stretch-necked gentle gliders coasting across the blue. Later that eve I saw him catch a rattler closing on Stella, and choke it to death. In that same darkness I found a name for him, all the while feeling his solid belly for lasting health. I squatted in the dirt and spoke to him while two broad-winged crows dipped and lifted in the purple sky above us.

I said, "Can't keep calling you 'boy.' I'm going to name you Benjamin, after my father."

Still, he didn't speak, but now he had a name. He was Benjamin. One white boy was mine with an Indian name; one Indian boy was mine with a white man's name. We were a hazard little group meandering along the escarpment, looking for peace up-canyon.

To get from the Brazos to the Red River's forks was a week's overland ride, scant of water or food, and all in hot sun. Yet Arakka took our group deftly down the old Kioway hunting trails, as close to small creeks as we could descend until at last we rode into a canyon formed by the ruddy outcrops. We discovered a narrow fringe of hackberry and black walnut, of raspberries and tiny, wild plums, and above this broad valley were even broader sandy hills atop the cliffs of this deep canyon. We found old winter camps of Kioway and Comanche, and a large abandoned beaver-town habitation of those most intellectual and humorous of creatures, where we came upon the stream that he sought.

A wide unmuddied bend lay before us, about a hundred yards across with waterlogged trunks fencing the farthest shore. We halted on the crusted bank, the children leaping from wagon and horse, rushing to this glistening place. To our astonishment the water tasted sweet as berries; that first gulp in our cupped palms was one we would all remember till the end of our days.

Arakka walked into the river to his ankles to measure the strength of the current, and once satisfied, he waved the children forward. They ran past him, diving and ducking into the bath, screeching water games in the hot sun, while my adopted boy stood tall, listening for the whispering of the river reeds. He had allowed his hair to grow past his jaw, and he wore no shirt. His back was burnished to the color of baked clay, and he cocked his head forward to hear some shared calling of blood. After all these years, he had never been ground to a different core than his Comanche soul.

After days of hard hot driving to reach this place, we threw camp early, on a slope of the riverside meadow. We feasted on elk, slow roasted in the rocks so the flesh would melt apart as it passed our lips. Arakka collected cottonwood bark-sticks for the mules and horses to chew, a practice he assured me was traditional for Comanche animals. The girls cleared and cleaned our tools, while James took my rifle and set off to scout the trees beyond our camp.

I lay by the fire, in the soft blue gama grasses with the light darting about me, thinking so hard about Micah I could feel his breathing inside me. Where we were venturing, there would be no letters, no telegraph, and if he lived I would not know it but through his spirit. I clung there with my eyes closed, unable to deny or hide from him.

Only James's voice broke through my dreams, suddenly running and tumbling to ground. "Ma! Ma!" he called out, although he knelt next to me. "There's a ghost out there!" He breathed hard and coughed as well, staring at me for an answer. The others gathered round us clamoring for the story.

"No such thing as ghosts, James," I said calmly.

"What did it look like?" asked Arakka.

"Big and white, come up out a' the weeds and groaned. Went down again till I lost sight. Biggest ghost I ever saw."

Lucy laughed at him. "You never saw a ghost, Jimmy."

James scowled at her. "Ten feet tall. Goin' up and down and up and down. You don't know it all, girl. You don't know what I saw."

"I will go see. You come with me," Arakka said to him, but all of us went, every child anxious to witness James's cast-off from paradise.

James led us beyond the beaver dam, to a place that had once been an Indian camp yet was now overgrown with rough weeds, three or four feet tall. There was barely any moon shining, and we pressed hard to see our way. About a quarter mile from our camp we reached the top of the bank, and all at once we heard movement in the prickled thicket and James raced away from us through the forking shoots and leafy stalks, while the rest of us were left behind to hear a call that sounded like a bellowing stag. Arakka, who believed in the half-life of spirits but did not fear them, walked ahead about two hundred yards. Behind him trundled our Benjamin, bending his head forward to hear and to see.

Soon I made out the shape, a large white head rising from the weeds. Without caution, Arakka and Benjamin approached the figure and touched it. Both put their hands on its long neck, for it was a slender-bodied white horse, sick with a bad case of colic and lathered with sweat. Arakka called to Evie to run for medicine and a tether, although that horse wouldn't be escaping for it couldn't even stand. Through the night, those three stayed with the animal, ministering to it with medicine and touch.

At dawn and no sleep behind me, I followed the river to their spot. She was a fine horse with a handsome body, and she was now standing quietly in the shallows, drinking that cool sweet water. Arakka held the rope while Benjamin sat astride her back, his body lying forward to warm her neck and his little arms wrapped across her mane. This small boy, no larger than our five-year-old Stella, made an inky outline in the river dawn against the mare's shock white hair.

Arakka grunted but once, and Benjamin sat up. He made several soft sounds with his tongue and lips, and brought the horse round slowly to step up the shore.

I smiled at Benjamin and put my hand on his narrow naked back.

"The plates on this horse are light," I said.

Arakka grunted again, and uttered words I did not recognize, but in response, my daughter levered herself behind Benjamin and wrapped the rope to form reins. She and the boy trotted forward, then galloped over the field, and returned to us, all within the space of a few minutes.

"She was a racing horse," Arakka said. "That is the cause of her thin shoes."

"Stolen?"

Arakka shrugged. "Someone rode till it could ride no more. Now it is Benjamin's horse."

I opened my mouth to speak, but Evie said this first, "It's only right, Mama."

I folded my arms and considered this. James had found her but was afraid of her ghostly soul. Evie and Lucy had horses of their own, and Stella rode with me in the wagon so was not in need.

"Can you teach him to care for it?" I asked.

"He knows," replied Arakka. "I told you, he is Comanche."

"How can he be the owner of a horse? He can't even talk."

"He can talk. He has just pulled the cloth over."

I shook my head and looked away. The sky was washed with milky blue, and mists hovered over the river. This new young boy had joined our family and he would need a horse, but he was too tiny and sickly to be riding this land on his own.

"Arakka, he is a small child and that is a big animal."

He laughed and stepped forward to take my hand. "One thing we know, Eliza, the boy will grow and the horse will not. I will help him. Allow it."

Of all the mysteries she had seen in her five years of living, my Stella still only viewed life in simple sides. Her bossy little soul insisted she be allowed to name the horse, and that she did.

She told her new friend that his mare would be called Cloud, and to my surprise, she made him speak that word aloud. I even heard her tell him that it was partly her horse. Unable to understand, Benjamin did not protest, and Stella announced to all of us that Cloud belonged to the two of them, equally.

CHAPTER 37

Our little congregation moved up the river slowly, the water depth diminishing each day as the canyon walls of sandstone and quartz rose higher around us. The grasses were luxurious for the animals, but the only varieties of timber were cottonwood and hackberry. Still, the density of these woods was thicker than any I had seen in our journey.

We traveled on, deep into the whistling cliffs where neither town nor lone hunter dwelled. When at last we reached a place of narrows, where the cliffs above were near three hundred feet high, the soil banking our creek was dark brown loam, and coated with wild rye and mesquite, giving the impression of cropland. Arakka and James walked the stream through the canyon's pillars and returned that afternoon for supper with tales of a wide meadow for tilling, plenty of wood for building, and fresh water flowing.

"We must build where we sit," Arakka said. "Farm on the other side. And above on the plains, we will find game, buffalo even."

"If we are to settle here, should we not be hidden beyond the narrows in case of attack?" I asked.

"The war will not find us between these tall bluffs. And we have no neighbors beside us, only a few Comanche or Kiowa hunters will pass by." He held out a hand. "Come see your new field. The seeds you brought will make many rows. Our family will eat well."

He strung our boots over his shoulders and guided me barefoot through the slow-flowing stream between the sandstone scarps.

"I will build a small bridge here," he said, blushing about the difficulty of our passage over the river stones and gesturing toward them.

A sheltered valley opened to us, about half a mile across, covered with grasses and pale blue cornflowers. The stream divided the land into one large parcel and a small one, became a creek, and after, disappeared entirely into the far gypsum rock wall. We advanced to the center of the meadow and looked back at our passageway. The late sun struck the white gypsum, causing the cliffs to glow with silver light.

"You see, Eliza. Sun and water. No wind. We will build shelter on the other side, where there are ways to leave quickly, and here can be your farm."

How well I loved him then. He had brought us hundreds of hard miles to such an eternal fountain where we might live out the days till the end of the war or the end of our lives. It was a haven for the children where the earth called us to drink our fill and survive. From the glints of sunlight dazzling on the calm water, I turned to Arakka and smiled. I moved to him and took his hand. I could feel the warm tears on my cheeks, and I put my arms around his shoulders, my sorry soul slacking. This boy we had saved had now saved us. Spasms rose from my gut until I found myself crying aloud for the mercy of his prodigious gift.

∼

We were alone, and what needed doing, we did ourselves. This was a wild place, and we shared the burden and the bounty. Rarely came a voice that was not ours, that was not the sound of my children laughing or arguing. Each of us struck axes through trunks and fitted latches; each coddled seeds for food. And word by word, this new child, Benjamin, joined our small family.

He was kind but ferocious in loss; he was loyal to Stella, and covetous of respect. We determined he was seven, although his body seemed smaller, and we began to educate him in the ways of Comanche and white alike, of horsing and cooking and crops, of letters, numbers, and the kill and gut of beasts.

By the last days of summer, we had raked and planted our rows of corn and squashes, yams and beans, and some were popping their shoots through the soil to form leaves and blossoms. The warm windless shelter of our farm gave us the bounty of Bluebonnet Ridge even so far from home.

Our night cover was a simple lean-to using the wagon box and the canyon wall. We stretched broad flaxcloth pieces to hackberry poles for our summer quarters, but after the crops were planted and came the first cooler weeks, Arakka and James began to build us a small cabin. The girls and I weeded the floor down to soil, wet it with the streamwater we brought in buckets, and leveled it out with our planting hoes. The boys cut hackberry trunks in half, leaving them with the bark undressed, and saddle-notched them together.

This would not make us a long-lasting build due to the destructive nature of even a few droplets of damp clustering in the spaces between logs, but we held a hope that the house was only needed for a season or two until the war ended. We had no clay or bitumen, so we chinked up the gaps with river mud, making the single room of shelter even damper, as that close to the water the chinks never crusted and dried.

We all slept in one room without windows, and we cooked outside in a firepot. Lucy insisted we build a proper door, as she feared wild animals, so Arakka split more logs and pegged them together. He used leather straps for hinges and built a lock beam across that Lucy could confidently latch shut each night.

By early harvest time, our creek began a wilder flow, and from the top of the bluffs we could daily hear the whirliwinds busting across the plains. Such heaving weather befell the mesas, that I thought I heard their pillars shaking at night. Hailstorms hurled about through the fall and winter, with deep rains across the flats above us that torrented down to our canyon crops.

In November, before we saw the snow dusting, a comely group of Comanches passed our way. I had never been this close to so many of a tribe, and as they were painted in black and traveling without women, we concluded they were a returning war group. Like Arakka, they were naked above the waist, but unlike him their skin was the color of copper pots.

Arakka went to welcome the group and invited them for supper. Although straight from battles, they were soft and kind with us. We roasted an elk they had killed up the far creek, and served them such delights that the men complimented our feast, and told jubilant stories of the re-taking of their prairies. Evie alone of my children had learned their language, and they were impressed when she smiled at their humor and clapped her hands at their bravery.

Far into the night, she came to sit by my bedmat, quietly at first until I sat up and saw her eyes wide and frightened.

"What is it, girl?" I asked and took her hand.

"Those men came from the North, Mama. From the Oklahoma Territories. They heard the blues lost a big fight in Georgia. Thousands of our men were killed. They said hardly anyone who fought is still alive. Could've been Father, Teddy Blue or Absalom, couldn't it? Arakka said could've been anyone, there were so many."

I paused a moment, staring at her, then quickly took her narrow shoulders between my hands. "How would those men know, Evie? No Comanches have ever been to Georgia. They just heard tell from someone who heard tell." What I most clearly knew at that moment was the smell of the fresh water, so close to us, not the butchered heroes left on the plains nor the horses left on the fields, but the sweet smell of water we had found in the canyons.

"They been battlin' everywhere, Mama. Dozens of fights and burnin' down whole towns. What if the greys win this war? What will we do?"

I led her across the packed floor and away from the cabin. There at the stream bank, by green willows and sweet shallows, I whispered to her. "You and I must keep these thoughts away from the children, Evie. You are old enough to help me keep their hope."

The child, as she will always seem, tapped her foot, and mindlessly, trembled her legs.

"The truth is," I said, "we don't know if our men are still living, but I'll tell you this I do know. Some nights I see your father's face in my dreams, and I believe he is not far, not on the other side."

Her expression was muted, angelic ice no axe could break. I put my hand out to stroke her dark wavy hair, knowing that if in harm's way, Evie and the other children would be seized as slaves.

"But we have Arakka now," I said, "and James and little Ben, and in this place we are well hidden and will always have crops and water. Maybe one day we won't be able to go home, but we can stay here, or even keep on to California."

At the mention of the western territory, her eyes brimmed up with tears. "But I don't want to go to California. I don't want to stay here. I just want to go back to Bluebonnet Ridge."

~

The next morning, we found fresh bear tracks and the men, ours included, took their horses skyward, following the scent and marks up the trails to the tabletop plain. A hunt with Comanche might take days, but a white man's hunt was to feed a much smaller group and without celebration, so we set to preparing roasted delights for I knew they would be home by supper of that same day. By dusk, we had yet to see our boys, and after we ate, I put Stella to bed in the thinning light while Evie swept the scraps away so not to draw the night animals to our home.

Lucy had disappeared off to her secret place on the riverbank, beside a lone cottonwood she had named the Lord's Tree. Not entirely secret, this idyll was where she went to pray to the god she had brought with her into the wilderness. She was a girl of thirteen years, poised for womanhood yet hostage to a war that had forced her onto our lonely frontier, and times I would find her there, eyes closed and swaying with rapture to a hymn she had learned at the Bluebonnet Ridge.

I followed the path by the river to an open circle of stones the children had laid, and I saw Lucy sitting in the center at the foot of her holy tree, staring into the darkened water.

"Girl!" I called. "Hometime now."

"A few more minutes, Mama. I'm askin' blessings."

"Now. You and Evie have work before bed."

"Yes, I'm coming."

I turned back on the path. After rounding a few bends, the earth vibrated and soon I saw Cloud's head poke through the trees and brush, carrying our little Ben with his bright smile, and the others riding behind him. Hanging from the saddles of each horse was a full pack of meat that would keep all of us fed for weeks. We paused in that clearing, examining our bounty while James chattered to me uncontrollably about the work of the day. All of them were tired and filthy with blood and dried soil from the plains above.

"You boys must wash in the river before bed. I'm not sharing a room with this smell."

Softly through the trees came an echo of deep chirping, a sweet sound but the Comanche snapped their heads round to look toward the river.

"Let's go now," Arakka said sharply, as the gentle chirp rose to a scream of the forest. "A panther is out and is smelling this bear." They pulled their rifles up and clucked their horses on.

Arakka offered his hand to me. "Eliza, you must ride with me. You cannot walk when a panther is near."

"Lucy is at her tree!" I cried out. "Alone by the river. Go quick!"

My boys wheeled their mounts immediately and shifted to a gallop, tearing the soil furiously as they rode.

I have never been fleeter than this moment. I ran the trail behind the Comanches, flying through the brush, and arrived at the cottonwood clearing just seconds behind my boys.

"Lucy, stand up, and wave your arms!" shouted James in his bravest voice as he leaned over the horn. "We come to save you!"

The panther was six feet long, its shoulder muscles rippling in the moonlight as it paced leisurely, gazing at my poor child pinned in terror against that infernal tree. Its small ears swiveled slightly at the sound of me crashing through the scrub, but its stare trained on Lucy, unwavering.

"Look away!" I shouted to her. "Don't see it straight on. And yell your heart out, girl!" But she sat frozen on the ground, trembling like the prey she was.

Arakka and James pulled up behind the tree line, both dismounting and moving toward the panther, and that is when I said my dreadful prayer, opening the door between the living and the dead. I whispered this aloud, thinking it a last cry for God's grace, not knowing it was a curse.

Oh Lord, save my Lucy. Do not let this animal take her. In Jesus' name I pray it. Amen.

The panther stalked closer to my girl and growled low in the back of its throat. Arakka lodged his rifle butt into the pocket of his shoulder, curling his fingers around the shaft to steady his aim. In an instant he aligned and fired at the moving animal. The bullet but grazed its haunch, and the panther, with emerald eyes glowing, crept forward toward my child. In two strides it was within the killing distance, and it opened its jaws before jumping at Lucy, its white teeth gleaming at the dusky sky.

Arakka and James dropped their rifles and ran to her, both plunging their knives into the animal's back. The panther released its prey, and lashed round to face those two while my girl ran to me, free and alive.

Arakka jumped upon it, fierce as cruelty itself and slashing hard and deep, while James lifted his knives, taking one heavy step back to balance himself. And in that instant the panther threw Arakka from its back and leapt forward, its jaws closing on James's head, cracking my boy's skull with its long fangs. It lifted him overhead and flung him aground, but my child, my dear James, had already died by its jaws.

From afar the Comanches shouted, and one put a bullet into the animal, bringing it finally to that soft damp earth.

Come the morning beyond that desolate night, we buried James in the same grave as the panther that had killed him. This was the plea of Arakka, and I could not refuse for Arakka had saved my girl and nearly lost his own life doing so. We dug deep into the clearing before that lord's tree and lowered them together by ropes. The children and I swept the piled earth back into its hole, while Lucy carved a cross on the tree trunk with James's name, and they all toed an imaginary line around it. She gave her brother a Christian service for unlike me, he had been a believer in the immortal soul of Jesus.

After, I wandered silently in the forest following the line of cottonwoods to the rivulet, clenching my fingers to fists as I watched a lone water snake slither down the stream bed. I squatted in the sticky mud, my ankles nicked by damp brambles, my heart rotting like a leper's until deep and reckless wailing pumped hard from my gut. I had not been able to save my son from his melancholy affliction, nor from his desire to escape it.

When Arakka came, he lifted me from the waterside. "Dear Mother," he said and put his arms about my shoulders. "Do you hate me?" I peered at him for a long time, and he put his hands timidly on my hot raw face.

"Why would I?"

"I did not save him," he said simply, touching me, inspecting my pain for blame.

"Oh, my son," I whispered, shaking my head. "My sweet child," and finding his torture larger than my own, I took his hand and held it to my cheek.

$\mathcal{M}$y children expended their sadness while the cold set in, toiling as instructed by Arakka. They harvested our food and preserved what they could in the frozen hole that had become our river valley. In thin winter sunlight, they dried the vegetables under cheesecloth draps, and Arakka taught them to make pemmican bars of powdered charky and fat that would keep us through the season. And I, well, I did little to help, filled as I was with my own hellish thoughts and guilt.

I believe it was January, although I had begun to lose track of time advancing. Arakka and I sat before our cook fire, and he saw to the chore by himself while I merely watched.

"Is there a story I can tell you, Eliza?"

"No, boy. No tale will bring James home again. I am sick and there is nothing."

He held the roasting body of a wild turkey on a stick over the flames, plunging it deep to the heat, and the rich sweet smell rose around us while he moved it back and forth to cook it evenly.

"By spring you will not have such pain," he said quietly.

"How are you able to know when this agony will stop? It may never stop."

"The sadness will not stop, but the pain will. That is how it was with my wife and boy." He called to the children to sup, for he had become father and mother in our family as I drifted in my monstrous delusion.

"I can't stay here that long," I said. "Certainly not until spring."

Simply, he asked, "Where will you go?"

A great gulf broadened between us while my sorrow grew. I heard the children wildly scuttling at each other in the woods, but I did nothing, said nothing. I planted the corn and squashes, drawing little of my previous joy from this land. The evenings I spent alone, listening to the cuckoos call out across the river, and every moment of unearthly sweetness from my children led me farther astray.

Some nights I woke in the dark to my own shouting, and often I would find Benjamin and Stella beside me, their arms stroking my own. I dreamed of wolves, never of panthers, and I stared at the faces of my children without speaking. I cried seldom, but ruminated on Arakka's question every day. Where could I, a dark and ruined soul, take these broken children? Where on this Earth would be kinder to them, and where would I ever be free of the vision of my poor son's face when he leapt with such courage toward the panther and his own death?

One afternoon, weeks hence, when the sun had taken the last of the frost, I squatted alongside Benjamin as we plumped the soil for sowing yams and beans. I stopped to remove my wool jacket, folding it beside me in the field. I looked over at him for a few moments.

"Why are you staring, Mama?" he asked.

I smiled and reached my hand to touch him. "Because you are a good worker."

∼

A few weeks later the warm rains brought those raw bean shoots up through the earth. Across our sheltered fields our food began to show itself, and even some wild blue cornflowers sprouted between our rows. Without me knowing or particularly caring, we had survived the winter.

Come the longest days of sun, this land released bountiful victuals to us. Our meals became times of music, as Arakka had carved a bone flute for Benjamin, and Evie's sweet voice never faltered. They were old songs and old stories of the Bluebonnet Ridge that Benjamin loved greedily for the adventure of his new family. James's death had brought us vigilance and care for each other, and at times we even stopped our garrulous blather to hold each other's hands across the table of tenderness. There were no others, no mail packets or telegraph from far places, no news of presidents or generals, just the elegant blackbird song faring across the bright blue sky.

Deep into summer we divided for the plains hunt. Arakka had told stories of great woolly creatures, larger and softer of soul than any others traveling in such great numbers they appeared like a magnificent ocean swelling and ebbing on the Llano Estacado above us. He intended only one kill, because he said a single animal would feed our family into the winter, give us warm blankets and tallow for the darker days.

Benjamin and Arakka planned to ride up the steep trails, but without James they needed a third in their party. Evie and I argued for the spot, she the better rider, but me the skilled shooter. Finally, I simply would not be ousted by her youth, and to her protest I put her in charge of Lucy and Stella while I rode up the hills with my boys to observe this mad nature on the summit.

We three carried rifles, and knives for the butchering that we would complete on the plain. Benjamin traveled with a bow that Arakka had carved for him from a long hedge apple branch, tough and supple, and strung with elk ligament. Only Arakka carried a lance and insisted this was the proper way to hunt a buffalo. They rode ahead of me in file, for the path up the vast mesa was slow and crooked, broad enough for only one horse at a time.

We crept through the mulberry and mesquite tangles until a couple of hours had passed and we lit upon the sight of the flattest calmest horizon I had ever encountered. No sign of weather touched the sky, nor cloud nor breeze, no hill or bush, purely the immense earth far to every side of us. And I, but a single woman gazing to this empty plain, was certain I could see the curve of our world before me.

"Where are these creatures?" I asked.

"Follow," he said, and clucked his mare to a Canterbury gallop.

We increased our speed across this land, my Comanche boys both moving with lordly joy and ease. Though carefully watched for so many years by Europeans, these prairie men had never been understood by the white invaders and their vain opinions. Fleet and precise, formidable in a hunt, the Comanche's deepest concern was the welfare of their animals, for these were beloved limbs of their own bodies.

Arakka stopped his ride a half-mile in advance, and Benjamin pulled Cloud to stand alongside him while they waited for me. My older boy dressed my head in a scarf.

"Benjamin will go on. When he finds the herd, he will stop and ride a ring for us to come." Arakka put his hand on Cloud's white rump, stroking it. "Benjamin, you will prowl the rim of the herd. Do not ride into the animals." He offered his rifle to me. "You take this, Eliza, and be my shadow. You ride fast at my side and protect me. Stay speedy and clear in your mind or they will trample you."

I must have looked like a bird in a thicket, suddenly confused from my tiny world. I had been confident; I had been proud. I stared at the horizon of copper mallow and grasslands, suddenly wondering if my curiosity on this plain would bring my final day on this Earth.

"I will choose the animal, and we will be three sides to it. Do not shoot it with the gun."

He touched his spear that lay laced to the side of his horse. "I am killing it with this." Putting his hand down across the chest of his horse, he stroked the area of the lung cavity. "If you penetrate here, it can only walk a few steps. It has only one breathing sac to lose and cannot breathe more. The buffalo will stumble and fall. The others may gather around it, but we will not be greedy," he said. "We only need meat of one for the cold season."

Benjamin turned to ride on, this small boy driving brutally over the plain until I could no longer see his shape on the horizon.

"I will tell you when to ride, Eliza," said Arakka. He dropped to silence, without raising an eye.

Around me settled the bitter smell of the grasses and thistles, heated and rising thick. I watched Cloud until she was only a smudge of white across the distant mirage of color.

"Now go," Arakka said calmly, and we shifted our mounts.

We moved into an easy Canterbury, rocking back and forth for a few lengths with the ambling hammer of hooves, until Arakka leaned over the neck of his horse, pressing himself to its back and urging it into full gallop. I kicked my own ride faster, gulping the yards of prairie behind us as the pounding numbed all other sound.

Apace like that, I could smell every plant, feel every rise or drop in moisture. I shifted my weight with each hoof beat to keep from crashing to the earth, for balance at this clip is the savior. My eyes teared in the wind, and I took the mane and reins with one hand while wiping my face with the other, desperate to see what I might. Riding fast with such a pitiless heart, I bared my teeth and jutted my jaw forward. Wildly, I lifted my voice to a ruthless scream and howled at the desert until my throat was raw.

As we gained on Benjamin my heart rose to my gullet, but we flew past him in this smooth gallop, trampling a narrow path between the animals. We lopped off a corner of the moving herd of buffalo. Against the sheer wind of speed and flying dust of the land, I clenched my thighs around my mount and lifted the rifle to my chest. Fixing it between my arm and ribs, I held the reins in my other fist. We slowed through the jumble of broad furred backs and horned skulls until at last, I focused on Arakka.

We two-beat among them for a quarter mile, all the while Arakka examining each for meat and hide, for weakness and isolation from the rest. When he found his sinner, he brought his horse to a faster uncomfortable trot. The animals quickened their pace, spreading over the plains toward the larger herd, and this grand gulf of foul-smelling creatures sped to meet their own until they raced out of our sight, but for the one we had trapped. It was an animal six foot tall on all fours, weighing two thousand pounds if any. It tried to escape, but Arakka and I galloped alongside, flying still while my boy lifted his spear high over his head.

The buffalo rumbled down the earth with a fearsome pound. I stopped breathing, watching Arakka while the grit and dust of the prairie rose around us. At last he chose a moment and, leaning far to the right off his center toward the beast, he flung the spear. The buffalo took two deep strides, a wobbling third, then bent its knees and slumped dying to the earth, for my son had pierced its only lung sac.

We remained safely astride our mounts until the last of the living disappeared into the haze of horizon. My breathing calmed slowly, my brawling guts settling at last. All around was silence, and the sliding afternoon sun blushed the sky with orange and violet.

I slipped from the horse and put my hands on its hot sweaty

side, stroking to calm it. The boys were already unfolding their carving packs and tarred agave cloth, but I didn't bow to help. I squatted in wonder by the steaming carcass, my wide-open eyes to its own glassy look, still rucked by its enormity.

From the Mississippi gators we killed for food to the cows and hogs on the Bluebonnet Ridge, creatures had kept us alive, but kneeling there beside this one, on the edge of the desolate desert, nothing seemed to separate me from the spirit of this dying animal.

We rode home with the weight of its shambles on our backs, slow across the prairie and even slower lurching down the moonlit mulberry trails to camp. Benjamin led, his little arms like dropped wings in trilling victory. I felt my heart beating hard to leave this tabletop mountain, and once we trod upon our rivergrass, I urged my tired mount to dip its hooves into the cool dark stream. Arakka, Benjamin, and I sat astride these horses, allowing them to drink the fresh water. They had seen our butchery on the plain, had saved us anyway, and had brought us home.

Head down and motionless almost at the world's end, we followed a path I knew well until we reached our pen. We unloaded our brunt at midnight into the storing shack on the other side of the narrows, those cliffs I had named Aphrodite's Pillars from a book I once read as a slave.

At last to our cabin in the deep night, we woke the girls only briefly. I slept in my killing clothes and dreamed of blood in webs over the river. When I awakened I could still see trembly bodies in the lick of fire-dream across me.

CHAPTER 39

$\mathcal{A}$t the tail end of the next wintertime, as we chewed down the last of the pemmican chunks, my children pulled their wools up over their shoulders against the seeping freeze, sitting round a fire we had stoked. Little Stella wrapped her arms round her waist, trying to hurple the cold from her bones.

All that week, only the slender grey light of day lay above us. Evie had lost her silky voice to the quinsy, so I painted her throat with Arakka's potions and draped her in bedquilts. Benjamin, the healthiest of all, strutted about our sad little circle calling for play, but none was to be had from my other children.

"We have been in this canyon for nearly two years," I said to them. "Soon the frost will go, and it will be time to send for news of the war, and maybe we can think about returning home."

Arakka steadied, and said this without looking at me, "Is this not our home now?"

A kingfisher bolted blue from the shadows across the narrow stream of light between us, and the smell of musk followed it. Still, my son did not look at my eyes, nor did I look at his, but nonetheless I replied, "The Kioway passing through last month told us the whites have given up on their battling. If this be true, we must figure our options. The children can't live here forever. We haven't even brought books with us to teach them."

He nodded without reply, and the children stared wide-eyed at me.

We all slept early, though not from exhaustion. With little care save feeding ourselves and our animals, with sickness and the fever of our lost James about us, sleep had become our kindest refuge. But before the morning, Arakka awoke, and I heard him among our horses in the little corral.

When I faced him across the crusty ice of the yard, he said, "I'll head first for the buffalo trading post to find the true answer to your question. If not there, I will move to Rescate until I hear news. My travel might be weeks, or months."

I nodded. "Stay off the main trails. You're of age to fight, and some might take you under."

Arakka put his hands on my shoulders, standing so much taller than I now, and stronger.

"Thank you, son," I said.

"Your soul is starving for word about Micah. It's time to begin home if we can."

Arakka pulled himself into his saddle, and rode off slowly into the white winter mist that lay on the floor of our canyon.

Three full moon cycles hence when he still had not returned, poor little Benjamin attempted to take his place in our workdays. Pulling himself from sleep before dawn, Ben leapt into the farming, until one early morning when I heard him shout his brother's name.

Arakka rode wearily to our cabin and slipped from his mare, turning to lean against it. The girls and I stood beneath the overhang, and watched him wipe away the dirt from his cheeks and forehead.

"Boy, you look thirsty and hungry both," I said softly, and suddenly we all put our arms around his waist while he smiled patiently. "You've become scraggly thin."

"Maybe, but I found your answer, Eliza." He pulled from the saddle pouch a folded broadsheet and handed it to me. "Far to the east I found Prussians who had this."

I stared at the paper.

"What's it say, Mama?" asked Evie. "Can we go home?"

"Give it to me," Lucy said. "I'll read it."

"What day are we?" I asked Arakka.

"The month of July. I do not know the day."

The old page had the date of the twenty-eighth of May, one thousand eight hundred and sixty-five, and I began reading to them of the end of our war, the success of our United States, and the murder of Mister Lincoln.

Within the week, we mounted our horses and followed the water onto the broad southern fork of the Red River. We chucked in a single line the six of us, our animals packed with all we owned and could carry. As the river bent north toward the old Indian territory, I believed I saw Micah in the distance, Teddy Blue, and Absalom too, watching them spring walking toward me. I swept and swayed across the horizon like a net in water, feeling they might be near but knowing all the while they might be buried by now.

I had never been that far to the north, and each day brought us a colder wind than the last. We journeyed near the old Wichita village, where one hour we trod in Texas and the next on the Indian lands of Oklahoma. We reached old Holland Coffee's trading post, a relic of history now. The government men who relocated the site three times in ten years to accommodate the movements of the tribes, had left behind the raw log footings in the mud of the riverbank. Going home as we were, we had no use for any of it, so we but set our camp within its lines, and made our fire in the ruins where others had before.

Arakka and Benjamin killed a fine wild turkey, and we ate it beneath the bright moon. Deep into the night, Lucy stirred herself awake and pointed to the sky. A cloak had cast over the moon, and carrying no almanac, I did not know the meaning at first. The shadow commenced below and went off at top, covering half the glow of light as it passed.

"What's happening, Mama?" Lucy cried.

"It's nothing, Lucy. Just the eclipse passing above us. One of the beauties of the frontier."

"It's God, Mama," she said firmly. "It's in the Scriptures. The Lord is telling us something."

I took her hands and squeezed them; she was wrapped in men's dreams, even at that age.

As we entered the prairie and closed on the stockyards at Fort Worth, we began to meet kindred refugees, whether Comanches traveling east to take on supplies or starving Texans seeking wild corn. Land in the county of Tarrant was never good for anyone but stockmen, treeless and sloping with but thin soil over limestone, and the cattle having been slaughtered to feed the soldiers, ranching families now passed us as they fled west. We intended to swing wide of any cowtown, avoiding the armed anti-abolition men still wearing their ragged butternut jackets and wool slouch hats.

We followed the Trinity straight into the heart of the damnable sight of Fort Worth. The field crops had been scrapped years past, and the school door broken to its hinges. The town itself was emptied of most, leaving but a hundred folks from its former thousand to the desolate broken economy. No livestock existed in this place, though it had been the king of cowtowns years before.

Many stores had been lost to passing scavengers, and these we eyed from our mounts. Angry women in soiled cotton dresses scurried in and back through the doorways, searching with scared eyes, stealing the stuff of home and piling them into their wagon boxes.

As we neared the south edge of the river bluff, a gaggle of ruffian children rushed onto Main toward us. They launched at my family, glimpsing our full saddlebags in this sorry chapped wilderness. Only one of them wore shoes, and his forehead shone in the hot sun as he reached my Lucy and grabbed at her legs to pull her from her mount.

"Ride on, children!" I shrieked. "Ride on hard!"

My babes took flight while I galloped to my girl, my heart spilling with anger at her scrawny attackers.

I took Lucy's reins and kicked the boy hard, yet no sooner did he fall than another leapt upon us, and another, each of them screaming like starving banshees, punching at our legs with their sticks. We lurched our horses forward, but these children grabbed our ties, our saddles, our shoes, and closing their small fingers tight around this contraband, dragged us to a halt, for what was left to them anyway but hell and will?

Lucy cried and cried to me as I kept pummeling the boys with my crop, until at last I heard a rifle crack.

"Go now!" shouted Arakka, and as I turned our horses, I saw him holding the Henry to his shoulder, one eye squinting, ready to shoot again as he kicked his mount to a gallop behind us.

We pressed on to the river's far edge where we hoped to water our mounts, but our animals pulled up about a hundred yards from the bank and refused to approach. Even Cloud, the bravest of all, bucked and circled back when Benjamin urged him on. My children stared to the river and cried out to me with such fearful vows that I lifted my rifle to ready for another attack.

Evie put her arm out to stop me.

"Mama, what is that creature?" she asked, pointing to an animal near a far-off tree by the river.

"Just an old horse," I said, scarcely attending to her question.

"Ain't a horse, Mama," said Lucy.

Arakka coaxed his ride toward the animal, and suddenly leaned over the horn with loud laughter.

"Whatever it is, this one is having a back scratch against that pecan tree." He moved his mount a few steps more, and the animal turned to him and spit. "This is a foul smell it gives and foul fluids. Eliza, this is taller than a horse, with a high back like Sugarloaf Hill."

I dismounted and walked slowly forward. The creature stood on four hooves in saltbush scrub, chawing at the prickles with its huge sloppy lips, and swallowing gulps of soft dust.

"We will leave it be," I said. "Just one of those camels the old army brought from faraway. I only ever saw drawings of them before."

Stella walked her mount to my side. I saw the thought hovering over her head, clear as if she had spoken it. Blind to all but the need of creatures, she reached her little hand out to touch my arm.

Before she could utter out her piece I said, "Soldiers let them go free because they were mean and full of stink, and we are not adopting it either for those very same reasons."

"Oh, Ma," she whispered. "Look at it standing so sad, needing a home and a family."

"No," I said. "We have enough to care for already."

She straightened her neck, pulling her little head high, topped as it was with brown curls like my own. Her mouth set stern and tight, Stella said, "You always are telling us we need to care for creatures."

"This animal has been wild for years. Too long to be your pet now. Isn't that right, Arakka?" But he and the others were laughing at us, mother and child engaged in such an exchange about a dromedary on the frontier.

"You have been showing her this path since she first breathed," he said and turning, rode on.

Once we passed wide of Waco, the low-slung hills spread out into our familiar cropland. There by the Brazos at the mixing of two prairies, the soil was black and moist as I dreamed it those long years apart. We rode hours until we reached the forking of the Little River and the Brazos, merely one day of travel from the Bluebonnet Ridge.

My winding old home river had not raged over its banks that summer, so its bottomlands were well timbered with all manner of wildness living in them. Birds abounded in those tall trees, unafraid deer salted at the licks, and though we were observed by wolf and bear, Arakka took the children to fish the banks for supper. Through the thick cover of cedar scent, I believed myself breathing in the faraway mulberries and the fresh black miracle of our own soil.

That night we feasted on tender bass with wild tubers and persimmons. Arakka dug among the riverside marigolds for deep clay, which he pasted around the whole fishes, covering them thick until not one scale was exposed. We built a deep hot roasting pit and lay these creatures in the embers until our fine meal was perfected. When cooled to touch, the clay cracked apart, taking the scaly fish skins with it, leaving but the sweet flaking flesh of the wild river.

The children were giddy with memories of their home,

knowing that the following eve they would sleep in what remained of their own rooms. Their laughter and breathless tales of the Bluebonnet Ridge drowned out any swarming sorrow of our years in canyon exile. All but Benjamin snored deeply through the night. He lay on a bedroll near his horse, and I could hear him shifting and turning across the fallen cedar needles.

"Benjamin, come," I whispered, and he crawled with his roll and blanket to my side. "Here, you must be cold." I swept my arms and quilt round him. "Close your eyes now, it is time for sleeping. Long ride home tomorrow."

He squared his little shoulders away from me and did not close his eyes.

"What is it, boy?" I asked.

"What happens then?"

"We build the Bluebonnet Ridge again. We work hard. Go to sleep now."

"But what happens to me? Where will you send me?"

I stared straight at his black eyes with all the comfort I possessed, but still my heart split in two, for however I loved his torn soul or what I might whisper to him, it would never be enough. Such devilry possessed this frontier to have thrown a lifetime of sadness on this child!

"You are my son," I said. "Wherever I am, you will be." I put my arms around him and pulled him tight to me, but his heart was utterly empty of hope. "This is my oath. You are part of this family."

"But I'm not your blood."

"Here is love, Benjamin," I said and held his small dark hand, smudged still with the mud of the day, against my chest. "Blood is not love. Little puzzling lunar child, you will always carry my love with you."

CHAPTER 40

*W*e rode out easy the next morn, with Evie insisting on leading our file. Her singsong of the fiddle melodies she had learned as a child seeded light around us, until the late afternoon when she brought us to the ridge overlook. She pulled up on her horse and slid from the saddle, gazing upon our dear cabins in the valley below. One by one we followed, my children standing knee-deep in the bluebonnet meadow. Angles of light lay across the field, and I stared ahead with the others, the sun and wildflowers calming my heart. Arakka walked his horse alongside mine and, lanky man that he had become, lay his arm across my shoulders.

"Walls are broken in places," he said.

I nodded.

"Door is open. Porch rails are broken, but the roof looks good from here."

"Don't see any stock or men. You?"

"No, Eliza. No living food. No tended crops. I will ride down first. You wait here with the children."

An hour hence as we sat in the soft sloped meadow hugging ourselves and watching our destiny before us, Arakka mounted his horse at the front of the house and rode a ring round, the Comanche signal of beckoning. The girls helped each other saddle, shrieking like triumphant warriors while racing down the bluebonnet hill to their home.

And my Benjamin, encumbered and unconvinced as he was, climbed slowly atop Cloud and paused till I was ready. A racing horse he had indeed, and the very sight of children charging down the ridge urged that great white animal to follow, but Benjamin held it steady, pulled up at its jerks and starts, and forced it to walk apace with me.

We tied our horses in the broke down corral, allowing them prairie grass. Evie set off to seek buckets for water, and I found our old well, the walls but a heap of stones. The porch rails were gone, the door at the front too, and we did not find a single ironware piece, not laying in the ruins nor affixed where we had left it. Those pecan trees we had planted so many years ago bore leaves aplenty that had mulched in piles on the steps and weedy ground. Dead damp foliage and crackling branches covered my dear porch rocker-bench.

Once Arakka declared the floors sturdy, the children rushed to their rooms seeking a wooden top or painted babe doll they left behind. But it was gone, all of it. Taken from us, just as we had stolen from others on our refugee journey.

I left them to their sad accounting and took Benjamin into the bumped-out kitchen shed that Micah and the boys had built for Cookie. Not a single pot could be found, nor even the pump or bowl left behind. High above the cook fire ledge, the chimney had cracked and the daub crumbled about the busted floorings. A broken chair lay tumbled upside down against the bricks, and beneath it, hogweed crept up through the boards from the earth itself.

Arakka stood at the jamb, waiting.

"Not everything is gone," I said, holding tight to Benjamin's calloused little hand.

"No. Some months of hard work for all though."

"We need to start growing victuals so we can trade for items."

Arakka moved closer to me. "As long as we remember what it was, Eliza, we can make it again."

I grinned at him. "Never remember Comanches being such hopeful ones."

We heard the doodle-doo of a far-off rooster, and Arakka said, "I will go and catch it."

But before he could move, Evie came shouting, "Ma! Ma!" flying through the doorway to us. "I found an old woman, Ma! In our corncrib." Her rampaging voice was righteous and stuttering.

"Cookie?" I asked, my spirit lifting with that sweet thought.

"Not Cookie," she panted, "just an old woman seeing to a sick babe. A mulatto babe." Evie stopped to gulp at the air.

"I will find her," Arakka said.

"We both will go," I replied.

And to our backs, my daughter whispered, "She is begging for food, Mama."

Arakka and I opened the loading door and peered in to find the woman. The light in the crib came through the broken slats, showering needles of silver dust across the sod floor.

"Hello?" I called out. "Someone in here?"

Arakka put his hand on my arm and shook his head.

"I see her. She is crouching in the corner."

"Be careful, boy. She may have a gun."

He walked to her. "She is no rounder, Eliza. This is your sister."

I walked straight to her and knelt in the dirt, grabbing her shoulders to my chest and breathing hard in the dark. I held her that closely only to find she was but a body near to bones.

"Are you hurt?" I asked, and she shook her head slowly. "How long you been here?"

A Mulatto babe lay in her lap without moving. I covered its little tum with my hand and felt a slight rise of breath.

"How long you been here?" I asked Lou again.

"Levi tried to kill our babe, so I shot him." Her eyes were bleary, and she rolled them closed, leaning her head against the planks. "I stole a hack and rode it all the way from Marlin. And my damn body won't make any milk for her. She's so hungry, Ellie." I stroked the hair back from Lou's temple, but a clump of it came away in my hand.

Pulling the babe into my arms, I whispered, "I'll take it to the house. Arakka, please can you lift my sister and bring her?"

Evie was assigning chores to the little ones in preparation for our supper. Arakka unrolled a pad and lay Lou near the kitchen fire, for she was trembling with cold even in this summer's heat. He made her a tea of cocklebur to warm her gut, and at last we covered her sad, bony frame and let her fall into a dark heavy sleep.

When all had eaten, we settled the children into little blanket forts they had built for the evening sleep. Evie and I sang songs to lay them back, *Tramp* and *Johnny Marching*, soft tunes in minor notes over the evening hush.

Much later, in deeper darkness and without a lantern, Arakka took his quiver and crept into the woods near the Sugarloaf Hill to find meat for our next day.

I set myself on the stoop with the poor babe, and this time it woke, grinding out starving shrieks that were sure to cut open the stars. She had lived but a few weeks, and with no sweet cow's milk to give her, I crumbled pemmican charky into water and let her suck the savory goodness from my fingers. She had no muscles nor fat to her, just a little sack of fading life. Who knows what pain that babe felt in her abused bones? I rocked and swayed this no-name child, guessing she might have a few days of life left in her. And may I be forgiven this, but in that moonless night, I wondered if it might be simple kindness to extinguish her life there and then, and allow her spirit to lift away to paradise.

The next day we helped Lou to sleep and sup, one of us in vigil beside her in the kitchen through the day's light. I took the children down to the stream where twenty years before I had discovered wild victuals, and I saw that even the clean rows of our old farm could not stop those fruits and tubers from returning. We brought sacks and baskets-full back to the porch to clean, and cook or dry to deliver to our bellies in faraway seasons.

At dusk, I took the babe to sit on the steps again, this time with a thick broth boiled down from wild turkey and sweet potatoes. A silent one she was, except for hunger, I had never known such a child. Focusing on her feeding, I did not hear my sister padding behind me, but when she sat so close, her shoulders touching mine, she breached the watermark of my love and I began to weep and smile.

"Viola," she whispered, and put her hand to the babe.

"Whose child is this?" I asked.

"Levi's."

"Well, who's the mother?"

She shook her head. "I am her mother, Ellie. And this Viola is my child."

"But she is not your color."

"Ellie, you are not my color, but I never said you weren't my sister."

I nodded as though I understood any of it.

"We're all a mix in these lands, sister. All your life you thought it was just you, but the blood of every one of us has secrets. Even Levi's. Even mine."

"And Levi is dead now?"

"I told you that," she whispered. "I shot him when he tried to kill the babe." She shook with righteousness, vault of bones that she was. "He could not love her. Look at her! He would not. I swaddled her and tried to rub her little head with ochre to cover her color, but he came after Viola and me. Ellie, he never loved the babe, nor me, nor anyone."

I only half-remembered the face of that devil who brought such a lifetime of pain to my sister. I took her hand and squeezed it, like long ago on the exotic soft beach of the Matagorda Bay.

"Pray for us," she urged, "pray, Ellie. Pray for the babe and myself. Baylis folk are gathering to come after me."

We fell to sleep with our arms about each other, and in the morning the sunlight broke over us through the heavy pecan foliage. I scrambled to my feet at the sound of my children inside the house.

"The pecans need pollarding if we're going to save them," I said to my sister, but she was still in sleep. "Nut yield this year will be small with all that wildness about."

Evie had roasted us wild potatoes and onions, and we sat on the floor planks reaching to them with our hands.

"A table is called for," Arakka said. "And stools for each of us. I'll work on that today. What about the rest of you?" He leaned back against the cobwebbed corner waiting for us to answer. There we were, sitting on the floor for our morning meal, been raided of doors and beds and chairs, of curtains and pots and spoons, of stock beeves and every bright thing we had brought to this Bluebonnet Ridge, and this boy I had loved as kin for near twenty years, just like that, became the obstinate fortitude for our family.

"Hoeing and planting," I said and smiled at the others. "And all you children will help me. We have got to get our seed in quick."

Poor little Viola murmured on the porch, and Lucy leapt up to attend. She brought the babe to us and said, "Child is hungry, Mama. What we got for her?"

I looked about the kitchen. "Can't give her onions. And she has no teeth. Try crushing the charky in broth and water and let her suck it from your finger nubs. Somehow we must acquire a goat or a cow."

Arakka took his knife from a rollpack and with the rounded handle began pummeling a pemmican bar. Lucy fetched water and stirred a few drops with the powder in the palm of her hand. We moved into a tight round, holding the babe at the center while Lucy let her suck the goodness from her fingers.

"Maybe she is cold, Mama," our Stella whispered. "Like Auntie Lou."

I shook my head, but Stella had already run for her bedroll. She spread it beside us like a skilled fiddler, smoothing the creases and squaring the corners with precision.

"Put the baby here and I will swaddle her," she said. The size of the cloth overwhelmed that scrawny child but Stella persisted until Viola was tucked neatly away. "See, she stopped worrying now."

"How did Aunt Lou get a dark-colored baby anyway?" Evie asked.

"This is your cousin. Aunt Lou's daughter," I replied.

"But she is the wrong color child," said Evie.

"There is no wrong color," Stella said, glancing at Benjamin.

"You're too little to know about such things." Evie picked up the breakfast roll and took it outside for washing, wobbling like a haughty madwoman between the dark trees of morning.

We planted our rows that day, kneeling elbow to elbow while Arakka brought the old well to life. In the orangey sun of dusk, we poured buckets of cool water across our new-seeded ground, believing that victuals would rise for us and that we had begun our farm anew.

In the early evening, as the children sat on their raw sapwood stools chattering about dreams of their old home, I went to the baby Viola to give the feeding. I hunkered on a stool and lifted her to my chest, pulling her to my own warmth, staring at those tiny black eyes while she sucked the broth from my fingers.

Every night I lay alongside my sister, taking her hand and closing my eyes. My sleep was deep and kind, for when I stretched my old muscles out on the bedroll, I knew my frightened thoughts would disappear. That was the sweetest time for me, not with my children or the rich earth at Bluebonnet Ridge, nor even with my memories of the years with Micah, but with my eyes shut as I sailed into a place of sleep and peace.

Come each morn, I stretched before the light to stoke the fire and wake the children, because try with the strongest hope I had, nothing could stop the new day's dawn.

CHAPTER 41

*A*rakka and Benjamin rode out each week, bringing us home deer or bear, as well as all kinds of birds abounding among the trees. By the weeks we grew in health and strength, all save my Lou, who lay upon her bedroll through the days and nights, barely able to take the porch steps without a stumble. By the last suns of the summer, her flesh began to swell with dropsy so that when I put a finger to her over-soft skin, a pock was left, little caves telling a trail of how she had been touched that day.

Some days she seemed fish-cold and nearly blind as she lay beside me. The children urged to send for the doctor at Nashville, but the surgeon I could trust with the truth of my sister and her babe, old Doc Leahy, had not survived Elmira Prison and only a midwife remained for nursing needs in the whole of our Milam County.

Day upon day we cleaned and repaired the house until it glossed like a pearl, and each night I held a bowl of soup for Lou, feeding her so that she might live another day, and telling her stories of the years we spent apart.

But her deepest medical truth was this: she had lost the

reckoning of why she remained on this Earth. For me, it was my children and the Bluebonnet Ridge, and the dream of Micah safe somewhere, that kept my heart throbbing as I lay in the dark. But Lou feared her babe was dying, and she had lost her hearth, her husband, everything that pushes the will forward across the damned frontier.

One night as I slept in my sweet peace, I heard a pair of doves calling to each other. I woke with my head swimming at this sound for doves never called till the dawn. I turned to see Lou's dark outline against the moonlight through the window. Her lips shone silver as they moved in those dovecalls. Just as suddenly, she chanted a long tale of cruelty, gnawing out of her like curses for bread, names I had not heard, till the veil of her dreamlife was rent open.

"Lou!" I whispered. "Lou! What are you saying?"

Her lovely blonde hair had nearly all fallen out by then, and she shook her skull from side to side. In the deep voice of a cunning hunter, she began anew. "We were troubled at noon. I prayed to the light I saw through them branches. I prayed. The cockles were cold, laying in river dung."

"Lou, please stop. I don't understand."

She turned her face to me, her eyes bitter. "They can never break the bond of sisters," she said firmly.

By dawn, my Lou had expired her hard life, and we buried her that day in the old Bluebonnet Ridge graveyard, with Three-Legged Willie and the others. I lay a cluster of wild roses on my sister's chest, young sprigs of pink, and green petals soaked clean through with light. That evening I took a tallow lantern and ventured alone down to the river, on a track through the cornrows where a bird glinting like flint wheeled above me.

The creeks have never been far, whether we were milling the Colorado or the Brazos. The sound of the water always brought me peace, escaping one life for another. Back when I was a girl, I belonged to those who were not my kin because crooked judges said my mother's blood was the wrong color.

When Micah and I had moved up on the Bluebonnet Ridge, it was my husband who brought me that peace, a life I would not likely have again. I lay back on the warm soft riverbank, clutching my rifle to me like a babe, and I fell quick to sleep in a dream of Micah, his eyes turned to ash.

Sometime before next light, the spoonbills started in to quacking and those ducks to whistling across the stream. I knelt beside the lapping water, drinking it fast till it spilled down my dress, drinking until my stomach would hold no more. I started the path back to the Bluebonnet Ridge, where thorny moss and verbena had grown over the trail. Where neither leaf nor acorn lay, the muddy way was slick and shiny like the back of a water rat.

My passage was tedious and strange on my own land, and so I scarcely heard the other's steps before me until I joined the wagon road to the corral and saw the man leaning on an oak trunk in the shadows, staring at my home. I lifted my Henry to my shoulder and took a step nearer.

A small fellow with a broad hat, he held his rifle and crouched behind a low-slung branch. By the time I halted, he had heard me crackling through the twigs and husks. He turned, and with gun raised and pointing straight for my heart, this man, this Frederick Braun, opened both eyes wide.

"Why Missus Moore, word in Cameron was you had gone abroad."

Without quaver in my voice, I stood strong in my dark culvert and stared at him. "Why are you on my land today?"

He moistened his dark pink lips and allowed a slow smirk to spread across them. "I will speak with your husband, girl."

"Mister Moore is on a hunt. What are you doing here?"

"Hunting with the Union, you mean? Killing our rebel boys and honest families has been his evil work these years past."

"There are no more rebs or bluecoats. The United States beat those who tried to tear this country apart, and now the fighting is finished."

Braun shifted forward, planting his feet square, still with scattergun raised. Without speaking again, he trained the barrel on me. "Nothing is finished. Plenty of us are still fighting for freedom. General Lee may have given up but the rest of us haven't. Your people will be back where they belong soon enough."

"Get away now!" I shouted, my voice fluttering with fright. "This is my Bluebonnet Ridge and you are not welcome."

"I am afraid, Missus Moore, that my current situation requires me to be here." He dipped his head slightly forward to admonish me with a round badge pinned to his hat. "In this state of Texas, murder is still a crime. I been hired by the Falls County Sheriff to avenge the death of a sad man, a true patriot, who was murdered by his adulteress wife. I am seeking that murderess, and I believe she may be hiding here at the Bluebonnet Ridge."

A bird in my gut began beating its wings furiously, while the bitter taste in my throat dried to dust.

Braun continued. "I think you know that murderess is your sister. The family of her poor, dead husband is appealing to the sheriff to bring her to justice."

The whistlers flew over us, making their maimed music, and I prayed to all the blight and hunger that had surrounded us these years past, to the laboring creatures and their ruler god, begging for mercy.

"Get off my land," I repeated, and motioned with my rifle for him to leave.

Braun frowned slightly. "Now, girl, this is not the way to do things." I saw his shoulders relax into a thought of some new connivance. "I do my duty here, that's all." He lowered the gun an inch and I could see his whole face squint. "I come for your whore sister and her bastard nigra child."

Quick I had been my whole life to know my place, a biddable girl following the law or running from it. I held his haughty gaze for only a second more until my fury and the justice I sought for my sister bellowed up inside me.

I fired at his chest and my body pitched back while the man slumped to earth, his gun falling from his hands. I walked over and took his weapon. Circling round him, I poked the flesh from every angle with the toe of my boot, until I was certain the mud of his life had drained away.

A clean breeze blew off the river and looking up I saw my distant family scatter into the corral, seeking the source of the single gun strike. With a pleasure that shames me unto this very day, I lifted my rifle again and for good measure shot one more hole through the head of this Braun.

I leaned over to see him true, his wide-eye scaredy-crow face. In his pockets I found a broadsheet with a drawing of my sister and a bounty announcement of $100 promised to the man who returned her to Falls County. I grabbed Braun's hat and pulled the badge from it, only to find it wasn't what he had claimed. He was no lawman, and the circle of tin pinned to the felt of the beaver was carved with the cross and star of the Knights of the Golden Circle.

I held it in the palm of my hand until I could stare no more. Slipping it in my pocket, I pulled his belongings from the saddle bags, bullets and a Colt, three hook knives, a handkerchief with a tiny garland of red geraniums needled across it, a small flask of whiskey, a pair of rusted iron shackles, and nothing more to witness his life. I pulled these items together, rested a rifle on each shoulder, and headed down the ridge to home.

Stella and Benjamin fell upon me before the others, clamoring for tidings of the gunshots.

"I killed a trespasser," I replied. "One who tried to kill me. Just a man come to raid what's left of our home. If your father were here he would have done the same because we all must work to protect the Bluebonnet Ridge now."

Before the workaday began, Arakka and I packed Frederick Braun upon his horse and rode him out to the edges of our land, where we buried him under a ravaged landscape of gopher holes, deep beneath the underground city of vermin. Arakka took the man's horse down the Little River over to Bell County, removed all evidence of Braun's ownership, and set it free near the Kioway camp, while the children and I did our planting and hoeing chores for the day.

One week on, our county sheriff appeared at our corral with a man he called Ezra Baylis. They came through the southern riding of our land, where Arakka spotted them along the creek. By the time they hitched their mounts, my boy was standing on the porch, rifle beside him.

"We are seeking a woman accused of killing in Marlin," the sheriff said.

Arakka crossed his arms over his chest. "Who is that?"

"Your mother's sister, Louisiana Baylis. She is called to trial in Marlin, and I have been sent to bring her."

I stepped through the door and stood on the porch beside Arakka. Before I spoke, he put his arm out to stay me.

"She was here," Arakka said. "But only lived a few days before she died. You are too late to take her. Follow and I'll show you where she is buried." Descending the steps, he motioned to the men. Rounding the house through the swaddles of weeds covering the graveyard path, he strode out to the pecan tree where Micah had begun to bury our dead so long ago.

We stood at the edge, and I pointed to the new-dug mound. "She came to me for succor and died in my arms," I said, my voice deep and loud.

Ezra Baylis ignored me. "How do I know she's under there? Need to dig it up and make sure."

"Not ever," I said. "You may not disturb her soul."

Arakka stepped in front of me, his voice calm. "This is a graveyard for our farm's dead. No one may dig these."

"I understand, son," the sheriff said. "But the Baylis family won't leave it be. They demand the woman, alive or dead."

"Before trial and judgment?" my son asked.

"Yes," said Ezra Baylis, lurching forward. "My brother got no trial or judgment 'fore she shot him." Baylis came within inches of Arakka, who remained still, straight-backed, and wordless. Had my child been a stranger to me, I would have missed his intention, a small side-shift of his lips, his curled fingers loosening slightly across his gun belt; I saw that this boy of mine was mere seconds from striking.

Folding my hands quick together, so tight and hard that our visitors looked from Arakka to me, I said, "Come then, gentlemen," and pointed at my sister's grave. "Satisfy your grudge against Louisiana Baylis with one last desecration." My voice was hoarse and my throat dry, but I turned to Arakka and said, "Find them digging tools. And tell the children to stay away. I'll wait here."

Ezra Baylis crossed in front of me, smelling of stale smoke and rotten meat, and strode to Lou's new mound. He knelt on a single knee and spat alongside my sister.

"Mean you no harm, ma'am," said the sheriff.

"We are Milam farmers, sir, and this man is from Falls County. You are obligated by nothing, but come, make short work and then pray for salvation as I suspect you will find yourselves in burning hell one day."

They brought their horses into the graveyard and flung their jackets in the dry soil. They removed their holsters but carried them in looped leather pockets onto the gravesite, setting them nearby as they took to hand the pick and shovel Arakka had brought.

I waited through those hours without offering water, watching them shift soil, holding Arakka's hand tight. I gulped at the dust of Lou's grave, trying to wean from the memory of her sickly skin. In the end, and girded with the sound of the shovel as the two men descended into my sister's hole, I leaned on the butt of my rifle, embracing the root and rock, the plow marks of hate on my body, and waited for the knock of iron to pine that would signal her coffin.

And when it came, I shouldered what my father would have called manhood, the prying open of the nails, my dead sister with glistening eyes in a dull-brown shroud; I stood it all and took a last long look at her reddened skin and sudden bloated belly, and sucked the smells of her death as though I was inhaling the water of violets. Love does not stop at death, then; it is protected and petrified, and stored to rise again.

"Your brother's wife?" the sheriff asked, and the other nodded.

"I'm sorry, ma'am," he said.

I glanced at him without answer. We had been released from his crime because my sister no longer wept.

"Here, Baylis, hammer the casket up again and shovel the dirt in."

They filled more quickly than they had dug, and said little until strapping on their Paso loops and guns.

Baylis lifted himself into the saddle. "I'll take the hundred dollars and be on my way."

The Milam man looked up slowly and pulled his revolver from its holster. "You'll be on your way without the money. You want a reward, you take it up with your own sheriff. Now, go on home. You been in my county too long."

Baylis opened his mouth to speak, but Arakka lifted his own rifle high and aimed it. "Leave our land," he said, and Baylis, looking at each one of us, pulled the reins out and moved off.

CHAPTER 42

*B*efore the war, we had gotten our tidings from broadsheets fed by telegraph wires, but once the Blues downed Vicksburg, most of our lines rotted in the ground. After the war we had given up on getting quick tidings from far away and kept watch for simple mail carriers to come riding across the county. Many brought broadsheets to us, often months past their printing dates.

One of them came riding hard to our tether post in September, waving a copy of the New Orleans *Picayune* from June, telling us the last battle of the war had finally been fought in Texas. And when Major Granger arrived in Galveston on June 19, 1865, proclaiming again that all slaves were free to leave or work for pay, we in Milam County did not hear until far into August and even then stacks of the news sheets were set afire by vigilantes.

The first overland carriers hired on to deliver the mail packets were old men who had been left behind when the others went off to fight, lonely ones who had lost their kin or been starved of grandchildren. Chop Coggins was such a man, alone but for his postal customers and any kindness we might offer.

Every week he fetched letters from Waco, rode down the river delivering to the towns and farms, and picked up more packets at Marlin, where he forded the Brazos near the falls and headed south to Milam County.

His day to pass the Bluebonnet Ridge was a Thursday, but when the river was on a rise that winter and he could not swim his horse across, he was often a day or two late. Down in January when the rains brought our Brazos to the floodbrim, we heard the bad news that old Chop had been seen to slip with the powerful current and plunge over the falls into the angry river below. Folks went out to rescue him but did not find a trace. A neighbor delivered us the story of his demise, but the very next day Chop Coggins came trotting up our path to the house, shouting his story with prideful joy. He had taken his horse and the mail to float down past the bend and had climbed out the west side of the river.

"Took a day or two to dry the letters," he said, climbing our porch stairs, "but now I be here, and present you with your packet. Still naught from Mister Moore though. I predict he be riding home to you as we speak!"

"I sure hope so, Chop. Never had news this whole war."

"He was fighting behind cover, I expect, ma'am."

"Well, come and have a grog." I pointed to the new chairs that Arakka had fashioned for us. "My son just built these out of green cedar, but they'll age and season soon. You'll appreciate their comfort."

Grabbing his hat from his balding scalp, Chop gave me a quick nod and followed through the door. He shut his eyes tight and nestled about in the chair.

"A fine job," he said. "I apologize, but I'm a little lightheaded from the last ride. Any water?"

I called to Evie, who brought a pitcher and cup for our dear hellion rider.

"I thank you," he said, and Evie returned to the kitchen where

Viola lay in her new rocker crib. Arakka sat in a chair alongside the fire, pushing the cradle to and fro to soothe the babe, and Evie worked around him, preparing a dinner bird for roasting.

"Your daughter's child?" Chop inquired.

I stared at him, disturbed that a person would think my daughter grown enough to have her own babes. "Why no, that is my sister's babe. She died shortly after the birth."

Chop nodded, lit up his pipe, while the babe's gravelling cries overtook us. Arakka lifted the child in his arms and spoke deep and soft to it. In doing so, the swaddling fell away from Viola's sweet dark face and shoulders.

Chop Coggins turned to stare at me. "This is your sister's child, my dear? Of that color?" He planted that question like a standard before me, a kindly man nonetheless ousting the story of my family. Our neighbors would surely burn this tiding across the county once Chop delivered it, and I thought about silencing the truth there and then. I could concoct a tale of the babe being abandoned near us, or a departing slave entrusting me with her; so many simple lies could explain away this child's color and shield my children until their graves.

Chop turned from the child to me, waiting still for my answer. I had been running from my mother's blood for most of my forty years, and in that bloated moment I decided this: *If I am to live out my time without my husband, I will at least live my truth.*

"Yes, my sister's babe," I said. "A delicate child, but so pretty."

Chop nodded his thoughtful lonely face. "I heard of them stories. Heck, we all mixin' together in this state. I don't give a dibble shite. You should see some of the folks I run into on this route." He coughed aloud from his tobacco piping. "Would you mind if I held her? I always had a soft spot for babes."

Arakka brought the child to the man. He held her like a seasoned one, but Arakka did not leave his side, watching every touch Chop made.

"You Moses?" he asked my son. "I heard a' you down the river."

"That is his name," I replied. "But the Comanches called him Arakka more years than we called him Moses, so the Comanche name just stuck."

Chop rocked the child and nodded to me. Suddenly, he looked to the floorboards and muttered, "You done some good things in your life, Eliza Moore."

Arakka took a step towards me and laid a tentative hand on my arm, stripping us both naked of all these years and memories, right down to the very day our lives first collided.

"I'll tell ya this though, ma'am," Chop continued, "best be cunning. Be careful who ya tell her story to. There's men about McLennan County, Falls and Milam too, who ain't give up yet."

Chop Coggins began courting us on his trips down the river. This garrulous kindly old man would hitch in just before suppertime on Thursdays, take a meal with us and stop the night, telling tales and bringing gifts of crab apples or fire matches, a tool for Arakka or a spinning bobbin top for Stella and Benjamin. He was on the trail to the next farm before the first light of Friday, slipping silently out the back door like a preacher for his mission.

Truth was, Chop Coggins had once been a circuit pastor down in Matagorda for the old Mother Church on the bay. Accustomed as he was to sermonizing in his distant life, he took to saying our blessings before meals, but he showed the soul of a joyous old gentleman who did not shrink from work, neither from babe-caring nor from post-pounding.

With Chop's occasional help, Arakka rode out each morning in search of wild beeves to populate our herd. Beef was aplenty, and we built a small congress of longhorns quickly, as so many had been left to wander during the war. We even acquired a couple gentle milk cows that I kept in the old barn where the children played. It was to Benjamin and Stella to bring the milk each morning, and those two little conspirators did so with the regularity of a well-trained militia.

By March the rains had turned away and came then warm days of early spring picking. Our victuals failed the harvest, and some that we plucked even squeezed to slime in our hands. We had little to barter and we desperately needed flour and seed for the next planting, cloth and fresh blankets, and tools for the farm. We had meat, but no bread; we had timber, but Arakka could not prepare it for trade alone; some wild fruits remained, but no legumes.

Against scurvy, I checked the children's gums and skin every day for crusts or bleeding. Of the day's necessities, we lacked a few, but I seldom gave voice to these worries. I should have sensed Arakka's contemplation, yet when he approached me one morning with his conclusion, I was utterly empty of response.

My futile chore that day was mixing our earth with rich manure for seeds we did not possess. I knelt among the rows I had hoed with my hands for lack of the tool, grinding through the dirt with an old axe handle. I wore the broad straw toiling bonnet from my mother. I had carried it with me for years and though I no longer believed in its luck, I used it all the same.

"We could do this work better with tools." Arakka squatted alongside me, supple of limb like his Comanche family. "What seeds will you sow, Eliza?"

"I scavenged a few from the wild onions and yams."

"We need corn and squashes too. Stringers and collards."

"Need? What we need is to stay alive. We will accomplish that."

He had taken his favorite blade from its sheath at his waist and held it in his hands. This Bowie knife, his most prized object, glowed of over-polished steel in the rising sun. His was one of the first made in Gonzalez by Mister John Sowell himself, not long after James Bowie acquired the original. Normally a stranger to irony, Arakka's pleasure at owning the knife of a Comanche killer, made by a gunsmith who despised his Indian family, had caused him to carry it and care for it with gentle reverence for many years.

"You been shining that thing? Not enough real work to do then?"

He smiled slowly and looked straight at me. "Going to sell it. No use for it these days."

"Oh, my boy," I whispered. "You don't need to do that."

"Going over to Nashville today, Eliza. I hear a new monger set up a blackie shop there. See what I can get for it. May not even be worth a Confederate note, in which event, I will return by supper. If I get a goodly price, I will stock provisions for us. Seed and tools. Maybe a sack of flour so Evie'll make a pie for us all." He grinned at me.

What could be said? He had been a willful boy all the years I knew him, and oft spoke the stubborn truth.

Sad as I was to see Arakka attempt the sacrifice, I was doubly pleased when he returned the following afternoon in a rented buckboard laden with purchases from Nashville. The children and I crowded him, except for Evie who oddly hung back on the porch watching us.

"You're like a Magi at the holy baby's birth!" shouted Lucy. "Let's see those precious gifts."

He handed my girl a sack of sugar wafers. "This is candy they eat in New York," he said. "Be sure to share that with the others, Lucy." She called Benjamin and Stella to her side and counted them out equally as though they were Indian pennies.

Arakka climbed into the box of the buckboard and handed me down its contents. Two large sacks of flour, seeds for planting, nippers and a hatchet, a tiny pair of shoes for Viola who had just begun to walk, and a bolt of the most beautiful periwinkle colored cotton I had ever seen. I called out to Evie for help, but she had slipped inside the house without a word.

"I will fetch her," Arakka said. "I have a pie plate for her bakery."

But fetch he did not, and when finally he emerged from the cabin, he called out to me for help.

"The baby is not well!" he shouted, and I emptied my hands to run to him.

Viola lay in her trundle bed, trembling with fever, her scrawny arms waving with her cries, her little face hot as a heated brick.

"I instructed Evie to make bone soup for the bath," Arakka said.

"Son, this child could pass quickly. What medicine is bone soup?"

"Boiled beef bones, cooled and strained. This will give the babe strength and break her fever."

"Or we could send you to Cameron for the new doc. Boiled bones may not be enough now."

"You forget, Eliza, I was married before to a Comanche girl. We had a babe. My father was chief of peace and knew healing. If Viola is not to die, we need to pull the sickness from her."

We soaked her in the foul-smelling bone soup, and swaddled fresh linen around her for the night. Arakka and Evie split their hours watching the child sleep, sharing the cold comforts of the deep night.

On the next morn, as suddenly as the fever had gripped Viola, so it left her, and left behind an appetite unusual to this babe. Stella and Benjamin brought the milk pail from the barn cows, and then another as our little girl sucked and burbled all the way into the dawn.

Whether it had been the beef bones or the natural course of the sickness, the babe grew more precious to me in that saving. Some fevered part of the soul's nature it is when a person saved carries more currency than one without need.

CHAPTER 43

One Tuesday at the turn of April, I woke to a fog thick across the Bluebonnet Ridge, crouching low into our corral and pastures. The air was warm when I poked my head out my bedroom window, and beyond in the meadow and our rows there were great numbers of tiny birds, red at their crests.

By the time I scurried down to the kitchen and stoked the fire up, the sun shone out over our pecan trees, touching my cheeks with daps of spring heat. I was at the well, watching this glorious day unfold, when Chop Coggins came slowly down the path to the house.

"Why Chop, didn't expect you. You're days early, my friend. All fine with you?"

He did not reply till he had wrapped the reins round our hitch and plumped to the ground from his mount.

"I come here today begging, Missus Moore." He grabbed his hat and held it limp at his side, shaking his head sadly. "I come begging. I'm sorry, ma'am. I got nothing and nobody else for hope."

He carried my bucket to the kitchen and filled the new iron boiler pot.

"Now Chop, take your seat and tell me," I said, but no sooner than my words were out, my children came rushing to the table. He shook his head again.

"My tale will wait, ma'am."

The children greeted Chop with hugs. They brought the milk and piled our table with Evie's preparations. Cold beef from the larder, biscuits with honey, and a plate of yams. The butter was thick and sweet, and Arakka had even brought a small amount of precious powdered coffee back with him from Nashville. All sat round but my boy who grinned at our family and left through the back door, returning shortly carrying a plate of roasted acorns.

"What you got there, boy?" Evie asked him, sounding so like myself that I turned to stare at her. She had raised her brows and crossed her arms over her chest, with a smile that bounced around the room like sunlight.

"Nothing you ever had before, girl," Arakka replied. "Tender roast oak apples. We'll cut down the mid and spoon butter in. Better than the yams."

We ate such a fine meal that morning, laughing at stories like old about Micah and Teddy Blue, Three-Legged Willie and Absalom, family that came and went but left their love behind for us. At last cleared of my rabble of children and farmhands, I turned to Chop Coggins.

"What is your story then, Chop? Has someone harmed you?"

"No, ma'am. But I am skinned now without a job. When I got to Waco this week, they gave my route to a man back from Elmira Prison. They said he needed it more'n me, and he could ride faster and hand out more packets in a week."

"That's wrong-headed, Chop. You did a good job and you do have stamina."

We heard our beasts in the paddock heaving across the clay of cow dung as Arakka drove them to the far meadow for morning feed. Chop did not lift his head at the noise, and his shoulders were sagged with the calm of the helpless.

"I have nothing now. Been renting a room in town but got no money this week. I tried for a job at Bartlett's store in Marlin, tried the Westbrook lands over at Lorena, Tomlinson's holdings, and Port Sullivan too. Can't even get a place preaching anymore. Nobody is hiring the older folk. Without family to keep us, we just been thrown away."

"Where is your birth family, Chop? You ever been married?"

"I got one boy who went off to the Sandwiches years back. Don't know his outcome. My wife died of yellow jack in the last season of the pestilence." He lifted his old head, his hair shot through with smokers of grey, and looked straight to me. "I never killed a man, never stolen so much as a apple. I'm just old, but that is a crime to most now, even family." He rubbed his eyes till his lids turned red, such an ordinary face with frontier skin the texture of porridge. His voice was rough as a brush from years of pipe tobacco, but he got the words out quick. "I'm begging, Eliza. You got any work for me?"

"You aren't needing to beg, Chop. We love you here at the Bluebonnet Ridge. And you are a good worker. You are part of this scraggly family. I can't right the wrongs done to you, but you got a position here. I'm not clear on your sleeping place yet, but we'll sort you one."

"Don't need much. Just food and a bedroll. Heck, I got the bedroll myself."

By late April of 1866, the first beef trains after the war set off, and we made sure our Bluebonnet Ridge longhorns were among them. The economics were clear: a wild beef left to rutting during the war could be bought for two dollars now or caught wild on the prairie for just the cost of catching. The stockyard men paid twenty or more on delivery at the Kansas grasslands station, and driving the animals only as far as Waco would still bring five dollars apiece.

Chop and Arakka put together a herd that could be taken up the Texas road and sold to the trail boss on the Brazos where the droving trail crossed. First time out, they brought back one hundred dollars, both of my men laughing and dancing like young fools with their treasure.

"This can be our trade," Arakka said. "We will work this for two years and become rich." His eyes were gleaming with such a call of money that I hardly knew him.

"There is nothing better than living off your own land, boy," I said, and frowned as he dug into the pork pullins that Evie and I had been slow cooking all day. "I'm not opposed to getting the Bluebonnet Ridge back to its former state with this enterprise, but don't be looking for riches. We're building a family here, the way your father would've done if he'd survived the war."

Suddenly, Lucy stood from the table. "Father's coming home. Don't you be saying anything else," and she ran outside to the porch steps where she stayed that long plum-dusk eve.

Late in that night when the children were bedded and Chop sat out on the porch smoking, Arakka came to sit by me as I finished my kitchen tasks for morning.

"Going to seed in those potatoes tomorrow," I said. "It was thoughtful of you to bring me the eye pieces from Nashville, son."

He twirled a stone between his fingers, one he had polished to glowing green, but he didn't speak.

I handed him a plate of raw yams and my sharpest knife.

"Here, help me with these." I took another knife and we set to peeling the skins away. I handed him water in a big red clay mug. He bent his forehead down toward the chore. The plop of the naked yams into a bowl of water broke our silence now and then, soft little splashes that made us look at each other, our deft knives bringing us closer than words ever did.

At last, when no more tubers lay waiting, he spoke. "I am not a greedy man, Eliza."

"I know that."

"What I meant about beef trains is I can catch and herd animals, sell at Waco until I save enough."

"Sounds a good plan."

"Not rich, but enough."

"So, you are wanting your own ranch?"

"No."

"What is your aspiration then, boy?"

I never saw him thus inadequate in all our years. This stubborn angry child, this Odysseus in our escapes from harm, sat before me now with his hands trembling on the burl knots of the table he had built. He twined those tanned fingers together, worker hands grown to manhood.

"I've known you Moore family all my life."

"Known? You are my family. My first child."

"But not blood."

"That never mattered to me."

"I know."

"Explain yourself. You're hard as flint tonight."

"I am not your blood or your band. I can marry a girl of the Moore family, if you allow it."

I gulped without meaning to, and the poor boy flinched.

Sitting still as the horizon, he said at last, "I want to court Evie." In a corner of the room a light burned, and he turned to it, looking away from me. "I will not be a reckless husband, Eliza. I will not be cruel."

Conversing with Arakka was never easy, and he stopped suddenly, waiting for me to speak.

"What thoughts has my girl on this?"

An ox in the barn paddock made itself known to us, lurching against the old cowpoke bell.

Relieved at this interruption, Arakka scraped his stool back from the table.

"I will see to that beast." He grabbed his hat from the door and was gone.

I propped my elbows on the table and rested my head in my hands. Neither good nor evil was in this decision he had put in my lap but judging Evie's best life was no less weighty. Across this frontier neighbors were building back lives lost, yet I knew we awaited the next pile of tattered bodies in some damned new fight. A god's mockery was all we were ever given, to keep farming or fighting or moving.

Evie lugged a sack of warm fresh ash into the kitchen toward the back door. She glanced at me as though in wait for prey and in doing so toppled the sack across the floor. "Oh, Mama!" she exclaimed. "I'm sorry."

We knelt with damp rags and short-handled brooms, sweeping and wiping together like we had done, day following day, together for all her years. We heard Arakka lower the cattle gang plank in the barn, and I nodded at my girl. "You in this with him?"

"Yes, Mama."

"Well, tell me true. No answer is the right one except yours."

"I love him."

I shook my head and stared at the soft piles of ash left before us. The gold dawn over our fields would not lift off the dark plain for hours, yet I knew she desired my answer to her destiny now. Now! What a decision had been put on my shoulders!

Evie leaned back on her slender haunches and straightened her neck, watching beyond me to the open door where her gentleman stood, my adopted son. I held my hand out to her and nodded.

"Your father loved you both so. I know he would be joyful to hear of your news. I can only decide as I think he might have, and knowing we need to populate the Bluebonnet Ridge over again. You have tall virtues, children, but promise me you will invest them in each other."

And like in an ancient prayer, Arakka whispered, "Eliza, I will," as he stood beside my daughter.

"Of course, Mama," Evie said. "Now that our father is lost, this family will have Arakka to lead it. He's a kindly man and a good farmer." She turned her head back to him, and followed his gaze as he watched my own.

CHAPTER 44

$\mathcal{B}$y the light rains of June in the year 1867, the Bluebonnet Ridge had come fresh to life. Our rough war memories disappeared in the polishing and rebuilding of this farm, and this family, found along trails and patched together as we were, settled to chores and arguments like any kin. Arakka and Chop burnt off a few acres of cane and brush for the fall planting, and by July, that fine earth had brought bright young grasses dotted with vermillion flowers just like old sketches of Elysian fields I had seen in a book while a slave at Cairo.

Evie and Arakka began courting after supper most nights, sipping milky bedtime drinks on the porch as they planned a wedding and a life. And always settling himself between the two was Chop Coggins, rocking his evening with his pipe, blowing billows around them till the two lovers could scarcely see each other.

For me, the mornings were thinking time, drawing in my mind the compound of our Moore family akin to that of the Bartletts of Marlin, or lush Bereminda so many years past. Arakka built a new sleephouse for cowboys he planned to hire, and I thought of high hedges and flowers to surround us all, for

Arakka and Evie would one day give new children to the Bluebonnet Ridge and I dreamed of red roses and buttercups and violets to teach those unborn children their colors.

On a dusky evening in early August when the heat across the golden hills oxidized the horizon to purple, our family rested on the broad porch of our house with a cool drink of honey milk before the last chores of the day. In the deep shadows of the fields beyond our paddocks, two riders approached, outlined black and moving with a lazy rising trot toward us.

Arakka set his cup on the railing and lifted his Spencer Repeater to aim, but as the visitors pulled through the darkness into our lantern light, I made out the ghosty face of my husband, hair and beard grown to a scraggle, followed by Teddy Blue Corlies.

I leaped from the porch, across all three steps and ran the path to them.

Micah slipped from his mount, and stood before me, straight as a beam and smiling in the tallow light. "Well, Eliza," he whispered, and covered me in his body, opening his mouth wide and sinking his tongue deep in my throat.

I pushed him back finally and felt his arms and chest, the cloth hanging like drapes across his bony body. Two years after the end of war and with no letter for five years, no warning, he had made his way back.

Finally, he smiled and said, "I'm all here. Two arms and two legs. No great harm after our time in Confederate prison, but we both are hungry and weariful."

"Got any food for us, ma'am? Seems like we ain't eaten for a couple hundred miles." That old dear voice of Teddy Blue came from the weakly man cloaked by shadows behind Micah. "They sent us home, free but poor as Lazarus," Teddy said. I turned and gave him a kiss, clasping him to me. "Eliza," he said, with a chuckle, "be gentle."

Evie and I led them to the well where they might wash off the bloodshot wounds of their trails, and then inside the warm house to bring them supper from the larder. Sounds carry through walls of a house like the Bluebonnet Ridge, and soon the children were about, and Chop was among us.

Evie held Viola on her lap, and beside her sat Arakka.

"Who is this child?" Micah asked.

"Auntie Lou's girl, Father," said Lucy, her arms round Micah's neck so tight he had scarce ability to twitch a muscle. "Auntie went to the Lord but we saved her babe, didn't we, Vi?"

Micah held Stella close, and she, being a willful loyal child, took Benjamin's hand, and stared boldly at her father.

"I'm sorry to hear your sister passed, Eliza. My memories of her are kind." He pulled Stella closer to him, while Arakka lit the lamps, throwing a touch of light across Micah's gaunt jaws. He reached a hand to Viola, who stepped forward tentatively and offered hers. "Pleased to meet you, niece," he said.

Stella moved from her father to the far corner of the room and grabbed Ben's arm, pulling him toward Micah. "Pa," she said, waving her hand in a broad, formal gesture toward our Comanche boy, "this is Mister Benjamin. He's our new brother and we found him in jail."

Micah raised his brows to me, nodded, and offered his hand. "Pleased, boy."

"We have some new and we lost some old," I said, not taking my eyes from my husband as he looked round our family.

"I am Chop Coggins, sir. Helpin' on here recently. I can ride and read, and some other chores, and your wife kindly gave me a place on the ranch. But I can move on tomorrow if you prefer."

Micah shook the old man's hand. "Don't know you, Mister Coggins. If Missus Moore says you are welcome, then you are. One of our best pokes, Absalom, went on to Mexico, and I hear we lost my son, James, last year." Micah put his hand across mine.

"You know about James?" I asked.

"I do. I heard this morning in Cameron." Micah leaned across his bowl of beef stew, soaking a chunk of bread in it and then putting it to his lips. "Mister Coggins, we have plenty of room here for men worth our trust." And to me he whispered, "I've contemplated this first meal for years. With all my family 'round me."

"Much to tell you, husband, about our travels and losses."

"We have a lifetime for that, Eliza," he said. "And my story is simple. Teddy Blue and Absalom and me joined up the 7th Kansas Cavalry, ranging and fighting in Mississippi. Spent a year at Belle Isle Prison and then to Andersonville. Nothing else to tell tonight. This night I would like to eat and sleep and hold you all. Teddy and I been soaked in blood these last years. In leaf and bloom, we saw more than most. Battle meadows with men's innards hanging from the hawthorn, houses burned to the ground with families still inside. We spent these years keeping on the breathing side of angels, waiting to see you again. We're home tonight. That's all."

The next morning before the first grain of light slipped the cracks, I crept into the raw, cold dawn where the wind was blowing so strong I could not stick a fire to save myself. My efforts with matches and kindling coming to naught, I sat back on my stool to contemplate a day without heat yet with a husband.

I stood on our porch with my huge and useless grin, watching the gossamers of light shoot gold up the ridge of bluebonnets. And just as he had done a thousand morns before, Micah came behind and pushed his rough warm hands about my waist, holding me in and watching that same horizon.

"Bitter out here, Ellie," he whispered. His touch was sweet thunder and his voice tentative with the lost years between us. "We alone?"

I turned to face him and dropped my shoulders in bewilderment. "You're a vision of devilry, husband."

He laughed long at that, and soon the dogs set barking and I heard Chop's old wake-a-day cough from the back lean-to.

"Now, you did it, girl." Micah took my hand and led me into the kitchen. "Let's get the fire glowing before they all clamor down on us."

Come October, a few weeks before the wedding, I marched my men up the Indian Mound beyond the smoke house to examine a view of our ridge and valley, of our Little River fork, and the lone red hill beyond.

"Here, you see, is the better place for a new home," I said. They followed the wave of my hand obediently as I described what I desired. "The river will never rise this high, no matter the rains, and we can see from one home to another. We need more rooms now, but Arakka and Evie will want their privacy. Families ought to have their spaces but be close for aid. The trail between is here," I said, pointing to the natural fabric of orange nasturtium trumpets winding down the hill.

Teddy Blue looked to Micah for a clear eye, but my husband only shrugged.

"We just built a bunkhouse, Ellie," said Micah, "why do we need another new house?"

Unconcerned by his question, I took his hand and pulled him higher up the mound. "We will clear a kitchen garden for them here and build a little pen for the softy creatures who will be pets to their babes."

Arakka lagged back and watched me.

"Married in October," I said, "you will be having your first babe by next summer, I guarantee that."

"Girl, it won't be that way," Micah said.

"Course it will, Micah. They both are healthy and close in love." I laughed at his innocent thoughts and leaned my head against his shoulder. "Just like all our Moore tribe."

Teddy Blue shifted his weight from the butt of his Yellowboy, shaking dry earth from the muzzle. "Got posting to accomplish this morning," he said, ignoring me. "What other jobs, Micah?" Teddy was set to walk abroad without a word or nod for my planning, back to the day's work as though the shivaree for these two children would be a fairy tale.

We stood round the silence, tightened out like a drumhead.

"I want you to tell me," I began slowly, "what is wrong with you men. Am I the only one among us to understand the future needs of Evie and Arakka?" I started with a cajoling voice, yet still those three were dumb, hiding even in my sight. "Go pound your damned paddock poles into our land and ignore me today. But I tell you this, Micah, I am not a loon and we will build them a house here, and to hell with the bunch of you!"

I turned hard and shanked, raving down the path. At the bottom I forked off for the hackling barn and found Evie scutching at the flax with her sisters, and little Viola beside them playing in the dust. Sitting on my spinning stool, I let my anger shake over me, watching my hard-working girls from the shadows.

"What's the matter, Mama?" asked Lucy. "You're boiling over."

"I tell you ladies this. I am perturbed today."

"What'd we do?" asked Stella.

"Nothing, girl. It's the damn men this time."

"What'd *they* do?" she replied.

I shook my head, quieted only by my fury.

My corner was drawn in morning shadows, with the tart smell of the scattered linseeds pressing about. Within moments the heavy door opened, freshening the air and swinging light into the barn. There stood the boy, Arakka, peering into my dark corner.

"Eliza, will you walk with me?" he asked. "I gave you anger. I am sorry."

He offered a hand and I took it.

Immediately, Evie stood and said, "I'm coming too."

We three passed his damned big-eyed cattle, droning at the new day, on to the hay barn where he and Chop had stacked our fresh-split logs for winter. Sharp smells of spice rose from the dew-covered pile, but we kept on toward the river, stopping finally by the salley thicket. Arakka removed his jacket and spread it across the muddy bank for me and Evie.

"You are similar," he said, stopping a moment to watch his mother and his intended.

"It would be surprising if we weren't," I said. "Boy, be quick about your story." I grabbed a handful of moldy blooms and leaves from the weedy water at my feet and crushed them together in my fist.

"Evie and I did not tell you our plans. Now is the time."

I did not move, did not even acknowledge that he had spoken, so he gathered himself up and said, "After the wedding we will leave Bluebonnet Ridge. Rafael Bereminda built a new hacienda on the Monterrey plain. He wrote and offered me a position."

"Mexico?"

"I will be *caporal*. Absalom is there now. Evie and I leave the day after we wed."

I leaned back with a deadly smile while my gut hard-chucked side to side and the raggedy seams of my heart tore open.

"Mama?" Evie asked, bewildered.

"These are harmful plans, and I will not approve them," I said quietly.

"Bereminda has cattle and mules. Cane and corn. Evie and I, we talked about this long and deep." His blue eyes opened so wide with a youth I could only faintly remember, and in remembering, hated.

"We?" I shouted at them. "We? Who is this 'we' you say, and why did you cut me out of it?"

"Eliza, we did not. We love you."

Evie put her hand across her lips soon as she heard that word uttered again, her brow domed and afraid, but Arakka did not stop.

"We are not brave like you. To disappoint is not easy. But new Bereminda is safe and rich for us and one day for children."

"Children! I will never know these children of yours! Listen to me, I didn't scrap in the Palo Duro to bring us all home only to find you traveling out again. I gave you everything, girl. And you," I glared at the boy, "everything I had and it still isn't enough? Well, you have broken me. The two of you together, and all the others at this forsaken ridge who knew your secret and kept it from me. God damn your deeds to hell."

"I'm sorry, Mama," she said.

"Don't waste your sorry, girl. Do your job, love your family, and look for nothing in return. For nothing is what you'll get."

CHAPTER 45

*T*hose were silent days like I have never known, watching my traitorous family in shivaree preparations and lust for the vagabonding fortune of the young couple. I knelt the rows with neither hat nor water, nearly sunstruck with chores, and when a voice dared to corner me or offer shade, I staggered off, borne back to the mud banks to contemplate the deceit of families.

On her day, my girl wore an unhemmed white cotton gown, and the boy a simple white linen shirt. Chop Coggins said their oaths, and blessed their infernal 'we'. After, the guests stood outside their window, banging pots and spoons and singing vile and raucous words about rutting goats.

And I, well, I sat alone in my room, bowing in agony to the unspeakable moment when yet two more of my children would be gone from my care.

The morning of their leaving came like a warning from the belly of the dawn. I watched from my window as the boys loaded in the schooner with gifts, pots, blankets, and dried provisions, with anything that the Bluebonnet Ridge could bestow for their month of trailing down into Mexico. Micah hitched up their rides, and two mules more, while Teddy Blue handed over his new Yellowboy rifle in exchange for Arakka's old Henry.

After the packing, they all piled to table for full bellies and farewells, and I could hear their laughing echo up the stairwell, my little ones dreaming right beside the couple, about the joy of such an adventure away from their home. By the time Micah lifted the latch to our door, I was past sobbing.

He eased himself to the bed beside me. "Time for goodbye, girl."

"I hate this day."

"Make no error here, we both do hate it. But you are obliged to let her go. Let them both go free. Much as it is opposite of what you desire, we both still are obliged. We are just the watchers of our children. Got no law over them."

"Some do," I said sharply. "All families aren't like this one." We sat hip to hip and shoulder to shoulder for such a time, but I found no more strength in his touch than in a book of manners.

He turned to me and stretched his arms out. "I been quiet about my time gone north and east, Eliza. I know you wanted to hear, but the battles I saw were not for speaking, or remembering. And getting back to Bluebonnet Ridge, well, coming home was worth the fight of the journey." He put his hands under my sleep shift, and held my breasts, smaller now than in our youth, the skin looser. "These are warm," he whispered, and leaned to kiss them. "Better than I ever dreamed."

"We both killed to keep this place safe, Micah. For our family. It doesn't matter to you that we are losing two more of our children?"

"It matters. But they're fledged, and moving to their own lives. Don't make them leave without a word. Letters later won't patch it like giving your heart now."

He took my hand and we walked to our fine broad porch, washed and sturdy, waiting for this family that might never be whole again. The children were jumping in and out of the wagon, giggling and pretending to be hiding along for this overland heel.

"I am not so strong," I whispered to my husband.

"Course you are, Ellie. Course you are."

Just then Benjamin came dashing from the house with his hands folded in front of him carrying a parcel. He held it fast, even as he tumbled over the rocks and clods at the bottom of the steps.

Arakka handed the reins to Evie and slipped down from the bench. "What you got, Benjamin?"

My Comanche child handed the small gift to his older brother. Arakka, or Moses as he had been named so long ago, pulled the linen rags from around it, and found himself holding a thick chunk of cedar bark, planed and polished flat.

Lucy moved closer. "What is it?"

Arakka smiled slowly into the rising sun. "This is a drawing of Cloud."

"I made it," declared the child.

Arakka leaned down to the boy. "Thank you, Benjamin."

I took my hand from Micah's grasp. When I reached the wagon, my daughter tied off the reins and jumped down to meet me. We stood in the damp dog daisies, arms round the other in the deep shadows of the gable. I covered Evie's slender shoulders with my fingers and said what first entered my head.

"Be generous to the oldest folks you meet, and give rides to strangers, for you will learn some things." I slipped off my own mother's straw bonnet and handed it to her. She took it and held it across her belly like a warm soother. I looked both Evie and Arakka straight on and said, "I am on your side, you two. I will always be on your side. No matter what feels broken between us."

I put my arms about Evie's body, small and cold as a chisel, and cradled that child once more for my own pleasure. Turning to Arakka, I stretched up to kiss his cheek, and held his face in my hands. "You got the heart to travel out?"

"Yes, Eliza," said the boy.

"I do," Evie said. "I want to travel on."

"Then you remember how dearly I have loved you. And that I will forever."

They nodded, and our farmhands pounded the last nails into the provisions crate, so I held my tears and let my children go.

Arakka lifted Evie up on the bench, and pulled himself up after. She called out 'So long!' while he chucked the mules around. I nodded at that boy, quietly watching him leave again as he had done so many times.

I stumbled back to our porch and stood calf-deep in the old seeding parsley, lifting my trembling arm to wave them off to the fearful morning. Arakka drove the oxen up the ridge, while one bel hen waited beside me, clucking in a broody growl at my small elegy.

CHAPTER 46

*J*n the end days of 1869, a new industry cast out across these cotton lands, driven by planters who needed to gin their crops and send them to Galveston. Powerful men put money on the railways so farmers could move their cleaned cotton quicker, starting with the international line headed for Palestine and Christopher Hearne's old plantation, and with the Great Northern up from Houston.

I got the sense of this dark operation clear enough from the road boss, Andy Ward, no gentleman to be sure, who stood at the bottom of our porch in a rainstorm one January afternoon. The light from our day lanterns spread across his sodden shoes, while his wide-brimmed hat streamed a torrent over the limestone path at his feet.

"Mister Moore in?" The man removed his hat as he spoke and came up the steps, staring at me. His hair was short and bristly, forming a widow's peak on his forehead. He had small blue eyes, clear and squinting, and his cheeks were mottled with small pits.

"No," I replied, and swung the door wide for him to enter. "But he won't be long in this storm."

Ward shook the water from his hat and swept it off the

epaulets of his coat. He stomped hard at the threshold and dipped his head to me. "I'm Andrew Ward. Of Dewey & Ward. We're running the railroad work outta Hearne. Come to talk to Mister Moore about a lease of his little dock on the river."

"That dock was never finished," I replied, "but come and sit. We've got hot coffee and grog, and I'll send for my husband."

Ward followed me into our morning room aside the cookery, and took a chair, folding his hands on the tabletop. The hearth firelight behind us revealed a stitched wound, a crude jag across his forehead, so fresh as to still glow purple.

After a few moments and still no steaming coffee, I excused myself to fetch it, only to find Stella, shivering under the shelter of the back porch.

"What are you doing out here? Just standing there!" I said. "I need you to fetch Mister Ward hot coffee while he waits for Father."

"I heard bad stories at school about him and the railroad," Stella said.

"Girl, get on, will you? I don't need your theater, I need the coffee served."

She went swiftly and poured our drinks, serving bread and persimmon jam as well. She stayed beside me and watched him eat as we talked of the dark wet day, and listened to his fork clacking against his plate. Stella would not leave me with him, but busied herself with folding and stowing blankets, watching this fellow all the while until Micah and Teddy Blue came noisily to join us.

"Your household is a hospitable one, Mister Moore," the man said, nodding at Stella. "Good jam. I seen them persimmon trees down by the Little River."

Micah nodded. "I understand you have an interest in my dock. It's in disrepair, but wouldn't need much work to make it functionable."

Andy Ward nodded. "My men are capable. We have a need for

most of a year, and for your logs too. Oak trees are preferable, but if you can't spare them, we can settle for the yellow pines near the hill."

"What use do you have for the dock, Mister Ward?"

"We'll be shimmying them logs down to the fork of the Brazos. To our mill there."

"East then?"

"Yes, to the east."

"Because the river west and south will not accommodate shipments. Too many lografts."

"East. We're still building down from Hearne."

"Hearne," Micah muttered. "I heard about that new town on Ellen Hearne's land." He stood from his chair and shoved it to table. "Well, Mister Ward, I'm open to such a temporary contract. Teddy Blue Corlies here will fix the rate with you. But one thing. The news of your company arrived before you. I will stand no trouble on my land." He paused and took a shell from his belt, idly shaking it in the palm of his hand.

Andy Ward leaned back, taken by surprise. "What news?"

"Hearne and Hell, they say. Why, I was told when the sun rose after the last payday, your guards left four dead men on the street there."

We heard the pounding chords of Lucy's piano practice from a far room, and Andy Ward looked toward it.

"Your criminals are rough men," Micah added. "And the men who hold them are rougher. I want no trouble. Do the work and move along after your time."

"The convicts are driven by firm hands. That's all."

Stella opened her mouth to speak but stopped when I frowned at her.

"And we will make you rich, Mister Moore."

Micah shrugged and, his business finished, left the room abruptly.

~

Truth be told, two of our own pokes had already quit to join on as overseers with Ward, and in all, twenty Milam County men had become his field guards, commanding the hundreds of Huntsville prisoners who worked and slept on the plain, building the rail lines out to Palestine and then down to Bexar. Simple cowmen might become landowners within a few months if they were clever enough to save their pay, and farmers could make a fortune by selling logs or beeves to the operations.

Ward & Dewey's new convicts built a camp just south of the Little River at the upper metes of our land, and I often ventured alone up the woodland rise to Sugarloaf Hill to watch them.

Sitting atop it one early afternoon, with the horizon shimmering blue from our ridge and summer mice darting at my feet, I heard a warning voice come straight at me like a target from the old Tonkawa trail below. The voice followed the path, louder at times then silent near the working men, until at last I saw a woman chugging that ancient road, carrying a satchel and a bundle, standing and lurching, and being swallowed into the shadows of the woods.

As she persisted clear of the copse, she lifted her chin, pushed it forward and stamped on, deep in the tide of a hard dream. Across her back slung a single black pot, butting her with every step. She wore layers of long skirts and soiled blouses, and she carried her body like a musket. Her hair and neck were covered with a shawl that sheltered her face from the dazzle of the high sun.

What wretched tramper would cross our land in this way, so many years beyond the end of the war? Rarely did we entertain refugees now since the battle-crazed ones had all gone or died. The woman turned with the road round the base of Sugarloaf and paused in a field of prickly poppies to explore the horizon. I stood from the red stone to follow this figure in and out of the trees, and as we heard the far-off clang of the supper bell, she arched forward in her determined journey, while the shawl slipped from her head to reveal the ruddy face of my old friend, Cookie Mahoney, not seen on our land since before the war, her kind heart we had presumed long dead.

Quickly, I picked my way down the hill through the rocks and the mounds, scraped by thistles and the rough stems of berry plants, until I clattered onto the path and called to her.

"Cookie!" I shouted, and then, "Cookie Mahoney!" one more time for the sheer pleasure that name brought me.

Stirring about, she saw me run for her and when I caught her in my arms, she smiled. We stood wordlessly in the gama grass, my heart wrenching up the memories of the years since we left her alone to fend at Bluebonnet Ridge. Both of us were now just dark figures holding each other, suffering the long pain, the loss of pain, and the return of pain, of those years buried alive.

She coughed, putting her hand to her face, and I saw her fingers were covered with dried blood.

"Are you injured, my dear lost friend?"

She shook her head and said, "I'm lost no more, Eliza." She had no tears, and said this proudly.

As we approached the house, I heard the cattle clacking across the bridge of broken limestone; Cookie and I followed them in quiet. Our creek flowed deep beneath, shimmering gold from the sunlight, and once across, we bent to dip and clean our arms, and I seized this moment to speak.

"Thank you, for coming home, Cookie. We missed you. We've needed you."

She nodded, stood straight, and took my clean cool hand. I remained hunched beneath the wild sycamores, wiping my tears while the day crickets harped at me.

"I been far, Eliza. Saw my house burn around me in Mobile, took work as I could, mainly feedin' the railroad men comin' across this state, most of 'em not even worthy of the stew. Truth is, I'm runnin' now for I nearly killed a man. Though I didn't succeed, them other guards woulda killed me if I stayed." She put a damp rough hand on my wrist, lay it there while she watched my face, judging my reaction. "I come for my old job, ma'am. If it be available."

"It is," I said without thinking. "Of course. You hungry?"

"Ain't eaten since Hearne a coupla days past. I ran and took no sustenance in my pack."

We climbed the broad steps to the porch, and I pushed open the door. My family and workmen sat to the long narrow table while Lucy and Viola carried tin pails of milk to each. The June light flooded the warm room, and all these faces looked to us.

"See who I found!" I exclaimed but stopped when my throat clenched with tears.

Stella ran quickly to Cookie's side, oblivious to the trail filth and sour smell of her clothing. She held her tightly and brought at last some sunny laughter from within the ripeness of her tired body.

"Go now," Cookie said. "Go serve. I need to sit and rest."

Teddy Blue pulled a chair for her, and I took my seat at the end opposite Micah. I waited while the lot of them called out the grace, and at the crack of amens, the boys filled their plates with buttered potatoes and corn, while Lucy passed behind them carrying a wood platter piled with Scotch fillets brined in whiskey. Onto each plate she chuck-forked a slab of slow-roasted beef, and Stella carried a tin plate to Cookie. Seeing the wounds on her fingers, Teddy Blue cut the meat for her.

"What happened to your hands?" Stella asked.

"My fingers are the least of my tale," she replied. "But if you got a clean kerchief, I'll wrap them. Ran into some trouble in leaving them railroaders."

Stella brought one to her and helped with the tying off, standing calm and close at her shoulder, even while our Cookie ploughed through her meal. "I did the cooking," Stella said proudly.

"Then you learned good, Missy."

The work beginning anew, our farmhands stood and drifted away to their mounts and fields. Teddy Blue was last, calling time to the others while Benjamin led them out the door. On the polished floor shone a patch of sunlight, and with the butt of his rifle, Teddy Blue tilled at the shadowed edges as though seeking what lay beneath.

He grinned and looked suddenly to Cookie. "We are all pleased to see you, ma'am. Just let me know what you need for your kitchen and we will fetch it or make it before the day is over."

She nodded and thanked him but looked across the empty room. "I saw some new workers here, but I do not see all the children."

Stella inhaled sharply as Lucy turned her back to us.

"Yes," I said. "You are correct. And I think on it every day. Every day they pass through me like thread through a needle, Cookie. But I will explain tomorrow; you need sleep now."

She nodded, her eyes shot with veins of fatigue. "Thank you. Thank you for not forgettin' me."

I led her to the kitchen and closed the door. Lucy brought a pad and blanket, laying them carefully alongside the hearth.

"Sleep here until you've had sufficient," I said. "We'll find you a better sleep space tomorrow."

Cookie put her head down and whispered, "So many have been forgotten."

Often those days, I would find my Stella sitting astride the kitchen bench like a modern girl, listening by herself to Cookie Mahoney's old tales of war. Always so reluctant to disclose her stories to others, Cookie passed them to Stella, who became the storyteller on our farm, treating the children of Bluebonnet Ridge to dinnertime fables, thus irritating her older sister.

"This happened only thirteen miles from our Sugarloaf," Stella began one afternoon, settling onto the kitchen bench with Benjamin on one side, Viola the other. "Only thirteen miles to Hearne's plantation, where the prisoner men were laying the rails north to Palestine and Longview."

"What do you know about Hearne?" Lucy asked.

"Enough," Stella replied sullenly. "Where the rail kings're building their mansions with railroad money and slavin' sweat."

"Ain't no more slaves," Lucy said.

"That is correct," replied Cookie suddenly. "But the owners and their foreman, old Andy Ward, found theirselves new men to do their rail line work now that all slaves be free. They rented out the Huntsville inmates for fifteen years to point that railroad up to Canada and down to Mexico, or until the poor slobbers fall dead, whichever comes before. New kinda slave now. I been their cook at Palestine and I seen it all, girl."

A luna-moth, green and broad as a fist, bumped the window behind Cookie's shoulder, bringing its light against the glass. "Times when I walked across this country, before the war and even before you were born to this Earth, I knew a thing or two about the dark powers of Manadoo." She nodded and smacked her lips quickly. "Darkness of the devil residin' in folks lookin' just like us, men like old Andy Ward and his foremen."

And with that, Stella continued to relate the story Cookie had taught her, describing the power and gold of the railroaders, and of their frightened leased men, as though the milky light of her words was her very own memory.

CHAPTER 47

$\mathcal{B}$y the end of the winter rains, we had a hundred prisoners living along the waters at our farthest bounds. Sinking in the wet soil, the leased men labored in the pine grove, downing the trees and hewing the damp, green trunks to get them onto flatboats. They were transported by blue mule schooners each morning from their tent camp up the Little, arriving before dawn and working, chained and bent in rows, till dusk.

Stella and Benjamin found a limestone perch at the top of the Sugarloaf trail where they could see through the scrubby trees down to the little dock and the railing work. They stayed in the drizzle, or the thin sunlight, or the early spring winds; whenever my two had a moment from their own work, they came to watch the rotting lives of Andy Ward's men. One suppertime, Stella told us of their climb up the mount and the sights that she and Benjamin witnessed of those poor souls.

"There's all kinds," she said, "young boys and whites and blacks. They chain 'em in groups of six men, and each group has a boss on a horse and a boss on the ground. Sometimes they feed them, but sometimes they don't. We watched them fell a tree today, only it hit the ground off-kilter and killed a man."

Cookie stood at the door, her arms limp at her sides. "All you say, miss, won't ever be enough to tell their story. I seen the shackle poisoning cut into their skin, the ones who dropped from heatstroke or beatings. All of it." She turned and pushed open the cookery door. "I seen all of it," she called out over her shoulder. "My job was to cook for 'em and cure 'em to get 'em back to work."

Outside the window a barred owl landed on the flower box, holding something in its glowing black claws. It seemed to look through the pane with its huge brown eyes, then rose slowly toward the top of the pecan tree.

"Best stop your games atop Sugarloaf," Micah said to the children. "Hear me, Benjamin. And Stella. Stay off that mountain until the men move on. Won't be long now."

Age though is not immune to curiosity about wretchedness. The next morn, Micah and I climbed up from the brushy swale, alive with crickets, blackbirds, and moorhens; with crows and jays and javelinas, all of them humming from the clean earth, high and fine. Atop Sugarloaf, we found the children's spot, a clear line across the bottomland where the paintbrushes and bluebonnets grew down the slope. That day we saw a convict die, tumbling to the mud, and whipped from his life by a lean tall young man wearing a slouch hat over his ruddy-colored hair.

By April, I had seen seven of them pass. The weaker ones fell first, confused men without water, or those who were simply too afraid. Beaten to the ground and in their starvation, they were felled by whip blows and kicks. The overseers rarely used bullets, so the convicts lay on the line, unable to run because of shackles, crippled in their own blood.

Although Micah rarely accompanied me after that first day, I climbed the mount often and carried camphor and hartshorn those afternoons to keep my vision clear, for mine was the only free testimony to the demise of these people.

Micah refused to extend the lease of our dock, and by the last day of May, when the bluestem grasses and bundleflowers covered the plain, Andy Ward's men worked furiously felling and milling his quota of logs for the railroad. The warm summer rain had stopped at suppertime, and the Blue Geese bayed out from the horizon. I had taken my place on Sugarloaf where I could observe both prisoners and hired men, all laboring in the steamy bottomlands of the Little River.

I knew Benjamin was with me on the mountain before he showed himself; I felt his presence crouching in the red clover behind the boulders that crowned the hill.

"Father told you not to come up here again," I said without turning to him.

Benjamin stood and walked toward me, the humid shadows fading around him. We believed his age to be about fourteen years, but standing in the afternoon light, his hair black and silky like a crow's, a rifle balanced easily on his left shoulder, he might have been beyond the age of majority.

"Why are you here?" he asked.

The heat was pulling the oil from the grasses so that the air lay heavy and sweet around us.

I turned toward the dying pink light of the afternoon and said, "I need to see these things."

"But why?"

"Kindness is the only true faith. I have seen too much harm to look away."

He took a clump of rosemary from the earth and rolled it between his palms, crushing the narrow leaves. He held it to me to smell, but continued watching the watchmen with their charges.

We sat on Sugarloaf until the men turned to home, long after the gold in the sky had disappeared. The mossed oak trunks lay in rows on the bend, and the last convict job of the day was to roll them onboard the waiting flatboats for their journey to the mill. A few prisoners had been unshackled for this purpose.

Benjamin took my hand as we walked down the trail into the shadows, through deep woods that were amuck with foxes and squirrels slipping about the darkening dusk. When we emerged near the Little, I heard a flatboat up the bend slapping in the water and the call of an overseer across the backs of the convicts.

An otter crawled up the bank nearby, and Benjamin had stepped silently beside it, when suddenly four bullet shots exploded on the river. Quickly, he pushed me to the mud. We lay on the slope for several moments, listening to more bullets and not knowing if we were witnessing the hunting of rabbits or the hunting of men.

The shadows melted into the sycamores, and I closed my eyes and waited. The belly bark of dogs echoed through the woods, and footsteps thudded toward us. Benjamin stood quickly and moved onto the river trail, holding his rifle high.

"Stay down," he whispered to me. Seconds later three men and panting dogs encircled him.

"Down that rifle!" The taller of the men crushed forward over a clutch of golden chanterelles and shouted furiously at my boy.

I scrambled to stand and pushed in front of Ben.

"Who are you?" I asked sharply. "And why are you holding ready to fire at my son?"

"Prisoners have run free, ma'am," said one of the guards. "Two escaped into the river." They kept their rifles trained on Benjamin.

"This is my son and not your prisoner." The long-held note of a red wolf rose through the twilight. "Go on then. Put your damn shooters down and get back to your hunt."

None of us spoke again, or moved for what seemed like a deep wedge of time. I heard the north wind through the broad sycamore leaves, and the sound of men cutting at the river.

In a low growl, the tall red-haired guard said, "Boy don't look like no son a' yours."

"Get on with you! Or my husband will throw you all off our land tonight."

The three stared at me, then turned and ran east along the virgin bank. The dogs followed, as did the other two men. Night had fallen where we stood, leaving us in dark and silence. Benjamin took his rifle from the mud and nodded toward the Tonkawa trail.

Deep in that moonless night I lay in bed, listening to the dogs across our pastures, roaming still, even by the fading stars of dawn. Soon the light began to soften the sky, and Micah and I smelled bacon steaks frying from Cookie's hearth. We heard the clatter of plates against our long oak table in the room below our bedroom.

"Didn't sleep much," Micah said, sitting up on our bed, "listening for the pack to find the running convicts."

I stared at him without speaking; in our youth he had stopped owners and hungry dogs from claiming me.

He put his warm arm across my shoulders and I felt his fingers reach for the crevices of the brand left there, all these decades past. He pressed his lips to my cheek. He watched while I slipped my work dress over my head, and when I sat alongside him to pull up my stockings and boots, he put out a hand to stop me, just to touch me. The morning air was fresh and cool through our open window, and he carried the familiar scent of our bedclothes.

At breakfast, the escaped criminals and the night sounds of the pack dogs were speculative topics.

"If they survived the river, they are free now," Benjamin said, but none agreed.

"Those men will never be free, boy," said Chop Coggins. "Not with Andy Ward after them. They're railroad property. Might as well be slaves."

Stella, never one to shrink from the opinions of men, replied, "A good swimmer can always get away. If they crossed to Robertson County, they'll be long gone now."

"Robertson? They'd be daft to go east, straight toward Hearne and the railmen," Teddy Blue replied. "Lucky chance is they drowned against those river swells. Nobody crosses the bend of the Brazos without a boat."

"You forget that I did," said Chop, and he laughed hard and long.

Benjamin pulled back from the table. The boy was strong and thick, wearing farmers' clothes with his black hair sheared to just below his ears.

"Where do you want me first?" he asked Micah, who lay a hand on his shoulder and smiled.

"At my side, Ben. Ranging needs the best horsemen."

Cookie handed them dinner baskets of dried fish and hunks of alligator gar from the Brazos that filled the room with stink.

"I'd stay off of Sugarloaf today, Ma," Benjamin said to me.

"Maybe. But I think the chase has moved off our land."

Of course, I would not avoid the hill, that day of all days. I climbed to a sandstone outcrop on the northeast face, hidden in the shadows of a huge skull-shaped boulder that had long ago been the landmark for tribes trading goods on their way west to the high desert. From that vantage, I peered out at the ruddy horizon, over the tops of the elms and willows along the river, and watched the violent afternoon unfold below me. The men cracked to action at the warnings of their overseers, with dry summer dust rising around them until at last the strike of a bell collided with their work and they filed away.

Only then did I hear the brush breaking, and a voice behind me.

I wheeled round to face a lone Negro boy about fourteen and the size of Benjamin, grimy and gaunt, ferocious even, and more like a ferret than a human spirit. I backed into the shadows of the skull rock, from where I could see a patch of sunlight over him. I lifted my Henry to shoulder and chambered the copper, ready to fire.

"What are you doing here?" I asked.

He shook his head quickly, touching his lips together several times, the shadows shifting the angles of light across his face.

"Who are you?" I asked, but he turned and ran from me. And I, the fool, followed to watch him descend the path.

As his dark shape scrambled on all fours down the sandstone, gunshots sputtered from the far grasses of the slope, and the boy fell to the dirt without moving again.

I leaned back against the warm rock, still holding my rifle high and pressing my lips together to quell my breathing. I did not move but hid in the shadows while the larks quieted across the sun, until another voice came round the boulders.

"Ma'am?" the man called out. Tall and slender, he carried a rifle to ready, but let it fall to his side when he saw me. "Did the nigra convict harm you, ma'am?" Petals of grime lay on his cheeks, and his face was framed by damp red hair. He carried a coiled rope slung over his shoulder, rough rawhide that smelled still of animal life.

"That child? No," I said. "You the one shot him?"

He shook his head. "No, Andy Ward took him down. Sent me up here t'look for the other one. You must be Missus Moore, wife of the owner of this farm. I'm Gus," he said in a low hollow voice. He held his hand to me, but I did not take it. "I'm guardin' for the railroad. Don't worry, ma'am. We're closin' in on the last escaped man."

"Take that child's body and get off my farm," I ordered him.

This Gus grabbed a knife from his boot and slashed hard at the briars beside him, then stared at me, saying, "Child, huh? I s'pose things have changed now, ain't they? Now that the war's done."

He turned and left, and I sat on Sugarloaf for an age until I heard my husband's voice calling for me through the purple light of dusk.

"Ellie?"

I stood immediately and strode to the trail. "Micah, I'm here. Up here."

"I was worrying on you so," he said and walked quickly to put his arms about me. "Did you come across him? Did he harm you?"

"No. Just a fright. He was young to be a prisoner. Only a boy. Probably same age as Ben."

He held me as though I was his deepest secret, his head bent to cover me and his warm breath across my neck. "We been out searching for you. Come on then. Let's to home."

CHAPTER 48

*W*hen I saw this Gus again, it was by lantern as he waited on my porch the next evening. Cookie stood with him, her gun aloft while the light flickered across his face. I stood back in the dark, watching every twitch of his body, his sun-browned arms and face. Along a forearm hung a dried skinflap of about three inches, baring a cut deep into his flesh that glowed red. I stepped into the light and he stared hard at me, his dark blue eyes changing to black.

"Ma'am, I come to apologize for frightening you yesterday. And for my rudeness."

He wore the same soiled clothes as the day before, stinking of river water and sweat.

"I accept your apology," I said quickly.

"I wanted you to know that before I leave," he said, his voice tight. The pulse in his forehead had swelled the veins near his temples.

"I understand," I said.

"I don't think you do," he replied, almost as though he knew me. "I quit the railroad. Got enough now to get me up north to the Dakota gold fields. Headin' out tomorrow."

I nodded and against my heart's judgment, I asked, "What's become of your arm then?"

He followed my gaze down to the angry wound. "Nothing, ma'am. I ran into trouble with one a' the road gang, is all," he said in that same low voice from Sugarloaf, faintly familiar but then again, no. Now that I saw him close with the amber flame of the lantern on his face, I understood that he was young, perhaps no older than thirty.

Micah stepped behind me. "You'll need that seen to."

"It'll heal," Gus replied.

"Not without cleaning," Cookie said, and lowered her rifle. "Can't let any man die of infection out here. Come round the back and I'll wash it and do it up for ya."

We moved to the well at the back of our house, and while Cookie directed him to sit on her old three-legged stool, the rest of us stood in the lantern light staring at him.

"Mind if I have water from that sweet-smelling well," he asked, and Lucy brought a cup to him. He drank carefully and held the empty tin out to her.

"Could I have one more, please?" Lucy nodded. "You're a kindly girl," he whispered, so softly.

She dipped the cup again and asked, "You have kin in Texas?"

"Why, no I don't."

Our Viola shook her small head and smiled at him, moving toward the well to offer him another cup of water. The evening breeze blew across us, lifting her apron bib across her face and causing her to laugh, but Gus only stared at her without so much as a smile. I stepped quickly to the child and pulled her back toward me.

"What you doin' here then?" Lucy asked.

"Lucy, give the man a moment before you pry his life from him," said Micah, stepping in front of her. "Son, you got a place to stay tonight?"

"I'll throw camp somewhere, I guess. Hadn't really thought."

"I have a barn I can offer for one night," my husband replied, "if you prefer an early morning start on your journey."

We continued to surround him, gazing and wondering, while Cookie gouged and scrubbed his wound.

"I know I be hurtin' you," she said, "but you can't heal without pain. Whosoever did this did a deep job. May not ever heal."

He looked up from his arm, across the silvery grass to Lucy. He stared at her for several moments, and when she caught him watching her, he did not look away. Soon my middle girl would be sixteen years, not a beauty like Evie, but a woman with the clear creamy skin and blonde hair of the Moore family, and short of stature like us Bunches. She was a fierce religious girl who struggled always with that passion.

Gus stood abruptly from the stool and put his hand on Cookie's broad shoulder for balance. "You do good work, ma'am, but can I rest from the pain, please? Just a minute or two." The lean shape of his long arms glistened in the early moonlight.

Cookie pulled him back to the stool and offered more water.

Suddenly, Lucy knelt in the grasses and said, "I will say a prayer for you." She folded her hands and bent her childlike head, whispering to her god on behalf of Gus until, with her oath completed, she said, "The rest is yours to do. Bad or good, your life is with God now."

"Ma'am," he said boldly to my young daughter as though she were a woman of age, "I been traveling since a child, but in all my years I got nowhere in this life but older."

She pulled an overripe red persimmon from a box by the kitchen door and handed it to Gus. "This will be sweet now," she said. "It's from the bounty of last fall. Good for you."

"Thank you, ma'am," and that word again made my hackles rise.

He pulled the pulp from its wrinkly skin and swallowed it, smiling at her. "Before the railroad, I was just a hand in the barnyard, a good worker, but I can't read or add up. Not much use to farmers these days who look for all-rounders."

Lucy wore her hair up-pinned, and her pale blue cotton skirt touched the dusty yard. She crossed her arms over her bodice, and Gus gazed openly at her.

"May I ask your name, ma'am? So I can thank you properly for your kindness."

She glanced at me and I nodded. "Louisiana," she said. "Or just Lucy."

"Well, Lucy, I thank you for your care. It's not easy finding friends in these lands if you come without family or a stake."

Cookie returned with blankets and tossed them in his direction. "You'll be cold tonight. And remember this, mister, you be stayin' one night at Bluebonnet Ridge because we're Texans and hospitable, but it takes more'n that to make a friend."

He nodded, opening his mouth to speak, then changing his mind.

Benjamin stepped across the shadows and stood in the flickering light. My son watched Gus for several moments.

"Who are you?" he asked carefully.

"Boy, I been wandering," Gus whispered, "a long time. Before I worked for Andy Ward, I was just taking cash as I could."

"Well, you be good off that railroad gang. Nothing but evil there," said Cookie.

"Tell us then." Lucy smiled suddenly at him. "Where ya from?"

Gus dropped his head, but stared at her sidelong, the light in his eyes flashing and his mouth twitching slightly. "I ain't got no kin. All I knew were killed or died from fevers before I was seven years of age. I passed east unseen across the Sabine, sometimes stealing food to quell my belly. Old couple caught me in Louisiana and took me to be their servant. When I escaped that life, I ran for New Orleans and caught a ship headed 'round the Horn to Monterrey for the pelts of them otters. I been bad company for a long time, survivin' among worse. Truth is, I wrangled with another guard at the railroad and scuttled out on my contract. Ward'll be lookin' for me too, I expect."

"You stay the night, boy," Micah said, and picked up his rifle. "Then be on your way tomorrow. I'm not getting into the middle of you and Andy Ward."

Our curious congregation, led by my tall kindly husband, walked Gus to the horse barn, waiting while he plumped up straw for his bed and lay the blankets over. Teddy Blue stood in the black maw of the open door, leaning his rifle butt against the iron hinges and watching him closely. He pulled a soft chachalaca feather from his pocket. Looking at it and not at Gus, he passed it back and forth between his fingers. "What's your true name?"

"Gus is the only one I can remember," said the man. "And, sir, if you have work for a farmhand, I'd be honored to stay on and do it."

The reek of horses and the mellow smell of warm hay rose around us, as I heard our animals chewing their cobs in the far stalls.

"Sorry, son, but we don't need another just now."

Gus opened his eyes wide, seeming to burst inside of a wildness, a rage that slowly spent itself without a sound from him. At last, he said quietly, "Thank you for considerin' me, sir," and he tracked Teddy's rifle barrel across the ground as though it were a small creature.

Lucy pulled her fingers into tight fists and moved from my side. She pushed open the stall latch and walked quickly to the barn door. As she left, a bright sheet of moonlight fell across us. I followed her into the yard, but Lucy did not stop for me. Starlight streaked the sky, and I waited alone for the peace of the night to come.

∾

At sunrise, Cookie and I carried breakfast buckets to Gus, who yet slept on the hay mounds in the horse barn. The animals shifted and snorted at our presence, and the man startled awake.

"This is your morning meal," Cookie said, setting the food within his reach. "I'll check your wound before you set off."

After he'd eaten and been bandaged again, we gave him a mule for the journey and went to wave him farewell.

"Thanks for your generosity," he said, "but as you can see I have no protection. I left the crew quick, obliged to do so without gun or mount. How will I eat or advance through this country without one? Do you think you could spare me a weapon?"

"You got some chuck, man," said Teddy Blue. "You got water, a meal, and a ride. You best stop expectin' more. But I'll see you to Cameron today since I've got purchases there to fetch. After that, you're on your own."

Teddy pulled himself into the saddle of his own horse, clicked it round, and followed Gus west, holding his repeater steady till I could see them no more.

Teddy Blue stopped the night in town, returning the next day under a gold sky at the last milking. He pulled an old two-wheeled Mexican mule cart through our open gates, and in its box we found yards of yellow dressmaker cotton wrapped in new Butterick tissue, a crate of pins and tongs for our smithy, and a dime novel on adventuring for Stella.

"And the western mail," he said, handing the pouch to Micah.

"And?" I asked.

The dust of the Cameron road lay across his jacket, and the fading summer light threw shadows over the sharp hollows of his face; he knew what I meant and answered quickly, "Said he'd be off to the mines. But I waited through the night, and finally saw him make the turn west and not north. He's a fellow who has the worst time giving out truth. Falls into a lie whenever he starts up talking."

"He'll be smart," Micah said.

Teddy Blue shrugged. "That's one opinion, Micah. Honestly, I'm tired a' talking about him. I don't believe he'll be goin' far. Some folks just don't know what to do to survive."

Lucy came to the porch and spoke, but every word was covered with the sudden squawk of a flock of black grackles wheeling up from the hill.

"Breakfast is set," she said at last, coming to stand beside us. "That man move on?"

Teddy Blue nodded and handed her the yellow cotton.

A nest of beetles worked the dirt at the cart's wheel and Lucy stamped it with her boot, over and again until she had killed them all.

CHAPTER 49

*A*ndy Ward and his men paid up their lease and moved the operation south, laying rails toward Austin. By September, most at Bluebonnet had forgotten that sad summer; we had weaned off the calves and lay down the winter wheat. The violet autumn skies trailed behind the reddening afternoons and come morning, the mists lay early and high across our ridge. After breakfast and still with swollen tired eyes, we walked into the silence of the workday fogs.

On one of those ghosty mornings, Micah and I drove out to the Little River dock, newly built by the convicts and strong, where the boats from the east now left our farm parcels. The thin silvery sun cast weak light on the water, and pearly waves frothed around the low cedar platform that the prisoners had constructed. Tall dying reeds were clustered around the planks, their plumes gone brown with the season. I stood in the wagon while Micah handed the packages to me, all of them stinking of river water.

Back on the bench admiring his mighty anchorage, he turned to me, grinning. "You see, Eliza, this dock was a useful idea after all."

We both laughed aloud, our voices rising into the early day. He drove us fast through fields as he had not done for years, and I put my arm around his waist to keep from tumbling from the cart. We trampled through the meadow of Indian sunflowers, their petals red as blood, until at last Micah pulled up at the little limestone bridge before our house.

He put his hand on my arm, leaning close. "Remember our first ride from Cairo to my sister's place?" He kissed my cheek and jumped down. He held my hand, cradling it between both of his. "Old Cash and I, we got you jittery, didn't we?"

"Nothing you have ever done has given me jitters, boy, except leavin' for war."

We washed in the creek for dinner, and Micah led the mules toward the hitch rails, but I stopped at the bank, staring at what lay in the mud.

"What ya got there?" he asked.

"Shoes," I said. "A child's shoes left to dry here on the bank. Here, look at the stitching. This is the work of a fine Mexican cobbler." I carried them quickly to show him. "Why did a workhand bring their babe's shoes to our stream for cleaning?"

"Aw, girl, I don't know." He chucked the mules and the cart squeaked forward, releasing the animals into their paddock. "Stream belongs to all anyway. Just bring 'em with you and we'll return them to the owner now." He took my hand as we climbed the steps and opened the door into the room where our family and workers all sat to table and I took my place in the armchair at the end.

A single voice, a child's voice, carried across me, coming high and sweet from the kitchen, and for a moment I could hear my own singsong in it.

"How old are you?" the child asked, and then quickly like bubbling water, "Are you a *vaquero*? What's your name?"

Teddy Blue had not yet joined us, but I heard his laugh crackling from beyond the kitchen door. When he emerged through the smoky shadows of Cookie Mahoney's kitchen, he carried a coffee pot in one hand, and under the other arm, a smiling barefoot child waving tanned arms. As Teddy Blue moved forward to bring our coffee, an apparition remained behind in the doorway, a man of height and perfect form, blond like the child and silently watching us. Arakka looked to me, then about the room, and returned his stare to my face.

Immediately, I felt my throat parch. I shoved my chair back with such racket that it scraped all sound from the room, and I rushed to him.

"I can feel your heart moving, Eliza," he said, for I had clamped his body between my arms and refused to release him.

"Little soul," I whispered, "my little vagabond. Is this small child my kin? Is this Jack?"

He nodded. "Yes. This is my son, and Evie's."

The child came running, pounding his bare feet across the floor and flinging himself into his father's arms.

"This is your grandmother," Arakka said.

I smiled but could neither think nor speak. I reached out for the boy, and instead of recoiling from such a strange rough woman, the child scrambled to me, tangling his body in my arms. Such was his warm skin, soft and dry, it felt to be dusted by powder. I kissed his face several times until I could no longer contain him, and so put him down beside his father.

"Where is my daughter?" I asked.

"Sleeping. We came through the night from Bexar, with no rest, dark or day."

"Why journey like that? You been gone five years with naught but letters, and now come with my little kin and no warning. Are we welcoming our family home or hiding you?"

"You have not changed much, Eliza."

The first I saw Arakka, he had been wearing black rags, led to me with a rope around his neck. Now his shirt glowed white from bluing chalk, crisp and clean with silk thread embroidered down the front, but inside his heart lay the same stubborn spirit.

"Believe me, boy, no one changes. Now tell me why you came so quick."

"Mother," he said softly, and put his arm around my shoulders, "You aren't wrong. We hurried to you for safety, and we come with nothing. We drove all day and night without stopping, and now so tired. Jack is so hungry. Let us sit first, and then explain. Please."

"Jack," I repeated, looking toward the child, for it was the first word I had ever spoken to my grandson. "Come with me, Jack, and meet your grandfather." I put my hand in the child's, and inhaled.

He followed me down the bench of men, the boy straggling only to peer out the windows to our vast sky and pastures. The murmured current of voices rose once again around us, and we reached Chop Coggins sitting beside Lucy.

The old fellow put his arm out to stop us. "This be the child of Evie and Arakka," he grunted to me. "A fine little man. What's your name?"

"Jack," replied the boy. "What do you call yourself?"

Chop did not answer but leaned close to me and said, "Boys here said your mare ain't bagged up yet, Eliza. She be layin' in the hay now waitin' for her milk to come." He looked at Jack. "I'm Chop Coggins, son," he said, and pushed the grey hair from his forehead with a liver-spotted wrinkled hand. "Chop be what you can call aloud if you need me, and I will come."

I led Jack down the row to Micah, and the boy climbed onto his grandfather's lap, staring at Micah's face.

"I knew of you years ago, before you had a name even," Micah said to the child. "I am pleased to meet you today." He took a gulp from his tin mug of grog. Suddenly he looked the boy straight in the eye and asked, "Do you want to hear your blood?" Though fifty years old, Micah's eyes still lit with the joy of a secret just as when he was fifteen and we first met.

"How?" asked Jack.

Micah cupped his hand over his ear and nodded at Jack to do the same. "Be silent, Jack, and you will hear your blood move through your body. Maybe even your heart beating."

Jack did this, and I watched the two of them, elbows up and hands over their ears, thinking that whatever had occurred in Mexico, this child was home now.

Arakka sat beside his adopted father and began to eat and to feed his son. When he had sopped the last of the whiskey gravy from his plate, he spoke to us.

"Yellow fever killed Rafael and Lariza. And their children. Absalom too." Arakka said it calmly like he had buried a family of foxes; he had always spoken a quiet truth despite the many languages that had been forced through him. "One after another. The fever nearly took Evie as well. Soldiers from Saltillo claimed the ranch after the Beremindas died. The soldiers took all the stock and even our furniture. We left unseen at night and traveled to you. We're tramps without stores or trunks, Eliza. We have our son, but nothing else."

Chop Coggins scrambled up from the table and walked toward the door, rolling his shirtsleeves as he went. Stopping behind Arakka, he put a gentle hand on my boy's shoulder. "Good yer back, man. For long?"

Arakka shrugged and turned to Micah, waiting for his father's answer.

But my husband was no longer looking at any of us; he stared instead at the bottom of our staircase where Evie waited. Such was her beauty that those at the table, even those who had known her as a child, all of them looked to her in a hush.

A tall slender girl, a dancer of spirit and grace, she wore an old white cotton frock greying at the hem, perhaps one she had found in her sisters' trunk. Her hair fell across her shoulders, dark and thick, and like her father's without wave. Paler and thinner than I ever remembered her, she nonetheless stood so straight and so proud that she might have been walking to a church on the Sabbath.

She came to us and took a piece of hard tack biscuit from the table, cracking it between her hands, smiling timidly at long last.

"Hello, Father," she said and put her arms around his shoulders, leaning close for his kiss.

She put one pale hand on the lace at her throat, carefully as though hovering beside a candle flame. And then with a look that was meant for the two of us alone, she turned to me waiting, casting and rolling her chances.

I held my arms out, close enough to graze her wrists with my fingertips, and at that touch she moved toward me, shaking. My heart, for so long filled with the labor of loving while broken, now swung wide as a furnace door. For our wildest emotions are surely undeniable; as I touched my girl again, I scattered aside the years of my anger.

"Mama, I love you," she said, and her voice carried that same trace of Jack's, and of my own.

"Oh, daughter," I whispered.

"I would take it all back if I could, Mama."

The boy slipped from Micah's lap and stood beside his mother, taking Evie's hand.

"Jack, this is your grandmother."

"I know. Why are you crying, Mama?" the boy asked, and Evie turned back to face me.

"Sit to table, Evie. Your husband tells me you traveled fast and far to reach your home."

She took a seat alongside her father and lifted a spoon of soft warm potato to her mouth, while my other children rushed upon us, bringing sweet cakes and coffee to their sister.

"They're not visiting," Stella said. "They come to stay at

Bluebonnet Ridge." She touched Evie's arm, and grinned. "And look, all of a sudden I'm someone's auntie!"

Lucy sat between Evie and Arakka. "I had a narrow fantasy that you would come home one day," she said.

Evie hugged her. "I know Mama would have written if you got yourself married, so I guess you're still my same sister, but I do want to know, is there a special boy yet?"

Immediately, Lucy flushed bright and hot.

"Why, Louisiana," Micah asked, "should you be telling us some news?"

"No. Nothing at all to tell. I'm just pleased we are all together." She stood and took the hand of her new nephew. "Come with me, Jack. Cookie made taffy candy this morning. Like to taste it?"

Our ranch hands drifted outside, back to work or for a last smoke on the porch, and Micah turned to Arakka. "Firing some dead stock this afternoon, boy. We could use help. Built a big burn pile on the meadow for the job." Both of them stood, reaching for their hats and guns, but Micah paused and said plainly to Evie, "There's no name for what it's like when a child leaves. I'm not ashamed to be giddy now seeing you."

The sound of hammer blows of our blacksmith working on hot iron fell around us as though from the sky.

"Thin bitch of a black wolf scouting out there," Teddy Blue said. "We'll need to stoke the fire up quick before it gets close to our living stock."

Micah nodded, looking at Jack through the puckered light. "Ever burned a dead cow, boy?" he asked.

Jack shook his head.

"Come with us. We might need another pair of hands."

CHAPTER 50

*M*onday had always been wash day, and according to Cookie Mahoney this was a requirement on the frontier in order to maintain our manners. Each week we gathered wood and started a fire atop the brick platform behind the house, setting the big iron pot upright on it. Cookie devised a system of four wash tubs and a rub-board, a poke stick, some dolly blue chalk, and lye soap she had made.

She sorted the clothes into the tubs, and we poked at them in the boiling water and beat them until they were clean, rinsed them several times, and then cranked them through her special wringer. This involved the effort of every female at Bluebonnet Ridge for the entire day, as well as all the children whose main jobs were fetching firewood and poking.

Finding the wood for the fire was the least agreeable chore, because the child given it had to go out in the dark before breakfast to the far woods to collect the branches that would catch a flame quick. Yet, in the fall of Lucy's seventeenth year, she decided it would be her job, and I never saw her before the sun rose. So often she returned clutching her tinder to her chest, her dress and petticoats soiled with smears of mud or mossy mold.

On such a morning, Cookie Mahoney took the wood from Lucy's arms and sent her inside to dress yet again for the day.

"I'm not having a filthy girl at my breakfast table," she said, following her to the bedroom. "Give me those." Cookie grabbed the yellow cotton frock that she, herself, had sewn for Lucy, and brought it out to the boiling pot, where she tossed it, disgustedly, on the heap of waiting work clothes.

We poked and rubbed and rinsed that day in the cooling season, and ate, and toiled more until the boiling and wringing were finished. We allowed Lucy's fire to extinguish, while Evie and Stella hung the clothes on the drying line. Cookie and I heaved together against the huge iron cauldron, rolling it on its side to empty the soiled wash water into the weeds.

"I'm going to sup my coffee now, quiet on the porch, before the rest of 'em come stomping in expecting food," said Cookie, always a Monday martyr in the glow of the late afternoons. She turned for the house but stopped suddenly and bent her heavy frame to touch the tepid mud. "What's this here?"

She held out a smoothed piece of jet coal that had been rounded and carved into the image of a black angel. She put it in my hand, clean it was and bright, with tiny copper hinges hooking onto a flat top. I popped that smooth oval open and found a place where a thumb-sized portrait had been, the paper now sogged by wash day and lost to all.

"Coal," said Cookie. "Some cowboy carving a poor man's locket for his girl."

Before supper, Cookie distributed the clean shirts and trousers to the boys, asking each if he had lost a treasure, but none lay claim. When they sat to table, she held it up to show the room, and again not a soul admitted being the owner.

A day later when I worked alone at the pond beside the paddock, I squatted among the yellow lotuses, yanking their tangled weeds from the icy water, and Lucy came to stand behind me.

"May I have that locket, Mama?"

"Does it belong to you?"

"It does. I need it back." And with that she dropped to her knees beside me crying and nodding furiously.

Lucy told me her story as we sat by the creek alone, and suddenly, I saw her so clearly, estranged from her family and wild from the touch of a stranger. For weeks, she had been meeting Gus, who had hidden himself on Sugarloaf, waiting for her each day. She told him of our farm, and of each of her brothers and sisters, adopted or by blood. she said she seduced this man, an orphan, with only the story of the Moores who received with love all the lost or lonely in this world.

In turn, he told my daughter that he had traveled the summer through Nacogdoches where despite not knowing how to read, he claimed he had learned to preach for the Disciples of Christ. He served through Waco, and finally on a farm near Marlin, until he arrived at Bluebonnet with his intention to marry my child. He told her he had lived hard but never harmed man or animal, that now his greatest passion was the church, and with each of these lies Lucy believed, she moved farther from us than I had ever imagined possible.

"She is forbidden from Sugarloaf," Micah said, "forbidden from meeting him." Sitting in the warm fields of an Indian summer eve alone with me, he swore to kill the man the following day.

"Before you move to make that gesture, husband, know that if you do, we will never see her again."

The moon began to glow nearly full, throwing seeds of light through the sheered stalks around us. It comes and goes, and comes again, cutting the day to night, yet offering nothing to help us over this ledge of life. I sat quietly on an old oak stump beside a cluster of orange maples and heard the black-bellied ducks whistling through the darkening skies.

Micah cried out, "Then what? I can't hold my own tongue from what I know. The man is a fraud. You know that, Ellie. No more a preacher than Teddy Blue."

I closed my eyes and didn't answer. When I looked again, he stood a little apart and his beautiful eyes were empty of kindness. He turned, showing me his back as he stepped out farther across the oak roots that lay thick as a man's arms in the dirt.

"I am well bruised," he whispered. "I want to beat this man to death with my hands. Hear his bones cracking. See him raw."

"You killed men before, Micah. And I have." I picked a stick from the grasses and held it against the palm of my hand. "But if you follow your pleasure now, Louisiana will never be ours again. She will run. And we both will be driven dumb from our bad judgment." I took his hand, always rough to my touch from his years of hard ranching on this frontier, and I walked with him through the evening shadows toward our house.

We stopped at the bridge and for a moment we stared at the creek water trembling in the moonlight. "This is a slow game," I said. "We must take our steps with care. You and Teddy Blue must go tomorrow and find Gus and bring him to Bluebonnet Ridge where we can see for ourselves if his new spirit has been shaped by God or poison."

Gus came proudly the next day, and unafraid. He turned beside his Morgan stallion, standing in the soft low ferns by the post, and watched me for a moment, squinting in the sunlight. Finally, he pulled a leather pouch from his saddlebag and put it in my hand.

I nodded uncertainly and shoved it in my pocket.

"Please, Missus Moore. Have a look at my gift to you. I been waitin' on your mountain with no chores so I been spendin' my days carving."

I opened the pouch and found a simple jet ring, smooth and dull with no embellishments.

"I hope it's right. I measured it from Lucy's hand."

Micah tensed, his fingers clenched colorless, when he heard this man speak so of touching our daughter.

"Thank you," I said quickly. "Come on in."

Gus put an arm on his horse and smiled broadly. He carried a Bible that he could not read, and strode in front of me up our porch steps. He didn't pause at the threshold, but walked confidently over it. Here went a boy who had never followed his mother to the hearth or his father down a trail. All that he knew, he had learned by observation of the acts of strangers, cruel or kind.

Teddy Blue followed us inside, but leaned against the jamb, his holstered Colt at his waist.

We were alone in that silent house, with the high sun bending through our pocked window glass. Lucy had ridden out with her brothers after supper to work the new wild ponies in the far fields. Perhaps she had an idea to seek her beloved on Sugarloaf as well, for neither family nor hands knew of our plans to bring this man in for questioning. Even dear Cookie had chopped a stew and set off for the high meadows seeking Dutchman's rue for her potions.

I pointed at a chair for him, and we sat across at the long table.

"I am thirty years old this year," he began. "That's what I tell, and that's what I think. And now I've been called to serve the Lord."

Micah said low and cold, "Hell, I don't believe a word out of your mouth anymore. Left the employ of Andy Ward, you said, but then we find out you ran from a fight without horse or weapon. Saved a stake, you said, but you didn't even have cash to purchase a gun. Off to the north gold fields, and suddenly you're back here a preacher wanting to marry my daughter. You didn't even have the manners to come to me first. You been seeing her alone without my knowing." My husband's hands lay curled together on the table shaking with anger. "Don't even know your true name, boy. You never even told us."

"Why, you never asked me. I'm called Gus Whipple." He touched the Bible laying before him. "Look, I ain't the same as before. I didn't think ya'd believe me, but I learned a thing or two about the Lord, and in these three months I been gone, I accepted my duty to him. I'm here now to make amends. God threw me hard to the ground and declared that I must love your daughter as her husband."

He had slipped a palm to his holster unlooping it, but Teddy was faster. "You move and I'll pull this," he said. "You're a damn fool."

Sweat trickled down Gus's forehead, and his ginger hair lay flat and wet on his scalp line.

"You cross back here with a lie about love and God," Teddy said. "Hiding on our land, waiting for our girl. You been told once to leave." He trained the barrel on Gus Whipple's head, his gun hand calm and strong, though his jaw was tight.

"Teddy," Micah said. "Take a breath, man. No point in killing him here and now."

"It would be easy, and nobody'd miss him."

A flicker of a smile crossed Gus's lips, slight and swift and with the pride of a man whose only skill was stalking the edges of community.

"I seen our girl from a baby," said Teddy. "She surely can't love a grifter like this. He's nothing but poison."

The smell of greasy beef and rosemary seeped into the room from the cookery, with the sound of the hard boil puckering through. As sly as a rat in its shadowed grove, Gus raised his head toward the cookery door.

"I mean her no harm," he said, still looking past us. "Nor anyone."

From afar I heard the crack of a single horse's hooves across stone, and I watched through the glass until we heard the rider dismount and climb the porch stairs.

Arakka opened the door, bringing the fresh smell of the field grasses in with him. Over his shoulder was slung a ruddy brown turkey, its tail feathers tipped black and its red head and neck rocking at the shadow of my boy's back.

Arakka lay the turkey on the table and smiled at us as he took a chair. "What's this? You didn't say a guest was arriving."

I looked to Gus. "This is my eldest son, Arakka."

Gus nodded. "Kinda name is that?"

Arakka did not respond, but continued to stare at our guest.

"Arakka is a Comanche name," Micah said. "My boy was raised by them for a time."

"Heard 'a you," said Gus Whipple. "Folks up in Waco tell a' one of them kidnapped boys growin' up in Milam. Heard on the line you be here with the family at Bluebonnet, and Lucy says you still got some Comanche ways about you."

Arakka nodded and turned to my husband. "We got a bull down pasture with a whistler's cough. You got time to have a look?"

"I do," Micah replied, "but for now we are discussing some business with Mister Whipple."

Arakka sat back into his chair, squinting. "Whipple?"

"Gus Whipple," the man said grinning suddenly, with the tip of his tongue showing between his lips and teeth. This suitor then said to my boy, "And what is your white name, man?"

With jacked fortune roiling in his eyes, Arakka replied simply, "My birth name was Moses Whipple."

CHAPTER 51

*G*us leaned across the table and put his hand on Arakka's arm. "Moses," he whispered, "why then, might you be the brother I lost?" He glanced to the far window, a smile growing sharp across his mouth, but without the slightest gleam in his eyes.

My son stared at Gus's fingers laying across his shirtsleeve, and then stood free of them.

"You from Nacogdoches?" Gus asked. He looked quickly from Arakka to Micah, and back again.

"Family farmed north of there, but I don't remember more. Yellow jack killed some kin, Cherokee killed the rest. As for me, Duwali's people sold me on to the Comanche."

Quickly, Whipple said, "That's my story too." And in a wild man's voice he added, "I been looking for family my whole life. Glory to the Lord to find you now, at the house of my beloved."

With narrowed eyes, Arakka replied, "They shot my father deep with arrows, and he hung on the horse plough till my brother and me pulled him down. Maybe you're him. Maybe not. Don't remember his name, but it doesn't matter. I got other brothers now."

"But I am a brother of your blood."

Arakka grabbed the slaughtered bird from the table. "I'll be down the fields," he said to Micah, and walked stiffly through the cookery door.

Gus stared after him, tallow-eyed and quiet.

"What're you doing here, Whipple?" Teddy Blue asked. "If Whipple be your name. You been circlin' us lookin' for a way into this family?"

Gus lay his hands on the tabletop and looked toward the door. "I don't understand," he said, his sturdy dirty body taut.

Micah pressed his hands around the grog cup. "I'm no fool, man. Remember that." He exhaled, his strong breath sounding clean as a sickle through grass. "If you are a Whipple you will prove it to us. For now, you're only a drifter tangled with my daughter. We'll return you to Sugarloaf, where you may stay until we have deliberated. And keep away from Lucy during these days or I will end your life without a thought."

Gus measured the frown of my husband, then gave his tart reply, "Yes, sir. But will Lucy stay away from me?"

Long after Micah rode the man back to Sugarloaf, I sat alone with Lucy up the slope beyond our creek. The warm haze of our Indian summer fell across our field and covered us with the gold of the disappeared sun.

My sad girl poured out her loveslung gut to me, expecting my shelter in return. I listened to her tell of promises they had made, and of the moments he held her hand to touch her heart. It was a child's voice, one believing so heavily in a savior or a ranger, or even in a wandering preacher seeking a congregation.

"He's good, Mama. He wants to join our family, work the ranch and work for the Lord to help us and our neighbors. Please Mama, you won't regret it. And he wants to marry me. Besides, he's Arakka's kin and we must help him." She smiled grandly, and added, "Think of it! Two Moore sisters marrying two Whipple brothers!"

Her words, more common than water, dropped like shadows in the dusk light.

"We don't know if he's a Whipple. He presented nothing for proof, girl."

She stood from the grasses and the last of the year's blue asters, and suddenly raised her voice. "I believe him, Mama! That's enough, isn't it?" Shouting and begging at once, she added, "You'll help us, won't you?"

And in this moment, I understood that my daughter was as mad as a murmur of starlings clenching across the dying light.

By the sabbath, we had seen three days of a long rain from the east, hard winds blowing the sheets aslant, while the blackened branches of the pecans began splitting apart. The soil of our paddocks was drenched and clotted, and the calves stood in the muck and chill, waiting quietly for attention. The men went out before dawn, propping rails and clearing roads for wagons, while Cookie and I fought to light the hearth fire again. Once it sparked, I stood on the porch watching the ruined sky choke its torrent across us.

At late morning our farmhands and family had eaten and washed themselves for the ride to the Baptist tent. They staged in several wagons, and the Moores prepared to lead them off with Micah and Arakka driving on the front bench, our children and Jack spread behind in the box. All of them wore the dark colors of worship, their broad hats and waxed coats making small protection from the drumming rain. Teddy Blue and I huddled on the covered porch, both of us having long ago removed ourselves from worship.

A silky tawny mourning dove sat drenched beside me, pecking at seeds we had put out on the railing, lifting its pinky feet in and out of the water pooling on the wood.

"Look at poor Lucy," Teddy Blue said, nodding toward my middle girl who sat silent and alone on the broad bench at the back of the wagon box.

"Maybe she'll find some comfort today," I said.

"Her heart's like a griddle for that grifter. Ain't no comfort from a parson for that."

"Teddy," I whispered, and his look-back was drawn with deep lines. "Please don't say that. I loved her since the first day she slipped so easily from me. I'm worried for her." I pressed my lips together and closed my eyes.

He put a gentle hand on my back, and I bowed my head so the others couldn't see the tears. We heard the twick and palm of the drivers, readying to roll out, when Teddy Blue said, "Look now, Eliza. She's alone but she's playing it proud, trying not to break."

My girl, narrow shoulders covered in black wool, stared straight into the cold rain, her friendless face taut.

Suddenly Teddy Blue took my hand. "Come on, Mother Moore. I'll go if you will."

And through the trails of rainwater, we hurried down the steps toward the procession. Teddy jimmy-footed me up into the wagon, and we sat aside Lucy while the others looked at us through the heaving rain, gawking in disbelief.

Micah pulled us through a thick arch of post oaks on a road of sandy soil, and I put my arms around Lucy to keep her warm. Our first alert that we neared the tabernacle tent was the snortling of a button box accordion playing out *Friend in Jesus*; by the time we skidded clear of the last cottonwoods, two fellows had joined, fiddling that song with frontier lust.

As we rolled onto the field, my children's voices sang out as well, and our wagon at last halted near the tent lines. Our wheels had crushed over blackhaw and wild rye, and we ran through the fragrant rain.

I followed my family to a bench near the front, but Lucy separated herself by taking the last lonely spot at the row end. As the preacher approached his platform, he paused at her side and rested a hand on her shoulder. Lucy looked up and smiled at him; from the nod of his head, I knew that some message had passed between them. He moved beyond her, leaping up the deep step to the stage, his big hands held high for quiet.

Our Jack pulled a face at the fellow, and turning quickly, squirmed free of Evie's hand. Crawling beneath the seats and between our feet, he scrambled row by row toward the back of the congregation.

As the pastor's piercing lesson began, Lucy chased after the boy, but the preacher's bellows drew my own attention forward.

"What have you sought?" he cried, scurrying across the platform like a thief, his voice rising grimly through the hammering rain. One woman behind me stood weaving and wailing in words I did not even recognize, until he jumped from the stage and touched her face with both of his hands, covered it and squeezed it while she howled in pain. When the button box player returned with the fiddlers beside him, we sang a final hymn of marching soldiers to release us from their lord's vise.

As we stood to leave I found Jack again, squirming no more, but sitting quietly at the end of our bench, holding a dark new toy.

Evie brushed passed me and grabbed her son's shoulder.

"Where have you been?" She unfolded his hands and found they had been clenched around a broad disc of coal, polished smooth like a coin and carved with a rising sun and the letters KGC. "What is this? Where did you get this?"

"Aunt Lucy gave it to me."

"Where is Lucy, boy?" my husband asked quickly.

"Don't know." He had a purply blemish on his left cheek, and heated pink spread up his jaw.

I knelt beside him and put my hand on the warm skin. "What happened to your face, Jacky?" I whispered, but he only shook his head and reached for his father.

"Tell me," Arakka said, lifting him to his chest. "Did someone hit you?"

Jack nodded. "Lucy. I asked her not to leave. Her friend said I cried, but I didn't."

"What friend?" I asked, stirring beside him. "Where is Lucy now?"

My husband stepped away from the crowd around us and lifted his head to stare about the tent. "I should have killed him," he muttered. Blackbirds scattered in the wet rafters above the pulpit, while he and Teddy Blue started toward the hitch posts. "We'll stop them at Sugarloaf," Micah said, mounting a horse he had untethered from our wagons. "See the family home for me, Arakka."

Without looking at Micah, Arakka said, "My duty is with you." The rain had begun to swallow us again and a shaft of thin wet light fell across my son's face.

"No, boy," said my husband. "This is not your brother. Just some charlatan who heard our story."

Arakka clamped his lips together and put his hand on his holster, nodding.

"I need you with the family, son," Micah said. "Not with me looking for revenge."

Out of the black mirror of his frozen stare, Arakka said, "I will keep them safe." And with a distance still to go, he put his hand out to me.

CHAPTER 52

*A*s we came over the ridge toward home, the sky closed darker around us. We crossed the slippery stones of our bridge, and once inside, Chop stoked the hearth fire while we stripped from our sodden outer clothes.

"I'll put a pan on," Cookie said. "Get some hot milk going for us all. You'd like that, wouldn't you, Jacky? Hot milk and honey to warm up your innards." She pulled the boy to her body and held him.

"And taffy?" Jack asked.

Cookie smiled. "Of course, my love."

The sour smell of a week of rain began to fade from the damp room as Chop brought the fire to roar.

"Stand over here, children," he said. "Evie, my darling, you'll fetch them dry clothes, now won't you?" He handed the iron poker to Benjamin. "Keep poking it, boy. Don't let it dim. We'll need to be cooking and drying all night." Chop pulled a chair to the edge of the hearth. "Here, Eliza, set down now. Soon Mister Moore and Lucy'll be coming through that door to catch this warmth too."

Chop had stripped down to his drenched Hendersons and a

sheepy-smelling wool shirt. He took my hand and pulled me close for a hug. "Ah, don't worry, love. She be coming home. I know it!" He smiled hard and walked me awkwardly back to the chair. Ducking low with a groan over the hearth basket, he gathered an armful of sticks and tossed them onto the grate. The fire flamed suddenly up the stones while the sweet smell of roasted cedar filled the room.

Evie brought a pile of dry clothes and blankets, spreading them across the table. The rain still pitched at the window glass, and the dark sky slowly darkened deeper into evening. She spread out a dress and shawl for Stella last of all, pausing, then turning to face me.

"No bed clothes on Lucy's mat, Mama," Evie whispered. "Her hope chest is sprung empty too."

Young and agile, always so clear-eyed, Evie gave me a weary frightened look. Yet before I could stand or speak, we heard Cookie calling out.

"What you doing there?" she wailed. "Stealing from your own kin?"

Arakka peered through the door chink into the kitchen. "Lucy, by herself. I'll go to the back and look for the other."

"Get out of my way!" Lucy shouted at Cookie.

I heaved through the passage calling until I reached the broad shape of Cookie's back stooped over in the shadows. Just beyond, between the cool stone tabletops, stood Lucy alone, holding in one hand a sack of meat haunches and in the other a Colt and a small prayer book.

"Move aside," Lucy said to Cookie. Then she turned to me and in a voice wild and thin as a hound, she said, "You can't stop me."

I reached my fingers across the cold stone to touch her, but when I did, she pulled away.

"He's hiding? Making you do the thieving," Cookie said. "Like a snake in the weeds."

"Watch yourself! You're nothing but an ignorant old harpy," Lucy snarled. "Gus is my husband now."

"Girl," I said. "Come here to me. You're not legally married."

"Oh, yes we are, and I belong to him, and you can't change that."

"He's a coward!" Cookie shouted. "Afraid to face us! Is this the man you chose for your life?"

I grabbed my daughter's wrist, and she dropped the lootings to the floor. She yanked her arm from me and ran for the back door but stopped short as Arakka dragged her lover up the steps.

He shoved Gus Whipple flat between us, holding him down with one foot and a rifle pressed to his back. Gus's face was soaked in rainwater and mud, and he turned his head against the porch planks to reveal dark juices of tobacco drool sliding down his chin and neck.

"Let go, brother!" he shouted, his glare focused on my face. "Lucy and me are just hungry."

"You are not my brother," Arakka said quietly.

"Let him up, son," I said. "He has no weapon."

Arakka looked to me and slowly released him. Whipple stood, crouching first, then pausing as he watched us, his eyes clear and unafraid.

"I'm a little lightheaded," he whispered sharply, neither tired nor in surrender. My daughter bent over and reached for his arm. He pulled his body tall, his grimy white shirt smeared with mud just as the day he had arrived. He took a single step forward toward me, bringing the smell of rot and lye across the room, and with a hollow calm voice he said, "Give us the food and the Colt and Lucy's prayer book, and we'll be leaving. I never meant you no harm. Whatever you want to believe, I am your kin, Moses. Maybe you'll see that one day."

Lucy stood close to Gus, silent and straight-backed, but her eyes were fierce. The curl of her mouth was utterly without reason, but I did not dare look away. Lifting the lantern from the stone slab, I held it high to see her face better, a woman now with only a dark lobe of the unfinished child nestling behind the light. This new creature, her golden hair tied in a thick green ribbon, had chosen a broken man, one bereft of all the dreams I had for her, and I could not force it otherwise.

"How foolish I have been," I said gently.

"Yes," she hissed, "you've always been a fool." She grabbed Gus's hand. "You can't keep me here. Only the Lord can do that."

"Go on then," I said. "Take the food and your damn prayers. Make your own way. You'll soon see, Louisiana, it's a lonely journey, girl, without your family."

She walked slowly past me, grabbing the sack and the book from the floor and returning to Gus. Into the mist and the moonlight they went, thirsting for that reckless half of life, and the pearly harm of it all.

"Come back here!" Cookie shouted after them, but the lovers continued toward the ridge. "Don't let them, Eliza! Do something. He'll be her death!" Cookie said frantically, scanning the room for what might stop them. But it was Chop Coggins who crossed the threshold before any of us. Teetering between the curing shelves and carrying his old Henry rifle to the cookery door, he lifted the gun to his shoulder.

Beneath the softened sky, he pulled the lever, shouting, "Stop where you stand!"

Lucy turned to see the barrel pointing at her trembling lover. She grabbed his hand and urged him to run as Chop pulled the trigger.

Whipple stumbled and fell across the muddy weeds, and my daughter stooped to lift him to run again. But she struggled with his unconscious body, and by the time we reached her, Gus had bled out and his heart had stopped. Lucy lay across him sobbing, but Arakka lifted her and brought her into the warmth of our house.

When her father and Teddy Blue returned, Micah sat with

her, whispering and reasoning and finally tying her with hemp ropes to the bed that night to keep her from escaping us.

Quiet as a serpent, after the others had finally fallen to their dark sleep, I peeked into the bedroom, to see my two daughters, Lucy and Stella, on their beds, one bound and one unbound. Stella was quiet but Lucy lay jittery, shifting back and forth, moaning with each turn, and sweating under a mound of bedclothes.

Then I saw the ropes, the stiff hide pulling her wrists to the bed, just as my owners had bagged me so many years ago. My daughter, my own child, however far astray she had fled was no less astray than her own parents, than the people of this land, or any land. I knelt beside her, taking her fingers between mine.

She opened her eyes and asked sharply, "What do you want?"

"To hold you," I whispered. "And love you."

Lucy turned her face away and would not speak to me again.

Micah stood in the doorway, waiting for me in the dark. He put his arm across my shoulders, but I shrugged him off.

"Free her," I said. "We can't hold that child with rope."

"She's no child, Ellie."

"You tied her like a damn slave. And we'll both rot in hell for that."

"It's no sin to keep a daughter safe till her mind comes right. If I let her go, she'll run again. Alone or with that devil, she'll be open to crimes on every turn of every road she takes."

"You free her now," I said again. "Or I will."

He breathed heavily and touched my hand. "I can't. She's not safe on her own. Not tonight anyway. Let it rest for a day or two."

I watched his kindly blue eyes as they glistened with grief, so slowly until his tears brimmed over and tumbled down his cheeks. His rough fingertips trembled on my wrist, and he whispered, "Girl, I know this isn't right, but how else can I protect her?" He moved closer to me, and between us there was not even a shadow. He let his shoulders sink around my own as though he could not bear another grain of light to touch him again in this life. "I can't lose another child."

I nodded and stood with him until he returned to our room. I wiped my dry brow again and again, and all the while inside me struck the aching echo of an anvil, pounding in my gut. I stayed with Lucy, though she did not speak to me but only moaned and pitched wildly at her ropes.

Within hours she had grown completely mute, watching me like a sentry lamp blazing over her.

When at last she closed her eyes in sleep, I pulled my apron away from my chest and feeling no tools in the pockets, I slipped into my bedroom and found a knife for her ropes.

Later, I lay alongside Micah, breathing the cool air in my sleep, as the moonlight lay greasy grey over the ridge when Stella came pounding on our door.

"She's gone. I don't know when. I didn't hear it." Stella sat beside us in a breath of white linen, weeping.

"It was bound to happen, Stella," Micah said gently, putting a hand on her head but watching me. "Not your fault. Nobody's fault."

We searched for weeks, and then months, and at last, years. When messages came back of a tramping girl to the south, in San Antonio and El Paso and Matamoros, Arakka traveled out but returned with nothing. She was seen in Deming working with the Harvey people, and Micah followed that tale all the way to the silver mines of New Mexico and Arizona. We sought my girl across circuits west and north, and every far sighting they lay at my feet caused me to weep, into my dreams of those hot foreign nights.

One afternoon at our Milam County Fair, I met a young woman who stood thigh deep in sedge and marigolds. She wore a simple shift cut low across her chest and held a jar of cider in her hands. With her eyes closed, she threw her head back to swallow it all in a gulp. When she opened her eyes, she looked straight at me, pensively watching with her head tilted. I moved toward where she stood under the bracketed tavern sign, thinking her blonde hair to be a clue, but the closer I approached, the deeper I understood she was not my own child.

"You look familiar," she said to me suddenly. "I've seen you somewhere."

"If you're from Milam, that wouldn't be unusual." I smelled the tart alcohol on her breath, and I looked around her for a husband or a friend.

"I'm not. I come from out west." Her pale skin was heavily rouged over the apples of her cheeks, and her voice was bold and smooth.

"Well, I can't tell you then," I replied, but she kept watching me, putting unclean fingertips to her chin.

"I think I seen your picture once," she said. "Out on the Gila, last year maybe."

My skin crawled when she said it, and I questioned her for hours, fed her and bought her gifts and necessities, but she could remember nothing else. Eventually, Micah and Teddy Blue began the search again across their old rangering territories on the Apacheria, but by then whoever owned my tintype had moved on.

To this day, I know in my heart the holder was Lucy and that she spoke to the girl about me, and perhaps, still loved me a little.

CHAPTER 53

BLUEBONNET RIDGE, 1883

On the table by my bed sits a crock and into it I long ago slipped the sacred fragments of this family: a purple basketflower Stella dried from the Palo Duro, a tiger's eye marble that once belonged to James, little Benjamin's old shackles, and that coin of coal, that curse, with the letters KGC carved into it that Lucy left behind. I even saved the Mississippi bank note belonging to my mother.

These are the ciphers of my story; my father brought us here not knowing what we would find, and we stayed because this land was all we had. I have endured its seasons under five different flags, and I raised six children in kindness, blood kin or not, as best I could. But enduring is not healing or prevailing; it is only persevering; this, a refugee's rough duty.

Most days I can feel the percussion of the iron locomotive wheels as the cars lurch along the lines and bolts, crossing over the deep river bridge above the metes of our land. Last year, Micah brought me to see the new Mundine railroad hotel at Rockdale, a mass of shiny windows with a veranda stretching the length, and another veranda high up on the third story.

Four hundred people came for the speeches and the bunting

on that day, and we listened to brassy musicians from broad white steps alongside a dozen galleries for guests. Such a place had only ever been built as a fortress in my time, and there we were, humming and waving little flags with our backs to carved columns. We stayed the night watching the grand parade and the fireworks, all of it for the hotel, for nothing more than the victory of the birth of a railroad hotel.

The look of a countryside becomes that of those who work it, and so the Bluebonnet Ridge, a proud and handsome acreage, reminds me of Micah, sheltering and enduring. Still that same decent boy, he rises in the dark and ventures out with Arakka and Jack, Teddy Blue and Benjamin, driving the cattle and trimming the crops before breakfast. Evie is up at their first stirring with her girls, frying bacon and boiling coffee, moving about the kitchen below just as Cookie Mahoney and I did, out every morning drawing water in the vanishing moonlight.

And my lazy job now is only to stoke the hearth fire before our men come plodding up the porch stairs. I fetch the fallen branches of our nearest pecan trees, throw them in the dying flames, and wait while the sweet vanilly smell humbles the other pleasures of our house.

Here now is my final gift from these blue hills and cool rivers, the thick gama grasses of the plains, and the scarecrow's raised and dreaming arms. The finest house in this county is what neighbors say about our Bluebonnet Ridge. They are all new folks, refugees themselves from some hard life, escaping to a job or a promise of acreage to farm.

They travel like cattle by railroad from St Louis or Memphis, families who never saw their kin's blood spattered on whitewashed walls, never purchased deed title to a man or woman, and likely never killed one. Some will give up and return to the comforts of their birth homes, but those who stay will learn that this land is only one thing: a look-back glass to their own mettle.

～

On this April day, by the time our old Goodie rooster finished crowing, the workers had swallowed their potatoes and ham, their coffee, but none had returned to the fields. I found my place in the rockerman on our porch, watching my children bring a wagon over the limestone bridge, the cobbles pale as eggs in the chilly dawn light. Benjamin gathered our late winter vegetables to sell at Rockdale and packed up the box for the journey, while Stella and Evie sat holding hands on an old log near the stream.

I walked down the slope to meet them, and staring at my Stella's small brow, I said, "Your father packed everything he thought you'll need, but write us when you get to San Antonio and let me know what we forgot."

She came to me, and then Evie did the same. We three held tight with the cold fresh air around us. Those old damp pecan trees, their bare branches and trunks musty with the rich odor of our land, hid us from the family. I bowed my head to my girls, my rights to their futures having at last disappeared.

Micah came down the porch steps, open-faced and big-limbed, carrying a new cabin trunk full of Stella's clothes for the journey. He loaded this last in the wagon and followed the muddy path down to us.

"It's time," he said. "Train won't wait for you, Stella."

She nodded and left us, Evie wiping her own tears and Micah's arm tight around my shoulders.

We watched Benjamin lift Stella into the wagon, as he called to us, "I'll be home by supper."

My husband brought me a clay crock brimmed with our well water. "Take a sip, Eliza," he said. "This won't be the last time we see her. She's not running like Lucy, just off to teach."

"How do you know?" I asked. "Running has many faces."

"I know," he replied firmly. "And you know."

I stared after my children, across the early spring ridge still with fading stars above, while their wagon disappeared over the slope of bluebonnets, shimmering in the morning light. That was myself riding out that day, on to a land farther than I had ever known.

THE END

STONES IN THE GRAVEYARD AT
BLUEBONNET RIDGE

Eliza Green Moore: born at the fork of the Yazoo River and the Mississippi, 1821 and died at Bluebonnet Ridge, 1889

Micah Moore: born in Macon, Georgia, 1816 and died at Bluebonnet Ridge, 1890

Arakka Moore (Moses Whipple): born near Nacogdoches, Texas, 1835 and died at Bluebonnet Ridge, 1912

Evie Moore: born at Bluebonnet Ridge, 1848 and died at Bluebonnet Ridge, 1916

James Henry Moore: born at Bluebonnet Ridge, 1849 and died in the Palo Duro canyons of Texas, 1863

Lucy Moore Whipple: born at Bluebonnet Ridge, 1851 and believed to have died in the desert of West Texas, year unknown

Stella Moore: born at Bluebonnet Ridge, November 1854 and died in Los Angeles, California, 1952

Benjamin Moore: born among the Comanches on the Texas plains, year unknown, and died in the Garza War in the Rio Grande Valley, Texas, 1892

Jack Moore: born near Monterrey, Mexico, 1870 and died in Havana, Cuba during the Spanish American War, 1898

Chop Coggins: born in Orange, Virginia, 1799 and died at Bluebonnet Ridge, 1878

Louisiana Green Baylis: born in 96 District, South Carolina, 1819 and died at Bluebonnet Ridge, 1865

Viola Louisiana Baylis: born in Cherokee County, Texas, 1864 and died at Marlin, Texas, 1941

Teddy Blue Corlies: born in Kentucky, 1815 and died at Bluebonnet Ridge, 1891

Hon. William 'Three-Legged Willie' McCann: born in Culpeper, Virginia, 1802 and died at Bluebonnet Ridge, 1861

Benjamin Franklin Green: born in 96 District, South Carolina, 1785 and died at Becky Creek, Matagorda County, Texas, 1837

Deirdre "Cookie" Mahoney: born at Drogheda, County Louth, Ireland, 1814 and died at Bluebonnet Ridge, 1881

ACKNOWLEDGMENTS

With love and many thanks to Eliza, who spoke to me from behind the veil for so many years to make sure it was right; to my agent Peter Riva; my betas Carmen Flores, Mary Ann DeVlieg, Julie Starr, Lynne Lockwood, Tina Sansone, Teresa Heine, Cathy Nolan, and Kathie Flamm; workshoppers John Fetto, Joe Belden, Patricia Lutjic; my goddaughter Camila Fernandez; editor Linda Watanabe McFerrin; critic Jesse Kornbluth; sweet readers Doug Hulyer, Kimberly Nichols, Angie Glielmi, and Joanne Hardy who took time from their busy schedules to give me opinions; Lea Goodsell, Princess Karen Cantrell, and Len Kubiak of Fort Tumbleweed; and of course, to my darling girl, Nicky Polidor, my forever inspiration and greatest love of my life, for her ongoing support, applause, and love.

A NOTE FROM THE PUBLISHER

Thank you for reading this book. If you enjoyed it please do consider leaving a review on Amazon to help others find it too.

We hate typos. All of our books have been rigorously edited and proofread, but sometimes mistakes do slip through. If you have spotted a typo, please do let us know and we can get it amended within hours.

info@bloodhoundbooks.com

Printed in Great Britain
by Amazon

21844741R00209